Howl of the Banshee

A Lou Gault Thriller

Dave McKeon

For Sandy, always

The Territory

Preface

Banshee

The **banshee** is a mythical creature who dwells in the spirit world. The name comes from the old Irish *bean sídh,* which translates to "woman of the fairy mounds."

Banshees are clairvoyant, and capable of crossing over from the spirit world in a shadowy form.

In Irish folklore, the banshee is considered an omen of death, or an impending peril that will soon beset one's family. The sound is often described as either a series of mournful wails or a shrill scream.

Chapter One

IT DIDN'T MATTER to her that it was near midnight when she finally decided to call her twin sister. Nor did she care that traces of dried blood were still visible in the crevasses around her finger nails. She felt no remorse for her actions, nor was she burdened with conscience. She never had been. The only behavioral traits Beatrice ever displayed were aligned with her immediate gratification and self-fulfillment.

When she finished punching in Anne's number, Beatrice sat back in the massive leather chair next to the huge fireplace, lifting a cocktail glass to her lips, she took a long greedy swallow, then finished off yet another French martini. As she held the phone to her ear, her eyes focused on the hand-carved ornate alabaster panels framing the shallow hearth in her father's study.

"Hello?"

"Are you dressed?"

Anne sighed before saying, "Beatrice, it's late. . . why on *earth* are you calling me so late?"

"It's done."

"What's done?"

"He's dead."

"You *killed* him?"

". . .Yes."

"How?"

"Is that really important?"

"No, I . . . I just thought . . ."

"What?"

"Nothing. It . . . it doesn't matter."

"You said you wanted *revenge*, didn't you?"

"Yes."

"Well, revenge costs money my dear sister, and he wasn't willing to part with any."

"Father refused us, *again*?"

"The damned fool actually looked me straight in the eye and said, 'Over my dead body.'" The smirk in her voice could be heard over the phone.

"Oh, God, Beatrice. . . what if they find out it was *us* who . . .?"

"*Trust* me they won't."

"How can you be *sure*?"

"The inquest into the death of Aaron Yardley, former Earl of Surrey, will be permanently closed by the end of the week."

"That's *ridiculous*; it's way too soon."

"Believe it."

"Why?"

"Because I've made *arrangements* to squelch it."

"How?"

"Our young coroner seems to have an insatiable desire to bed *older* women."

"Oh God! Beatrice you can't . . . "

"I'm not leaving *anything* to chance. Remember what I said? 'No loose ends!'"

Anne closed her eyes as she took in a deep breath. "So, when will you file?"

"Tomorrow."

"That quick?"

"Yes."

"Won't that raise a lot of eyebrows?"

"Perhaps."

"Will the Crown approve it?"

"They *could* deny the transfer of father's title, but it's unlikely. Once the prime minister's office creates the writ and places it before our beloved Royal Sovereign, he seems to sign anything involving a first born."

Anne, paused briefly before saying, "Then what?"

"Then we go after the *bitch*."

"Beatrice, we'll have *money* again! Let's just go live out our lives."

"No! That bitch is going to suffer . . . like *I've* suffered."

Beatrice waited for a response. When nothing was forthcoming, she said, "Anne? Are you in or out?"

"I'm . . . I'm *in* . . . I guess."

"Then *act* like it. Evelyn said she was in."

"You've *spoken* with her?"

"Yes."

"When?"

"Just now. She's on her way over to my flat. I'm leaving father's study shortly."

"Do *I* need to be there?"

"Yes."

"I won't be able to stay long."

"Anne, you and I have talked about this."

"They have me going into work early tomorrow."

"I don't *care* . . . I need you to *be* there."

"I'll come; but I can't stay long."

"Anne, there are no *buts* allowed . . . you'll stay as long as it takes us to finish talking this thing *through*."

Anne closed her eyes; a heavy sigh escaped her lips. Beatrice had always been the dominant twin.

"Anne, I hope you're not going to disappoint me. Was that sigh I just heard a 'yes?'"

Anne closed her eyes again and thought: *No, it wasn't . . . why do you always try to manipulate me?* But she was an appeaser. As the younger twin, Anne had always yielded to her domineering sister's demands.

Now Beatrice waited for Anne to finally say the word she wanted to hear.

"*Yes*, I'll be there."

"Good. Use the back stairway this time."

"Why?"

"Because I *told* you to. Isn't that enough Anne? For once in your life, will you just go along with what I *tell* you without giving me such a bloody royal hassle? It's tiring Anne, it really is *tiring*! You do this to me *all* the time!"

Anne sighed heavily. *You're right, Beatrice, it is tiring because it's always about you . . . what you want.*

"Look, I'm leaving father's estate now. After what *I've* been through tonight, I don't need a hassle. Just be there . . . okay? *Please*?" With that, the line went dead.

ACROSS THE POND, Lou Gault had no idea people were plotting against his wife. . . against his lovely Kate.

Chapter Two

I T WAS CLOSE to midmorning when the first sound of an approaching float plane interrupted the natural serenity of the beautiful valley nestled deep within the wilds of central New Brunswick. For the rest of the morning, Twin Otters and de Haviland Beavers would line up offshore waiting their turn to taxi in to the dock at the resort known as *Harve de Poisson*.

As soon as the incoming passengers disembarked, the sportsmen who had arrived the previous week would board the same float planes and head home. Most would fly west to Grand Falls, others would head north to the Kedgwick Airport where they would take connecting flights back to civilization.

A decade earlier, Lou Gault had inherited the remote sportsman's retreat when his grandfather, Grey Elk, had died. The resort was situated on the southern shore of an obscure lake created during the end of the Pleistocene Ice Age as the glaciers retreated. In the area, few logging roads existed; the only practical access to the resort was by float plane. As for other settlements, the nearest one even coming close was a small Abenaki village over six miles away "as the crow flies."

AS THE LAST plane taxied in. Lou and his remaining two guests stood up, grabbed their gear, and walked down the well-trodden path to the dock.

"Hey, fellas, I've got you in the same cottage, same week, for next year."

"Thanks, Lou! We really like that one."

"Refresh my memory," he said, "how many years have you been coming up here?"

"This is our sixth year, Lou."

"I knew it was something like that. We had a group up last week that's been coming for nineteen years.

"How large a party?"

"Eight. A few years ago, they brought down a deer that actually made the Boone and Crockett record book."

"Is that the same group that caught the lunker trout you've got mounted inside the lodge?"

"Nah, that was a different group. I was actually surprised when they brought that fish in. Every one of them is a catch-and-release guy. But they figured *that* one would set a new record, and it *did*."

"Helluva girth on that fish!"

"Yeah, well, it was gorging on smelt all summer."

For some trophy-hunting sportsmen, returning to Havre de Poisson year after year was a strong calling akin to the call of the wild or a sacred pilgrimage.

The lake itself was obscure and listed on maps merely as "Number 980." Yet it held the record for the largest lake trout taken by rod and reel in Canada. Twice, rainbow trout hauled up from its depths topped New Brunswick's provincial record. The potential of hooking a record-breaking fish had always been the allure for most sportsmen who came to the resort.

"We enjoyed the Abenaki guide we had this year, Lou."

"Glad to hear that."

"Lou, I gotta tell ya'," another said, "every time we leave here, we say to each other that we need to come up and do a little *spring* fishing."

"Then, *do* it."

"We're gonna hint around to the wives, so maybe that'll be our Christmas presents."

"First part of May is prime fishing, fellas," Lou said. "The days are warm, the smelt are running; you can use light tackle, *and* there are no black flies."

"Can't ask for more than that!"

"If you decide to come up, get your reservations in before the middle of January. You won't have your choice of cottage, but you still should have your choice of week."

"You book up that quick?"

"Over half of next season is already booked."

"Lou . . . you should add a few more cottages."

"Nah, I'm at just the right size now."

"You think?"

"Definitely. Any more than twelve and running this place would feel like work."

"Well, hell, ya' can't let *that* happen." Everyone laughed.

As soon as the plane reached the dock, the men picked up their pace. Once they were gone, Havre de Poisson's twenty-three-week season would officially come to an end. Both men climbed aboard the plane, stowed their bags, and took their seats. Once they settled in, the man in the rear leaned forward. "Ya know, there's an enviable independence about Lou, isn't there?"

"Yeah, he's certainly found his niche in life. Doesn't seem to have a care in the world."

To the most casual observer, Lou Gault projected a calm self-confident demeanor, yet it masked a warrior's spirit which lay hidden deep within him. His tall, wiry physique belied the tremendous strength in his limbs. Even though he was no longer a member of Canada's elite *Joint Task Force Two* commando unit, he still wore his hair clipped close on the sides. He lived a quiet life now, far away from the daily carnage he faced back when he fought in the Afghan war.

As the plane taxied away from the dock, Lou's eyes scanned the natural beauty of the valley, always looking for anything unusual . . . anything that might be out of place. It was a habit of his that would never go away.

Other than a flock of geese winging their way south, it was a typical fall day with deep blue sky and just a hint of wispy white clouds in higher altitudes. Snow clouds were weeks away, but still, there was a chill in the air, and thin layers of ice had begun forming along the shoreline the last few mornings.

Lou had grown up with the knowledge that nature, itself, told the story of how close it was to winter, not some computer-generated weather model. For weeks, the tree tops had resembled an artist's palette filled with fiery reds, brilliant yellows, deep purples, and various shades of orange. The once-colorful treetop canopy now carpeted the forest floor, contributing to the rich, earthy smells of fall. Clumps of balsams were more noticeable now; their dark green color contrasting with the naked grey branches of the hardwoods.

Movement suddenly caused Lou to zero in on the far shoreline. *Well, the loons are still here,* he thought, *they're always the last to go! They're the real bellwether for when fall will give way to winter.*

As Lou turned to walk back to his cottage, the furthest thought from his mind was how abruptly this quiet, peaceful life he was living was about to end . . . and this time, the target would be the love of his life.

WHEN KATE O'GRADY-GAULT heard their porch screen door open, she looked up from her laptop. "Hey, Lou, was that the last plane out?"

"It was. You ready? Let's go. Angelo will have our celebratory drinks ready."

"Give me a moment. I just need to save what I've been doing, before I log off."

Lou, leaned against the door jamb, and stared at his lovely wife. By any man's standard, Kate was a desirable woman. Standing five-six, she had shimmering chestnut brown hair, vibrant hazel green eyes, an alluring smile, an hour-glass figure, and was smart as a whip; a true partner in every humanly way possible.

Standing up, Kate announced, "There! Okay, now I'm done! And I also know where I'd like to have the reception, after we renew our vows in Ireland."

"Good."

She brought a few dishes over to the sink. "It's a grand place, right on the river, just before you leave Abbyfeale."

Lou stood there smiling, listening to the dulcet tones of Kate's Irish brogue.

Drying her hands on a dishtowel, she glanced out the window. "It's only a short walk from the church. But it's more expensive than some of the others, though, are you okay with that?" She didn't wait for his answer. "It has a grand view of the river Feale, too; we'll have the whole place to ourselves." As Kate donned a sweater, she went on. "I think it'll be grand."

"I'm sure it will. Ready?

She walked over to her husband, stood on tip toes, and kissed him on the lips before whispering, "I am *always* ready for you!"

They stepped out of the cottage and closed the door. "You seem to be in an agreeable mood this morning Lou."

"I am. I had a good season; it's over, and now I'm looking forward to my celebratory drink."

"Have you always celebrated the end of the season this way?"

"Actually, it's only been a tradition since Angelo came over from Italy."

"So, are there *other* traditions, I should know about?"

"Not really . . . well, maybe one, but it's just something *I* do. I wouldn't call it a tradition."

"And that is . . .?"

"Well, later today, I'll take a look at my notes and decide on what changes I want to make before next year."

"I like traditions, I think they're important. I'm glad you haven't forgotten 'lesson number one,' now that you're married to this Irish colleen?"

Lou, smiled as he squeezed his wife's hand. "You make me feel complete, Kate. Why wouldn't I want to hold your hand when we're together?

Kate, looked up at her tall, handsome husband, leaned

into him and squeezed his arm as they walked toward the lodge.

"It's funny, Kate, in the spring I can't wait for everything to begin. I love what I do. But by the time the season draws to a close, my tank is so low . . . I'm ready for it to end."

As soon as they entered the lodge, Angelo emerged from the kitchen, both arms raised in a welcoming gesture. *"Mio amico, vieni a festeggiare!"*

Lou sensed more than saw the inquisitive look on Kate's face, and whispered, "It translates to: 'Let's celebrate my friend.'"

"You speak Italian?"

"Some . . . but it's mostly Tonto Italian."

"Is that a dialect?"

"Years ago, there was a western called the Lone Ranger. Ever hear of it?"

"Of course."

"Well, like Tonto . . . I basically speak in nouns and verbs."

As soon as Angelo's wife finished pouring the *prosecco*, he raised his glass and shouted: *"Salute e la pace!"*

"Yes, to health and peace, my friend," Lou echoed the sentiment as everyone took sips.

Chef Angelo and his wife, Alessandra, were the only other year-round residents at Havre de Poisson. The middle-aged couple had arrived from Italy years ago, and decided to stay on. He looked like a shorter version of Pavarotti and she could have passed for a mature Marisa Tomei. Chef Angelo was also a favorite among the guests. Not only did he come out of the kitchen and sing Italian songs upon request, he was also an accomplished chef. Whoever brought him their catch of the day would find that Angelo had transformed it, or any fowl presented to him, into the most delicious, mouthwatering epicurean delight anyone ever tasted. Alessandra was the housekeeper as well as her husband's sous chef. They treated Lou like the son they never had. Kate and Alessandra's relationship could be compared to mother and daughter.

After refilling everyone's glass, Alessandra disappeared into the kitchen, and returned with an assortment of delicacies while shouting, "*Mangia! Mangia!*"

Lou reached for a *bruschetta*. "Okay, *mangia,* but I'm eating light, I'd like to get a few things done this afternoon, and don't need to feel like a boa constrictor who's just swallowed a wild boar."

Alessandra shook her finger at Lou, "You're just like my papa. You try to do too much. Slow down! Rome wasn't built in a day."

"I just need to get a couple of things done before Jake flies in. We'll be starting on the big stuff soon; then I'll sit back and enjoy the peace and quiet."

Kate looked at her husband. "Lou, you and I are off to Ireland in a few days, and we have a lot to do once we get there."

"What's there to do? We're going over to renew our vows in front of your family in a simple church ceremony. Then we'll traipse around Europe for a month."

"Well, that's what I'd *hoped* it would be."

"That's *not* what we're doing?"

"It is . . . sort of, but there's a twist now. The whole thing has turned into a rather big deal, thanks to my cousin, Claire."

"How?"

Kate let out a sigh. "Well, Claire's like the town crier.

Everybody on both sides of my family now knows we're coming, and they all expect to be invited to the wedding."

"Did I meet this cousin?"

"Remember the redhead you met the time we were at the pub . . . who never stopped drinking and talking?"

"Kate, that pretty much describes everyone in your family."

"She wants to know how many I'm planning to invite."

"So, what's the count?"

She rolled her eyes. "It's ridiculous, close to two hundred."

"If we weren't already married, I'd say let's elope and send them a postcard."

"That's just it, Lou, in the eyes of the O'Grady clan and the McKiernan clan, we *aren't* married! And we won't be a married couple *until* we exchange vows in the Catholic Church."

Alessandra reached for a piece of *focaccia*. "Kate you *are* married. You had a beautiful wedding this summer over at the Abenaki village."

"I know that. It's just that my family . . . they're just so . . . they're just so damn *Irish*!"

Lou grinned. "I've been thinking of getting a Mohawk and bringing my formal Abenaki attire. What do you think?"

"You'll do no such thing!" Kate snapped. "You're wearing a tux and be thankful that it's trousers, and not the traditional kilt!"

"Whoa, Kate, slow down! I was only joking."

She was breathing heavily now. "I'm sorry. It's just that my cousin is pressuring me to book the flights. I need to get over there and corral this thing before it gets out of hand any further. Claire can be an 'English breakfast' at times."

Alessandra looked at Kate. "An English *what*?"

"An 'English breakfast' . . . it's just a saying."

Kate could tell Alessandra was waiting for an explanation. "If something needs to be done and you don't address it straight on, it'll keep coming back on you like an English breakfast does."

Lou placed his hand on Kate's forearm. "Hey, forget your cousin. Give my travel agent a call. She'll handle everything."

"*Claire* is a travel agent, Lou. That's what she does. Her agency just merged with a British group and she says she has terrific deals to offer."

"Well, handle it however you want," Lou said while standing up. "Now, I'd like to stay here jawing, but there are things I need to get done before Jake shows up. Great drink, and now the season's over. See you all later."

Chapter Three

B Y THE TIME Jake taxied the Twin Otter up to the dock, the sun was a huge orange ball sitting low on the horizon. As he climbed out of the plane, he saw Lou waiting.

"Sorry, I planned on being here earlier, but they gave me a few extra stops today."

The two first cousins had grown up as brothers, which created a strong bond between them. They shared the same values, however, their personalities and approach to life were completely different. Lou was serious, the stoic one. Jake was a fun-loving free spirit who flew the mail plane out of Kedgwick five days a week. During the off-season, he was a fixture at Havre de Poisson.

"No worries," Lou called. "It actually gave me a chance to go over to Rocky Point and think about changes I'd like to make during the off-season."

"So, whatcha got in mind this year, cuz?" Jake asked as they secured the Otter's tiedown straps to the dock.

"Well, after watching the number of float planes lined up, waiting to get to the dock this morning, and overhearing a few guests grumbling about the delay, I think it's time I expand the dock."

"That'll help."

"Yeah and I think I'll replace the outboards too; more than a few of them are getting along in years."

"Nah, a little elbow grease and some new decals will have them looking like new."

"I think it's a lot more than that, Jake. I keep adjusting them, but they're getting harder to fire up. It could be just the recoil starters, or it could be corrosion. New ones will be quieter and easier to start. I'm thinking of outfitting all the boats with those new kickers that Honda just came out with. I think they'd do well and make a nice impression."

"I've read about them."

"The electric start model?"

"Yeah, there's a small nickel cadmium battery inside the housing."

"The reviews are good."

"Pricey, though."

"Yeah, but I'll save money on fuel."

"What else?"

"The inside of the lodge needs to be redone. Angelo wants to expand the kitchen. A couple of cottages are looking pretty tired and Alessandra says she thinks it's time to replace the mattresses." They were both silent for a moment, then Jake changed the subject.

"When did you pull the boats ashore?"

"Are you paying attention to me?"

"Yeah, of course."

"I brought 'em ashore last night, so there'd be more room

for the planes to pull up to the dock this morning." They turned to walk toward Lou and Kate's cottage.

"So, when do you wanna go up?" Jake asked.

"I figure we'd do it tomorrow."

"Is Kate coming with us?"

"Yeah, it's time she found out."

"What? You haven't *told* her?"

"Every time I planned on telling her, all she wants to talk about is this Irish wedding she's planning."

As the two cousins walked away from the dock, Lou had a flashback. He was reliving the moment he first met Lieutenant Kathryn O'Grady. How she shook his hand with poise and confidence. He could hear her saying her first words to him: "I go by 'Kate.'"

It all happened well over a year ago, yet the memory was as fresh in his mind as if it happened only yesterday. The Mounties had decided to take a covert operation off the grid and establish a base at Havre de Poisson. He remembered how surprised he was to learn this young, attractive and demure gal was the INTERPOL liaison, sent to help the Canadians coordinate with MI6. Yet in the end, she was the one who almost single-handedly brought down a ring of international smugglers.

Then his thoughts raced through the memory of how conflicted he had been to partner with her on an undercover assignment and having to act like a couple . . . until it had stopped being an act. Images of her playfulness, her courage, her sexuality, and her perseverance, all popped into his mind like flash cards.

It wasn't until well after Operation Delta-Tango had ended, and the three British ringleaders were in custody, that he realized Kate had a mischievous side. He smiled now, recalling how she had never let on that the Mounties were aggressively recruiting her, and how creatively she had conceived a ruse to be with him by pretending to be a guest and arriving unexpectedly at his lodge. Yet, she had come with so many belongings, it was clear that she intended to stay.

Before long, she held dual citizenship and Havre de Poisson had become her home, albeit she still owned a wee cottage in Abbyfeale, Ireland, which she vowed she would never give up, not even for her new husband, Lou.

LATE THAT NIGHT, a fast moving, powerful storm roared up the valley. The howling winds pelted the rain against the windows of their cottage with such a vengeance that it woke Kate from a sound sleep. Thunder following flashes of light sounded almost choreographed to the rhythmic beat of hailstones pounding down upon the metal roof. But it was the frightening howl of the wind which brought Kate to stand near the window on her side of the bed, more than once.

The next morning, the smell of bacon sizzling in the pan and the aroma of freshly brewed coffee drifted into the bedroom and drew Lou into the kitchen. Hearing her husband's footsteps, Kate turned from the stove to look at him.

"That was quite a storm we had last night. Did you hear it?" she asked.

"No, as soon as my head hit the pillow I was out like a light," he said.

"Well, it certainly woke me out of a sound sleep. Is your cousin awake, yet?"

"He's long gone. He was going over to Angelo's for breakfast."

"The winds were really fierce last night, Lou, they had me up twice. It was howling outside like a banshee. Gives me goosebumps just thinking about it"

"Howling like a *what*?"

"A banshee."

"What the hell is a banshee?"

"Oh, it's just Irish folklore. You might as well know now we Irish are a superstitious lot."

"Does that include you?"

"Well, there are many who believe the banshee will come to warn you when something terrible is about to happen."

"Terrible . . . like what?"

"Well, usually it's when there's about to be a death in the family . . . but mind you, it can come for other troubles, as well."

"You believe that?"

"Well, no . . . not really. It's . . . it's just folklore . . . that's all it 'tis."

"Yet, you're not dismissing it?"

"Well, my mother and my mother's mother would often talk about the banshee, whenever the wind howled, like it did last night. My grandmother, God rest her soul, said her own mother looked out the window once and saw the banshee, wailing outside her home. The very next day, her father had a stroke and died. I guess the howling just brought back a few memories for me, that's all. There's nothing more to it than that."

As Lou poured himself a cup of coffee, something was on his mind. "So, did you get up and look out the window last night, Kate?"

"I did. How would you like your eggs this morning?"

"Over easy." He studied her for a moment, noticing that she didn't seem quite her normal self. "Are you okay?"

"I'm just tired. I had a terrible time going back to sleep last night."

Lou took his usual seat at the table. "Yesterday, I gave some serious thought to the changes I'd like to make before next year, Kate."

"Have you, now?"

"You recall the Styrofoam ice coolers I started giving out during the second half of the season?"

"Yes."

"I think I'll upscale those to plastic-lined wicker baskets next season with two wraparound leather straps. I'll go with a little larger size and have them imprint my logo on the inside of the lid."

"That will be a nice touch."

"I've also been putting off expanding the dock for long enough. I need room for at least two planes to be able to tie up at one time, without having to jockey the boats around."

"That will help."

Lou took another sip of coffee, still looking at Kate's reactions. "Angelo has been after me for a couple of years now to expand the kitchen. So, I'm going to tackle that, too."

"Be careful you don't take too much away from the dining area, it's already cramped."

"I'm thinking we'll do a bump-out. I'm also going to replace the outboard motors with new Honda electric starts."

"Really?"

"Yeah."

Kate raised her eye brows. "How much will that cost?"

"Not much. I'm only going for the twenty-five horsepower kickers."

"How much?" she repeated.

"They're running about four grand a piece, but if I buy a dozen, I'll get a break."

"Lou, between the kitchen and the motors, you're talking about some serious money."

After leaning back in his chair, he stretched. "Kate, I take in over three quarters of a million every year. I can well afford it."

"And you spend a lot. What's your bottom line look like for the year?"

"I don't know yet, but I'm in the black."

"You're talking close to fifty grand for just the motors. Heaven knows what the kitchen will cost."

"Here's what I'm concerned about Kate. I've noticed a few of the old timers, the guys who come up year after year, struggling with the pull cords this season. I've taken those things apart a few times and looked at them but can't figure out if the problem is the recoil starter or just plain corrosion. The last thing I want is for someone to have a heart attack pulling on those damn starter cords while they're here. Besides, I can depreciate them."

"What else?"

"Well, Alessandra has been telling me for the last two years to think about replacing the linens and the mattresses. So, I'm going to do that."

Kate just shook her head.

"I've got it covered, besides the guests will love it. A few of the cottages need some sprucing up, too. I want to get these things done before they start showing up on the comment cards as an issue."

"Lou, you're talking about some serious money. Don't forget, we'll be spending a small fortune on this trip we're taking."

"Ah, that's just chicken feed."

"Lou Gault, you are hardly talking about chicken feed!"

"Kate, word gets around pretty damn fast in this business. Even the little things matter. If it looks like I'm cutting corners, it won't take long before people start looking elsewhere. Everyone I compete against has the same fish I do. I'm only able to command the rates I charge because of our high-end quality reputation."

"Lou, I'm really concerned about the amount of money we're spending."

"Relax, I've got it covered."

Upon hearing the word "relax," Kate rolled her eyes and let out a sigh. "Lou, this celebration in Ireland isn't going to come cheap; and then, we'll be spending some serious money traveling around Europe for the better part of a month!"

"I know, I know. Kate, relax, I've got it covered."

"You've just gotten your life back, Lou, after stepping onto the tribal council over at the village, and now you're going to take on all of this? Lou, we'll be leaving shortly." She was showing anxiety that Lou hadn't seen before. Now it was etched on her face.

"Kate, will you *relax* . . . none of this is going to interfere with any of our plans. With the exception of the kitchen design layout, I'm delegating everything."

If this man says the word 'relax' to me one more time . . . I'm going to scream, she thought.

"Trust me, this is not a big deal."

As they continued talking, neither gave in to the other's concerns.

We're having our first real disagreement, Kate thought.

Then, Lou pushed his chair back and stood up. "Go put your hiking shoes on." Without another word, he walked out the front door and headed over to the main lodge.

Did he just tell me to go 'take a hike,' she thought, *or did he mean I should actually put my hiking shoes on?* Clearing the table did nothing to help clear her head. At that moment, she was miserable.

Chapter Four

BY THE TIME Anne walked up the back stairs to her sister Beatrice's flat, their lifelong friend, Evelyn Maxwell, had already arrived. After entering quietly, Anne paused at the doorway and listened to what they were saying in the next room.

"Beatrice, are you *sure* we can pull this off?"

"Evelyn, I majored in criminology, remember? And you took a few criminal justice courses, yourself. Between that, and all the ridiculous true crime books we've read, we know who the people are who get caught. They either *don't* have a plan, or are flat out *stupid*, even *careless*, and they leave loose ends. We're not stupid, we'll have a plan, *and* we're not leaving any loose ends."

With that, Anne cleared her throat and walked into their presence. Evelyn stood up. "Anne, dear, my sympathies on the death of your father. I had no *idea* he was in such poor health."

"Thank you, Evelyn," Anne replied.

"Did he suffer long?"

"No, actually," Anne said, "I heard he went rather . . . *quickly.*"

For the next hour, the three women huddled in Beatrice's flat going over details of how they planned to take revenge on the one person who had collectively ruined their lives.

"I'm looking forward to digging my nails into the *bitch*," Evelyn said at one point.

"As am I Evelyn, as am I." Beatrice said.

"Yes," Evelyn added, "but I really want her to *suffer.*"

"Trust me. She's *going* to suffer. She's the reason everyone's turned against us. It's because of this self-righteous bitch that we've been ostracized." Beatrice inhaled deeply as she closed her eyes and thought, *I was made to feel like I didn't even belong at my own father's damn funeral. It's because of that bitch I'm being shunned.*

A YEAR EARLIER, Lou's wife, Kate O'Grady, had led the INTERPOL team that successfully brought down an international smuggling ring run by the husbands of all three women. British courts had shown no mercy when sentencing the three men. They had all been stripped of their titles, property, and accumulated wealth, then condemned to life imprisonment.

Like a house of cards, the respectable, aristocratic lives of all three women, and their affluent social prominence, came crashing down.

The three women were now living lonely, miserable lives in the outskirts of London. Their only means of support was a modest income they each received by working in a travel agency catering to the very commoners they had looked down upon their entire, pampered lives.

Beatrice Hastings, who never had a moral compass, was consumed by revenge. The only thing she lived for now was getting even with the one person she held accountable for the humiliating life she was now living - Kathryn O'Grady.

"BEATRICE, I NEED to go," Anne said, interrupting her sister's thoughts. "I need to get at least a few hours of sleep before I go into work."

"Anne, we haven't finished with our meeting yet."

"They have me coming in on the early shift tomorrow, well, it's *today*, now," she said. "I really must go."

"Sit down, Anne. I *said* I wasn't finished."

Anne reluctantly did as she was told while Beatrice sipped her tea. "Here's what I know: Kathryn O'Grady now lives in Canada. But soon the papist pig-bitch will be traveling to Ireland and getting married in Abbyfeale."

"How do you know all that?" Evelyn asked before taking a sip from her cup of tea.

"Remember me telling you about that little backwater Irish travel agency that Royalty Travel picked up a few months ago?"

"Somewhat."

"Well, once that was finalized, the bitch's cousin, and everyone else in that damn office, was aligned under *me*."

"Who's her cousin? Do I know her?" Evelyn asked.

"Claire O'Grady. She was on the conference call last week."

"The one who kept interrupting?"

"Yes, she's the bitch's cousin and a *total* sieve; talks incessantly. She *thinks* I'm her best friend. I had no idea she was even related to the bitch until she started blabbing about her. She's taken it upon herself to make all the travel arrangements for the bitch's wedding."

"*R-e-ally*," Evelyn said in a long, drawn-out manner. "Is she a wedding planner, too?"

"Who the hell knows." Beatrice smiled. "Evelyn, believe me, I have *dreamed* of this, and now it's all falling right into our laps."

Anne spoke up, feigning interest. "So, what's the plan?"

Beatrice ignored her sister's question.

"I'll see the itinerary once it's settled," she said. "Then I'll book her flights."

Evelyn shifted in her seat. "Her *cousin* can't book the flights?"

"Of course, she can. But I told the little fool I could save her some serious money by using *my* supervisory discount, but she would need *me* to book it."

"So, what are you thinking?"

"Hopefully, I can find a way to separate her from her husband. Then, we'll snatch her."

Anne turned to her sister. "Husband? Beatrice, I thought you said she's *getting* married."

"Oh, the bitch is *already* married." Then she turned to Evelyn. "Get this, they got married in a ceremony somewhere out in the *woods*."

"You can't be serious," Evelyn scoffed.

"I am *dead* serious. Her cousin has pictures and she brags about it."

"So, what's the plan?" Anne asked again.

"Thanks to my father, we now have the funds to do whatever we choose to do. I'll stay in contact with The cousin. Once I find out what their itinerary is, we can regroup."

Anne looked at her watch. "Beatrice, I *really* need to go."

"Anne, we're nearly done. Besides, I'm going to transfer you over to my group. I'll work that out tomorrow."

"No, don't do that, I'm fine where I am. I just need to go."

"No, I'm *going* to transfer you. I've been planning to do this; it'll make things easier for me, if you're in my group."

Anne put her tea cup down and stood up. "Beatrice, it's nearly two in the morning, I *really* need to go."

"Anne, dear, we have more to discuss."

"I don't care…I don't care about this…I need to leave."

"Anne, please, don't disappoint me, you don't want to *disappoint* me, do you? I need your support, Anne. Look, Evelyn is staying, she's tired too. I'm tired and you *know* I've had a long night. Don't forget Anne, you agreed to be a part of this."

"I just need to leave. And stop trying to manipulate me, you always do this to me."

Beatrice sighed, as she shook her head, watching her sister slip out the door.

"Are you sure she's *in*?" Evelyn asked.

"We'll need to watch her."

"So, what's *really* the plan?"

"I need you to be my number two in all of this, just like you have always been. Can I count on you to follow my lead?"

"Why would you even *question* that?"

Beatrice, reached out and placed her hand on Evelyn's forearm. "Thank you. We'll run this one just as we ran 'The

Triplets' back in the day, even if it turns out to be just you and me."

"So, are we going to ransom her, or are you thinking of just snuffing the bitch?"

"No . . . *ransoming* her is still the plan, but I want her to *suffer.*"

"I'm fine with that."

"I can't wait to throw a damn hood over her head, like we did with that fool of a headmistress. Remember how we beat the ever-living crap out of her?"

"Ha, yeah for all her talk, Mrs. Humphreys turned into a whimpering sack of shit when she didn't have the upper hand, *didn't* she?"

Beatrice smiled. "No different than Professor Hutchinson."

"Ha, what a joke *he* was . . . the bastard thought he was going to have us expelled."

"I still remember my hands shaking when I brought him his last cup of tea." Beatrice said, closing her eyes and remembering. "'Here's your tea, your *Lord*ship.'" She mimicked the moment. "I couldn't *wait* to watch him drink it."

"Did they ever do an inquiry on that one?"

"Yes, don't you remember how we sweated it out?"

"Vaguely."

"They were both so old and stupid. Neither one knew enough to retire. So, we had to help them do it."

Then Evelyn stifled a yawn. "Enough of this memory stuff, let's get back to the plan."

"I'm working on it. I know they'll want to fly First Class. I need you sitting next to her on the plane, so I'll come up with a way to separate the bitch from her husband."

"Won't they ask me to switch seats with him?"

"They will, but I'll put him in the second row. All you'll have to say is that you're just getting over knee surgery and need the extra leg room in row one to stretch out."

"I thought all the rows in First Class had the same amount of leg room?"

"You and *I* know that, but *they* won't.

"What if they board before me?"

"Won't happen, I'll have you cleared to board as a Priority Advance."

"So, where do we grab her?"

"It'll have to be at the airport."

"Dublin or Shannon?"

"Shannon, the security at Dublin is too tight. I'll have her change planes at Shannon."

"Didn't I just read that Shannon is upgrading their surveillance system?"

"They're planning to, but they don't have the funding yet."

"So, what's my cover?"

"You're traveling for the same reason she is, and you're traveling *ahead* of your soon-to-be husband. I figure that would give the two of you something to talk about."

"How will you and I stay in touch?"

"You'll have a burner phone. Anne doesn't know this yet, but tomorrow, the three of us are having passport pictures taken. I've found someone who makes really good passports."

"So, we're going *incognito*?"

"We need to, our faces have been in the society pages for years."

"Okay, so who am I?"

"I'm not sure yet; I'll come up with names tomorrow."

"Just remember all my luggage has the initials 'E.M.'"

"Here, take this."

"What is it?"

"Hair dye. Use it tonight, I want you to have a different hair color on your new passport."

"You think of everything."

Chapter Five

EAGER TO GET started, Lou returned to the cottage, wearing his hiking boots. "Are you ready, Kate?" he called out.

"Lou, it's overcast; it's going to rain, can't we do this another time?"

"Come on, Jake's waiting for us down by the brook. I need to show you something."

Choosing not to argue, Kate rolled her eyes, got up from the table and grabbed her hiking boots. As soon as she finished lacing up, she stood. "Okay, let's go."

When they met Jake, he bowed slightly and made a gesture conveying, "ladies first," then took up the rear of their single-file column. Lou led them up the grassy knoll, toward the old saw mill. The brook was fairly wide near the mill, but just beyond it, was a narrow spot with a series of stepping stones one could use to cross over without getting wet. When they reached the far side, Lou paused slightly to adjust the straps on his back pack, then chose a path which obviously hadn't seen much wear.

"Lou, where are we going?"

"Up to the stream's headwater. Watch yourself here, Kate, these roots are slippery."

As they entered higher elevations, they began penetrating a heavy cloud cover that hung over the valley. Their breathing became more labored in the heavy, moist air. Rich earthy smells of the forest were replaced with musty, damp air. The fog limited their vision now to only a few feet in front of them as they continued climbing upward. Everything they touched felt wet, even the sounds of the forest seemed to have disappeared behind them. The only thing present was the sound of cascading water as it splashed over the rocks in a stream bed running parallel to their path. They were at a point where few humans ever tread.

Sections of the uphill trail were steep; footholds had been chiseled into an exposed granite ledge periodically. A few sections had been quite challenging. Kate began to sense the fog was lifting as they continued upward and the air no longer seemed quite as moist.

I have no idea why we're doing this. I should be home packing for our trip to Ireland, she thought. "Lou, how much further are we going?" She didn't like being kept in the dark for no apparent reason.

"Not far, it's just up ahead," Lou answered.

Then, as suddenly as if they had emerged through an invisible trap door, they broke through the fog and were looking down on the clouds. Lou turned to his cousin. "It sure is beautiful up here. Jake, do you get to fly above the clouds a lot?"

"Nah, I fly with a special VFR clearance. I need to stay

clear of clouds and maintain visibility of at least a mile. And, yeah, it's beautiful up here."

Fifty yards later they reached the source of the brook. The force of water gushing out from the jagged fissure in the ledge reminded Kate of an open fire hydrant. "I thought water pressure was supposed to be strong at the *bottom* of a hill, not at the top!"

"It is," Lou said. "Can you imagine what this would be like if it was coming out somewhere down below?" He knelt down next to an opening in the rocky ledge, rolled up his shirt sleeve, and reached into the cavity. "Kate, hold out your hand."

When he withdrew his arm, Lou placed a handful of walnut-sized nuggets into Kate's hand.

"What's…what's *this*?"

"Gold."

"I can *see* that," she said, blinking her eyes and trying to understand.

"Then, what's the question?"

"Where did it come from?"

Pointing with his thumb back toward the hole in the rock, Lou said, "From in there."

Kate locked eyes with her husband. "Lou, you *know* what I mean."

"Jake, hand me the waterproof bag in my knapsack, will you?"

"Sure, cuz."

"So, how did it *get* in there? Is *that* the question, Kate?"

"Yes."

"Jake and I stashed it there."

She stared at Lou, shaking her head, unable to speak. Lou

scooped out a few more handfuls of nuggets, then looked up at Kate.

"What?"

"Earlier this summer, I was surprised to find that among the Abenaki, you are known as 'Raven Claw.' Yesterday, I discovered that you understand and speak Italian, to a degree. *Now,* I find out that you have a *gold* mine. Are there any *other* secrets I don't know about? Do you own a coffee plantation somewhere? Maybe an island in the tropics?"

"Kate, I wasn't purposely trying to keep this a secret, okay; but every time I planned to tell you, all you wanted to talk about was the wedding in Ireland, and touring Europe."

"*That's* your reasoning? That *I've* been singularly focused?"

Lou smiled sheepishly.

"I may be going out on a limb here, Lou," she said, "but I'm pretty sure if you had said something like, 'Hey, I have a gold mine. Wanna hear about it?' I just *might* have put the wedding talk aside. No, actually, that's not correct. There is no *question* in my mind that I would have given you my *utmost* attention!"

Lou continued filling the waterproof bag with nuggets. "I'm sorry, Kate, I didn't intend to surprise you with this, but . . . well . . . now you know."

"Just tell me . . . is it *legally* yours? Where did it come from?" Placing her hands on her hips she added, "Without any leprechaun malarkey business…if you please."

"Yeah, it *is* legally ours, Jake's and mine actually. . .and now, of course, *you.* It came from the brook down by the saw mill. Years ago, the brook was loaded with these things. Our grandfather was always concerned one of the guests would wander over there and see them in the water. He didn't want that to happen. So, one summer, he told Jake and me to gather up all the nuggets we could find and haul them up here to the source of the stream, which we did. There were a *lot*. Now, when either of us needs a little extra money, we just hike up here and get some."

Kate looked at the two of them, her eyes wide in disbelief. "I don't know what to say, Lou, I'm dumbstruck. I need to sit down."

A WHILE LATER, after they had rested, Lou stood up and looked around one last time. "All right, we got what we came for, let's head back down."

Shortly, after heading down the trail but before reentering the fog , Lou slowed the pace. Kate's mind had been swirling with questions; she took this opportunity to ask one.

"Lou, are there more nuggets in the brook down below?"

"Occasionally, I'll find a nugget or two."

"What do you do with them?"

"I just pick 'em up."

"And?"

Lou stopped and turned around, "I put 'em in my sock drawer."

Kate laughed. She thought about this simple, unassuming approach to life that her husband had: Hiding gold nuggets in his sock drawer. "Lou, you are one of the most amazing creatures I could ever hope to find. . . kind of like a unicorn. . . if they even exist; but you always hope they do, like something magical."

"Hey, what about me?" Jake said. "Aren't I magical, too? I'm kinda feeling left out."

They all laughed together, then started walking again.

Whenever they came to a ledge, Lou paused to help Kate navigate the footholds in the rock before moving on. As soon as they reentered the dense fog, their world became opaque again. Even the familiar sounds of the forest seemed to vanish into the thick shroud of mist surrounding them.

As they continued their descent, Kate found herself alone in her thoughts again, thinking about Ireland and the cool, damp and cloudy days which so often embraced the Emerald Isle.

Suddenly, without warning, Lou, came to an abrupt halt and held up his hand. After a moment, Jake whisper from behind, "On the right, maybe fifty feet. . . no more."

"What is it?" Kate whispered. Lou turned his head and held up his index finger while making a shushing sound.

"What?" Kate mouthed the word silently.

Lou leaned closer and whispered. "I heard a snort. If we were down on flatland, I'd say it might be a feral hog, but not up this high."

"So, what is it?"

Lou didn't answer. Thick fog limited their visibility to about six, maybe eight feet. The heavy air muted the sound of a huge chunk of bark as it was ripped from the trunk of a tree and fell crashing to the ground.

"Lou, please, what is it?" Kate whispered more urgently.

"A black bear."

"What! Are they still around?"

"They're grubbing for food. . . need to fatten themselves up. It'll be a while yet, before they den-up for winter."

"Will this one bother us?"

Lou held up his index finger again. The beast had moved closer. If it smelled them, it could be onto them in a heartbeat. Lou cupped his hand around Kate's ear, and whispered. "It doesn't know we're here. The wind is coming *toward* us so it hasn't caught our scent. Breathe in deeply through your nose; you'll get a slight scent of clover."

"Clover?" Kate mouthed the word.

Lou nodded, then leaned over and cupped his hand around Kate's ear, again. "They smell like clover this time of year."

He unclipped the bear repellant from his belt, undid the safety, and held it up so Jake would see. Jake already had his cannister ready and mouthed the words: "Locked and loaded."

"What do we do now?" Kate whispered.

"We listen."

"Then, what?"

"If I tell you to get down, do it fast, and get into a fetal position."

Jake whispered from behind her. "Sounds like just one," Lou nodded in agreement.

"Is that good or bad?" Kate whispered.

"Good. It's not a sow, with young'uns to protect."

"Offense?" Jake whispered. Lou nodded, held up his hand and counted down with his fingers. When he reached three, both he and Jake let out a bloodcurdling yell and clapped their hands together as loudly as they could. The sudden noise coming through the fog startled the bear enough to send it crashing through the underbrush in the opposite direction.

"You'll have to teach me how to do that, when we get back," Kate said, very relieved.

Lou replaced the canister on his belt. "I will, but the first thing I'm doing is outfitting you with one of these canisters."

FINALLY REACHING THEIR cottage, Lou opened the door for Kate. As she walked passed him, he said, "I'll need to book a trip to Winnipeg."

She furrowed her brow. "Winnipeg?"

"Ya. Jake, you coming?"

"Nah, that's a busman's holiday for me, Lou. I'm gonna pass."

Kate looked at her husband and raised her eyebrows. "Lou, we're leaving for Ireland in a few days. *Why* would you be going to Winnipeg?"

"Because that's where the assay office is that we use for the gold."

"Are there no assay offices in the whole province of New Brunswick?"

"There's a few, but it's far too risky to use one of them."

"Why? What's the risk?"

"People would try to figure out where the gold came from."

"And?"

"Have you ever heard of the Cariboo Mountain gold rush?"

"No."

"Google it, sometime."

Placing hands on her hips, Kate said, "How about just giving me a synopsis."

Lou took a deep breath. "Back in 1870, when word spread about the strike in Little Horsefly Creek, people with gold fever poured into the Cariboo Mountains from everywhere. The governor of what is now British Columbia even had a road carved out of the wildness just to haul supplies into the camps, and help bring the gold out. They overran the lands of the native people who lived there, took what they wanted, killed off the game, and squatted along the streams until the claims ran dry. We can't risk anything like that happening to our ancestral lands if anybody suspected that we've found gold there."

"So, you travel all the way to Winnipeg because of what happened a long time ago in British Columbia?"

"Yeah, people don't change, Kate. Gold does funny things to people. Manitoba has four areas that are actively being mined for gold, today. In Winnipeg, they don't even ask where the gold comes from. Hell, if I went into an assay office in New Brunswick with a five-pound bag of gold, word would travel pretty fast. People would be trying to figure out where it was coming from, and we'd have a real problem on our hands."

"Is that how much this bag weighs?"

"Just about."

"How much is that worth?"

"Between this little bag and what I have in my sock draw, I'd say over a hundred thousand."

Kate's eyes opened wide. "Oh, my gawd. Is there much more up there?"

"Jake, how many times did we each lug a knapsack up there?"

"It has to be at least a half dozen times, I guess."

"The stream bed was loaded with nuggets, Kate. It took us weeks before we cleaned out everything we could find. There are a lot more nuggets still up there."

She tousled Lou's hair. "Well, I guess it's a moot point now whether we can afford the changes you want to make around here *and* have enough to tour Europe."

"I kept telling you to relax, didn't I?" He turned to his

cousin. "Jake, do they still fly direct to Winnipeg from Grand Falls?"

"Only on weekdays, Lou."

"Kate, you wanna come with me?"

"No, I have too many things to do before we leave for Ireland."

"Ah, come with me."

Kate took a deep breath and looked at her husband.

"*Please.*"

"All right . . . but we're not staying over!"

"Okay," he quickly agreed.

LATER THAT EVENING, Lou and Kate were relaxing on the couch watching colorful flames dancing between the logs. The huge fireplace covered nearly a third of the wall. After a while, Kate lifted her head off Lou's shoulder.

"Lou, when will you be ready to leave?"

"What's today, Monday?" he let out a sigh. "After we get back from Winnipeg, I should be okay to go by Thursday afternoon."

"Oh, Lou, that's way too late!" She said, sitting up straight.

"Kate, I'm trying to get everything squared away, so when we come back in a month, everything will be done. The Abenaki guides are coming back for a couple more days to work at the saw mill. We're redoing the kitchen design that Angelo wants to put in another oven. It's all taking a little longer than I thought."

She took a deep breath and let it out slowly. "It's just that my family wanted to spend a little time with us before the wedding."

When Lou didn't comment, she continued. "I spoke with the priest today."

"And?"

"He said he wanted us to go through pre-marital counseling before he marries us."

Lou furrowed his brow. "Why?"

She paused. "Because you're not Catholic . . . and that's the way it's done."

"So, what'd yah tell him?"

"I told him, that if he *insisted* on it, he could kiss his damn inflated stipend goodbye and we'd get married in the Church of England."

"*That's* my girl! No pulling any punches. What'd he say to *that*?"

"Well, he huffed and puffed a bit. Then he backed off . . . he knew my Irish was up."

"*What* was up?"

Kate let out a sigh. "He knew I was *angry*. You might as well know it now, this Irish colleen you've married, doesn't suffer fools gladly."

Lou smiled and looked at her a long minute. "So, how'd it end up with the priest?"

"He said he'd make an exception, but he's upped the ante."

"So, he waved the counseling?"

"Money still hasn't lost its influence within the church." She smiled, then was silent a moment, before taking a breath. "Claire has been on me again . . . about booking the flight. She says, she can work in an extra discount, if I book soon."

"Kate, take your time; we don't need any discounts."

"I know that. She's just trying to help."

"You know, it's your call if you want to go through her.

But if you change your mind, remember that Travel by Tatten helped me put together a nice itinerary for our honeymoon."

Kate was suddenly alert. "Care to share?"

"No, I don't. Our honeymoon is *my* surprise and don't bother calling Linda either. She's been sworn to secrecy. Just pack for fall weather, and bring some provocative sleepwear."

"Like the one that belongs to my cousin?"

"Exactly."

"I bought a new negligée. Would you like to help me try it out tonight?"

Lou smiled. "I'll be your huckleberry…"

Chapter Six

T HE FOLLOWING MORNING, Kate was preparing breakfast as Lou came in from the porch while pressing the "end call" button on his phone. "Kate, the kitchen design crew won't be flying up with new plans until Thursday, sometime before noon."

She waited a long minute before answering him. "Lou, I *really* need to get over to Ireland."

"I know."

She hesitated and carefully thought about how to phrase the next thing she was going to say. "Lou, I think Angelo could handle the kitchen design, don't you?"

"I can't saddle him with that. If anything goes wrong, he'll blame himself."

It completely surprised her that Lou wasn't budging; she decided to try a different approach, "Would you be terribly upset, if I flew over to Ireland ahead of you?"

"Kate, I didn't plan for this to happen, but, look, if that's what you want to do, go ahead."

"Fine."

It was the icy way she said it that caught Lou's attention. "Did you say 'fine?'"

"Yes, I said *'fine.'* It's not what I want, but . . . *fine.* I expected to fly over with my *husband,* but I have no problem flying over *alone.*"

Lou kept his mouth shut, which surprised Kate even more. *Is our honeymoon time over?* she wondered. *Is finalizing the kitchen plans more important than traveling together? If so, I won't press it,* she decided. *But I'll not be hogtied by anyone.*

After breakfast, Kate picked up her phone and called her cousin. "Claire? Kate here."

"Hey, Kate, are you ready to book your flights?"

"Yes."

"Are you excited?"

"More anxious, than anything."

"I know, right?" Claire said, "flying can be such a drag. When do you and Lou want to fly over?

"Actually, I'm going to fly over ahead of Lou."

"Oh?"

"He has a few things he needs to tie up, before he can take off for a month."

"Oh, sure, understandable. So, when would *you* like to leave?"

"Tomorrow."

"Great! Now, I'm sure it's absolutely delightful where you live, but, Kate, I gotta tell you, you're really living out in the sticks, dear."

"I know."

"So, first, I'll need to get you to an international airport. There's Toronto, Montreal, and Halifax. Take your pick, any preference?"

"Halifax seems like the most logical one."

"Grand, and you wanted a First Class, aisle seat, right?"

"Yes."

"How many bags?"

"Three, and a carry on."

"Grand. What else?"

"Nothing, really…oh, I'll need a taxi when I arrive in Dublin."

"No, you won't, dear, I'll pick you up."

"Oh, Claire, you don't have to do that. I don't want to be a burden," Kate protested.

"Hush. We'll have *no* talk about that. I'll be back in touch after I put a call into my supervisor. She's a bit of a bore, always prying, but she has a discount that I can't access."

"I'm not really worried about the money at this point," Kate said, "Just the time I need to get there and do everything." They talked only a few more minutes before saying goodbye.

As soon as Claire hung up, she called the London office.

"Hastings, here."

"Beatrice, it's Claire. Listen, I'm ready to book a flight for my cousin, Kate. You spoke about an additional discount that we could apply?"

"Party of two?"

"No, her husband will follow later."

R-e-a-lly. How wonderful, Beatrice Hastings thought as she sat back in her chair. A huge smile appeared on her face. *Things just got a lot easier.*

After a full moment of silence, Clare said, "Beatrice? Are you still on the line?"

"Yes, I'm here. What's the route?"

"Halifax to Dublin, First Class, aisle seat."

"Give me a moment." After a short pause, Hastings came back on the line. "I can do a huge discount, if she flies into Shannon and changes planes going into Dublin."

"First Class?"

"Yes."

"How much of a discount?"

"Nearly half price."

"How long's the layover?"

"Really just long enough that she won't have any luggage transfer problems. She'll go through Customs in Shannon which is way easier than Dublin."

"That's grand! What code do I use?"

"I'll need to apply it from here. Send me the complete itinerary, and I'll do the ticketing."

"Thanks, Beatrice."

"You bet."

Beatrice Hastings sat back in her seat, very pleased. *It's payback time, and she's traveling alone. I couldn't have asked for a better scenario if I had scripted it myself.*

AFTER BEATRICE BOOKED a First-Class seat on flights from Halifax to Shannon, then from Shannon to Dublin, for a passenger named Kathryn O'Grady, she booked a second passenger on the first leg of the same flight and put her in the seat next to O'Grady. Then, she dialed Evelyn Maxwell's extension.

"Evelyn, I need to speak to you."

"We're talking . . ."

"Privately."

"Oh, then I'll be right over."

When Evelyn arrived at Beatrice's office, Beatrice said: "Close the door and take a seat."

"Okay."

"You need to go home and pack."

"Why?"

"You're on a flight to Halifax in three hours."

"What's up?"

"The bitch is coming over solo."

"You're *kidding*?"

"No, can you believe it? How beautiful is that?"

"This is too sweet."

"Exactly."

"So, what's the plan?"

"You're flying over to Halifax today. Tomorrow, you're on a flight to Shannon, sitting beside you-know-who in First Class." Beatrice paused then retrieved a vial from her desk drawer. "I want you to become best friends with her."

"What if she doesn't want to talk?"

"She'll talk. Your cover is that you are traveling for the same reason she is - to get married."

Evelyn's focus faded and she appeared to be lost in thought.

"Look, it doesn't matter *what* you talk about. Tell her you're afraid of flying and you need someone to talk to; just make friends with her. Sometime before you land in Shannon, find a way to put this into her drink. It will dissolve instantly without an odor. The drug won't kill her, but it'll make her very slow and shaky."

"Then, what?"

"She's supposed to change planes in Shannon. She'll be out of it, so request a wheelchair to get her off the plane. Tell the flight attendant that she's your friend, and that you'll accept responsibility for her. Go with the wheelchair, I'll meet you in the baggage area once you clear Customs."

"What about her luggage?"

"Come on, who gives a *shit* about her luggage? That'll go on to Dublin . . . without her."

"Then, what?"

"I'll have a limo waiting; we'll put her in the back and take her to a remote location."

"Where?"

"I've narrowed it down to two places, both off the beaten track."

"How much is the ransom?"

"I'm staying with the nine million pounds, that's what we all agreed on. We'll split it three ways."

"So, Anne is *in*?"

"Yes."

Clapping her hands Evelyn rose from her seat. "I need to go pack! Which airport am I flying out of?"

"Gatwick."

As Evelyn turned to leave, Beatrice called out: "Wait." Then she opened her desk drawer and pulled out a package. "Here, you'll need this."

"What is it?"

"Your tickets, a burner phone, and your new passport."

"You think of everything."

Evelyn turned again to leave as Beatrice yelled out, again: "Wait." This time, she reached into her credenza and pulled out a Boston Red Sox baseball hat. "Here, take this, too."

"What's *this* for?"

"There will be a security camera taking pictures when you get off the jetway in Shannon. Put this hat on her head and pull the peak down to cover her face."

WITHIN THE HOUR, Claire rang Kate back. Recognizing her cousin's phone number, she answered with her name.

"Hi, Clare."

"Kate, I just spoke with my supervisor. I was able to get the supervisor employee deal for you."

"And?"

"You're flying First Class on both flights, and you leave tomorrow."

"Claire, I said I wanted to fly *direct*."

"I know, I know, direct is easier, but by doing it *this* way it's half the price of going direct. The tickets are nonrefundable and nontransferable, so it's all set, but that shouldn't matter."

"Which airline?"

"*Hello*, Aer Lingus, of course."

"How do I get down to Halifax?"

"Smyth Air will pick you up tomorrow afternoon at four and take you down to Halifax."

"Perfect."

"Now, how many rooms will you need?

"None. Lou and I will be staying at the cottage; everyone else can fend for themselves."

"Understood."

"Thanks, so very much, Claire. See you soon."

"Wait, wait! What about Lou? How's he getting over?"

"He uses an agency over here. He'll book his own flight."

"Got it. I'll be waiting for you in Dublin when you get in."

As soon as Kate ended the call, she walked into the other room. "Lou, I'm flying out tomorrow afternoon."

"I'll be only a couple of days behind you, Kate, promise."

"I wish you were coming with me."

"Believe me, Kate, so do I. It's just that I need an extra day here. You're anxious to get over there; it'll all work out."

"We're a couple, now," she said. "I don't want us to travel like this ever again, okay? Will you promise me that?"

"I promise." Lou saw the hurt in Kate's eyes. *Ahh, crap, I hope I won't regret not flying over with her.*

Chapter Seven

OVER THE PAST several days, Alessandra and Kate spent a little extra time together, enjoying each other's company before Kate left for Ireland to prepare for the wedding.

"Kate, you know Angelo and I would fly over and attend your ceremony in an instant, but we respect your wishes about this being a low-profile event," Alessandra said.

"Thanks, Alessandra. I'm beginning to wonder how 'low-profile' this shindig will actually be, no thanks to my cousin, Claire." Kate said. The idea of going "home" to Ireland was somewhat conflicting. She now thought of New Brunswick as her home . . . with Lou.

WHEN KATE RETIRED to their bedroom that evening, she put on a negligée she had borrowed from a different cousin. It was the same negligée she'd worn when she prepared herself for bed the day they were married in an Abenaki ceremony.

Unaware of the evening ahead, Lou finished banking the coals in the wood stove and walked into the bedroom to find Kate sitting on the bed, legs crossed in yoga fashion, wearing the provocative negligée.

"Whoa, *Kate*. You're wearing that sexy little thing, again."

Without a word, Kate pressed a button on her smart phone and a track from a Mickey and Sylvia's song began to play. Instantly, Lou recognized the melody to "Love is Strange."

Sylvia . . .

Yes, Mickey?

How do you call your lover boy? Kate, motioned with her finger and began mouthing the words.

"*Come here, lover boy!* The recording continued.

"*And, if he doesn't answer?*

"*Oh, lover boy!*" Kate tilted her head as she continued mouthing the words.

"*And, if he STILL doesn't answer?*"

"*I simply say, bay-bee…oh, oh, bay-bee…my sweet, bay bee… you're the one.*"

No longer able to keep a straight face, Kate laughed while her attention was fully captured by Lou's now naked body as he approached her. Knowing they'd be separated for the next few days, Kate wrapped her long legs around her husband and they made love to each other with every ounce of passion they had.

Eventually, Lou rolled over onto his back. "Promise me one thing, will you?"

"What's that?" she answered, smiling in the dim light of the room.

"That you'll never give your cousin back that nightgown, okay?"

She playfully punched him on the shoulder. "It's not a nightgown, it's a very *expensive* negligée."

"Frankly, my dear, 'I don't give a damn' . . . just be sure you pack it."

Kate tousled Lou's hair. "Why, Rhett Butler, you are simply *incorrigible*!" she said in a somewhat Southern drawl.

THE FOLLOWING MORNING, Lou arrived at the breakfast table, phone in hand. "Kate, you'll be happy to know the business manager I hired to run things over at the village is working out swell. Heck, even Kicking Bird seems satisfied with him."

"I'm surely glad; that must take a huge load off your shoulders."

"It does. Hey, I didn't mention this before, but the marina over in Five Fingers gave me a nice discount on the Honda outboards. They're taking the old Johnson outboards from me on trade."

"Good."

"And, we're almost finished cutting the lumber. The only thing I'm hanging around for now is one last meeting with the kitchen design team. Once we sign off on that, Angelo will be running the show."

Angelo should be running the show now. Kate thought. But out loud, she said something different. "Lou, I expect you over in Ireland right after that, okay? We're getting married on Sunday, and there are things I'll need your help with, before then."

"I know, and I won't disappoint you. Are you all packed?"

"Just about; how about you?"

"No, but I know what I'm taking."

"I'll have a tux waiting for you over there, but remember to bring your black shoes and a pair of black socks."

"I will. I already have them put aside."

Kate spent the rest of the morning visiting with Alessandra, while Lou oversaw the work over at the saw mill.

When the Smyth Air charter arrived, Lou walked Kate down to the dock, feeling even more conflicted than before, now that she was actually leaving. He knew he should be traveling with her, but he just wasn't comfortable going until the kitchen plans were finalized.

"Kate, I'm really sorry I'm not traveling with you. Call me as soon as you get there."

"Lou, it'll be the middle of *your* night when I land."

"I don't care what time it is; I want you to call me. Will you promise to *call* me?"

Kate kissed him and tousled his hair. "Yes, I'll *call* you."

"Travel safe. I love you," he whispered to her.

Once Kate boarded the plane, Lou passed her luggage up to the pilot and closed the door. He watched the plane taxi down the lake and take off, never moving from the dock, until it was out of sight.

I hope I haven't made a mistake by not going with her, he thought. *But, for better or worse, I'll own it.* Then he walked back to his cabin and dialed up the kitchen design firm. "Pierre, Lou here. What time will you be here on Thursday?"

"We should be there no later than eleven that morning."

"Could you make it even earlier?"

"We'll do our best."

He hung up, then dialed the number for his travel agency.

"Travel by Tatten," a pleasant voice answered.

"Linda, it's Lou."

"Hi, Lou, what's up?"

"I need to leave here on Thursday afternoon, then catch a flight over to Dublin."

"Both of you?"

"No, Kate's just gone on ahead."

"Okay. I'll get on it and call you back tomorrow morning."

"Thanks, Linda."

"You bet."

IN THE EARLY evening, another fast-moving storm came roaring up the valley. The sound of the wind whipping through the trees brought a smile to Lou's lips. *Kate would be at the windows for sure, stretching her neck to see if it was a banshee doing all that howling.*

His phone pinged and he saw a text from Kate: *In Halifax. . .boarding flight now. . .luv you.* Twenty minutes later another text arrived: *Backing away from the gate on time. . . luv/miss you.*

By the time Lou banked the coals in the stove and retired, Aer Lingus, flight 219 had already flown a third of the way across the Atlantic.

IT WAS AFTER FIVE the next morning, Atlantic Standard Time, when Lou's cell phone rang. Normally a light sleeper when out in the forest, Lou slept soundly in his own bed. It took a while before he realized the sound of the far-off noise he heard was his cell phone. By the time he grabbed it, the call had already bounced to voicemail. He looked at the clock. *5:12.*

This has to be Kate letting me know she's arrived, he thought.

Half awake, he sat on the edge of the bed and thumbed through a number of unread voices messages until he reached the most recent one and listened to it.

Lou, it's Claire. Have you heard from Kate? Her luggage is here in Dublin, but she didn't get off the plane.

He replayed the message but still wasn't processing everything when a text came in from Claire: *Pls call me!*

Now Lou was wide awake as he punched in Claire's phone number. "Claire, Lou here. What's the problem? Kate got on the plane in Halifax and left on schedule."

"Lou, she never arrived in Dublin."

Lou's heart sank. "Are you *sure*?"

"Lou, I've been standing here in the airport talking to Aer Lingus people for the past half hour trying to figure out where the hell she is. Her luggage made it, but they're telling me she got off the first flight in Shannon, but never boarded her connecting flight to Dublin."

"That doesn't sound like Kate, she's a savvy enough traveler that she wouldn't miss a connection."

"I know, that's why I'm concerned."

"Was there a problem with the flight?"

"No, her flight into Shannon was on time. The only thing the airline reported was that when they landed in Shannon, they took a passenger off in a wheelchair."

"Was that *her*?"

"I'm trying to check on that."

"Look, Claire, I'm awake now so keep me updated, okay?"

"Will do."

"And, Claire, if it *was* Kate they took off the plane in a wheelchair, maybe she's in a clinic or a hospital somewhere near Shannon."

"I'll check with the first aid station in Shannon; they might know something. I'll also check with Aer Lingus; maybe she rebooked and is coming in on the next flight."

As soon as Lou hung up, a wave of regret washed over him; his mind flashed back to an incident that happened a short time ago when he and Kate had gone up to Quebec City on an undercover assignment. They had met with a retired Mountie who had been doing minor surveillance work for them. The SOB had kidnapped Kate. The same hollow feeling Lou had back then, was once again churning in his stomach. He closed his eyes.

Damn it. The kitchen design wasn't that friggin' important . . . I should have let Angelo handle it and gone over with Kate. She knew it, too.

Chapter Eight

EVELYN MAXWELL TRAVELED from London to Halifax, Nova Scotia, under the alias "Ellen Marshall." The following afternoon, the gate agent in Halifax immediately recognized the special Priority Advance designation on Evelyn's ticket and allowed her to pre-board the plane.

Later, when Kate boarded, Evelyn looked up, smiled, and waited for Kate to settle into the seat next to her. A few moments later, she looked over at her.

"Business or pleasure?" she asked.

Kate turned her head slightly and smiled. "Pleasure." Then took out her cell phone.

"Me, too." Evelyn answered.

Kate punched in a text to Lou saying she had boarded. *I hope I'm not sitting next to a 'Chatty Cathy,'* she thought.

Evelyn waited for Kate to put her cell phone away before speaking again. "I'm looking forward to a relaxing flight."

Without turning her head, Kate answered, "Likewise."

"I'm heading over to Surry; we're renewing our wedding vows in front of my English family." Kate did a double-take upon hearing that and turned to look at Evelyn, but said nothing. Letting out a sigh, Evelyn lamented, "It hurt them deeply when they found out we'd eloped. Now, we're doing this to hopefully mend fences."

Kate's antenna was on high alert. *What are the freaking odds that two strangers would end up sitting next to each other on a flight from Halifax to Shannon and traveling for the same reason?*

When Kate didn't respond, Evelyn tried a different approach, "That's a beautiful wedding band you have on; may I see it?"

Kate held out her hand to show the Abenaki ring Lou had given her at their ceremony.

"It's very different; I don't believe I've ever seen one quite like it."

"It's one of a kind; an artisan friend of my husband crafted it."

"How lovely. Have you been married long?"

"No."

"Same here."

Evelyn sensed that Kate wasn't ready to talk yet. She didn't want to push it, so she backed off and took out a book. But a short time later, she put it down. "Can I ask you something?"

Kate turned her head and waited.

"I'm really upset that I ended up flying alone," Evelyn said.

"Why is that?"

"Because we're a couple now. I thought he'd be flying *with* me, instead he's coming over later."

Kate took a breath and let out a sigh. "We're doing the same thing. I'm also on the 'advance team.'"

"I don't know about you, but it's been such a hassle trying to plan everything over there from over here," Evelyn said, shaking her head. "I'm just looking forward to exchanging our vows in front of the family, then spending a few weeks traveling around the Mediterranean."

Kate began to relax a little. *This is totally crazy; maybe this is one of those coincidental, serendipitous things that happen.*

"My husband has never been to Provence," Evelyn said, continuing to talk.

Kate smiled, not having noticed that Evelyn hadn't *really* asked her a question. "We're doing the exact same thing."

"No way!"

"Yes, we married this past summer. My family didn't come over because we told them we planned to fly over to Ireland and renew our vows in front of them once we closed the lodge."

"My husband is flying over in a couple of days; he just couldn't get away."

"Neither could mine; he has his own business, it's seasonal, you work around it."

Once they started discussing the hassles of making wedding arrangements from across the pond, Kate was hooked. The two continued exchanging stories as the plane took off and climbed to a cruising altitude. Eventually lights were turned down for the red eye flight. Later, after they had both dozed, then woken again, they were enjoying breakfast mimosas and continuing to talk.

Shortly before the pilot announced they were about to enter an approach to Shannon Airport, Kate rose from her seat to use the unisex lavatory. As soon as her back was turned, Evelyn Maxwell reached into her purse, took out the the vial of clear, odorless substance Beatrice had given her, and emptied the contents into Kate's unfinished mimosa.

When Kate returned to her seat, the plane was beginning to descend. As the flight attendant came to pick up their glasses, Evelyn quickly lifted her glass into the air. "Come on Kate, let's toast to *us*, the advance team!"

How could Kate refuse? She drank all the liquid in her mimosa glass.

By the time the plane reached the gate, Kate was slurring her words and starting to slouch in her seat. The first-class flight attendant noticed and came over to assess the situation.

"Shall I call ahead to have a medical response team at the gate?" she asked Evelyn.

"No, she's just had a little too much to drink. She's not an early drinker. I think if you simply call for a wheelchair, that will be sufficient."

"You're sure about that?"

"Yes, thank you," Evelyn smiled. "We're together," she lied. "This isn't the first time. I'll stay right here until the wheelchair arrives." Evelyn and Kate were the last to deplane. When the wheelchair was brought onboard, Evelyn helped the attendant lift Kate out of her seat and into the conveyance. "I can take it from here," Evelyn assured the attendant. "Thank you so much."

The elderly wheelchair attendant didn't even hesitate before saying, "Ma'am, you just lead the way and I'll follow you."

Evelyn looked at him for a long moment, then placed the Boston Red Sox baseball cap on Kate's head; they exited the plane and headed into the terminal.

"Thank you so much, but you've done enough. I can handle it from here," she said, trying to dismiss him again.

"Sorry ma'am; it's airport policy. I'm responsible for the safety of anyone who sits in my chair." Evelyn decided not to challenge the elderly volunteer and reluctantly led the way over to the baggage claim area.

"Ma'am, do you have your luggage stubs?" the old man asked.

Knowing Kate's luggage was checked straight through to Dublin, she said, "No, we only had carry-on luggage."

He looked at her with surprise. "Didn't you just come in from Canada?"

"Yes."

"And you *don't* have any checked luggage?"

"That's what credit cards are for," Evelyn said, thinking quickly. "We girls have to travel light so we can buy new things." The elderly volunteer slowly shook his head.

"I'll be darned, always something new," he said. "Okay, then, we're on to Customs."

When the Customs official questioned the way Kate looked, Evelyn explained that her companion had a stomach bug and between whatever meds she'd taken, cocktails on the plane, and a rough flight, her companion had obviously had a bad reaction. The customs official shook his head, took their passports, and stamped them both.

When they exited the customs area, Beatrice Hastings was waiting. She motioned Evelyn over to her and whispered, "Why didn't you get rid of the old guy?"

"I tried, twice!"

When the wheelchair attendant asked if they were finished with the chair, Beatrice said, "No, we need the chair to get her into the car. Follow us, please." She started walking and they all trailed behind her toward the exit.

Evelyn leaned toward Beatrice and whispered: "How can we shake him?"

"We'll ditch him in the garage; there are only a few cameras there. We're coming up on one now. Tilt your head down so they won't get a clear shot."

"Are you parked in the garage?"

"No. I told you I'd have a limo, remember?"

Then why are we walking to the parking garage, Evelyn wondered.

Beatrice continued across the street and when they reached an elevator at the closest garage building, she pushed the button. The door opened and the wheelchair attendant said, "Ladies first; go ahead, I'll need to back in." After the doors closed, Beatrice pushed a button for the third floor. When they reached it and the door opened again, Beatrice was the first to step out.

"This way," she commanded, and headed toward a dimly lit area near the rear of the garage. As soon as she sensed they were alone, she discretely fell behind the old man as he kept pushing the wheelchair alongside Evelyn.

Beatrice reached into her purse, whipped out a blackjack, and in one fluid motion, delivered a crushing blow to the back of the elderly man's head. He dropped into a heap on the concrete floor.

"Evelyn, hold the chair while I drag him out of the way."

"Do you need help? This chair has a brake."

"No, I've got it." Once Beatrice dragged the old man between two parked cars, she reached down, fished around for his wallet and took out the small amount of cash in it along with a credit card. She dropped the wallet next to him and turned to Evelyn.

"Okay, back to the elevator. I've got a limo waiting." As they approached the elevator, Beatrice warned again, "Keep your head down, there's a camera up ahead of us."

When they reached the limo area, the driver Beatrice had engaged helped them lift Kate into the back seat.

"You can put the chair in the trunk."

"Sorry, ma'am, that chair is airport property. We're not allowed to take airport property off site."

Beatrice hadn't counted on that little wrinkle. Opening her purse again, she took out a two-hundred Euro note and held it out to him. "I'd very much appreciate it if you would put the chair in the trunk for us."

"The pole that's attached is too long, ma'am, it won't fit in the trunk."

"Then *make* it fit."

The driver looked around to see if anyone was watching before he bent the hollow aluminum pole in half, snapping it off. Then he collapsed the chair and put it into the trunk. He helped the women into the back seat where they had put Kate; she was still unconscious but now slouching between the two women. Starting the engine, the driver looked into the rearview mirror. "Where to ladies?"

"Don't you have the address I provided?"

"I do, ma'am, but I always like to ask, just in case there's been a change of plans."

"McDermott's Castle, County Roscommon, the ferry landing," Beatrice said in an annoyed tone.

"Right, that's what I have, ma'am."

WHEN LOU HADN'T heard from Claire by five-thirty, his time, he punched in her number. "Claire, have you located Kate?" he asked as soon as she picked up the call.

"No, I can't figure out where she is."

"You're *kidding*!"

"No, this is the weirdest thing. She boarded in Halifax, but she's not in Shannon, she's not in Dublin, she's not answering her phone, she not in the first aid station, and she didn't rebook. I can't believe it, but I've totally lost my very own cousin!"

"This may be a wild guess, but could she have rented a car in Shannon?"

"Now, why would she do that? She had a plane ticket."

"Maybe she missed the flight?"

"It's unlikely, but I'll check."

"Claire, she's *somewhere* over there. Have you spoken with the airport police?"

"Yes. I'm waiting to hear back from them."

"Keep me in the loop," he said, more than worried at this point.

"I will."

AT 1:00 P.M. DUBLIN time, Aer Lingus called Claire and verified that the passenger who had been taken off the plane in a wheelchair was, in fact, Kathryn O'Grady. However, the first aid station in Shannon's airport had no record of anyone with that name being seen, treated, or examined in the past twenty-four hours. In fact, no one remembered seeing her at all.

Chapter Nine

McDERMOTT'S CASTLE, tall and imposing, sat alone on an island in the middle of a small lake in County Roscommon. The castle had not been occupied by a member of the McDermott Clan for well over a century. Its large, gray stones were weather-beaten and in need of attention. Beatrice had been attracted to it because of its remote location. She had rented the island castle for two weeks and arranged for two large wall tents, four bunks, tables, chairs, a portable toilet, a field kitchen, and several weeks of provisions to be delivered and set up on the island.

As the limo pulled up to the ferry landing, Beatrice turned to Evelyn. "Anne's already over there. I'll help you to get this one back into the chair, then I want you to wheel her over to the dock. I'll let the old man who operates the ferry know we're here."

"Aren't you staying?"

"I'll be over later. I need to take care of something first."

As the limo driver took the wheelchair out of the trunk,

Evelyn looked across the water. Springing up from the middle of the small island was a huge, partially dilapidated edifice which at one time would have been the castle keep. In its day, the tower and massive stone walls would have been an impressive stronghold, but those days were long passed. Sections of the fortress wall had now collapsed and the land surrounding the castle was completely overgrown. Vines were trailing up the sides of the walls, and a colony of brown long-eared bats had taken up residence inside the tower.

Hmph, not quite the venue I'd expected, Evelyn thought.

A moan slipped from Kate. Beginning to arouse, she was vaguely aware of movement, but kept fading in and out of consciousness. She had no idea where she was nor that she was being held captive.

BACK IN NEW Brunswick, Lou was waiting for a call from either Kate or her cousin, Claire, when he received a text:

Nine million pounds and U get her back . . . unharmed.

Who are you? Lou immediately texted back.

No reply.

Quickly, Lou punched in the cell phone number of his friend, Fletcher Martin of the Royal Canadian Mounted Police. The two had fought side by side in Afghanistan years earlier. Recently, Fletcher had been promoted to the rank of sergeant major for the province of New Brunswick.

Fletcher was deep in thought when his phone rang. He had been laboring over the uncertainties inherent in the upcoming year's operating budget that he would soon be bringing forward, when he answered.

"Sergeant Martin speaking."

"Fletcher, someone has kidnapped Kate! They want nine million pounds to release her."

"Say again?"

Lou, held his cell phone at arm's length and yelled: "FLETCHER, SOMEONE HAS KIDNAPPED KATE . . . KATE O'GRADY HAS BEEN KIDNAPPED!!"

"Lou, is this you?"

"*Yes*, it's me! Fletcher, I need your help!"

"Did you just say *kidnapped*?"

"Yes. They just sent me a text. They want *nine million pounds*."

"Who does?"

"I don't know."

"When did this happen?" Fletcher was trying to sort out what Lou was saying.

"Overnight. Today. I don't *know*, damn it . . . I'm not sure, it just *happened*."

"Where?"

"I don't *know* . . . somewhere between Halifax and Shannon Airport in Ireland.

"Lou, I don't have jurisdiction in *either* of those places."

"I don't give a good *damn* if you do or not! Fletcher she's been *kidnapped*! We need to find her!"

"Right. Sure thing, Lou, I'll get a missing person's bulletin out as soon as we shut off.

"A missing person's *bulletin*? Are you *shitting* me? Fletcher, for God's sake! That's not good enough! She's a friggin *Mountie!* You have a Mountie in your own command who's been kidnapped!"

"We'll get it up on INTERPOL as well, Lou, right away."

"Fletcher, you're acting like a friggin bureaucrat. Don't be an *asshole!* you need to launch a friggin investigation! This *has* to be related to that damn smuggling thing all of you were involved in last fall."

"Now, *that's* a pretty big stretch."

"The hell it is, and you damn well know it!"

Fletcher paused. "Lou, I'm going to put Duffy on this."

"Good, have him call me back right away. *Damn it!*"

LOU WASN'T EXACTLY sure what to do next. His mind was going in several different directions at once. Then, he dialed the Irish Directorate of Military Intelligence.

"Irish Military Intelligence. How may I direct your call?"

"Hello, this is Lou Gault, a former member of your group has just been kidnapped. I need to speak with whoever is in charge."

"May I have your name, sir?"

"Lou Gault, Royal Canadian Mounted Police."

"Is this an official call, sir?"

"Look, my wife transferred from the Irish Directorate of Military Intelligence to the Royal Canadian Mounties seven months ago. Now, she's *missing.* I need your help. I need to speak with whoever is in charge."

"Sir, this sounds like a matter for your local police. Have you contacted them?"

"Look, *I need your help*! She's *still* an Irish citizen."

"Where did the abduction occur?"

"I don't know. . . somewhere between Halifax and Shannon Airport early this morning. Look, they texted me. They want nine million pounds ransom."

"Stay on the line. I'm going to place you on hold."

It was over five minutes of excruciating silence as Lou

waited on the line, all the while staring at the kitchen chair where Kate usually sat.

My God, he wondered, *where the hell is she? Damn . . . Kate!*.

Finally, the operator came back on the line. "Who are you holding for?"

It took Lou a second before saying, "Field Investigations."

"One moment; I'll put you through."

There was a click on the line and Lou heard, "Field Investigations. O'Malley speaking."

"Hi. Listen, this is Lou Gault. Here's the deal: My Irish wife has been kidnapped. I need some help."

"Start at the beginning and tell me what's happened."

Lou began relaying everything he knew along with what he suspected. Periodically, O'Malley asked a question, but for the most part he just listened and took notes.

"Okay. So, you say your *wife* is a Royal Canadian Mountie, but she previously was a member of the Irish Directorate of Military Intelligence. Is that correct?"

"That's correct. Her name is Lieutenant Kathryn O'Grady."

"All right, now look, we're coming up to a shift change over here. So, I'm going to give this to the incoming watch commander. Now, the number you're calling from . . . is that the best number to reach you at?"

"Yes, but I'll stay on the line."

"That won't be necessary, sir, the watch commander will call you back; you can be sure of that." Lou heard a click and the line went dead.

Lou, inhaled deeply. *Friggin damn bureaucrats.*

A few minutes later, Lou's phone rang. He answered and heard the voice of Duffy. "Lou, what the hell is going on? Fletcher said something about Kate being kidnapped?"

"I put her on a Smyth Charter yesterday, around four in the afternoon, for Halifax. She sent me a text when she boarded an *Aer Lingus* flight to Shannon. She was supposed to change planes in Shannon and fly to Dublin. She got *off* the plane in Shannon in a goddamn *wheelchair*, but never got on the next flight, and she's not answering her phone. No one knows where the hell she is. Her cousin was supposed to meet her in Dublin, but Kate never showed; then I just got a friggin' ransom note on my cell that somebody just sent me."

"Do you have a copy of her itinerary?"

"Yes."

"Fax it to me."

"Okay"

"*Who* was supposed to meet her?"

"Her cousin, Claire. Claire O'Grady. She's a travel agent."

"Text me her contact info. And you have a ransom note?"

"Yeah. They sent me a text; they want nine million pounds."

"Save that text and *don't delete anything*, and I mean ANYTHING on your phone, I'll have our guys pull off everything that's hit your phone in the past twenty-four hours. Are you at the lodge?

"Yes."

"All right. Here's the deal: Because no minor is involved, and there's no evidence that the kidnapping occurred on Canadian soil, the Abduction Unit won't deploy. So, we're going to handle this a little differently."

"What the friggin' hell does *that* mean?"

"It means, pack up your gear and get your friggin' ass down here to headquarters. Bring your passport, Kate's police sidearm, and any recent photos of Kate. You and I are going over to Ireland."

"Will do." He felt relief at something beginning to happen. Next, Lou placed a call to Smyth Charter requesting an immediate pick up at the lodge. After that, Lou called his cousin, Jake, who answered on the second ring.

"Hey, cuz, you're up early. Wassup?"

"Kate's been kidnapped, Jake, I'm heading down to Fredericton."

"Very funny."

"I'm serious."

"Come on, cut the clowning."

"Jake, I'm *serious*!"

Jake paused to internalize what he had just heard. "*Holy crap!* How? When? Where?"

"Sometime in the last twelve hours. I received a ransom note. They want nine million."

"Who does?

"I don't know. All I know is that she boarded a plane in Halifax last night heading over to Ireland. She was supposed to board another plane when she reached Shannon and fly to Dublin. But she never made that flight, and she's not answering her phone, or texts. Nothing."

"Shit, man, this doesn't sound good."

"I'm on my way down to meet Duffy. Fletcher's put him in charge of the investigation. We're going over to Ireland. I could use you as my wingman, Jake."

"You know I'll give you everything I have in the tank, and then some, cuz!"

"That's why I called you."

"I'll let my guys know they need to line up a replacement to fly my mail route," Jake said, starting to think things through. "You want me to meet you at the lodge?"

"No. Smyth Air is picking me up shortly; catch up with

me in Fredericton. We'll most likely follow Kate's route and fly out of Halifax."

"Got it. You're heading out fast, anything I need to do at the lodge for you?"

"No. Angelo can handle things while I'm gone."

"All right, gotta go, cuz. I'll see you in Fredericton."

Closing off his phone, Lou walked over to the dock, turned on the flood lights so the incoming float plane would be able to safely navigate to the dock, and headed over to Angelo's cottage.

Lou shared everything he knew with Angelo and Alessandra, including the fact he was heading out shortly. "Angelo, I'm not sure how long I'll be gone, but I'm not coming back without Kate. The kitchen designers are flying up later today. If you're happy with their revised plan for the kitchen, give them the green light. If you want them to make a few minor adjustments, tell them what you want, and get things going."

"Lou, don't worry, you do what you need to do. I'll take care of things here."

"Jake is coming with me, so you're in charge of overseeing and managing the kitchen expansion and all the projects underway. I'm trusting you to hold down the fort until I get back."

"Don't worry, *mio figlio,* I will take care of all these things for you."

As Lou turned to leave, Alessandra grabbed his shirt sleeve and embraced him. With tears in her eyes, she hugged her adopted son tightly. "Lou, *non ti scordar di me!*" Then she repeated it in English. "Do not forget me. Do not forget to call us and tell us about Kate. We love her, too."

"I know. I won't forget." His heart was beating fast as he walked out the door.

Chapter Ten

THE ONE THING Beatrice Hastings always strove to avoid in life was loose ends. As she sat in the back seat of the limo she thought, *I should have made sure I killed the old man with the wheelchair, if he's still alive, he could identify us. At least I wiped my fingerprints off his wallet. The evidence will point to a simple robbery, but I need to be more careful.*

As Evelyn started wheeling Kate over to the ferry landing, the limo driver tapped on the back window. Beatrice rolled it down half way.

"Are you getting out ma'am?"

"No, I need a ride back to the airport."

"The reservation didn't say anything about a return passenger, ma'am. I imagine that'll be an additional charge."

She waved her hand in a dismissive manner. "It doesn't matter, I need to go back to the airport."

"All right, I'm headed back there anyway. I'll call it in; shouldn't be a problem."

"Fine." In Beatrice's mind, the limo driver was another loose end. *I need to deal with it.*

WHEN THE TWINS and their friend, Evelyn, were young, they were often referred to as 'the triplets' and had a nefarious past. Not only were they quick to physically punish anyone who gave them even the slightest grief in school, but they had actually killed two faculty members . . . and had gotten away with murder.

Later in life, a member of their yacht club had died under shady circumstances. The dead woman had, for some unknown reason, decided to run against Beatrice for the prestigious role of "Lady Commodore." Beatrice had waited years for a perennial favorite to step down, now she wanted the role. Early in life, Beatrice had learned how to manipulate and bully people to get whatever she wanted. This other woman had no idea who she was trifling with, but on the day she died, she found out. In the days that followed 'the triplets' were never considered as suspects in the cause of death.

NOW, WHEN THE limo left the area adjacent to the ferry landing, it traveled across a long stretch of undeveloped land which had once been the productive fields and pasture lands of the McDermott Clan. Well before they reached the main road, Beatrice, moved from the very back to the front bench seat directly behind the driver, and knocked twice on the privacy window. The driver toggled a button and lowered the glass.

"Yes ma'am?"

"Pull over."

"Say that again, ma'am?"

Beatrice shoved her arm through the opening, held a pistol against the driver's head, and said it again. "Pull over."

The driver glanced in the rearview mirror, saw the gun next to his head, and cried out: "Jesus, Mary, and Joseph, pray for us!"

"I said . . . *pull over*!" Beatrice growled.

"Don't shoot! I'm pulling over! Take the limo and my money!"

As soon as the limo came to a stop, Beatrice said, "Put it in 'park,' shut it off, and hand me the keys."

The driver's hands were shaking as he handed the keys over to her.

"Now, get out," Beatrice demanded. She wasted no time exiting the limo herself, but by the time she was out, the limo driver was already running down the road.

She fired one shot into the air and the man stopped running. When he turned around, she said, "Come back here."

With his hands held high, the man cautiously walked back. "Ma'am, I am not going to resist you in any way, shape, or form. You can take the limo."

Ignoring the man's plea, Beatrice waved the pistol with an air of indifference. "Move into the field, and be quick about it."

WHEN JAKE FLEW into Fredericton, he walked over to the Aer Lingus counter, booked a seat on the same flight from Halifax to Ireland that Lou and Duffy would be on, and took a taxi over to RCMP headquarters. As he entered the building, he flashed his auxiliary officer's badge at the duty sergeant and walked through the lobby.

"Lou!" he called out. "Where are you?"

Duffy emerged from an office. "Jake, over here."

"Duffy! Where's Lou? What's the plan?"

"The only plan right now is for us to head over to Ireland; after that, it's all freestyle."

"I like that."

"It's far from being a textbook operation, know that."

"Is *Fletcher* okay with that?"

Duffy smiled. "We talked."

"You got someplace I can stretch out for a while?"

"In here; but don't get too comfortable, we're flying down to Halifax soon."

"The word *comfortable* just ain't in my vocabulary, right now, Duffy."

"Understood. Are you 'carrying?'"

"No."

"Then get your ass over to the supply sergeant, draw a Glock and some shells, and hurry back. We're moving out within the half hour. Tell the sergeant I had you and Lou moved to 'active status,' otherwise, you won't get anything from him." Without that move, the men wouldn't have been able to carry firearms and live ammo on the commercial flight from Halifax to Shannon.

As Jake walked away, he called over his shoulder: "Where's Lou?"

"He's on the phone talking to a travel agent in Ireland."

Fifteen minutes later, Jake returned wearing a shoulder holster with a Glock and carrying a box of cartridges.

When Lou finished talking with Kate's cousin, Claire, he

walked over to Duffy's office. "Nothing further on that end, Duffy."

"All right, Jake's here, let's go. There's a chopper waiting on us at the airport. I don't have enough clout to hold the flight going out of Halifax, if we're late arriving."

As they walked out the door, Lou looked at Jake. "Thanks, cuz."

ALL THREE MEN had flown in enough choppers to know that inflight conversation would be damn near impossible once the bird was airborne, even with headphones. So, each man sat back, closed their eyes, and sat alone with their thoughts.

Jake recalled the many times he and Lou had ridden choppers after being called out on search and rescue missions for lost hikers and hunters. This mission would be different, though, and his thoughts were focused on the role he needed to play for his cousin. Lou pushed aside whatever regrets he had about not traveling with Kate; now, he was focused on what lay ahead. In his mind, he was sorting out what had happened, what he thought he knew, and what he didn't know, trying to get his head around it all. The only thing for certain was the fact that he'd allow Duffy to run the administrative side of this for now. But when the time came for actual field work and rescuing Kate, he would take the lead.

Duffy reflected on how Fletcher Martin had broken protocol by passing over three Mounties of higher rank to select him to lead this strike force. His thoughts shifted back and forth between all the times he and Kate had worked together in the past and about the bond he and Lou shared going back to the dust and heat of the Afghan wars. He also knew this was his last opportunity to regain the sergeant stripes he'd lost, twice now, due to the shenanigans he kept pulling on the higher ups. If they failed to rescue Kate, he also knew that Fletcher would be criticized for not choosing one of the higher-ranking Mounties to lead the effort.

By the time the chopper landed in Halifax, all three men were mentally prepared for the mission that lay ahead.

Chapter Eleven

T HE LIMO DRIVER had walked no more than thirty feet into the tall grass when Beatrice fired two slugs into his back. He fell to the ground with hardly a sound. She walked over to the dying man and coldly finished him off with a third shot directly into the base of his skull.

This time . . . no loose ends, she thought. When she returned to the limo, she slid into the driver's seat and drove herself back to the landing without a single ounce of remorse.

The old man who ran the ferry had just returned from the island and was securing the ropes to the cleats when Beatrice stepped onto the dock.

"I need a lift over."

The man stood up straight and looked her directly in the eyes. "Well, give me a damn *minute.* I have to go take a pee before I wet myself."

From the beginning, Beatrice had been repulsed by the man's slovenly appearance, but his crude, uncouth language caused her to take a step back. He, too, was a risk . . . another loose end that she didn't need. But she needed him a while longer.

Within minutes, the ferry master returned. The crossing went without incident, but Beatrice watched his every move. She expected she'd need to run the ferry boat herself very soon. As they docked, Beatrice stepped onto the wooden platform and looked back at the old man as he pulled the ferry boat away.

Another time, then, she thought. She started up a small incline to the pitched tents and heard Anne call out.

"Beatrice, you're here!"

"Yes, is everything in order?"

"I . . . I believe it is."

"You don't *know*?"

"Beatrice, don't you *dare* start with me." Her tone indicated she wasn't up for her sister's manipulation right now. Beatrice ignored Anne's warning.

"Evelyn, where's the bitch?"

"She's in the other tent. She's not going anywhere."

"Let's go pay her a visit."

Evelyn had secured Kate to the wheelchair using a set of handcuffs and ropes. She had also tied a gag across her mouth. While still physically immobilized from the drug, Kate's vision had returned; she was becoming cognizant of her surroundings and what was happening.

Beatrice smirked when she saw Kate. "Believe me, *bitch,* this is only the *beginning.* You're going to *suffer* like you've *never* suffered before."

Kate defiantly locked eyes with Beatrice. Seeing the defiant look, Beatrice stepped forward without warning and slapped Kate twice across the face - hard. Then she turned to her sister.

"Anne, stay with her. She gets *nothing* to eat tonight."

She would have objected, but Anne sensed that Beatrice was in another of her foul moods, and decided against it.

"I'm going to check these ropes," Beatrice said while bending over the wheelchair, "just to make sure our little *kitten* isn't able to wander off during the night." The light inside the tent was low, but once Beatrice walked behind the wheelchair, Evelyn, came into view.

Kate's eyes opened wide in total disbelief. Evelyn saw her recognition.

"That's right, *bitch*, it's me! Surprised, huh?" She walked over to Kate and slapped her on the side of her head. "This is only the beginning." Then, she slapped Kate a second time, only harder, leaving a red welt on her cheek.

Satisfied that Kate was secured, Beatrice began barking orders. "Anne, watch her; this is *your* tent. Evelyn, I'd like *you* to get something going for us to eat. I need to spend some time on the Internet."

AFTER THE THREE women ate a meager dinner, Evelyn asked, "Beatrice, is there a toilet here?"

"Yes, I had them bring a portable one over."

"An *out*house?" Evelyn said in disbelief. "Oh, *please* don't tell me we've sunk *that* low."

Beatrice, glared at her. "Put a sock in it." Evelyn was speechless. She had never been spoken to in such a dismissive manner before. Yet, as shocked as she was, she dared not confront Beatrice at this time.

That night, while Anne slept on a cot four feet away, Kate sat upright, secured to the wheelchair. The night air was chilly and moisture off the lake made it damp. She shivered as she sat alone with her thoughts, shuffling her feet and rocking back and forth in the wheelchair. The one thought that constantly entered her mind during the night was that Lou would use all of his tracking skills to find her. At some point during the night, Anne inexplicably got up and placed a blanket around Kate's shoulders.

In the morning, Anne again showed kindness and loosened the rope bindings, but left the handcuff in place that secured Kate to the chair. Then she wheeled Kate over to the portable outhouse. When they reached the small structure, Anne helped Kate swing herself onto the seat and looked away, giving her some privacy, as she passed her morning water.

When they returned to their tent, Beatrice called out, "Anne, is that you?"

"Yes."

"Are you up?"

"I am up, Beatrice."

"Good, then get some breakfast going."

Anne, said nothing, but had thoughts of her own. *I don't recall giving you permission to treat me like Cinderella, dear sister.*

During breakfast, Beatrice said, "If either of you have any interest in looking inside this dilapidated old castle, you'd best do it today."

Evelyn let out a sigh. "It looks like it's going to rain; I've got all week to do that."

"We may not be staying here, Evelyn."

Anne looked at her sister in surprise. "I thought you said we were going to be here for a couple of weeks?"

Beatrice was annoyed. "What I *said* was that I *rented* this place for two weeks. There's a difference, my dear."

Anne looked away, upset with another putdown of her feelings.

Evelyn broke the uneasy silence. "Well, I, for one, will be quite pleased to go *any*where else that has a proper water closet."

Chapter Twelve

BEFORE DUFFY LEFT Fredericton, he called the police chief in Limerick, Ireland, to let him know the Canadian government would be sending a delegation over to work with his team on the kidnapping of a Royal Canadian Mountie.

"We'll welcome the assist," the chief said. "Hold on; I'll connect you to the man who I've assigned to the case."

It took a few minutes before someone with an Irish brogue thick enough to cut with a knife, came on the line. "Hello, this is Francis O'Connor. Now to whom is it that I have the pleasure of speaking to?"

"The name is William McDuffie-Ferguson, Royal Canadian Mounted Police. But you can call me 'Duffy.'"

"Well, 'tis a fine Irish name that you have. I go by 'Fran-O,' me-self. Tell me now, will you be coming over?"

"Yes, I will."

"Is it *just* you?"

"No, two field investigators will accompany me."

"Well, it certainly sounds like you mean *business*."

Duffy ignored the comment. "Fran-O, if at all possible, I'd like you to have some information ready for us when we arrive."

"And what would that be, lad?"

"I'd like a list of the passengers who traveled in First Class on the flight coming from Halifax along with Lt. Kathryn O'Grady, and the names of those who *boarded* a connecting flight leaving Shannon and going to Dublin."

"Easy enough."

"Also, I'd like you to detain the flight attendants who were assigned to the First-Class section on O'Grady's flight from Halifax. We need them to remain in Ireland for the time being."

"There was only one, Duffy and we've already questioned her. But I'll have the lads let her know that she needs to stay put."

"Were you able to impound the trash and glassware from the First-Class section on the flight from Halifax?"

"I believe the lads did that, yes, but I'll check to be sure."

"And one last thing, I'd like to have copies of all the surveillance camera footage from Shannon Airport available, beginning from a half hour *before* O'Grady's plane landed until two hours afterward. Can you do that?"

"That won't be a problem. The lads have already put in a request for that very thing. Is there anything else?"

"That's it for now."

"Grand, and I'll have a report waiting for you on what we've found. Now, where will you be staying?"

"I haven't made those arrangements, yet. Any suggestions?"

"I'll get rooms for ya' over at McDougal's; that's where we tell all the lads to stay."

"Do they have Wi-Fi?"

"I think they all have it now. But McDougal's has a decent pub, too."

"Thanks, Fran-O. I need to shut down now; I've got a ride to catch."

WHEN THE CANADIAN team arrived at Shannon International, a police car was standing by waiting to bring them to the station house where Fran-O was located. Like many older police buildings in Ireland, the Limerick Station House was built in the early part of the twentieth century. The interior design was typical for that era, and beyond continual investments in new technology, it hadn't been modernize one iota in all those passing years.

When Duffy, Lou, and Jake entered the front lobby, each felt as if he had stepped through a portal and traveled back in time, or had somehow walked onto the set of a long-forgotten television show called *The Twilight Zone.*

A massive, oak-paneled desk on a riser stood front and center in the lobby. At both ends of the imposing structure were pedestal lights, each topped with an opaque blue globe the size of a soccer ball. The only lobby light came from a recessed fixture directly over the desk which sent a subliminal message of who the alpha authority was in the room. The chair behind the desk was also on an elevated platform, further conveying a strong message of superiority. The stereotypical image was definitely "old school."

After visually taking it all in, the men approached the sergeant sitting behind the desk. "I'm William McDuffie-

Ferguson, here to see Sergeant Francis O'Connor," Duffy spoke loudly.

"He's been expecting ya'. I'll call him out."

In less than a minute, a barrel-chested man who stood well over six feet tall, came from out of nowhere and stuck out a hand as large as a baseball mitt. "Ahh, so, it's yourself, is it?"

Duffy immediately recognized the deep booming voice while he shook the massive hand offered to him. "Fran-O, these are the two detectives I told you would be coming with me." He turned to indicate Lou and Jake beside him. "This is Fran-O. He and I will be running this operation." Fran-O stuck out his mitt once again, first to Lou, then to Jake, and with a voice that sounded like it was coming from the very bottom of his shoes, welcomed them heartily.

"The pleasure is all mine," he said. "Most o' me lads are out now, but Pat is still here." He turned his head to the corridor from where he had come and called out. "Pat! Will ya' come out and say hello to the lads?"

Pat appeared at the doorway and waved. "Welcome."

"Now the pleasantries being done and all, let's get on with it. Duffy, ya' said ya' wanted to see the surveillance tapes. Well, come along; we've got the tapes all set up for ya.'"

Duffy turned to Lou. "You'll recognize Kate quicker than any of us. I want you on the tapes."

"The lads have it all set up in the next room." Then Fran-O called out again. "Pat, are you there?"

"I am, Sergeant."

"Pat, show the lads where the tapes are." Then, he turned to Duffy. "Pat's my technical guru; the lad can do anything with these computers. I don't know how we'd get along without him these days."

"What about the passenger lists?"

"Ahh, come with me, we've got those, too. And the flight attendant is waiting around, just as ya' asked. We weren't able to figure out which trash belonged to the First-Class section, so, I told them to keep everything. There's a lot to look through."

"Jake, take a look at the passenger lists. We want to know which First-Class passengers on Kate's flight had a connecting flight to Dublin, and who remained in Shannon."

"Got it."

"Oh, and find out where the other First-Class passengers on the flight came from."

"Got it."

Fran-O put his hand on Duffy's shoulder. "Come with me, I told the lads to pull together a report; it's got everything in it that we know so far."

As they walked down the corridor, Duffy noticed that Fran-O's breathing seemed labored. "How long have you been on the force, Fran-O?"

"It 'twas fifty years this past spring."

"So, you've been at this for a while?"

"I have. The wife keeps telling me that I should step down, and take the pension. But then, I say to myself, 'and what the hell am I going to do *then*?' This is the only thing I know."

"You must have handled quite a few cases like this over the years."

"We've had our share of runaways and domestic quarrels, where one parent takes off with the youngers, and doesn't tell the other, that's for sure. But this is the first time we've had a situation like *this* one here at the annex."

"This isn't *headquarters*?" Duffy asked.

"Well, technically, we're still part of headquarters, but once they built the new station, we've become known as 'the annex.'"

"So, what's the *role* of the annex?

Well, we're about keeping the peace, mostly. We're not what you'd call 'crime fighters.' We handle the local stuff. Like I said, we'll get the call when there's a runaway, or domestic troubles, and of course, when someone's had a few too many down at the pub and is knocking heads about. We did have a situation when Mahoney's touring car was taken two weeks ago, but we got that one back for him. And then there was the fella from County Kerry earlier in the month. He kept coming around and stealing things. He was no good for sure, that one was, but we put a stop to him."

"Sound like things stay pretty quiet, eh?"

"For the most part they do. I've learned that if you just sit back and wait, you'll get a tip, and the whole thing will be over in no time at all. Here, sit down now, and read this report."

"Fran-O, so tell me," Duffy persisted, "is there a central unit over at headquarters that handles kidnappings?"

"Not really. We've all been schooled in tracking down runaways and finding those who go missing. The only abduction cases we seem to handle involve minors and one of the parents."

"So, you don't have anything like our FBI, who would handle an *international* kidnapping?"

"No, we're the ones who would handle something like that."

Fran-O was well-respected within the station house, and his lengthy tenure brought a set of experienced skills to the department. However, as the contingent from Canada would come to realize, Fran-O's investigative skills, along with a sense of urgency, were as dated as the building itself..

"I'll be in the next office, Duffy," Fran-O said, "should you have any questions about the report."

As he left, Duffy sat down and began reading:

Case #149 - Kathryn O'Grady,

Individual holds Canadian and Irish citizenship

Active Royal Canadian Mounted Police Officer.

Reported missing at approximately 10 a.m. local time Thursday 23 October by Airport Police at Shannon International.

O'Grady, boarded Aer Lingus flight 219 in Halifax bound for Shannon International as a First-Class passenger Wednesday 22 October

O'Grady was ticketed to board a connecting flight in Shannon to Dublin.

Three pieces of luggage were checked through to Dublin which are now in unclaimed luggage at Dublin.

Aer Lingus confirmed O'Grady failed to board connecting flight.

According to Aer Lingus, O'Grady had ample time to reach the connecting gate.

Aer Lingus at Shannon repeatedly paged O'Grady to proceed to the gate before the ground crew closed the gate area.

On 23 October, Airport police filed a missing person alert, at the request of a relative, after conducting a thorough search of the airport.

No record was found at the airport's first aid station of anyone with the name Kathryn O'Grady having been treated, or seen in the past thirty-six hours.

All onboard trash on the flight was impounded and remains at the airport awaiting inspection.

When Duffy finished reading the report, he yelled over to Fran-O, "Is this all there is?"

"It's only been a little over a day," Fran-O called back. "The lads are out and about. We'll be hearing more about it, you can be sure of that. The statement that the lads took from the flight attendant is in the top draw."

Duffy raised his eyebrows. *The first twenty-four hours are the most critical, hopefully, the flight attendant's statement will give us more to go on.*

He opened the top drawer and took out a folder containing a one-page document titled: *Flight attendant Fiona Burke, First Class attendant on Aer Lingus flight 219 on 23 October.*

Attendant stated that passenger O'Grady appeared to be in good health when she boarded in Halifax. She chatted with another woman passenger in the seat next to her for the better part of the flight. They appeared to know each another.

The attendant stated that the First-Class section ran smoothly throughout the flight.

The attendant stated that when the pilot announced their initial approach to Shannon, she observed passenger O'Grady returning to her seat after using the unisex lavatory in First-Class.

The attendant stated that when she went to clear the tray tables prior to landing, the passenger in seat 2-A, next to O'Grady, said something akin to: 'Let's drink up,' and saw them both finish their drinks.

The attendant stated that shortly after she secured herself in the crew seat and faced the passengers, she noticed O'Grady acting in a different manner and attributed it to their rapid descent.

The attendant further stated that when the plane arrived at the gate, O'Grady's speech was slurred and she was unable to stand on her own.

The attendant stated that O'Grady's traveling companion requested a wheelchair for her friend, which she ordered.

The attendant stated that O'Grady's friend said she would take responsibility for O'Grady's wellbeing because she knew her, and also stated: "This isn't the first time."

The attendant also stated that after helping the companion swing O'Grady into the wheelchair, she last saw them traveling into the terminal with an airport volunteer pushing the wheelchair. O'Grady seemed to be asleep at that time.

Taken on 23 October by Officer F.X. McGuire

Duffy reread the last statement.

I thought Lou said Kate flew over alone. He underscored the word "companion," and made a note to speak with the wheelchair attendant. As Duffy sat back in his chair, he reflected on what he had just read. *If Kate didn't board her connecting flight and she wasn't in the airport, she would have had to have passed through Customs. How could that happen if she was in a wheelchair, and wasn't able to communicate?*

"Fran-O, did anyone check to see if O'Grady went through Customs?"

"If it's not in the report yet, we'll find out when the lads come back today."

Duffy held the flight attendant's statement in his hand and kept thinking. *Maybe whoever this unknown traveling companion was took Kate to a hospital.*

Duffy, stood up and stretched. "Fran-O, I need some help."

"What is it Duffy?"

"I need a list of area hospitals. I'd like to know if a Kathryn O'Grady was taken to any hospital in the last thirty-six hours."

"Pat, can you hear me?"

"I can, Sergeant."

"Be a good lad, and print off a list of the local hospitals for Duffy here."

"Fran-O, I also need to find out who the individual was that was dispatched with the wheelchair, I'd like to speak with them?"

"I'll get one of the lads on that now."

Duffy got up and walked over to the office where Lou was watching tapes. "Lou, I thought you said Kate was traveling solo."

"She was."

"Then take a look at the flight attendant's statement. She says differently."

After reading the statement, Lou said, "I have no idea who that other person is. Kate sent me a couple of text messages. If she connected with someone she knew, I think she would have told me."

"We need to run down the name of the person who sat in that window seat."

As soon as Duffy had the list of hospitals, he walked over to the room where Jake was working. "Jake, give each of these hospitals a call, will you? Find out if anyone with the name Kathryn O'Grady has been admitted, or treated, in the past thirty-six hours."

Duffy then returned to his desk and dialed Aer Lingus headquarters. He wanted to know the name of the passenger in seat 2A on the flight from Halifax.

Friend, my foot. Duffy thought. *That's a lead.*

Chapter Thirteen

ONCE LOU IDENTIFIED the security camera of the gate where flight 219 from Halifax had deplaned its passengers, he had the tape rewound back to a time just before Kate's flight arrived. Then he watched the tape carefully as passenger after passenger exited the jetway and entered the terminal.

Before long, he saw someone slumped over in a wheelchair exiting the ramp. A blue Boston Red Sox baseball cap was pulled low over the person's face. At first, it didn't register with him that Kate was the person in the wheelchair, but she hadn't been among the others he'd watched walk out on their own. So, Lou rewound the tape to a frame where the wheelchair first appeared, and froze it. While the peak of the baseball cap hid most of the woman's face, Lou recognized that the hair color, and the carry-on bag resting on the woman's lap, matched Kate's.

"Duffy, take a look at this."

"Lou's got something," Duffy motioned to Fran-O. "Let's go."

Lou replayed the tape several times, showing Kate being wheeled out of the jetway and into the concourse.

"Are you *sure* that's Kate? I can't tell with that hat pulled down over her face."

"Yeah, that's her. I recognize the clothes, the hair, and the carry-on luggage. No other wheelchair came off the jetway and they were the last passengers off."

"Focus in on the woman who seems to be following along."

"Let me back it up; she didn't have her head all the way down when she first came out of the jetway." As soon as Lou had a decent facial shot of Evelyn, he froze the screen.

"Okay, save that one, and print off a copy. We'll send it over to INTERPOL. I wanna know who she is."

"Lad, is your wife an invalid?" Fran-O asked.

"No. They must have drugged her."

Lou sat back and stared at the image of his wife slumped over in a wheel chair. "Okay, now we're sure she left the plane like the attendant said. I'll follow these tapes and see where the hell they took her; this may take a while."

At that moment, Jake poked his head into the room. "Duffy, no hospital or clinic has a record of anyone named Kathryn O'Grady being treated, or even looked at. What else do you have for me?"

"We just got word that the guy who they sent over with the wheelchair for Kate was taken to the hospital with a head wound," Duffy said. "Go over to University Hospital and talk to him."

"Where?"

"University Hospital. Have someone take you over and get a statement on what exactly happened."

"Will do."

Before Jake left, he handed Duffy a sheet of paper. "Here's a list of all the First-Class passengers you wanted. It's split into who made a connecting flight, and who didn't. Nobody went on to Dublin. Those who *did* fly out, all had the same last name and flew on to Paris. Of the six who didn't, four live in Limerick. That just leaves Kate, and someone named 'Ellen Marshall' unaccounted for."

"That has to be the name of the passenger who was sitting next to Kate in seat 2A. I've got a photo I want you to run through INTERPOL's database with the name 'Ellen Marshall.' Let's find out who the hell she is. Then go through the police blotter of the local communities. I wanna know what's been happening since Kate's plane landed."

Before Jake left for the hospital, he sent a message to INTERPOL, requesting any information on an 'Ellen Marshall, address unknown'…along with the photo.

"DUFFY I'VE GOT something else," Lou called out a while later. He replayed the video of the wheelchair being brought through Customs, then followed it over to the parking garage. A third figure was now visible on the tape.

"Lou, who's the other woman?"

"No idea. She showed up when they exited Customs."

"Can you get a facial?"

"Not yet. It almost seems that she's aware of the cameras and is purposely looking away."

When the video showed them entering the elevator, Lou

switched to a different camera, and caught them coming out on level three.

"The lighting on level three in the garage is poor. We can only see them walking away from the elevator." Lou left the film running as he made a few notes.

"Lou, can you make it any brighter?"

"It's the video, Duffy, that's as bright as I can get it. In a minute, I'll switch to the camera positioned at the exit. We might be able to get a decent facial of the other woman then."

They watched as the wheelchair was pushed back toward the elevator from the shadows.

"Take a look, something's different," Duffy said.

"Yeah, the old guy is gone; it's just the two women and Kate, now."

"I see that."

"I just sent Jake over to the hospital to talk to the old guy."

"He's in the hospital?"

"Yeah, they found him unconscious up on the third floor bleeding from a head wound."

"Okay, I'll run through the exit ramp tapes. Maybe I'll get a good shot of them coming out." Just then, Duffy's cell phone rang. "I need to take this," he said, and walked back to the office he was using. "Yes, Fletcher?"

"They've just finished going through the activity we copied off Lou's phone."

"And?"

"The ransom text came from a cell phone with a London area code."

"Email me the number."

"It's most likely a burner phone."

"Well, email it to me anyway, Fletcher."

"How's it going?"

"We're making progress, but it's slow."

"Are you getting the support you need?"

"So far."

"How's Lou doing?"

"He's worried Fletcher, but doing okay. I'm keeping him busy."

"All right, call if you need anything from this end."

"Will do."

"Oh, and Duffy, just so you know, Ottawa has asked me to keep them appraised on this one. News of a Mountie being kidnapped traveled pretty fast."

"Don't worry, I'll keep you in the loop."

Moments after Duffy hung up, he received the text from Fletcher with the London area phone number and studied it for half a minute.

"Fran-O, I need your help."

"What is it, Duffy?"

"Could you have someone bring the flight attendant over; I'd like to talk with her."

"Right, I'll have one of the lads go fetch her."

A few minutes later, Lou got up and poked his head into Duffy's office. "They took her away in a limo."

"A limo?"

"Yeah, I ran through all the exit ramp tapes and was able to follow them over to the limo area. They put Kate in back and the driver did something to the wheelchair before putting it in the trunk. I only have part of the license plate."

"What's the time on the film?"

"Local time, 0950."

"Fran-O?"

"Yes, Duffy?"

"Can we get a list of limousine companies that picked up at the airport on Thursday morning?"

"I'll have one of the lad's get on it for ya'." Then, as Fran-O left the room, Lou looked over at Duffy. "Does this guy actually do *any*thing by himself?" he asked quietly.

"Yeah, he's teaching me about the art of delegation," Duffy answered.

"Well, don't try practicing any of that shit on *me*."

Lou's cell phone rang; caller ID showed the name *Claire O'Grady*. "I gotta take this. It's Kate's cousin, the travel agent. She might have something."

"Okay, I'll be right next door talking to the flight attendant when they bring her over," Duffy said as he left the room.

"Hello, Claire? It's me," Lou said.

"Lou! I'm a nervous wreck. Have you found Kate?"

"Not yet, Claire, but we're working on it. She's been kidnapped, and we know they took her from Shannon in a limousine."

"But she's alive?"

"To the best of our knowledge, yes."

"Thank goodness, Lou!" Claire said, pausing for a split second. "I hate to bring this up now, but there's a second reason I'm calling. I have to let everyone know that the wedding's being pushed out."

Lou felt a twinge of emotion, then quickly compartmentalized it. "Claire, I really can't talk about that right now. Just do what you think is the right thing, okay?"

"I understand, Lou. Sorry. Godspeed to you. *Please* call me if you hear anything . . . anything at all."

"I will."

After Lou hung up, he sent a brief text off to Angelo,

letting him and Alessandra know about the situation and that they were making some headway.

Down the hallway in another office, a small box popped up in the corner of Jake's computer screen notifying him that he had received an email from INTERPOL. The subject was "MARSHALL, Ellen."

Chapter Fourteen

DUFFY SAT ACROSS the desk from the flight attendant. The room was small, close. . . a tape recorder sat on the table between them. Duffy was interested in getting right to the heart of the matter. Still, making the subject feel comfortable could only help to earn her trust.

"Would you like a glass of water before we start?" he asked.

"No, let's just get this over with; I'd like to get back to work."

"Understood." Duffy said, relieved there would be no small talk. He turned on the recorder and noted the date, time, place, and gave his own name before beginning.

"I am speaking with Fiona Burke, flight attendant on Aer Lingus Airlines Flight 219 which flew from Halifax, Canada, to Shannon Airport, Ireland, arriving on 23 October of this year."

"Ms. Burke, how many flight attendants were onboard Flight 219 from Halifax?"

"We flew with a crew of four, sir."

"How many were assigned to the First-Class section?"

"One."

"And that was you?"

"Yes."

"Did you work the First-Class section for the entire flight?"

"Yes."

"At any time did you leave the First-Class section?"

"No."

"At any time did any other flight attendant join you in First-Class?"

"No. It was a full flight and my colleagues had their hands full in the main cabin."

"At any time did either the passenger in seat 2A or 2B push the red call button?"

After a slight pause, the attendant said, "Yes, before we took off, the passenger in seat 2A pushed the red call button."

"Was there a problem?"

"No, she wanted me to serve them a cocktail."

"Did you?"

"Yes. We're allowed to serve first class passengers prior to take off."

"Interesting. Okay, what can you tell me about the passengers in seats 2A and 2B?"

"Not much more than I've already given," she said. "Those two passengers were two of twelve I was responsible for on that flight."

"Did anything in particular stand out about them?"

"Nothing really. They appeared to be typical First-Class flyers."

"You didn't notice *anything unusual* about them?"

"No. They settled in, began to chat; it seemed like they knew each other."

"In your earlier statement, you *also* mentioned you felt they knew each other. What made you believe that?"

"I can generally tell if they've just met, or if they know each other, by the way passengers are talking with one another."

"And you thought they *knew* each other."

"It appeared to *me* they knew each other, based on how they were talking."

"Did you overhear any of their conversation?"

"I try not to listen, but I noticed their body language was relaxed. They seemed comfortable with each other."

"How so?"

"Their upper bodies were turned toward one another like friends do when they're talking. There was no tension between them, and they were somewhat animated, using hand gestures. Passengers who don't know one another tend to keep both shoulders against the back of their seats and only turn their heads slightly when speaking to the person sitting next to them."

"Is there anything else you remember?"

"Again, I try not to listen in on conversations, but it seemed these two passengers were engaged in a friendly topic. It also seemed like the passenger in seat 2A was asking more questions."

"What makes you say that?"

"Whenever I stopped by their seats, *she* seemed to be the one more or less leading the conversation."

"Can you expand on that?"

"Well, at one point, the passenger in seat 2B just wanted to sit back and relax, however, the other passenger's body language indicated that she wanted to continue talking. Like I said, I try not to listen in."

"Did anything change toward the end of the flight?"

"I noticed passenger 2B walk to the lavatory. Then I remember seeing her go back to her seat out of the corner of my eye."

"Was passenger 2B able to return to her seat from the lavatory unassisted?"

"Yes, she was."

"What were you doing at that moment?"

"I had gone to row three to begin picking up mimosa glasses and anything else that needed to be discarded so passengers could stow their tray tables before landing."

"Then what did you do?"

"I worked my way up the aisle to the front."

"Did you notice anything odd about the passenger in seat 2B at that time?"

"No, she seemed okay. They both finished off their mimosas and handed me their glasses."

"Then what happened?"

"Well, everything changed shortly after that. By the time we reached the gate, something was definitely wrong with the passenger in 2B. She was unable to function. It did seem odd that it happened so fast, she had been fine for most of the flight. That's when the passenger in seat 2A suddenly seemed to become her caregiver. She asked for a wheelchair to be available when we landed. She assured me that she would take care of passenger 2B and even said 'they were together.' She also said that it 'wasn't the first time.' Because she was handling it, I didn't see a need to get involved. I had a galley to clear and prep for the ground crew and figured they would use the call button overhead if they needed me."

"What did you do then?"

"I stayed up in the forward crew area, disposing of trash, stacking used glassware, and making sure the lockers and carts were secured for landing."

"How did the passenger in seat 2B appear to you at that point?"

"I was in the forward crew area with my back to the passengers. I wasn't able to see her."

"When *exactly* did you first notice something different about the passenger in 2B?"

"Just before we landed. I sat down in the crew seat which faces the passengers and that's when I noticed a difference in her behavior."

"How would you describe her behavior at that point?"

"She was slouching in her seat and didn't seem alert."

"What was the passenger in the seat next to her doing?"

"I'm not sure, she may have been looking out the window."

"Was the passenger in seat 2A *unaware* of what was going on?"

"I don't know how to answer that."

"Did she seem *concerned* about the passenger in seat 2B?"

"Not at that moment."

"Earlier, you said the passenger in seat 2A appeared to be acting like the caregiver, yet now you say she may have been looking out the window. Can you clarify that?"

"Perhaps she wasn't aware of what was going on with her friend at that moment."

"Did they *tell* you they were friends? You used that word in your earlier statement."

The attendant took a breath, "No, I should have said '*fellow* passenger.'"

"Would you have noticed if someone tried to put anything in her drink while she was in the lavatory?"

"No, like I said, I was up by row three. I'm pretty focused on my role when we're in our final descent. Unless someone pushes the red call button, I'm pretty much oblivious to what the other passengers are doing."

"So, at no time did you observe anything being put into the drink of Kathryn O'Grady, the passenger in seat 2B. Is that correct?"

"That is correct."

"Did anything else seem odd to you toward the end of the flight?"

"I *did* ask the passenger in seat 2A if we needed to call for medical assistance once we were on the ground."

"And what did she say?"

"She said that it wouldn't be necessary, that it wasn't the first time, and that they were together and she would take care of it. I assumed her friend just had too much to drink. The passenger in 2A simply asked me to arrange for a wheelchair."

"You just used the word friend again, did you actually hear her use the word friend?"

"She may have, I can't be sure."

"Is there anything else you can think of?"

"Well, I don't know if this means anything at all, and I did forget to mention it before, but the passenger in seat 2A was an 'Advance.'"

"What's an 'Advance?'"

"That's a passenger who's allowed to board early. It's called an Advanced Priority seating. Usually those are individuals who work for our airline or are one of our retirees."

"Was the person in seat 2A an employee of your company?"

"No, there would have been a designation on the passenger list indicating that if she was an employee, or a retiree."

"How else could a passenger board early?"

"Sometimes, as a courtesy, professionals in the travel industry are allowed to board early."

"Was that the case with the passenger in seat 2A?

"I would have no way of knowing; the gate agents handle that. I would guess that she was connected with the travel industry in some capacity."

"Anything else?"

"This is just an observation, but I've seen a dramatic change in people after they've done drugs in the lavatory."

Duffy bristled at the inference that Kate might have taken a drug. "The individual we're concerned about doesn't *do* drugs; she's a *lieutenant* in the *Royal Canadian Mounted Police*. But I get your point."

The attendant waited for the next question.

"Well, this has been quite helpful. I guess I don't have any further questions to ask."

"Am I free to go?"

"Yes."

"Can I go back to work now?"

"Yes."

"Thank you!" As the flight attendant stood up, she raised her eyebrows. "Oh, one thing I didn't mention: After we arrived at the gate, the passenger from seat 2A seemed to be constantly on her cell phone. I only noticed because I thought she would have been more concerned with the woman."

"Actually, I do have one last question. What *time* did Flight 219 land?"

"It was a little after nine in the morning. I don't recall the *exact* time, but Aer Lingus would have a record."

"Thank you for your time; you've been very helpful."

WHEN JAKE RETURNED from the hospital, he stuck his head into the office that Duffy was using. "I'm back."

"Did you learn anything?

"A little."

"Sit down."

Jake cleared his throat. "The wheelchair guy said that his pick-up appeared comatose when he arrived at the plane"

"He used the word comatose?"

"Yeah, and he said he had to physically lift her up and place her into the wheelchair. He said the other woman wasn't happy when he told her he couldn't release the chair to her. He waited at Customs while the other woman handled everything. He said a third woman was waiting for them when they came out of the Customs area. He also mentioned that nobody had any baggage which he *really* thought was strange. But he didn't make any comments and just pushed the wheelchair over to the parking garage."

"The woman who flew over with Kate didn't have any *luggage*?"

"No. I double-checked with him on it.

"Now, *that's* interesting."

"Yeah, what woman flies from Halifax to Ireland with only one piece of carry-on luggage?"

"Yeah, that's beyond strange. Anything else?"

"The only other thing he said that I found interesting was about the woman who joined them after Customs. He thought she was the 'queen bee.'"

"Why is that?"

"She was bossy, he said."

"Was he able to tell you anything about what happened in the garage?"

"Nah, he just remembers waking up in the hospital with a headache. It surprised him."

"I'll bet it did! Think he'd be able to identify them in a line up?"

"I asked him about that, and he said he thought he could."

"Here, take a look at this briefing report they worked up for us; give me your thoughts."

Jake read the report and handed it back to Duffy. "Not a lot of substance in it."

"Yeah, this laid-back approach that Fran-O has is bothering me. Go take a look at the local police blotters, will you? See if anything important was reported since Kate's plane landed."

"I'm on it," Jake said as he left the room.

Chapter Fifteen

WHILE SITTING IN her car outside Dublin Airport, Claire O'Grady hit the "send" button on her smart phone and an email went out to all 238 of Kate's relatives who were planning on attending the wedding. The email advised them that the wedding had been postponed because the bride had been kidnapped, and couldn't be found.

More than a few recipients on Claire's distribution list replied, asking what the new date was, or the *real* reason for the postponement.

"All we know is that she was on the plane from Halifax to Shannon, but then was kidnapped, and taken away in a limousine," Claire answered. She underscored the fact that this was the truth, and *not* a game being played. "You will be updated as the police investigation proceeds. Please remember our Kate in your prayers!"

WHEN JAKE RETURNED to his temporary office at the police station, he found an email message from INTERPOL. After reading it, he printed it off and carried it into Duffy's office.

"Take a look at this reply I just received from INTERPOL." Duffy reached out for the printout and read it.

The name Ellen Marshall is not in the INTERPOL database. However, our facial recognition software has matched the individual in the photo with a photograph of an Evelyn Maxwell, who is in our database.

"Did they include a dossier on her?"

"No, I'll ask for it."

"Good, let's find out who this Ellen Marshall / Evelyn Maxwell *really* is."

WHEN THE INTERPOL dossier on Evelyn Maxwell, came back, it identified her as the wife of Herbert Maxwell. At the end of the report, it listed Maxwell's present employer as Royal Travel Agency LTD, and included a picture of Evelyn Maxwell who looked like the woman leaving the plane with the wheelchair. The only difference was her hair coloring.

As soon as Duffy saw the picture, he threw the report on his desk. "*Shit,* she's the one who got off the plane with Kate! Jake, I think we just figured out what the motive is behind Kate's kidnapping. I know for a fact that some years ago, there was an unprecedented rash of attempted kidnappings among the British aristocracy. These well-to-do Brits had images of themselves, their wives, and their children entered into the INTERPOL database system for precautionary purposes. I'll put money down that she's the wife of one of those three big shots. If that's the case . . .we're dealing with revenge. I'll subpoena the phone records for all three of those wives."

IN LESS THAN A HALF HOUR, Fran-O walked over to Duffy. "Here's the list you wanted of limousine companies authorized to pick up passengers at the airport. The highlighted ones had drivers there on Thursday. I had the lads put 'em in order of the number of pickups they each did."

"Thanks," Duffy said and quickly scanned the list. "Could you add the contact numbers for each of these companies, so we can call them?"

"Pat! Are you free, lad?"

"I am, Sergeant."

As Fran-O walked out of Duffy's office, Jake poked his head in. "Duffy, I've checked out every police blotter in every county that borders Shannon airport."

"And?"

"Someone was brought in for questioning about a fire that broke out in the back room of Hanley's Pub. There was a domestic disturbance that ended up as a 'drunk and disorderly.' A limo company reported a missing vehicle, and a cow was found wandering out on highway M8."

"Give the limo company a call; let's find out what's up with that."

"That was next on my list."

"Good, then get to it."

Duffy pulled up the text that Fletcher Martin had sent over containing a phone number that had been used to send the ransom note to Lou, then walked over to Fran-O's office.

"Fran-O, can you have someone run down all the calls and text messages sent to and from this phone number?"

"That shouldn't be a problem."

"Make it for the past four months."

"You don't need to know who the phone belongs to?"

"I do, but it's probably a burner."

"Right. I'll have one of the lads get on it for ya'."

"Thanks. We're beginning to get a picture of what happened and what the motive is."

"If that's the case, then I'll give credit where credit is due . . . ya' work *fast*, lad."

"Kate means a lot to the three of us."

LOU TOOK IT upon himself to go over to the limousine area at the airport and ask around, hoping somebody might have seen or heard something unusual in the past twenty-four hours. After talking to several limo drivers, one told him, "Yeah, I seen something odd yesterday, something I ain't never seen before. A driver twisted the pipe off the back of a friggin' wheelchair and put the chair inside his damn trunk. Everybody *knows* you don't transport airport property."

"Say again?"

"Airport property *stays* at the airport. If you get caught taking airport property off site, you're banned from *ever* comin' back here, again."

"Is that right?"

"Damn right it is! Ya' can take *that* one ta the bank. I heard of it happenin', but it surprised me ta actually *see* somebody do it."

"What else did you notice?"

"So, I says to me-self, 'where's the bloke what shoulda

been pushin' that chair?' The ones who push them chairs around have to turn 'em back in 'fore they can go home. If they don't, they're written up, and you won't see 'em back, again, either. Hell, right over there in the gutter is the piece of pipe the bloke twisted off."

"Do you know the driver?"

"I seen him a few times, but, nah, I don't know who he is."

"Do you know which limo service he works for?"

"Ha, take a look around. Can't tell one company from the other, can ya? Nah, the only time ya' see a company name on a limo is when there's a funeral. As if the corpse gives a *damn* about who's haulin' him ta the grave, huh? Hell, half the time, you don't even know who's *drivin'* for the same company you are."

"You say he *twisted* the end of the pipe off?"

"Yeah, he bent it over and twisted it off. There was no other way he was goin' ta get that chair inta his trunk."

Before Lou left the limo area, he walked over to the gutter and found what he was looking for. He took out his handkerchief, and picked up the piece of metal pipe.

WHEN LOU WALKED into the station, Jake had just gotten off the phone with the limo company, and came out of the office he was using. "Okay, gather round, I'm not sure how significant what I've just learned is, but I want to put it out there." When Jake realized Fran-O was still in his office, he said, "Fran-O, can you join us?"

Once Fran-O had joined the three Canadians, Jake, began, "Okay, here's the deal: Both a driver *and* his limo are missing. The limo was hired to meet three people at Shannon

International, arriving on flight 219 from Halifax. He was to drive them to McDermott Castle in County Roscommon. The driver sent a text that he had picked up his passengers and was enroute. He sent a second text when he arrived at their destination. Then, he sent a *third* text saying one of his passengers wanted to return to Shannon International. The office calculated a return charge, sent a text, and he texted back that the passenger had agreed. The office ran the credit card on file, and that was the last time they heard from him."

Duffy said, "Anything else?"

"Nope, that's all I have at this point."

Duffy thought for a moment before saying, "Call them back and get the credit card number."

"Will do."

Lou shared what he had learned from talking with the limo drivers. Before going into his office, he handed Duffy the section of pipe he had picked up over at the limo area.

"Here's the metal rod the limo driver twisted off the wheelchair Kate was in. Maybe we can pull off some prints."

HAVING CONNECTED THE DOTS, Lou returned to his office area and googled "McDermott Castle." The first thing he saw was that the property was up for rent, or for sale. He punched the number of the listing agent into his phone and hit the call button. It was Saturday afternoon and most businesses had already closed for the weekend, but Lou let it ring. Finally, someone picked up.

"Tri-County Properties."

"Yes, I'm interested in renting the McDermott Castle. Do you handle that, and is it available?"

"Ah, yes . . . yes! As a matter of fact, I believe we *do*

represent that property. Just a minute and I'll check the availability, sir. We don't get many calls for that one." After a brief hold, the agent came back on the phone.

"Hello?"

"I'm here."

"Ah, yes, good, I have the sheet in front of me, now. Oddly enough, sir, it does seem to be rented for these next two weeks, however, it's open after that."

"How often is it rented?"

"Well, sir, truthfully, it's very rarely rented out. This is the first time it's been rented in, well, in quite some time. The last time it was rented was . . . *hmmm*, it doesn't seem to say when that was."

"How long ago did someone call to rent it out?"

"I'm sorry, sir, that's not information we give out."

"You're speaking to me on a police line. This property may be involved in a criminal investigation. Now if you don't want to be charged with Obstruction of Justice, I'll give you another shot at this: How *long* ago was it rented out?"

"Three days ago, sir."

"Who rented the property?

"Let me see." After a brief pause, the man was back on the line. "Someone named 'Hastings,' sir."

"Full name?"

"That would be *Beatrice* Hastings."

Lou smiled. Every instinct in his being told him he had just found where Kate was being held.

"The castle is on an island, is that correct?"

"Yes, I do believe that is the case, sir."

"Do you merely *believe* that is the case, or is that *actually* the case?"

"That *is* the case . . . sir."

"Is there a bridge over to the island?"

"No, sir, you reach the island by ferry."

"Can you take a vehicle over?"

"No, it's a pedestrian ferry. The island is only a short distance from the shore, sir."

"What's the phone number for the ferry service?"

"I have it here, if you'll wait a moment." Lou could hear pages turning. When the man spoke again, he gave Lou the number. "It's listed in the ferry master's name which is 'Owen Murphy.' I believe he lives on the property."

Lou ended the call, smiled, and walked back into Duffy's office, "I know where she is. We need to move out!"

"Whoa," Duffy said. "Lou, we need to plan this out first."

As Lou was dialing Owen Murphy's number, he looked over at Duffy. "They've taken her to a *friggin' island* in County Roscommon called McDermott's Castle. Somebody by the name of 'Beatrice Hastings' rented the place. The missing limo drove them there yesterday. One of the people Kate put away for life was named *Hastings*. INTERPOL just identified the person that sat next to Kate on the plane as Evelyn *Maxwell*. What the hell *else* do we need to know?"

Fran-O had been standing in the doorway listening; now he waited to see how Duffy would respond to this direct challenge from a subordinate. Fran-O was old school and was unaware that because of past relationships, the three Canadians were *a team of equals*.

Duffy sat silently thinking. He recalled that men with surnames of "Hastings" and "Maxwell" were two of the principals in the smuggling caper he and Kate had worked on together last year.

"Let's get a plan in place before we start moving," he finally said.

Lou placed his hand over the phone and pushed back, saying "Duffy, listen to me, we can do the planning in the car. I'm not sitting around here, wasting time while you check off every damn box on a *friggin'* sheet of paper. We need to move, *now!*"

Duffy looked at Fran-O. "Lou's right. We'll need a vehicle and a boat."

Fran-O, called out to one of his lads. "Pat! On the double now. Have a *Garda* utility hauling an inflatable brought over from the garage."

Jake, looked at Fran-O. "What did you just call for?"

"An inflatable. It's a large *dinghy*, lad."

"I know what a *dingy* is, but you said something *before* that."

"What, a Garda utility? That's an SUV."

"No. 'Garda!' What the hell is a Garda?"

"It's in the Irish tongue lad, *Garda Siochana*. Guardians of the Peace, that's what the police are known as over here."

IT WAS ON THE eighth ring when Owen Murphy picked up. "Murphy here."

Lou placed his phone on speaker. "Mr. Murphy, can you tell me if you've taken anyone over to McDermott Castle in the last few days?"

"And who'd be doing the asking, if ya don't mind?" his voice was strong, yet wary.

"Lou Gault, I'm trying to track down my *wife*."

"Well, in that case, aye, I have."

"Was one in a wheel chair?"

"Aye."

"Are they staying inside the castle?"

"Hell, *no*, the castle is fallin' down, not even a *fool* would stay there. They're roughing it in a couple of tents."

"Are they still there?"

Murphy was silent for a half second. "*Who* is this again, if ya don't mind me asking?"

"My name is Lou Gault; I'm calling on behalf of the Garda out of Limerick."

"*Well*, in *that* case, *yes* they're still over there."

"You know that for a fact?"

"They haven't called for the ferry yet today."

"So, you *do* believe that they're *on* the island?"

"Well, unless they're able to walk on water, that'd be a safe bet for any man ta make."

Lou smiled. "Thanks, Murphy."

In short order, the SUV was out front of the building. Duffy emerged from his office with a map of the lands surrounding McDermott Castle.

"Let's go. Fran-O, you're driving; Jake, take shotgun; Lou, you're in the back seat with me."

The SUV pulled away from the building with the dinghy trailing behind.

Chapter Sixteen

ONCE THE SUV was enroute, Duffy looked at Lou. "You're better at this tactical field stuff than I ever was . . . take a look at this map and tell me what you think."

Lou studied the map, then pointed to a spot on the paper. "We'll put the inflatable in right about here. That way, we'll approach the island without being seen."

Duffy pointed to the map, "You don't think it'll be easier to launch from the ferry landing?"

"It would, but that also puts us in the open. We can't risk telegraphing that the calvary is on its way. If they think they're under attack, it'll put Kate in greater danger."

"Well, they're going to hear the outboard motor."

"No, they won't, we're paddling over. We'll use the motor on the way back. Once we're ashore, we'll surround the two tents, and on command, we'll go in with weapons drawn."

"That's it?"

"Duffy, we're not going up against a seasoned battalion of commandos, tripwires and lookouts."

Duffy nodded, then leaned forward and tapped Fran-O, on the shoulder. "How much longer 'til we get there?"

"It's three counties over; plan on a good couple of hours from here, lads."

RAIN DRIZZLED FROM a gray sky. Beatrice spent most of Saturday morning and afternoon either on the Internet or her phone. Evelyn preferred not to venture out in the rain and had spent the entire day napping on her cot.

Without warning, the flap to Beatrice's tent was thrown aside and Anne walked boldly in, almost as if confronting her sister. "I know it's early, but I've fixed lunch, if either of you are interested."

Beatrice looked up. "Perfect timing, I'll be right over. Evelyn, get up and see if you can help Anne." During the primitive meal Anne pulled together, Beatrice surprised them by announcing, "Eat up. As soon as we're finished, we're heading out." Evelyn and Anne looked at each other.

"Why?" Evelyn asked, the first to speak.

Beatrice ignored her question. "I've just called for the ferry; we're leaving as soon as the old man reaches the island. Anne, finish up. Then, Anne, I want you to wheel the bitch over to the dock."

"But what about all this?" Anne motioned to the supplies all strewn around.

"Leave it."

"I thought we were here for two *weeks*?" Her voice had a complaining tone. Beatrice ignored it.

"Take your personal things; that's all you need."

Evelyn scowled. "Why can't we just stay the night?"

"*Because...I said...*we are *leaving*!" Beatrice's tone was icy. "I don't feel *safe* here." Evelyn could sense that Beatrice was slipping into one of her moods again, and backed off.

When they finished eating neither Beatrice or Evelyn made any effort to stow things before heading back to their own tent to gather what few items they would take. Once she was alone with Kate, Anne gave her some bread and a drink of water before wheeling her over the bumpy ground to the dock.

Within a short time, the old man arrived; they were able to load their few things onto the ferry and make the crossing to the opposite shore in one trip. When they docked at the landing, the old man looked at Kate, and for the first time, seemed to realize that something wasn't right. "Why is this one handcuffed to the chair? She don't look so good." Kate was weak and drowsy from lack of sleep.

Beatrice stared at him hard, and paused before answering. "Because we don't want her to fall out and hurt herself. She's not well." She carefully watched his reaction.

"Well, a *strap* would work a whole lot better," he shrugged and turned his attention to securing the ferry. Beatrice relaxed, knowing the old man wouldn't be a problem. She took out a spare set of cuffs and handcuffed Kate's free hand to Anne. Only then did she undo the cuff securing Kate to the chair.

Turning to the old man, she said, "Come over here and help me get this wheelchair into the trunk."

Looking at her sister, Beatrice directed again. "Anne, I want you in the back seat with this one. Evelyn, help Anne get this one to stand up." Kate was shaky from having sat so long. They shoved her toward the vehicle as the sound of a pistol firing from close range echoed off the ancient walls of the castle across the water. Owen Murphy had made his final ferry run.

"Beatrice! Why did you *shoot* that poor old man?!" Anne shouted.

"He saw our *faces*, sweetheart. He could identify us. We're not leaving *any* loose ends, remember?"

Without the slightest remorse, Beatrice ordered Evelyn. "Come over here and give me a hand with him."

At that moment, had Beatrice realized it, killing the old man or not killing him really didn't matter because of the number of loose ends she had already left behind. She was completely unaware that the authorities had already identified her and Evelyn Maxwell as two of the kidnappers. The proverbial noose was already beginning to tighten.

Without a word, Evelyn helped Beatrice drag Owen Murphy's body into the tall brush which lined both sides of the ferry landing along the shoreline. As Beatrice walked around to the driver's side of the limo, she noticed her sister and their captive still standing outside the vehicle. With a cutting voice, she invalidated Anne.

"Didn't I tell you to get *in*?"

"Beatrice, *I* am not a prisoner, and I *refuse* to allow you to treat me like one. Take this handcuff off me," Anne said, trying to stand her ground.

Beatrice walked over to the limo, reached in for her purse and took out the second set of cuffs. Then she walked around the limo to where Anne and Kate were standing. She cuffed Kate's free hand and brought that arm behind Kate's back, and applied the other cuff to Kate's other wrist. Once both of Kate's hands were secured behind her, Beatrice removed the other set of cuffs.

"Are we *better* now?" she snarled,

Anne bristled, but snapped back, saying, *"Yes!"*

"Then get in the limo, Anne. Evelyn, I want you in front with me." Beatrice slid behind the wheel and engaged the engine. "We'll have to ditch this shortly."

Anne was clearly surprised again. "Why?"

"It's a risk, dear. By now, they know the limo is missing. They'll be checking every limo on the road. No loose ends, remember?"

"Oh."

Beatrice looked at Evelyn. "I should have had the limo drop us off at a car hire, but I didn't *think* of that. If I had, maybe we could have remained here."

"So, what do we do now?"

"Evelyn, just take out your cell phone and see if there are any car hire agencies between here and County Louth."

"County Louth? Why County Louth?"

"Because *that's* where we're heading. We'll be staying in County Louth for the rest of the time. That was supposed to be my backup location."

AS THEY TRAVELED down the road, the two women in the front seat talked among themselves. Anne sat in the back, staring out the window while she slipped in and out of her own private thoughts. She glanced over at Kate who was slumped over, eyes closed, then turned to watch the passing terrain outside the limo's window. Although Anne detested the miserable, lonely life she was living, she had never been as consumed with revenge to the extent Beatrice and Evelyn were.

Growing up together, the three of them had been

inseparable; their classmates had referred to them as 'the triplets' since they were never apart. In many ways, they were exactly alike, yet with very different personalities.

Beatrice was the more domineering of the three. Even though she could be a charmer, she also had what the other two called 'a short fuse,' especially if she didn't get her way. She had always been self-focused, never showing even the least bit of empathy for others. As she grew older, she became even more narcissistic.

Evelyn was the most outgoing of the trio, always talking, laughing, and 'up for whatever' adventure was at hand. She, too, had a sadistic streak in her and would go along with anything Beatrice wanted, especially if she thought they would be the center of attention.

Anne and Beatrice were fraternal twins, not identical ones. Personality-wise, Anne was the polar opposite of Beatrice. Anne was the introvert of the threesome. More often than not, she saw things differently from Beatrice, or had little interest in what Beatrice wanted to do. Early on, Beatrice had learned how to manipulate her sister in order to get her way. Anne often gave-in to her domineering twin merely to avoid being ridiculed. Anne suffered from the same mental disorder which had afflicted their mother. The disorder was severe enough that when flare-ups occurred, she would be shuffled off for a brief stay in an asylum.

Anne was brought out of her reverie when she heard Evelyn shout. "I can't *believe* it! I can't believe we actually *have* the little bitch!" Then Evelyn laughed and clapped her hands.

"Believe it, Evelyn. It's like old times," Beatrice answered. "*No*body screws with us and gets away with it."

Anne felt completely excluded from the conversation going on in the front seat. She continued to quietly listen and was okay with *ransoming* Kathryn O'Grady, but she was becoming conflicted with the harsh treatment they were subjecting her to; that she didn't like. Anne was also unhappy with the way she, *herself,* was being treated. She was beginning to regret she had ever agreed to be a part of this . . *.little adventure.*

Chapter Seventeen

T HE LIMO HAD become a loose end in Beatrice's mind, which forced her to stay clear of the main thoroughfares connecting County Roscommon to County Louth. It wasn't long before she realized the back roads were not much more than unpaved, meandering, cow paths, many of which had been that way for centuries. These roads were mainly used by farmers moving their livestock from one field to another. The sides of the road were lined with ancient stone walls that stretched as far as the eye could see in the fields, dividing the land, keeping the livestock in check, and peace among neighbors.

As the limo navigated the road, Beatrice was forced to come to a complete stop several times and wait while flocks of sheep passed from their daytime pasture to where they would spend the night.

At one point Evelyn said, "This is absurd; press the *bloody* horn!" In response, Beatrice simply gripped the steering wheel tighter.

"Didn't you *hear* me, Beatrice? I said, press the bloody *horn!*"

Finally, Beatrice replied in a low, snarly voice, "They are *sheep*, Evelyn, bloody *sheep*. Blowing the horn won't make the slightest bit of difference to them."

"They're filthy things, aren't they?" Evelyn said, in an attempt to agree.

"While we're waiting, tell me, did you find a car hire shop?" Beatrice asked.

"Yes, there's a petrol station a few villages up that has one. Hopefully they'll have a decent selection."

"I'll let you out when we get there. Once you hire the car, continue up the road. I'll be waiting for you off on the side."

Anne spoke up from the back seat, "I do hope they have a toilet."

"Anne dear, we're only stopping to let Evelyn out to hire a car."

"I don't care, I have to *go!*"

"Well, you'll just have to wait."

"I will *not*. I may be sitting in the back seat, but I am *not* a prisoner, and don't you *dare* treat me like one!"

Beatrice let out a sigh and looked in the rearview mirror. "All right Anne, we'll stop long enough for you to use the toilet."

Kate had tried periodically to shift around and find a comfortable position. But with her hands bound, it was next to impossible. That being said, no matter what position she found herself in, she was always facing the side window of the car. The gag, which had been placed across her mouth, had now become little more than a thin strip of cloth, which pulled on her cheeks. Her face looked somewhat contorted, but the thin strip remained an effective gag.

Anne assumed that Kate's decision to keep facing away from her was either an act of defiance or some type of emotional withdrawal. On the contrary, not only had Kate been actively listening to the conversation going on in the front seat of the limo, she was actually taking note of every sign post they passed, hoping to get an idea of where she was being driven. For the longest time, the landscape looked unfamiliar and offered little for her to go on. Then little by little a few of the fields and county road markers seemed somewhat familiar.

When a half hour had passed, Anne spoke up. "Beatrice, how much further is this? I really *need* to use the toilet!"

"Patience, dear sister. We're on a main road now, it shouldn't be too far."

THE STEEPLE ON TOP of the old stone church adjacent to the common in the village of Lannat Cross had a very unique design to it. It was very recognizable even from a distance. When the limo entered County Louth and passed through the center of Lannat Cross, Kate saw the steeple and smiled. She knew *exactly* where she was now. Her mother had grown up in County Louth, and most of her mother's family still lived there. If they stayed on this road and stopped at a petrol station, as planned, it would be the one in Stonetown, owned by Sean McKiernan, a first cousin to Kate. She began to imagine how she might attract someone's attention.

After several more delays, while moving at a snail's pace behind countless shepherds herding flocks into different pastures, they finally came to a petrol station. It pretty much defined the village center of Stonetown, Ireland.

"Is this *it*?" Beatrice asked.

"It must be," Evelyn said. "There's signage for the car hire. Wait here, if they're out of motor cars, I don't relish the thought of having to take a hike up the road."

Beatrice let out a sigh. "Just go and inquire. Signal me if they have one."

As soon as the car came to a stop, Anne announced, "I'm getting *out* to use the *toilet*."

Beatrice, had inadvertently pulled in and parked at the petrol pumps. It wasn't long before a man dressed in coveralls emerged from the garage, wiping his hands on an oily cloth. He knocked on the limousine's window to get the driver's attention.

Beatrice lowered the window a few inches. Using a well-rehearsed condescending voice she said, "Yes?"

"What'll it be?"

"What will *what* be?"

"Do you want a fill-up?"

"What *are* you talking about?"

"Did you pull in for petrol, or not?"

Beatrice lowered the window a little further and stuck her head out. She hadn't realized she had parked next to the pump. "No, we're just waiting. My friend is inside hiring a car."

"Right." As the man turned to leave, he paused and looked directly at the face pressing up against the window of the rear door. The first thing he noticed was that the eyes looked familiar, as did the face, but there was something odd about the mouth, like it was being pulled at the corners. The woman was raising her eyebrows up and down in an unusual manner, like she was trying to catch his attention. But just then, another man emerged from the garage.

"Sean, your wife is on the phone." As Sean walked away,

he thought, *it might just be my imagination, but the woman in back looked vaguely familiar…the way she was moving her eyebrows was odd though.*

When Anne, returned to the limo, Beatrice announced, "Now you've got *me* needing to go to the loo." As soon as Beatrice, was out of the limo, Anne, tapped Kate on the shoulder. Turning toward her, Kate heard Anne say, "Tilt you head back and open your mouth. I want to give you some water."

Slouching down, Kate tilted her head back as best she could and felt the cool refreshing liquid pass across her parched lips. She felt the liquid travel all the way down her gullet.

When Beatrice came out of the toilet, Evelyn was standing in the doorway of the building waving her hand. Beatrice nodded, assuming that was Evelyn's signal that she had a rental. As soon as she reached the limo, she slid into the driver's seat, started the motor and proceeded to drive up the road. When she finally found a break in the stone wall running parallel to the road, she pulled over.

It wasn't long before Evelyn arrived driving a large late model, blue sedan. In short order, the women transferred everything from the limo into the trunk and Kate was sitting in the back seat of the new rental.

"Did you have any trouble?"

"No, but I didn't have any cash, so I had to give them my credit card. If they had asked for any identification we'd have been screwed. The card says 'Maxwell.'"

"I didn't realize you didn't have sufficient cash, Evelyn. We'll need to find an ATM and get more cash. You can't use your credit card again, that leaves a trail. No loose ends, remember?"

"Beatrice, *please,* don't scold me. I didn't have a choice. After all, no card, no car!"

Beatrice looked over at her friend. "Hopefully, there's no harm done." Then she turned to Anne and gave her a command. "Anne, get in the back seat of the rental and stay there. Evelyn, get in the limo, you're coming with me."

As the limo passed through the opening in the stone wall, Evelyn noticed the huge rusty hinges in both sides of the stone end caps. At one time, they would have anchored a gate. The grass in the field was tall and the ground just uneven enough to jostle both occupants inside the limo as Beatrice drove to the far end of the field. When she got out, she removed the license plate. "This won't stop them, Evelyn, but it may slow them down a bit. Use your hankie and wipe down the inside of the car. I don't want to leave any fingerprints."

"Why don't we just torch it?"

Beatrice looked at her friend. "What?" Then, shaking her head, Beatrice repeated the instruction. "Just wipe down the inside so we can go."

"Well, what's *wrong* with torching it?"

"We're trying to be discreet. We don't need any unnecessary attention, *remember*?"

EVEN THOUGH THE light was beginning to fade, the further the kidnappers drove along, the more familiar the landscape was becoming to Kate. Close to dusk, they turned into a long dirt driveway leading to a farmhouse situated at the top of a hill.

"Take a look at the cottage ahead of us on the hill ladies, *that's* where we'll be putting our heads down tonight."

Evelyn looked around. "Well, it certainly looks isolated."

"The WIFI is supposed to be good," Beatrice said. "That's all I care about."

"Well, is there plumbing *inside*?" Evelyn asked. "That's all *I* care about."

"Yes, for your information, there *is* plumbing."

Evelyn shook her head. "How do you find these places?"

"Online. . . and it's ours for two weeks. The rental agency agreed to provision the kitchen with a week's worth of food for two adults and three children by noon today."

"But we're *four* adults," Anne spoke up suddenly. Then, correcting herself, she said, "I mean *three* adults, and *her*."

Beatrice let out a sigh, "I *know* that, dear sister, I was trying to disguise who we are."

Evelyn rolled down the window and snorted. "Damn, there's that foul stench of peat, again. God, how I hate it, and it's *every*where. Don't these people have anything else to burn?"

The pungent smell of peat, and the long drive up to the farm house, had already brought back Kate's memories of happier times. At last, she felt a sliver of hope that she just might survive this ordeal and find a way out. This was her country. She knew this home.

Chapter Eighteen

I T WAS DUSK when the Garda SUV reached the access road to McDermott Castle. Lou leaned forward and tapped Fran-O on the shoulder. "Turn the headlights off. As soon as you see the ferry landing, stop, so we can put the boat in the water."

"Sure thing."

After passing through more than a quarter mile of fields, Fran-O called out, "I don't see the ferry landing yet, but it looks like there's water on the right side now."

Another quarter mile further on, as they passed a field, Fran-O called out, again. "There's something dead over there to be attracting all those buzzards."

Lou folded the map and sat up straight. "Find a spot to pull over; we'll deploy from here."

As soon as Fran-O, pulled over, Lou was out of the SUV and untying the straps that secured the inflatable to the trailer. "Duffy, get on the other side and give me a hand."

In minutes, the inflatable was off the trailer and resting on the water's edge. The boat was large enough to carry four adults. When Duffy motioned for Fran-O to take the forward position, Fran-O declined. "I'll stay with the vehicle. It's unwise to leave it unattended, even out here in the middle o' nowhere." Lou nodded.

Once Jake and Duffy were forward in the boat, Lou knelt down in the stern. He spoke in hushed tones. "All right, once we determine which side of the island the tents are on, we'll paddle around and come ashore on the far side. When we're ashore, the two of you will deploy to the right side of the castle and wait. I'll take the left flank. When you're in position, give the sound of the whip-poor-will. Wait for my reply; that'll be our signal to move in. I'm guessing the tents will be four-man wall tents, so, let's come in from different ends with weapons drawn. Don't fire unless you *absolutely* have to."

Lou held out his right hand, whispering, "Here, use these zip ties to secure the kidnappers' hands. Once the situation is under control, I'll call for the ferry."

Jake whispered, "It's going to be tight driving back with four extra people in one SUV."

"We'll deal with that later."

"I'm not sure I can mimic a whip-poor-will." Duffy whispered.

"Just follow Jake," Lou said. "All right, cell phones off and no talking from here on out." He waited for everyone to check their cell phones. "Let's move out, nice and easy."

As the three-man strike force paddled toward the island, Duffy whispered, "It gets dark early out here."

Jake whispered back, "We're further north than we are in New Brunswick; about ten degrees latitude, I'd guess."

Lou whispered, "Quiet! Sound travels on the water."

When Lou saw that the tents had been set up directly across from the ferry landing, he used his paddle as a rudder and directed the craft around to the back of the island. Once the inflatable had beached, and was out of the water, Duffy and Jake headed to the right, and disappeared into the darkness; Lou circled left.

Centuries earlier, the castle ramparts had been constructed by stonemasons who were aligned with the McDermott clan. Time had not been kind to the structure; entire sections of the once formative outer walls had collapsed after decade upon decade of neglect. Now, as the men circumvented numerous obstacles, they listened for voices. But the only discernible sounds came from crickets, bullfrogs, and the fluttering wings of bats as they darted overhead, feeding on swarms of insects.

When Jake was finally in position, he made the call of the whip-poor-will. Lou immediately responded. In unison, the three rescuers silently advanced on the tents, weapons drawn. Then, throwing aside the tent flaps, they yelled: "Police! Hands up!"

Duffy was the first to say, "*Shit.*"

Jake went over to the cooking station. "Lou, this stove is stone cold. Nobody's been here for a while."

Duffy looked at the ground. "Well, they *were* here; these tracks were definitely made by a wheel chair." He pointed to rut marks on the earth.

Lou took a deep breath. "They rented this island for two *friggin'* weeks."

Jake's head was on a swivel. "They must have figured we'd be able to track them here, and moved out."

It was Duffy who noticed a small envelope on one of the

cots. He picked it up, opened it, read the contents; then handed it to Lou.

Nine million pounds, and you get her back. Screw with us and we'll screw with <u>her</u>. The last word was heavily underlined. Lou folded the message up along it creases and placed it in his shirt pocket.

"Where to now, Lou?"

"Back to Limerick. I'll call for the ferry." Lou punched in Owen Murphy's number and waited. No one picked up. "All right, he's not answering his phone. Let's go back to the inflatable. We'll beach the damn thing over at the landing; that'll be easier."

As they walked back to the rubber boat, Duffy pulled out his cell phone and called Fran-O. "You can bring the SUV down to the landing; they weren't here."

When they finally dragged the inflatable up onto shore, Duffy looked at Jake. "Grab hold of the other side, and give me a hand loading this sucker onto the trailer, will ya'?"

As Jake walked around the far side of the trailer, he tripped. Duffy laughed. "Not quite as sure-footed as we once were, eh, Jake?"

Jake growled to himself, and tried kicking whatever he stumbled over further into the brush. When it didn't move, he bent down to pick it up, then realized he had taken hold of a human ankle.

"Duffy! Over here!"

"What?"

Jake ignored the question and walked up to the front of the SUV. "Fran-O, give me the flashlight, and pull this rig forward a few feet."

"Sure thing."

"Duffy, I said, come *over* here!"

As soon as Fran-O pulled forward, Duffy walked over. "What?"

Jake handed the flashlight to Duffy. "Just shine this light down here."

Bending forward, Jake grabbed both of Owen Murphy's ankles and with one heavy pull, the ferry master's body was stretched full out onto the roadway.

"Holy *shit!*" Duffy said, his eyes popping wide open. Lou and Fran-O hurried over.

"Mother of God! Saints, preserve us!" Fran-O muttered while blessing himself.

Lou bent down to examine Owen Murphy's lifeless form. "Looks like he was shot in the back of the head. Now, we know why he didn't answer his phone."

Fran-O just shook his head. "They've kicked it up to a new level now, lads. Kidnapping and assault was serious enough, but now they've *killed* a man."

Lou stood up and wiped his hands off. "They're on the run. Murphy was a risk. He could have identified them."

"I'd best be calling the locals in," Fran-O said. "It's *their* county, not mine." When he finished talking with the Roscommon station house, Fran-O again spoke aloud. "We'll need to wait here for the locals to arrive before we can leave, lads."

Meanwhile, Lou's hope for a quick rescue was now shattered. He was deep in thought and struggling to keep his warrior spirit at bay.

Jake was wrestling with the same challenge. *This certainly tells us a lot more about who we're up against.* He decided to make a quick trip back over to the tents with the flashlight to search for any additional clues, but found nothing.

On his way back from the island, Jake wondered how long before Lou would decide to take the lead. He knew it was inevitable, and now, only a matter of time.

Chapter Nineteen

BEATRICE GUNNED THE large sedan and fishtailed up the hill before coming to an abrupt stop in front of the main door to the small cottage. She turned to Evelyn. "This car you rented has some guts." Then, barely taking a breath, she yelled, "All right, everyone out!"

Inside, the cottage was broom clean. The windows were not large, but were certainly adequate. The ceilings were a little low, but typical of the centuries-old, thatched roof cottages which now only intermittently dotted the Irish countryside.

Evelyn immediately went to check that the toilet flushed. Once satisfied that the accommodations were suitable, she came back into the sitting room and looked at their captive. "Beatrice, let's get this one up into the attic. I can't stand the sight of her."

Kate smiled upon hearing she would be taken up into the attic. In spite of the gag, Evelyn saw her smile and immediately stepped in front of their bound captive. She raised her hand, as if to slap Kate.

"Was that a *smirk* I just saw? Go ahead, do it *again*!" Kate lowered her head. "Smirk again, and I'll *wipe* it off your face!"

Quickly, Anne stepped between them. "That's *enough*. I'll take her up to the attic." She helped steady Kate as she climbed the narrow stairway, with her hands behind her back. When they reached the upper floor, Anne led Kate over to a bed. "Sit down."

In a muffled voice Kate attempted to say 'take off the gag', but it came out muffled.

Anne seemed to understand what Kate was trying to say and at this point, she didn't see a need for the gag. "I will, if you promise not to yell. If you do, I'll get into trouble and that will just make things worse."

Once the gag was removed, Kate took a few deep breaths. "Thank you. Now, please release me from these cuffs, they're chaffing my skin. I'm not going anywhere." She sensed that Anne was struggling with how to reply.

"For God's sake, I'm in the damn *attic*. There's only one way out. Can't you just tie me up with a piece of rope . . . at least for tonight?"

Anne hesitated. "I . . . I don't have the key. But, quite honestly, right now I'm more concerned about keeping you hydrated and getting some nourishment into you."

She's a sympathizer, Kate thought. *She could be an ally*. Out loud she said, "Thank you, but please get the key. My arms and shoulders are killing me. I can't *go* anywhere; I'm in the damn *attic*."

"Be patient," Anne said, touching Kate's shoulder. "I'll do what I can, but Beatrice has the key. I have to go down now, but please don't make any trouble for me." With that, Anne walked over to the stairs and stepped down one step. Then, after turning around to look at their hostage one more time, she closed the door to the attic behind her.

AS FAR BACK as County Louth records went, the property surrounding this cottage at the top of the hill had belonged to the McKiernan clan. The last McKiernan to have actually lived there were Kate's grandparents, on her mother's side. Kate's mother was the only daughter in a family of nine children.

Even after Kate's mother had married into the O'Grady clan and moved to Abbyfeale, she would make the journey back to her mother's cottage every fall to help with the harvest being brought in from the fields. From the time Kate was born, her mother had always brought her along whenever she made the trek back to her own mother's cottage, the very cottage where Kate was now being held in the attic.

Kate looked around thinking. *The days and nights I've spent in this attic were among the happiest days of my life. My uncles would be in the fields early, and my aunts would arrive in the afternoon with all my cousins trailing behind. Some would help my mother with the canning, the others would prepare the feast we'd enjoy later when the men came in from the fields. Those were happy times, everyone was always laughing.*

Momentarily, Kate lost her train of thought when she heard a noise that sounded like someone coming up the stairs. When the door remained closed, she returned to her memories of harvest time, she reminisced. *Harvest time was really the only time during the year I saw my cousins on my mother's side . . . the younger ones would help clean and stack whatever my uncles brought in. Us older kids took turns whitewashing the cottage and the barn, collecting eggs, and moving sheep from one pasture to the next.*

Again, she thought she heard someone coming up the stairs. When the door to the attic didn't open, her mind wandered back again to happier days at this cottage on the hill.

I remember Sean and I were the same age. We'd end up doing chores with either group. She had always seemed to be everyone's favorite cousin, either because her cousins rarely saw her, or because of the joy Kate brought with her.

Back then, in the evenings after supper, there was always a game of hide and seek which wouldn't end until well after the fireflies came out. Kate's favorite place to hide was underneath the bulkhead doors which led to the root cellar. Not only was it a great place to hide, but she could sneak up the stairs on the opposite end, put her ear up against the secret door that blended into the kitchen wall, and listen to the grownups talk.

The original part of the cottage was well over three hundred years old, and sat on the highest point in the middle of over twenty-seven acres of fields. Each generation seemed to add something practical, making life on the farm a little easier. Kate's grandfather brought running water into the cottage. Her great- grandfather had put a second stairway up to the attic which Kate always thought was a secret passageway. It was her great, great grandfather who had dug out the root cellar underneath the kitchen.

When Kate had signed on with the Irish Directorate of Military Intelligence, she had stopped attending the fall harvests. The annual event still continued and everyone else in the McKiernan family put their lives on hold to participate every year. Now, her cousin, Sean McKiernan, owned the property and recently had installed indoor plumbing. Sean's wife loved the little cottage, but wanted to wait until he retired before moving here. So, for the time being, the cottage was a rental, except of course, during harvest time.

DOWNSTAIRS, AFTER THE three women had eaten, Beatrice looked at Anne, "Take some food and water up to the attic. Not a lot, mind you, just enough to keep the bitch alive."

As Anne, went about fixing a plate, Beatrice watched closely. "That's too much," she directed. "We're not trying to bloody fatten her up." Anne removed a small portion of what was on the plate, and tucked a roll into her pocket.

"Anne, come over here with that dish." Anne walked over to Beatrice, anticipating a complaint. Instead, Beatrice spit on the food. "There, now you can take it up to her."

Anne closed her eyes as she turned away from her sister. Suddenly, Evelyn put her hand out, saying, "Wait." She, too, spit on the plate.

Anne let out a sigh as she walked upstairs to the attic with the small plate of food and water, but no key. As soon as she entered the attic, Kate looked at her.

"Can you please take these handcuffs off?" she asked.

Realizing their hostage wouldn't be able to feed herself, nor relishing the thought of feeding her, Anne went back downstairs to the kitchen. Beatrice had already settled into the parlor and was busy on her laptop. Evelyn was at the far end of the kitchen doing dishes. Anne knew the key was in

Beatrice's purse, conveniently sitting on a side chair next to the stairway. She reached in for it.

Returning to the attic, Anne said, "I'm going to take one cuff off and loosen the other, on one condition, that you don't do *anything* that will get me in trouble." Kate nodded her agreement. The sense of relief that swept over Kate, when her hands were no longer constrained behind her back, brought renewed hope she might still find a way to escape this nightmare.

Famished, as well as partially dehydrated, Kate knew she needed to pace herself after having been denied nourishment for almost two days. Anne sat in a small chair directly in front of the stairway. "I'll stay with you until you finish eating. But before I go, I'll need to lock you back up again."

Kate nodded and continued to eat. She still needed time to create a plan, she was familiar with every nook and cranny of this cottage. Her bed had always been here in the attic whenever she came to visit her grandparents. She knew every secret the attic held.

Just before Kate finished the meager portion of food Anne was allowed to bring up, she looked at Anne and asked, "Why are you doing this?"

"It's not *me* really, my sister and Evelyn are the ones who are full of hate. I had little to no choice but to go along with this."

"No, that's not what I was asking," Kate said. "Why are you being *kind* to me?"

"Oh. I…I don't approve of how they're treating you."

"Will you help me escape?"

"No."

"Why?"

"I can't do that. You don't know Beatrice. I'm afraid of

what she would do if she ever found out that I crossed her and helped you escape. She can be . . . *very* unpredictable when things don't go her way. It would be very terrible for that to happen. You can't imagine how cruel she can be."

Oh, yes, I can, Kate thought. *That's how I came to be here, isn't it?*

Chapter Twenty

WHEN SEAN MCKIERNAN'S wife called him at the garage, it was only to tell him that her brother, Matt, would be bringing his car over for repairs and to put one of his better loaner cars aside for him.

That evening, when Sean arrived home, his wife greeted him saying, "Yer cousin, Kate's wedding is off . . . again."

He shrugged. "We'll talk about that later. Right now, I just want to clean up." As he walked away she called after him, "Be sure to put your work coveralls in the bag; they'll be here to pick up the laundry first thing in the morning."

After Sean had showered, toweled off and dressed, he returned to the kitchen. "Are the girls not here?"

"They ate earlier; they're over with the Dowd's."

"Now, what was it that you were saying about Kate, earlier?"

"Claire sent out another email today."

"And?"

"Your cousin Kate O'Grady's wedding is postponed. . . again."

"Did she say why?"

"Ha, get this. Claire said that Kate has been *kidnapped* and taken off in a limousine . . . of all the foolish things to say."

In an instant, Sean had a vivid flashback. The face of the woman he had seen in the back of a limo came to mind. He reached for his smartphone asking, "Did she copy the *both* of us?"

"I think she copied the world on it . . . she usually does."

He looked up the email on his phone and read it. "This isn't anything to be trifled with. Claire didn't make this up. The authorities are looking for Kate."

"I don't believe a word of it. It's just *crazy* talk," his wife said. "Who in their right mind would go to the bother of kidnapping one of your cousins, and for what reason?"

"There was a limousine that stopped at the pumps today. They didn't buy any petrol, but there was a woman in the back seat of the limousine. She somehow reminded me of Kate, just a little bit. Something was 'off,' about her though . . . I need to make a call."

"You'll be doing no such thing! I'm putting your dinner on the table right *now*. You can make your call after we sup."

Realizing the hour was late, and that his wife had waited to sup with him, Sean let out a sigh. "All right, we'll go ahead and eat first."

As soon as Sean finished his meal, he placed a call to the County Louth police. "Hello, this is Sean McKiernan. I'd like to speak with someone regarding a kidnapping."

"Are you *reporting* a kidnapping?"

"No."

"Well, then, go on; what do you have to say?"

"A cousin of mine sent out an email today that *another* cousin of mine has been kidnapped."

"And?"

"And I think I may have seen her today, but I'm not sure."

"Which one did you see?"

"The one that was kidnapped, *ya fool*!"

"Where was that?"

"In Stonetown."

"Does your cousin live in Stonetown?"

"No, she lives in Canada."

"All right, you're confusing me. Give me this one more time."

Speaking slower, Sean began again. "My cousin, Kathryn O'Grady, was kidnapped from Shannon International Airport. Word has it, she was taken away in a limousine. I think that very limousine stopped at my petrol station earlier today."

"And where is your petrol station?"

"In Stonetown, County Lough. They may have rented one of my cars for hire, too,"

"And where exactly was this cousin of yours *supposedly* kidnapped?"

"I just *told* you! She was abducted at Shannon International."

"Well, why in the *hell* didn't you call earlier? We've all been on the lookout for that one all *day.*"

"Because I just found out about it, ya' bugger. Is this *you*, Danaher?"

"It 'tis."

"Well, don't you be giving me any of your baloney, or you'll be drivin' yourself over to Castletown from now on to get your petrol."

"Is this *you*, Sean?"

"Ya' damn well *know* it 'tis!"

"Don't you go *anywhere*; I'll have someone call you right back!"

IT WAS LATE when Lou and the others returned to Limerick. As they walked into the station house, the desk sergeant said, "Fran-O, there's a message on your desk; it just came in from County Louth."

Once Fran-O read the message aloud, he said, "It's a lead on the limo. But it's late now. We can follow up on this in the morning."

"Are you *shitting* me?" Lou said, furrowing his brow. "I don't care *how* late it is, I'm calling this Sean McKiernan, *now*."

SEAN USUALLY SWITCHED the ringer on his cell phone off at this time of night, so that any after-hour calls would bounce over to his tow service answering line. But tonight, he decided to leave the ringer on. When the phone rang, he caught it on the second ring.

"Hello?"

"Sean, this is Lou Gault, your cousin Kate O'Grady's husband. I'm sorry to be calling so late; we just got back to the station. I'm working with the constables in County Limerick. What information can you share with me about this limo you saw?"

"Like I told Danaher earlier, there was a limousine that stopped at my garage this afternoon. I thought they wanted petrol, but they didn't. They just wanted to hire a car. But I noticed a woman sitting in the back seat. She looked familiar to me. Now, I'm not saying that it *was* my cousin, Kate O'Grady, but it damned sure reminded me of her. The only reason I remembered is that something just didn't feel right. She was looking at me, almost pleading-like. And her eyebrows. She kept moving 'em."

"When was this?"

"Like I told Danaher, late this afternoon."

"Where?"

"In Stonetown, County Louth."

"When they drove off, which way did they head?"

"I have no idea. By then, I was back in the garage, but then, I would guess northeast, toward Castletown."

"Did you say they hired a car?"

"That they did."

"Do you recall the name on the agreement?"

"I don't. I have a young fella who handles all the paperwork for that. Me? I fix cars for a living."

"So, you don't know who hired it, or for how long?"

"Not offhand; the paperwork's down at the garage."

"Sean, I need to see that paperwork."

"I'll fax it over to you first thing in the morning."

"That's not good enough," Lou said pressing hard. "I know it's late, but it's *urgent* we have that information."

"It's that serious?"

"They've killed once, maybe twice, and bludgeoned another man; that's how serious this situation is."

"Right. I'll go down to the garage straight away."

As Sean hung up, his wife asked, "Who was that you were talking to?"

"Kate's husband. I'll be back, I need to go down to the garage and fax him something."

"It can't wait 'til morning?"

"No. This kidnapping thing sounds like it's for real. I won't be long."

Chapter Twenty-One

A S SOON AS Sean McKiernan faxed over the rental agreement, Lou saw the name Ellen Marshall on the agreement. He sent a text back: *Notify me if and when they return the vehicle.*

It was late, but Fran-O was still in the station. Lou walked the fax over to Fran-O, saying, "I need someone to run the credit card used to hire this car."

"I'll have one of the lads get right on that."

For the next few hours, Lou and the team looked at maps trying to determine which direction the kidnappers might have headed.

At one point, Duffy turned to Fran-O. "What happens if they cross over from County Louth into Northern Ireland?"

"That would add a wrinkle we don't want to deal with," he said. "We can't just go traipsing around up there like we're doing a pub crawl."

"So, how do we work it?"

"Well, the way we've worked things out in the past with the North is having one of their own join our team."

Lou asked, "Is there a check point at the border crossing?"

"There is."

"Can't we have them detained if they try to cross?"

"I've already had one of the lads alert the North to be on the watch for the rental car. If they try to cross over, you can be assured they *will* be stopped," Fran-O said.

THE FOLLOWING MORNING a county Roscommon detective was dispatched to McDermott Castle, to take a few more pictures of the crime scene. As he traveled down the access road, he was surprised at the number of vultures roosting in the trees off to the side of the road and circling overhead. He thought to himself, *there must be something big that died in that field to attract these devils.* He made a mental note to check the field out on his way back.

MEANWHILE, THAT SAME morning, over in Stonetown, two young brothers had been out hunting partridge in Mulcahy's vacant fields since sunrise. The brothers were close enough in age that they were jokingly referred to as "Irish twins." Each had brought down a bird and they were allowed one more apiece.

Mulcahy's land was flat with the exception of one field with a hill in the middle. At the top of the hill was a lone oak tree that stood there like a monument. When the brothers reached the top of the hill, they sat down on a section of the tree trunk that had split off years earlier when a bolt of lightning had struck the ancient tree.

"It's a grand view you get from here," one brother said. "I can make out the top of the steeple over in Lannat Cross."

"I see it."

Looking up at the huge canopy of leaves overhead, the older of the two said. "You'd surely stay dry sitting under a tree like this in a storm."

"Do you think that's the reason Mulcahy has left it standing."

"Nah, it's a fairy tree."

"A what?"

"A *fairy* tree."

"Now, aren't you the one to be talking nonsense."

"Do ya' not see the ring of rocks around the base of the trunk?"

"Ah, some fool put those there."

"You can't deny that there's many that believes a lone tree, standing in the middle of a field, is a fairy tree."

"And you're the bigger fool if you believe in any of that rubbish."

The older of the two looked at his younger sibling for a moment. "Then you don't believe that it's a gateway between our world and the world of the wee folk?"

"No, I don't. That's a bunch of malarky, that's what it 'tis. I don't believe in *any* of that foolish folklore nonsense, and neither should you."

"Well, Mulcahy must, it's in his field."

"Then Mulcahy's a fool himself."

"You might try listening to the talk down at the pub about the night this tree was struck by lightning."

"Ahh, that's just the whiskey talking. Don't tell me you believe in any of *that* blarney."

The older brother took a deep breath. "Well . . . I won't say that I do, and I won't say that I don't, but there's been talk."

"Well, I *don't*." After a pause, the younger one continued, "But I do wonder why Mulcahy doesn't work the land?"

"He hasn't worked it in years."

"Then he should do like O'Doul does."

"What, rent out his fields?"

"Aye, that's what I'd tell him."

"And who are *you* to be telling the likes of Mulcahy what he should or shouldn't be doing with his own fields?"

The younger brother ignored the put down, and looked to his right. "So, would you be telling me then why Mulcahy would be parking a *limousine* in that back field of his?"

The older brother turned to look. "I have no idea."

"Well, if he's not going to *use* it, he should sell it, don't ya think?"

"If he needed money, wouldn't he be renting out the land?"

The younger brother took his binoculars out and focused in on the limo, "It looks like a fine one from here."

"Well, if it's sitting off in a field like that one is, there's a reason for it. You can be sure of that."

"It looks fine."

"The question you should be asking yourself is, does it *run* fine?"

"McKiernan could fix it up for me, if it needed fixing."

"Are ya thinking of buying it?"

"I might . . . if I get my price."

"And what would you be doing with a car like that?"

"I'd hire it out. Hell, McKiernan does it all the time, and look at him, he seems to be doing swell."

"Then, when we pass by Mulcahy's door on the way

home, give it a knock, and ask the man what he wants for it." With that, the older of the two stood up.

"Let's go, I just saw some movement in the field below."

"It's probably a fox. I saw one earlier."

"Or it could be a partridge . . . so get up, and get a leg under ya'."

IT BEING THE weekend, Sean McKiernan's wife decided to let him sleep in later than usual that morning.

When she heard the toilet flush, she called out, "Sean, your breakfast will be waiting, when you come down."

Sean hadn't worked a weekend for close to a decade now. The only thing that even came close to work on a weekend for him was checking in on the occasional tenants who rented the cottage on the hill. He'd had good luck renting the cottage out once he had brought the plumbing indoors.

As Sean sat at the table, he asked, "Are the girls off already?"

"My sister picked them up early this morning; there's a church fair over at Christ the King in County Meath. She promised to have them back for supper, but not before."

"Did it ever occur to you that I might want to see the likes of me own two daughters, once in a while?"

Ignoring her husband's comment, Sean's wife turned to him. "I was thinking I'd like to go over to Castletown today."

"Fine."

"And I'd like you to go with me."

"I'll go with you, if you can hold off until tomorrow. I need to check on the new renters; then I'd like to go back to the garage. The county sent me more forms to fill out with a short window on returning them. Every year, there seems to be more and more forms. It's getting so, I'm thinking that I'm working for the damn *county* and not for myself."

"If that's the case," she said, "we can go tomorrow. But that means we'll be going to church tonight, so we can put an early leg under us in the morning."

JUST BEFORE NOON, Sean drove up the long drive to the cottage on the hill. Everything looked quiet. As soon as he put the car in park, Evelyn stepped out of the cottage, arms folded across her chest.

"Can I help you?"

"Just checking in; is everything to your liking?"

"Are you the owner?"

"I am."

"Everything is to our liking."

"Then I'll be on my way. My card is on the fridge. Give a call, if you run into a problem."

"I'll do that."

When she stepped back into the cottage, Beatrice was standing just inside. "Who was that?"

"The owner. I saw him coming up the drive; he was just checking in."

As Sean turned his car around, he recognized the blue sedan parked beside the house as one of his rentals. *That's the rental I faxed over to Kate's husband last evening.*

By the time he reached the end of the long driveway, he had pulled out his cell phone and dialed the local constable's office.

"County Lough Constable Office, how may I help you?"

"This is Sean McKiernan. I think I have something else to share about the Kathryn O'Grady kidnapping."

"Hold, I'll put you through to Limerick."

AT THE EXACT time Sean McKiernan was sitting at the bottom of the driveway waiting to be connected to Limerick, Beatrice Hastings decided to toy with their captive's husband, and sent him a text.

Do you have the nine million, or would you like to purchase her one piece at a time?

Lou sent an immediate reply back: *I have the money. Where's the drop off?*

Beatrice smiled. She liked a quick response. *I'll send the drop off location soon . . . stay alert.*

Lou replied: *Ready now!*

Beatrice texted back: *Patience. It's a virtue.*

When Lou told Fran-O that he'd just received a couple of text messages from the kidnappers, Fran-O was quick to respond.

"Give your phone here, we may find out where they were when they sent you the texts."

"They're using burners."

"Makes no difference, the lads will figure it out."

THE TWO YOUNG brothers were on their way home from hunting when the youngest stopped off at Mulcahy's manor house to inquire about the limousine. It took a while before Mulcahy came to answer the knock at his door.

Removing his hat, the young lad said, "Good morning, Mr. Mulcahy."

"It is a fine morning."

"I've come to inquire about the limousine in your field, sir. Is it for sale?"

Mulcahy looked perplexed. He had no idea what the lad was talking about. After a pause, he said, "Lad, if there's a limousine in one of my fields, it doesn't belong there. And if there is, you're more than welcome to have it."

"Well, fine sir. I thank you kindly." With that, the young man took out his cell phone and called McKiernan's Garage.

"McKiernan's."

"Yeah listen, this is Michael Patrick. There's a limo sitting in Mulcahy's field that I'd like to have towed to Sean's garage, if you would."

"It's in Mulcahy's field you say?"

"It is. And I'd like Sean to give it the once over."

"Well, your timing is perfect, it's himself who just pulled in. I'll let him know."

BACK IN LIMERICK, Duffy and Fran-O had called for a midmorning team meeting. Fran-O began the meeting by saying, "Okay, lads, yesterday was a bust. But today is a whole new day. Lou received a few text messages from the kidnappers this morning. The lads are working on finding out where they were, when they sent them."

Then Duffy spoke up. "Fran-O, let's go over everything we know now. Roscommon is reporting that a body has been found along the access road to McDermott's Castle. That's very likely the limo driver; nobody's heard from him since the limo went missing."

As Duffy was about to continue, Fran-O's cell phone rang. After he looked at the caller ID, Fran-O announced: "I need to take this call."

"Hello?"

"Fran-O this is Danaher, over in County Louth."

"Good morning, Danaher."

"Listen, I'm calling to tell ya' that they just towed a limousine out of a field over here. I knew that you'd want to know about it straight away."

"Where was it found?"

"Stonetown, just a mile north of the center."

"Do you have the license tag number?"

"The tag was gone, but the VIN number matches that of the missing limo."

"I'll be thanking ya' for that."

Fran-O had no sooner put his phone down, when it rang again. He looked at the caller ID and raised his finger signaling for everyone to wait. Then, he placed his phone on speaker. "Hello?"

"Danaher, again. You hung up too quick. I wanted to tell ya that Sean McKiernan just phoned in to say that the rental car you were interested in is sitting outside a cottage he rents out over here."

"In County Louth?"

"Yes."

"Where?"

"He says it's on the outskirts of Stonetown, at the old McKiernan place."

"Thank you." Fran-O said as he put his phone away again. "Like I said, if you wait long enough, the tips start rolling in."

Lou had been struggling with Fran-O's lackadaisical approach, but this was the final straw. Rising to his feet, he could barely control his emotions. "Time is of the essence here, Fran-O. What's the quickest way for us to get over to

County Louth?"

"Well, by helicopter, of course, otherwise it's close to a three-hour drive."

Lou leaned forward; his body taut. "Then call a chopper in! This isn't some damn friggin' classroom exercise we're running!"

Hoping to defuse the situation, Duffy pipped up. "Fran-O, the life of a Mountie is at stake here. She's also Lou's wife. We need to move now!"

"I agree, lads. I'll call the Air Corps and tell them we need the Defender to transport us over to Louth on a priority code."

While chomping at the bit to leave, Lou realized he needed to put his impulsiveness aside and develop a plan. "Duffy, let's look at the map. I wanna see where this cottage is in County Lough so we have a lay of the land."

AFTER THE CALL FROM LIMERICK came into Dublin, a Britten-Norman BN 2T-45 Defender was quickly airborne. Twenty-five minutes later, the huge chopper was sitting on the front lawn of the station house in Limerick taking on passengers and receiving clearance to proceed to County Louth.

Before they lifted off, Duffy took Lou aside trying for a moment of calm. "Lou, the man means well," he said, referring to Fran-O. "This is all new to him. We're all concerned about Kate. Right now, we *need* this man and the resources he can provide."

Lou could only give Duffy a stone-cold look. *Maybe he's right,* he thought as he climbed into the chopper.

ANNE'S COMPASSION WAS growing. Before she went downstairs for the night, she had massaged Kate's shoulders and back. When she finished, she removed the other handcuff from Kate's wrist and bound her hands in front of her with a length of rope she'd found in the attic. Then, after placing the handcuffs, and the key on the table next to the bed, she wrapped another length of rope around Kate's body, securing her to the bed.

Alone with her thoughts, Kate remembered how she always went down to the kitchen from this same attic as a little girl using what she considered to be a secret passageway. Her grandfather had built the second stairway when half of the attic housed his daughters, and the other half housed his sons. If you didn't know where the opening to the second staircase was in the attic, you would surely miss it. The second set of stairs ran parallel to the original stairs, but were separated by a wall. Reaching the bottom, only a sliding panel door separated the hidden stairway from the kitchen.

Sometime during the night, Kate managed to wiggle out of the ropes that bound her hands and the rope that held her to the bed. Once free of her bonds, she tiptoed across the room, to the secret stairway she knew would lead to her freedom.

Chapter Twenty-Two

ONCE BEATRICE HAD a chance to evaluate their new location, she realized they were actually trapped at the top of a hill with only one way out. It was not what she had planned.

She had expected to remain at McDermott Castle while negotiating a drop point for the ransom money and terms for the release of their captive. However, as soon as she had arrived at McDermott Castle, she realized the location was a mistake. They were trapped on an island, and the limo company had a record of where they had been dropped off. That first night, she had laid awake well into the early hours of the morning before she decided to quickly move to her back up location.

Now this site, which had been her contingency plan, was proving to be just as much of a mistake as McDermott Castle was.

Beatrice was feeling more than a little antsy at being trapped on a hill. For the first time in her life, she was experiencing anxiety. Her intuition had never failed her before, nor had she anticipated being on the run. She had always been the one in control, doing the hunting, never the one being hunted. Now, she found herself questioning her choice of the second hideout she had selected.

After only a few hours at the cottage, Beatrice knew this location wasn't any safer than staying on the island next to the castle would have been. It wasn't until after dinner, when she closed her eyes, that her thoughts were clear: *We need to leave Ireland; otherwise, we'll constantly remain on the run.*

It took some searching on the Internet, but before she went to bed, she found an old farmhouse located on a different island. The only wrinkle in her new plan was that in order to get there, they had to risk traveling through Dublin.

It's a risk we're going to have to take, she finally convinced herself.

IT WAS WELL AFTER MIDNIGHT when Kate managed to free herself from the ropes that bound her. Once free, she quietly traveled down the hidden staircase, tiptoed across the kitchen floor, slid open a panel in the wall next to the stove, and stepped into the root cellar. When she slid the panel closed behind her, she breathed a sigh of relief, believing she had found her freedom at last.

THE NEXT MORNING, Beatrice was up at the crack of dawn shouting to everyone, "Get up! Everyone up! We're on the move today!"

Evelyn came out from an adjacent bedroom yawning as

she ran her fingers through her hair. "Beatrice, we just *got* here. You said we had the place for two weeks."

"It doesn't feel safe to me," Beatrice answered. "We need to move. Get dressed. Anne, bring the bitch down from the attic. We'll have breakfast on the road."

Evelyn reluctantly returned to her room and began to pack. Anne, only half awake, walked upstairs to the attic. Knowing it would take time for her to remove the ropes and place the handcuffs back on Kate before she could bring her downstairs, she hoped Beatrice wouldn't be too impatient.

The last thing I want is for Beatrice to come up to the attic before I'm finished making the switch, Anne thought. But when Anne opened the door to the attic, she froze in her tracks.

The bed was empty!

Horrified at the consequences she would face, Anne frantically searched every inch of the attic to no avail. Trembling, she came downstairs and simply stood on the bottom step.

Beatrice looked at her. "Well? Go back up there and bring down the bitch!"

"She's . . . she's not up there."

"What?"

"She's . . . .she's not in the attic, Beatrice. I don't know where she is."

Pushing her sister aside, Beatrice raced up the stairs two steps at a time. The first thing she saw was the empty bed. Then her eyes shifted to the handcuffs and key both sitting on the bedside table. Instantly, she turned around and bolted down the stairs. In a menacing voice, she pointed at her sister.

"*You* . . . come over *here!*"

Anne approached cautiously, but didn't move fast enough

and Beatrice literally pounced on her, slapping her face, her head, her arms, her shoulders and yelling.

"You *fool*, you stupid, stupid *fool*! You let her escape! I *trusted* you!"

Sobbing and shocked at her sister's violent treatment, Anne fell to her knees and covered her face with both hands.

"It's not my fault! She promised she would stay in the attic if I . . . if I took the handcuffs off! She *promised* me! It's not my fault!"

Evelyn was beside herself. "Anne, how *could* you do this? You've ruined *everything*!"

Beatrice took a deep breath and regained control of her emotions, "She couldn't have gone far. Evelyn, search the yard . . . and that barn. You, my dear sister, gather your things and *get* in the car."

From the root cellar behind the paneled door, Kate listened to the confrontation, wishing there was something she could do to help Anne; but there was nothing she could do without risking recapture.

Moments later, Evelyn returned. "She's gone. She's not in the barn, either. I even checked that filthy hen house."

"Let's go; everyone in the car. We're moving," Beatrice commanded.

A gray dawn was just breaking when the car scrubbed out from the side of the cottage and roared down the long dirt driveway, fishtailing, and kicking up stones along the way.

Though Kate heard the car peel out and travel down the long drive, she remained in the root cellar for a while longer. When she finally felt safe, she emerged from the root cellar through the bulkhead doors leading out into the yard. Quickly, she ran over to the barn and slipped inside . . . directly into the waiting arms of . . . Beatrice Hastings!

"Ha! Thought you could get away, didn't you, *bitch*!! But I *knew* you hadn't gone far."

Kate was flabbergasted. It had never crossed her mind that one of her captors might have stayed behind, hidden in the barn. In her weakened physical state, she wasn't able to put up much resistance. Beatrice was able to quickly secure a handcuff around one of Kate's wrists and then, pulling her other arm behind her back, she secured the second cuff.

As if on cue, the car came roaring back up the drive with Evelyn at the wheel, and braked to a screeching stop in front of the barn.

Pushing Kate out from the barn, Beatrice yelled, "Evelyn, open the back door so I can put this one inside with her little friend." As soon as Evelyn opened the door, Beatrice shoved Kate into the car beside a whimpering Anne More, who was lying on the back seat, curled up into a fetal position.

A FEW MINUTES after nine that morning, the Britten-Norman BN 2T-4S Defender set down in the parking lot of the County Louth Garda headquarters. Three unmarked SUVs were at the ready as the strike force from Limerick emptied out of the huge chopper. Within minutes, they had passed McKiernan's petrol station, already open for the day, and were racing toward the cottage on the hill.

Each vehicle had their hands-free police communication channel on. Fran-O pressed his mic. "All right, listen up now: Vehicle Three will continue on past the cottage. The other two will stop as soon as we have a visual on the building. I want three teams moving up the hillside at the same time. Be careful; these people are armed and have killed already."

Lou was in the third vehicle which would allow him the

opportunity to eyeball the landscape surrounding the cottage on the hill as his vehicle passed by.

Lou's SUV had barely come to a stop, before he was out, and moving up the hill alongside a stone wall before the others had even released their seat belts.

The terrain was steep, but certainly not a challenge for anyone like Lou or his cousin Jake. As Lou approached the top of the hill, he veered off to the right, circled around behind the barn, and entered it through a rear door. Then, he peered out through the half open barn doors. The absence of a car in the yard disturbed him.

Moments later, Jake entered the barn, and whispered to him. "It looks deserted Lou."

"That's what I'm thinking, too. Where are the others?"

"They're still making their way up the hill. Duffy will be here before the rest."

"If they're inside, they're bound to see everybody working their way up the hill."

"I agree."

"Then, let's go."

The two men ran across the yard and pressed their backs up against the thick, outer wall of the cottage. Then they inched their way toward the door. When they reached it, Lou held up three fingers and counted down. As he came to one, they both slammed through the door and entered the cottage weapons in hand.

The cottage was obviously empty.

"I can't friggin' *believe* it, Jake! *How* in hell did they know we were coming?"

"They didn't Lou; they're on the run. That's what this is all about." Jake went over and felt the stove. "The stove is stone cold; they've been gone a while."

"Damn it!"

Walking outside the cottage, Jake cupped his hands around his mouth and yelled: "Ollie, ollie in free!" Duffy and the rest of the men who had worked their way up through the fields, suddenly stood up.

Duffy walked over to Lou. "We have the make, model, and license tag of the vehicle they're in, Lou. Fran-O is down the hill. I've sent a man down to tell him to put out an APB. There's not many roads around here, they won't be able to get far."

"How the hell are they able to keep *beating* us?"

"Lou, they're on the run. And they're scared. That makes them unpredictable. It also means they'll slip up at some point. That's when we'll be on them. It's not like they have a network giving them shelter. They're out there on their own."

"They've been pretty damn lucky, so far."

"And that's all it is: They've been *lucky*. But hoping to stay lucky isn't a sustainable strategy."

"So, tell me Duffy, what the hell is *our* strategy? The only thing we seem good at is finding their cold camps."

As the strike force rode back to the station house at County Louth, Fran-O contacted Limerick and asked them to send two vehicles to the Louth station house to take them home.

Lou kept to himself on the ride back trying to figure out what signs he was missing. *Who the hell are these women, and how is it they're able to constantly beat us at our own game?*

Chapter Twenty-Three

BEATRICE WAS DRIVING away from the cottage on the hill when she announced, "We need to change cars."

"Beatrice, we only hired this one yesterday," Evelyn protested.

"I know that. But think about it. . . think about all the information you gave them. Not only do they know *who* you are, they know approximately *where* you are, and *what* we're driving. We need a different vehicle . . . don't you agree?"

"Well, if we hire another car, won't we be giving out the same information?"

Beatrice ignored Evelyn. Her thoughts were churning as she tightened her grip on the steering wheel. She pursed her lips and chastised herself for not having allowed for the potential they might get flushed out of McDermott Castle and even the cottage on the hill. Now they were on the run and she needed a nondescript vehicle, one that wouldn't call attention to themselves.

"We're not going to hire another one Evelyn; we're going to *exchange* this one."

"And just *how* do you propose doing that?"

"We'll find one at the shopping center in Castletown."

"We're going to go *shopping* for a car?"

Beatrice smirked. "I guess you could call it that."

LIKE EVERY WEEKEND, there were a number of cars in the parking lot by the time Beatrice rolled into the Castletown shopping center. Stopping near the outer edge of the lot, Beatrice put the car in park, and scanned around.

After only a few minutes, Evelyn couldn't hold back any longer. "Now, what?"

"We wait."

"For what?"

"For the right opportunity. . . and I think I see one approaching now."

"Where?"

"See the old lady . . . the one who just got out of that Volkswagen Jetta?"

"The one walking toward the pharmacy?"

"Yes. I'll pull around and let you off in front of the store. When she comes out, follow her back to her car. I'll be parked right next to her."

As Evelyn was getting out, Beatrice pulled a blackjack out of her purse. "Here, use this when she gets between the two cars."

When the elderly woman came out of the pharmacy, instead of walking back to her car, she turned in the opposite direction and walked down the long line of storefronts looking into each one as she passed. Evelyn, followed her at a safe distance.

When the elderly woman went into a bakery shop, Evelyn peered through the window as the woman stood in line, waiting her turn at the counter. As she reached the front of the line, she pointed to a cake and nodded. Shortly after that, she left the store with a bakery box in hand. Again, she turned right and walked further down to a luncheonette where she took a seat at the counter. At this point, Evelyn began to fidget and decided to walk back to where Beatrice was waiting, just to let her know what was happening.

"Evelyn, what the *hell* are you doing? Why are you *here*? You're supposed to be shadowing that old broad."

"I thought you'd want to know what was taking so long."

Shaking her head, Beatrice said, "Evelyn, just shadow her, *please!*"

A little less than half an hour later, the elderly woman finished her meal, got up, and walked out of the luncheonette. Once again, she turned right. Her next stop was the dry cleaners where she picked up what appeared to be a dress. When she left the dry cleaners, she finally turned left, passed right by Evelyn, and proceeded to walk back to her car.

Evelyn followed at what she felt was an appropriate distance. When the woman arrived at her car, she placed the cake box on the roof, folded the dry cleaning over her left arm, fished her car key out from her pocketbook, and inserted it into the door handle just as Evelyn made her move.

The old woman fell like a sack of potatoes when Evelyn bludgeoned her from behind.

When the old woman went down, the dry cleaning went one way and the cake flew in another direction. Her purse fell at her feet, spilling the entire contents directly under the car. When that happened, Beatrice jumped out of the rental car.

"Grab her wallet," she commanded. "Stand her up against the car; she's going into the back seat."

"She's coming *with* us?" Evelyn said with surprise.

"Yes, for a little while, she is."

"Why don't we just put her in *our* car and leave her?"

"So, she can tell everyone what type of car *she* owns that we're now driving? Really, Evelyn, why don't we just leave a note with all the details? Honestly, I can't be the *only* one doing all the thinking here!"

Beatrice, opened the rear door of the rental car and spoke harshly to Anne and Kate. "Okay, both of you, *out* quick, and into this car."

Anne didn't move fast enough for Beatrice's liking and she slapped her on the shoulder. "I said *move!*" Once Anne exited the car, Kate scooted across the back seat as best she could with her hands cuffed behind her back.

As soon as Evelyn pulled the limp elderly woman to her feet, Beatrice secured her wrists with the second set of cuffs and shoved her into the back seat.

"Evelyn, I want you riding in front with me."

It didn't faze Beatrice in the least when she found the elderly woman's car was a standard shift. She held the clutch in, turned the ignition key, gave the car a little gas and it started right up. When she reached for the non-existent stick shift, she realized everything was on the column. Beatrice had driven manual transmissions years earlier, but they had been floor mounted stick shifts.

Okay, she thought, *on the column, or on the floor, it's still an 'H' pattern*. But, as soon as they moved forward, Evelyn yelled, "Beatrice, *stop!*"

"What?"

"We forgot the wheelchair."

"Jesus, Evelyn don't ever do that again."

"But we forgot the chair."

"*Forget* the damn chair, we only needed it when the bitch was drugged."

Chapter Twenty-Four

LOU HAD GROWN weary of playing the game of "catch me if you can" with the kidnappers. He was fed up with the way the whole operation was being run. It took close to six hours before they were back at the station house in Limerick from County Louth. When they stepped out of the vehicles, Lou pulled Duffy aside.

"Duffy, you're a friend, and I'm not challenging you, or trying to usurp you. Make no mistake, you're in charge. But we need a different approach. We're being out maneuvered left and right by three friggin' amateurs. We're getting good intel, but we're arriving too late to the party."

"Lou, I'm struggling with this, too."

"The problem is that we keep coming back to Limerick; we're too damn far from the front line."

"Lou, it's where our base is."

"No, it's where the *Irishman's* base is. His feet may be nailed to Limerick, but ours don't need to be. We've just wasted six friggin' hours!"

"It only took three hours to get back."

"Yeah, and we waited around in County Louth for three friggin' hours before we were picked up!"

"Look, I'm not happy about this either, but lower your voice a little."

Lou ran one hand through his hair and across the back of his neck in complete frustration. "I will, but I'm not putting up with this crap any longer. Fran-O is *not* a lead investigator. He's an old friggin' warhorse, biding his time, hoping something will break."

"I'm not disagreeing, but this is Ireland, Lou, not Canada. There are no SWAT teams traveling around in mobile units. We leave Limerick, and we lose our communication link."

"Then you stay here. Jake and I are the field investigators, anyway."

"And how do you propose we stay in touch?"

"Cell phones."

Duffy thought a minute before nodding his head. "Okay."

Just then, Fran-O walked over to them. "There's been another development, lads, you'd better gather 'round."

Lou's heart skipped a beat.

When everyone was assembled, Fran-O announced: "Word just came in from Castletown. They found the car that was hired out from McKiernan in a shopping mall parking lot. They think they might have a lead on the type of car they're in now. But this being the weekend and all, it might take a little time before we get any details."

Duffy spoke up. "We need a helluva lot more to go on than *that*! What else do they know?"

"There were some papers on the ground next to the car they abandoned; we're hoping it might lead to something. One more thing though, Lou, I have a note here that says those text messages you received were all sent from the cottage we raided today. But that's it; that's all for now, lads."

As the others dispersed, Duffy looked at Lou and motioned with his head to take a walk with him. When they were out of earshot, Duffy turned to him. "Your point is valid. We're hours away from where the kidnappers are by now. I'll let Fran-O know that I'm deploying the both of you into the field."

"I just need to let the tiger out, Duffy, I can't keep it inside any longer."

"I know. I'll have them assign one of their vehicles to you."

"No, just get me a lift over to the airport. I'll rent something nondescript."

"Okay, but Lou, I expect you to stay in touch with me. You're still *my* responsibility."

"I'm not going rogue, just going out on forward point."

Duffy understood Lou completely. The two of them had often gone out together on forward point during the Afghan war.

Lou walked over to where Jake was sitting. "Let's go."

"Where to?"

"We're moving out."

"Point?"

"Yeah."

"Any rules?"

"Winner take all."

"About time."

In less than half an hour, the two ex-JTF2 commandos were headed north toward Castletown. It wasn't long before Jake noticed Lou wasn't staying on the correct side of the road. "Ah, you know they drive on the opposite side over here, right?"

"I'm getting the hang of it."

"I hope so . . . I'm not up for missing tomorrow."

"Neither am I…I'm good."

IT WAS WELL after dark when Lou and Jake arrived at the station house in Castletown. Fran-O had called ahead to let the desk sergeant know two members of the kidnapping response team were enroute. When they walked into the building, the desk sergeant looked up.

"How can I help you?"

Lou flashed his badge. "We're here to talk with someone about the lead you have on the kidnapping case."

"Then you want Detective Costello, down the hall, second door on the right."

Lou stopped at the doorway of Costello's office. It was open. Without looking up from what he was doing, the man sitting at the desk said, "Come in and sit down. I've been expecting you."

As Lou and Jake entered his office, the detective stood up and put out his hand saying, "Name's Costello, I go by 'Dinny.'"

He was of average height, greying about the temples, broad chested, mid-forties, with a thick stock of strawberry blond hair. When he shook hands with Lou, both men took full measure of the other.

Costello motioned for them to sit down and began talking right away. "All right, I don't know what you two know, or don't know, so I'll start at the beginning. I've looked at a copy of the surveillance tapes from the plaza. We still have them if you want to go through them, yourselves."

Lou waved his hand, signaling for Dinny to continue.

"It appears that a little before one o'clock today, the exact time is on the tape if you need it, a woman followed an elderly lady to her car and knocked her over the head. The angle isn't great, but we can tell the old lady went down like a sack of potatoes. Her pocketbook must have been open when she got clobbered because the contents were scattered on the ground.

"Next, we can see a third woman get out of a vehicle, which was parked on the far side of the elderly woman's car. She appears to hurry around between the two vehicles and opens the rear door of her own vehicle. Next, we see two more females exit that car and enter the back seat of the elderly woman's car. One appears to be cuffed. Then, we can see the elderly woman being hauled up and thrown into the back seat of her own car. The one who struck the woman from behind, got into the front passenger side, the other got into the driver's seat, and off they went."

"Anything else?"

Costello inhaled loudly through his nose, then continued. "The car they left in the lot is the same car that an 'Ellen Marshall' hired from Sean McKiernan just a day ago. Before we picked up the items strewn around the crime scene, we took pictures of it all, if you want to see them, I have 'em. We've taken finger prints off the vehicle they were in, but nothing is back yet."

"We're most interested in knowing the make and model of the vehicle they're in now."

"Right. We were able to track that down using information strewn on the ground. They're in a maroon

Volkswagen Jetta. License tag is a Eurostyle plate, number TB12-W7SB. I've issued an ABP on it. I've also notified the police service in the north to hold the vehicle, should they attempt to cross the border. And I've just added an 'assault with a deadly weapon' and a second kidnapping charge to the warrant."

Now, this is exactly what I hoped we'd hear, Lou thought.

Costello continued. "I've provided the north with the name 'Ellen Marshall' along with a warning that they're armed and dangerous. I've also updated INTERPOL's database."

"Any idea where they're headed?"

"Not yet."

"How far could they have gone since they left the parking lot?"

"That all depends on where they *wanted* to go. We're only a few miles from the border, they *could* have crossed over and gone into Northern Ireland before we even arrived on the scene. Or they could have traveled as far south as Killarney by now. They could even be sitting right under our damn noses."

"Until now, they've tended to stay in remote locations," Lou said, "so I don't see them in a city."

"We're all on the lookout for them. I'll get word to you, if we learn anything further."

Lou reached his hand out as he stood. "Thanks, we'll take all the help you can send our way."

"I wish I could do more for you fellas, but if you follow the money trail, you'll find them."

"Dinny, you've been more help than you know."

"It's late. Do you have a place to stay tonight?"

"We heard O'Brien's Road House was decent."

"Nah, you don't wanna go there. O'Brien's kids are running the place now; it's not the same. Go to Daley's. It's just beyond and always had the better pub anyway."

When they got back in the car, Jake phoned Duffy to bring him up to speed.

"Jake! I'm glad you called. I was just about to call you two."

"What's up?"

"Are you and Lou together?"

"Yes."

"Put me on speaker."

"You're on speaker."

"They stopped at a petrol station on the outskirts of Dublin just after four-thirty today. Then, just before five, they made withdrawals from three different ATMs, each for the maximum amount, all on East Canal Street in Dublin."

"So, they went south. Why Dublin? Any thoughts?"

"None other than Dublin's a hub. From there, they can go anywhere. I'm thinking we may wanna freeze their credit and debit cards."

"No, don't do that," Lou nearly shouted. "We'll lose the limited eyes we have on them."

"Are you heading down to Dublin?"

"We are now. If they're in Dublin, that's where I wanna be. Keep monitoring those credit cards, Duffy, if we can figure out where the hell they're staying, we'll take them *tonight*."

"The merchant service providers are notifying us within minutes any time something hits their cards."

"Which cards are you tracking?"

"Every active card in the merchant services database with any of their names on it."

"Good. They've been on the run for a few days now.

Hopefully, they're getting tired. I still need to hear where the drop point will be. Do we have the ransom money ready?"

"We're good to go on that end."

"All right, we've gotta pay attention to the road," Jake said. "Lou and I are coming up on a few road signs that say 'Dublin' right now. He's driving on the wrong side of the friggin' road again."

"I'm paying attention," Lou called out.

"Be careful, you two. I'll call you as soon as I hear anything new."

AS LOU AND JAKE were driving south toward Dublin, Beatrice Hastings, was leaving Dublin, heading north again.

Chapter Twenty-Five

WHEN BEATRICE LEFT Castletown in the old lady's car, she knew she needed a better plan. The law of averages would work against her the longer they were on the run. There were two things they had needed: cash and a safe haven. Now that they had reached Dublin and taken cash from the ATMs, she headed out of the city in search of the second one.

Evelyn had gotten into the habit of reading road signs. When she noticed a sign that read: *'Leaving* Dublin,' she turned to Beatrice. "I thought we were going *to* Dublin?"

"We already did; you were dozing. Now we're going to the airport."

"Then, *why* did we go to Dublin?"

"We needed cash."

"We could have gotten cash at the airport."

"Evelyn, think about it; they'll be *looking* for us in Dublin now. We just bought ourselves some time."

Kate sat in the back seat, silently taking it all in. She wasn't giving up hope for another chance to escape.

BEATRICE HAD BECOME obsessed with her need to flee the Emerald Isle. She knew that as long as they remained in Ireland, the feeling that the walls were closing in on her would persist. She also knew that flying commercial would leave too big of an imprint, if flying commercial was even still possible now.

When they entered the Dublin airport just outside the city limits, Beatrice drove straight to the charter terminal area. As soon as she parked the car, she turned to Evelyn. "You're in charge, stay here. I'll be right back."

Entering the terminal, Beatrice was surprised at the number of charter flight counters she saw. Blue Pelican, a high-end operation, was the first to catch her attention. Four people sat behind the counter, all dressed in the same fashionable light blue uniform.

They're big enough to be paying attention to any police alerts, so, they're out, she thought.

At Icarus Air, two young attendants were sitting behind the booth wearing identical sweaters with the Icarus logo on it. *Why would anyone name an airline after someone who fell from the sky trying to reach the sun?* she wondered.

Directly across from Icarus Air was the Emerald Air booth. An older man sat there and was motioning her over. Beatrice's instincts kicked in; she walked over to Emerald Air. Forcing a smile, she greeted him.

"Hello, sir."

"Hello to you, ma'am. How can I help you today?"

Standing only a few feet from the man, Beatrice thought,

Should I take a chance on this old man? He might be too inquisitive. If he is, I'll just move on.

"Are you looking to book a flight?" he asked.

Beatrice snapped out of her trance and answered. "Yes, I'd like to book a charter to Guernsey."

"The Channel Islands, huh? Not a lot of tourists going there this time of year. I haven't been there, myself, but they say it's *very* picturesque. When would you like to travel?"

"Now, would be fine."

"You're in a hurry, then?"

"No. Well, yes, somewhat. We have a wedding to go to tomorrow."

"That explains it." The old man reached below the counter and took out a form. "All right, let's fill this out. How many in your party?"

Beatrice paused, then said, "Four, we're four women."

"Okay. Luggage? How many pieces?"

"Why is that important?"

The old man put his pencil down and looked up, staring her squarely in the eyes. "Ma'am, I need to be able to calculate how much *weight* will be on the plane, so we can distribute it all properly."

"Oh. All right, then, we each have one piece of luggage . . . carry-ons."

The old man took off his glasses, and looked at her again. "Four women, traveling to the Channel Islands, to a wedding, with only carry-on luggage?"

"Yes. We . . . we shipped everything over in advance."

"Ah, I see," he said more relaxed. He put his glasses back on. "More and more people are doing that. And why not? It's half the price of the baggage fees."

Now, Beatrice was beginning to fidget. "Sir, I'm pressed for time. Do you have a plane available?"

"We have plenty of planes," he said. "Let me punch in 'Channel Islands' and see if we've got any *pilots*."

"You don't have any *pilots*?"

"Oh, we have pilots," he said, "but they're all on call." Just then, his phone rang. "Actually, one of them is calling in now, excuse me."

Beatrice half-listened as she scanned the terminal for another charter company.

"Yes, that's correct." She overheard the man say. "Yes, the charter is to the Channel Island . . . Guernsey. Four passengers . . . as soon as possible. That will be fine. I'll let them know, thank you."

When the old man hung up the phone, he looked at Beatrice. "Well, you are certainly in luck, young lady. The pilot will be here, with his copilot, in about thirty-five minutes. Is that soon enough for you?"

Letting out a sigh of relief, Beatrice nodded. "Yes. That will be fine."

"Then let's fill out the paper work. Maintenance will pull the plane over to the gate area a little earlier, so you can board."

"How much is this going to cost?"

"Four passengers to the Channel Islands then deadheading back . . . a little under ten thousand Euros, I believe. I'll work up the exact figure shortly."

Beatrice had no idea what the flight would cost, but quickly replied, "That's about what I expected."

The man simply nodded, and continued with his paperwork. Once the flight plan was completed, the agent ran the form through a scanner. When his computer finished processing all of the information, a report was sent to his printer.

"Ha! Eight-thousand, five-hundred and seventy Euros, plus four percent tax. I wasn't that far off. May I have your credit card, ma'am?"

Beatrice pulled out a credit card which had belonged to her father, hoping the old man wouldn't look at the name on the card. But he did.

"So, is your name, '*Lord* Aaron Yardley,' ma'am?"

Thinking quickly Beatrice answered, "Of course, it isn't, that's my husband's name."

"Is he here?"

"No."

"I'll need to see his photo ID."

With only a few seconds to think, Beatrice quickly said, "Our husbands flew over a couple of days ago . . . to . . . to play golf. My husband gave me this specific card and said to use it when we flew over." Then, finally regaining her composure, she asked, "Is there a problem with his card?"

"We require a photo ID."

"That would be rather difficult, since I've just *told* you that he's gone on ahead. Wouldn't you agree?"

The old man stared at Beatrice for a moment before asking, "If I may be so bold madam, just *who* is 'Lord Aaron Yardley?'"

After emitting a very theatrical sigh intended to convey her extreme annoyance, she replied, "My *husband*, the Lord Aaron *Yardley*, is the *Earl* of Surrey, Second *Viscount* of Horsham, and the Baron of Basingstoke. And, I might add, a sitting member in The *House of Lords*." All of which was quite true, had she been referring to her father when he was alive.

The old man hesitated for only a second. "All right, then I'll need to see your passport."

The only passport Beatrice had was the one with the alias she was using. Beatrice was becoming more and more antsy about leaving a trail. In a bold move, she said, "Our passports are with our husbands; *they* take care of those things."

"Well, I must tell you, depending where you're going next, you're likely to encounter difficulties without a passport."

"Our husbands will be meeting us."

"Madam, do you have *any* form of identification you can present, a driver's license, perhaps?"

Sighing again, Beatrice said, "Let me see what I have." She made a show of looking through her purse. "I'm afraid all of those documents are with our husbands. They intended to arrange a trip to Provence after the wedding and said they needed all of those things *with* them."

The man just looked at Beatrice. She avoided his eyes and continued looking through her handbag. Finally, she pulled out a document. "Here, I have *this*."

The old man adjusted his glasses as he looked at the yellowed paper she handed to him. "This is a birth certificate," he said.

Using an icy, sarcastic tone, Beatrice replied, "I am quite *aware* of what it *is*. I should think it would be *enough*."

The old man cleared his throat. "Madam, I need to see an ID with a photo on it."

"Sir, you are positively insufferable! I have presented my certificate of *birth* to you, and here I stand, the very same person *before* you. What further proof do you possibly need to believe that I *exist*?"

"Your birth certificate states that your name is 'Yardley.'"

"Sir, I am fully aware of what my name is."

"So, you were born a Yardley, and you *married* a Yardley?"

Beatrice shook her head. *This sly old coot.* Then, as if to clear her thoughts, she agreed. "Yes. The house of Yardley tends to marry *within* the family. It is one of nobilities' rather awkward, yet enduring traits, wouldn't you agree? My husband is a fourth cousin to my father. Of course, he's quite a bit *younger* than my father. Now, can we *please* move on with this?"

The man behind the counter hesitated.

Beatrice decided to call his bluff, "*Sir*, tell me, do I need to interrupt the Earl and take him away from whatever important business he is engaged in at this very moment, to settle this trivial matter?"

The man handed the birth certificate back to Beatrice. "No, I'll waive the requirement." But he muttered under his breath, "It's little wonder her husband went on ahead."

"Thank you."

Beatrice fidgeted as she waited for the credit card to process. When the light on the machine changed from a blinking red to a solid green, she relaxed.

"It looks like they took the charge ma'am, or should I address you as *Countess*?"

"It's not required. This isn't a formal setting, but thank you for asking."

"It'll be a little while yet, before the pilots arrive, ma'am. You can wait in here, if you'd like, or in your vehicle. Makes no difference to me. But, when you see a plane with the Emerald Air emblem on the tail arrive at the gate, come back in, so we can get you on board."

When Beatrice returned to the car, Evelyn said, "What took you so long?"

"Nothing. I just had to straighten a few things out. Hand me that bottle of water you're drinking." Beatrice put the bottle on the dash, opened her handbag and took out a vial full of liquid. Pouring half the contents into the water bottle, she gave it a couple of shakes before returning the vial to her purse.

"Here, Evelyn, give half of this to the bitch, and the other half to the old lady."

"Is this what I gave the bitch before?"

"It's diluted, so it will only make her groggy."

"But why to the old lady?"

Beatrice, inhaled deeply, then looked at her. "Don't be difficult, Evelyn, it's been a long day. Just do as I ask."

Evelyn got out of the car and walked around to the side where the old woman was slumped over. She opened the door and shook the woman's shoulder.

"Open up, sweetie, I have a drink for you." The woman obliged by opening her mouth and Evelyn slowly poured half the liquid in the bottle into the woman's mouth. Then she walked around to the opposite side of the car, opened the door, and spoke to Kate. "Tilt your head back, bitch, we don't want you dehydrated."

Having overheard the whispered conversation between Evelyn and Beatrice. She tried to resist, but Evelyn grabbed hold of Kate's hair, pulled her head back and forced the bottle between her lips. Kate tried keeping her teeth clenched and shook her head back and forth. The resistance worked to an extent, as a great deal of the liquid Evelyn tried to force into Kate's mouth ran down the sides of her cheeks, soaking her blouse.

When Evelyn returned to the front seat, Beatrice said,

"We're on a flight to the Channel Islands. The old woman stays here."

"When do we leave?"

"Soon. I see the plane being towed over now."

"Where?"

Pointing to the right she said, "*That* one."

"That's a bloody *prop*," Evelyn protested. "Why didn't you book a jet?"

"Evelyn, connect the dots. We need to be discreet. It's a dinky little company; they only fly dinky turboprops. If you think you can do better, sweetheart, then be my guest."

When Evelyn didn't respond, Beatrice looked at her. "Well? Do you think you could have done better?"

Not wishing to cross an imaginary line with Beatrice, Evelyn replied, "No. You did fine."

Then Beatrice turned around and reached over the seat to grab hold of her sister's knee. "Anne . . . Anne, dear, wake up. It's time to go. Our plane is here."

"I'm awake, but I'm not going. I'm tired of this, and I'm tired of *you*!"

Using a calm voice, Beatrice said, "Now, Anne, dear, don't do this. Be a big girl, and do as I ask. This will all be over soon, you'll see."

Anne sat up. "When? When is this disgusting nightmare going to end? I *hate* you, Beatrice! And I hate the way you're treating *me*. I've *always* hated the way you've treated me."

"Anne!" Beatrice commanded. "Get a hold of yourself! You're upset, I can see that. If you don't want to continue doing this, you can leave, just not *now*, not *here*. This isn't a safe place for you to leave."

"Why? Why can't I leave? Why are you treating me like

I'm a prisoner? I am *not* a prisoner. Do you hear me, Beatrice, *I am not a prisoner!*"

"Anne, please . . . you're working yourself up unnecessarily. Everything will work out, trust me. Just give it a little more time."

"No, I'm done! I'm staying here, and I'm not getting on that plane."

"Anne, I'll make a deal with you. If you come with me, this one last time, I *promise* you can stay where we're going to next. I promise, okay? Are we fine with that?"

Anne folded her arms in front of herself and looked out the car window.

Beatrice, shifted to a softer, soothing voice, "Anne, I *need* you to answer me. Are you fine with that?"

Anne hesitated, then realizing she couldn't win a fight with her sister, gave an answer. "Yes, but then I want *out*."

Beatrice looked over at Evelyn who appeared ready to say something. But Beatrice held up her hand and simply mouthed the word: *Later*.

Knowing she had her sister under control, Beatrice sat back and positioned the rearview mirror to see if the fast-acting drug had taken effect on Kate.

When Evelyn had tried forcing the water down Kate's throat, her clenched teeth had prevented much liquid from even entering her mouth. Then, when Evelyn had taken the bottle away from Kate's lips and let go of her hair, Kate had lowered her head and much of the liquid that had entered her mouth drained out. The small amount she did ingest was not enough to knock her out. Kate sensed a slight fog developing in her head and some tingling in her extremities, but for the most part, what she did next was purely an act. She slumped over, and let her head roll forward and to the side.

"Evelyn, I think the drug has kicked in. I'd like you to escort Anne over to the plane, I'll take the bitch. We'll have to go through the terminal. I'm sure we'll attract some attention. If anyone says anything, our story is that she did a little too much celebrating earlier."

"Got it."

"We'll leave the old woman in her car."

"Isn't she a loose end?"

"Well, she'll never be able to recognize us. Besides, from the looks of her, she may never be able to recognize anyone ever again. Let's go."

Chapter Twenty-Six

ONCE ALL FOUR women were sitting at the gate, Evelyn stood up. "I need something to read and something to munch on. Beatrice, would you like me to get you anything?"

"No, I'm fine."

"Anne, what about you . . . can I get you something?"

Anne just shook her head.

When Evelyn approached the cashier at the kiosk, she again realized she had no cash with her. Beatrice had insisted on holding all the cash they had withdrawn from the ATMs. So, rather than walk back and ask for some money, Evelyn simply gave the cashier her credit card.

WITHIN TWENTY MINUTES, Duffy was on the phone to Lou. "We just got a message that one of their credit cards was used inside the charter flight terminal at Dublin Airport."

"We're on it, Duffy, thanks."

Jake was riding shotgun and reading the highway signs. "Lou, take this next exit, we need to double back; we just passed the turn off for the airport."

The access road to the airport was a long causeway stretching across open water, but the airport could be seen off in the distance.

"Lou, something's going on over there."

"Yeah, I see the flashing lights. An ambulance just passed us, going the other way."

Jake sent a text to Duffy: *Anything new?* Before he received an answer, they tuned onto the airport property and were approaching a fork in the road. Lou read the sign. "Main Terminal, left; Charter Terminal, right."

"Left or right, Jake?"

"Go right . . . Charter Terminal."

As they approached the low, two-story terminal building, it was obvious something was going on. The number of flashing red and blue strobe lights bouncing off the building created a macabre, chaotic scene.

"Jake, we're not gonna get very close to the terminal."

"Get as close as you can."

Lou slid into a parking spot a distance away and the two men jogged toward the building. The police had cordoned off the front of the terminal. When Lou and Jake ducked under the yellow tape barrier, two uniformed officers approached them. Before being challenged, Lou and Jake held up their badges.

"Okay, fellas, come on in."

Lou walked up to the abandoned Volkswagen Jetta and looked around. "Who's in charge here?"

A man in plain clothes about Lou's height turned around and looked at him. "Who's asking?"

Lou flashed his badge. "Lou Gault. We're working a kidnapping case and this vehicle is involved."

"Then, come on over; we'll fill you in."

"Thanks."

"We received a call from the station house in Limerick to stop and detain this vehicle. Airport security had knowledge of the APB and reported they had located it in this parking lot. When we arrived, there was a woman inside, the EMTs just transported her to the main hospital ER."

Lou held his breath. "Can you describe her?"

"Older woman, late seventies, early eighties, had an ugly wound on the back of her head."

"Was anyone else in the car?"

"No, only this one woman."

Lou turned to Jake. "Let's go. They're inside the terminal."

With Glocks in hand, they raced up a short flight of stairs and entered the terminal's main floor. Passing through double doors, Lou went left and Jake went right. Both men scanned the benches and ticket counters. With the exception of a few agents behind the ticket counters, the terminal was empty.

Lou put his Glock away, walked over to the nearest ticket counter and flashed his badge. "Have any of you seen four women in here recently?"

The oldest among the young women behind the counter, spoke up. "I believe three or four women walked through here just a short while ago." Pointing left, she continued, "They went down the hallway to the gate area."

Jake was already moving before Lou said, "Thanks."

When they arrived at the end of the hallway, Lou motioned he'd go right and signaled Jake to go left. On the count of three, both men burst into the gate area, Glocks at the ready. An elderly man stood at a podium where he was shuffling papers; Lou looked around, there was no one else in the gate area.

"Did four women just pass through here?"

"Yes, they did," he said.

"Where are they?"

"On the plane."

"Which plane?"

"The plane that just lifted off the runway," he said. Then, looking up and seeing Lou's pistol, he quickly stepped back and raised both hands.

Lou took a deep breath, then let it out slowly. "Where's that plane headed?"

The old man hesitated, not quite sure what was happening. He hadn't seen any badges, only pistols. When he didn't respond, Lou squared off in front of him.

"I asked you a *friggin'* question. . . where the *hell* is that plane headed?"

Jake took his badge out. "We're officers of the law. We believe three of the women on that plane are kidnappers."

Seeing the badge, the old man relaxed slightly. "That plane is headed to the Channel Islands. But I don't think they're the ones you're looking for, fellas. They're going to a wedding. One of them is the wife of some Lord."

"Where's the paper work for that flight?"

"At the counter."

"Let's go!"

ANNE HAD RESISTED going to the terminal with Evelyn until Beatrice had confronted her. In a menacing tone, looking straight into her sister's eyes, Beatrice had whispered, "If you don't cooperate right *now*, I will beat the ever-loving *crap* out of you, do you understand? Do you want that? Is that what you *want*?"

When Anne hadn't responded, Beatrice dug her fingers into her sister's upper arms. "Look at me. Do you *understand* what I'm saying to you?"

Anne winced and tried pulling away. "I *hate* you," she whispered.

Kate offered no active resistance when Beatrice removed the cuff from Kate's left wrist and attached it to her right wrist. Kate was dead weight and Beatrice struggled to support her as they walked through the terminal, past the gate, across the tarmac and up the steps into the aircraft.

Once Kate was seated in the plane, Beatrice removed the one cuff she had attached to her own wrist and secured Kate to her seat with it.

The planes that Emerald Air used were standard *Piaggio* P180 turboprops. The seat configuration was 1 + 1 with an aisle in between. All seats faced the same direction, which was forward. The seats were quite comfortable, however, in order to accommodate the premium seats, the aisle was quite narrow.

Anne had boarded first, and taken a seat in the first row, with the hope of being as far away from her domineering sister as possible. Beatrice took a seat directly behind Kate and opposite Evelyn.

"Anne is not handling this very well, Beatrice."

"Evelyn, it will pass."

"This is so unlike her."

"No, it's not, actually. She's always had her little tantrums. She takes after her mother."

"I always liked your mother."

"She could drive my father up a wall."

"Anne could?"

"No, my mother."

"Well, I don't believe Anne really hates you."

"Who knows."

"Will she snap out of it?"

"She's unpredictable when she's in this state."

"Are you going to allow her to leave?"

"Hell, *no*. We can't risk a loose end like that."

"What if she doesn't come around?"

"Then . . . I'll take care of it."

A plume of white smoke billowed out from the rear of the propeller on the right side of the plane; immediately following, the engine on the left kicked in.

Kate was giving the illusion of being drugged, but she was fully cognizant of everything going on around her, including the entire conversation between Beatrice and Evelyn.

As the co-captain walked past, Evelyn tapped him on the arm. "Excuse me, Captain." The young man turned around and smiled down at her.

"I'm only the *co*-captain, but how can I help you?"

"How long will this flight take?"

"Once we're airborne, we should make Guernsey in a little over ninety minutes."

"Is there any food onboard?"

"No, ma'am, I'm sorry, there isn't. But we do have bottled water under the seat in the last row. Please, help yourself."

"Does the airport have a restaurant where we'll be landing?"

"Yes, ma'am," he said, looking at his watch, "and it should be open by the time we land."

"Thank you."

Once the co-pilot went forward, Evelyn asked Beatrice, "How long before the drug wears off this one?" She nodded toward Kate.

"She'll be out for at least another three hours."

Kate kept her eyes closed, but her mind was thinking. She still hadn't developed a plan of escape, but at least now she knew where they were heading, when they would land, and the fact that they expected her to be knocked out for another three hours. In any event, since her hands were no longer cuffed behind her back, the muscles in her shoulders, arms and upper back were finally beginning to relax.

BACK AT THE charter flight terminal, Lou was studying the form the agent had filled out prior to issuing the tickets to one "Beatrice Yardley." She had only provided surnames for the others, none of which matched the three kidnappers. Absent from the list was Kate's name. Finally, Lou looked up. "How'd she pay for the tickets?"

"Credit card."

"Did the name on the card match her photo ID?"

"She didn't have a photo ID. It was her husband's card."

"Did you check *his* ID?"

"He wasn't here."

"He wasn't *here*?" Lou couldn't believe the ineptitude.

"No, she said he'd flown on ahead."

"Let me get this straight: You took a credit card from

someone you didn't know, for roughly eight *thousand* pounds, with someone else's name on it, and you *didn't* insist upon a photo ID?"

The old man's hands began to shake as he responded. "I tried, but she said her husband had all their passports and every other piece of identification with him. But she *did* show me her birth certificate."

"Her birth certificate." Lou was taking it all in. "What was the name on it?"

"*Her* name . . . 'Beatrice Yardley,.'" The old man simply didn't elaborate about the father/husband/same name situation.

"The woman failed to produce any form of a photo ID, and yet you weren't the least bit suspicious?"

"I ran the card; it processed, so I waived the photo ID requirement."

"What type of card was it?"

"VISA."

"Show me the name that was on that card."

"It wasn't her name. The name on the card was 'Lord Aaron Yardley.' She said it was her husband."

"Don't go anywhere." Lou looked at Jake. Jake was googling the name: Lord Aaron Yardley.

"He's the Earl of Surrey, Lou, a sitting member of the House of Lords."

Lou quickly called Duffy. "Listen, Duffy, I need you to call the House of Lords; find out if the Earl of Surrey, Aaron Yardley, is on the Island of Guernsey attending a wedding."

"How is this connected to anything?"

"I'm playing a hunch. Someone just used the Earl's credit card and said he's on the Island of Guernsey. I need you to verify if that's true."

"And you think someone at the House of Lords would know that?"

"Yeah, my guess is that it's no different than in Canada. If you're a member of Parliament, and Parliament is in session, you're required to let the Chamber know where you are at all times."

"I'll get on it. Are you having any success?"

"If you consider success that we're missing these friggin' kidnappers by less and less time, then, yeah, we're having *phenomenal* success."

"Where are you now?"

"Dublin Airport, trying to determine if they're still here."

"Say more?"

"The car they stole in Castletown is sitting outside, so they were here at some point. They left the old lady who owned the car inside. She's been taken to the hospital."

"Is she alive?"

"She was when they took her to the hospital. That was before we arrived."

"Where's Jake?"

"Right now, he's trying to find out if any of the local taxi services picked up four women at the airport and took them anywhere in the past hour."

"What's your next step?"

"I'm not sure. I'm talking to a small charter flight company, trying to find out who the four women are who just left on a plane to Guernsey. Does that sound like a coincidence, or what? Maybe it will be a success.

"You're closer to the front line."

"Yeah, but I need to get *out in front* of the front line."

"You know there's a good chance they're still where you are. No further activity has been reported by the credit card companies, so that means maybe they're not using their cards to go anywhere."

"Maybe. But, there's one thing for sure: this chase is really getting old."

"All right, let me go run down this House of Lords thing; I'll get back to you."

Chapter Twenty-Seven

THE FLIGHT FROM Dublin to the island of Guernsey was uneventful. The noise and vibration from the twin turboprops lulled Kate to sleep, giving her body and her mind a brief respite.

As the plane began to descend, the sudden change in cabin pressure awoke her. Turning her head slightly toward the window, she noticed a faint glimmer of dawn on the horizon. Shortly after that, her attention was drawn to the conversation behind her.

"Evelyn, when we deplane, stay close to Anne; I'll take the bitch."

As the plane banked hard right on its approach to the runway, Kate could just make out the silhouette of the island, contrasting against the lighter ocean water.

She felt the plane descending, then the slight bump when the wheels grabbed the ground. Once the plane taxied up to the gate and came to a full stop, Beatrice walked up the aisle to the front of the cabin and sat on the arm of the chair across the aisle from Anne.

"I'm really sorry, if I've upset you, Anne. I didn't mean to. Please, let's not be this way, okay?"

Anne breathed in heavily, still looking upset, and paused before saying, "Beatrice, you always do this to me; I've had enough of it."

"Anne, dear, that is totally *not* true. Haven't I *always* put your needs first?"

"No, you *never* have. It's always about *you.*"

"Anne, that's not true, you know that's not true, why do you say that?"

"Because it's the truth."

"Give me another chance, Anne, darling. Please, you know how much I love you. Once this is all over, things will be different. I promise."

"You always say that Beatrice, but it never is."

"Now you know *that's* not true Anne. Things always turn out for the better. I'll buy you those special sweets you like."

But Anne was really fed up this time, especially with Beatrice constantly invalidating her.

"Anne, please, I *mean* it this time. Evelyn and I really need you, sweetheart. Come on, get up now, and join us. Don't do this to us, please. Put on your big girl panties and help us." But Anne simply continued staring ahead.

Beatrice continued 'gaslighting' her sister until the door to the cockpit opened, and the co-pilot emerged.

"Excuse me, please; I need to pass through. I'll have the rear hatch open and stairs in place momentarily, then you can deplane."

Beatrice put her hand on Anne's shoulder. "Anne, we need to go now."

Without saying a word, Anne rose from her seat, turned, and walked down the narrow aisle toward the rear of the plane. Once again, Beatrice, had selfishly manipulated her sister. Anne hesitated for a brief moment as she approached Kate, cuffed to the seat, a sweater draped over her arm to hide the metal, then she continued on. Beatrice motioned for Evelyn to follow Anne.

THE STRAIN OF constantly being on the run and shouldering the lion's share of the load, was taking its toll on Beatrice. Anne's behavior was beginning to affect her negatively as well. What had started out as her idea of a profitable game of cat and mouse, with her playing the role of the cat, now felt more like a game of fox and hounds. Lately she became more conscious of the game. She began to wonder if the tables had turned and she had become the hunted fox desperately trying to stay ahead of the hounds.

Beatrice felt tired. She hadn't had a restful night's sleep since Evelyn had left for Halifax and it was beginning to show. She had closed her eyes during the short flight, hoping to get a little rest, but her psyche wasn't at rest. Throughout the flight, her mind kept racing through a number of possible next move scenarios.

When she returned to her seat, directly behind Kate, she grabbed her handbag, rested it on the arm of the chair and reached into it as she searched for the key to the handcuffs. From the corner of her eye, she noticed Evelyn about to exit the plane. She quickly turned her body and waved her arm to attract Evelyn's attention.

"Evelyn, tell them I need a wheelchair." As she said it, her purse fell over, spilling the entire contents onto the seat and floor.

Damn it! I don't need this crap right now. She bent down, picked up the key to the handcuffs, placed it in her jacket pocket and threw everything else back into her bag helter-skelter.

Kate was fully awake but her eyes appeared closed. When she felt a tug on the wrist that was handcuffed, she shifted her head ever so slightly, and through the slits in her eyes, saw Beatrice undoing the cuff attached to the seat. Then she noticed Beatrice place the key in her left jacket pocket before snapping the cuff around her own right wrist.

Attempting to lift Kate out of the seat and into the cramped aisle proved difficult for Beatrice. Although Kate offered no physical resistance, she was dead weight. The two women were close in height and build, however, unlike Kate, Beatrice hadn't been working out, and had no knowledge of proper lifting techniques. After a few failed attempts, Kate allowed herself to be lifted out of the seat. But Beatrice wasn't prepared for the sudden shift in momentum and they both tumbled backward into the opposite seat. While Beatrice struggled to push Kate off her, Kate snagged the key from Beatrice's jacket. At that point, the young co-pilot came back into the cabin.

"Whoa, whoa, let me help you," he said, rushing forward to assist.

UNLIKE SHANNON AIRPORT, Guernsey had no wheelchair attendants, nor were there any restrictions pertaining to the use of a chair. With the help of the co-pilot, Kate was placed in the wheelchair and Beatrice wheeled her into the terminal building.

"Evelyn, where's Anne?"

"She said she had to use the toilet."

"Evelyn, are you a *complete* fool?"

"What?"

"Follow her and stay with her! She's a potential flight risk. Don't make me have to tell you that again."

Evelyn cringed from the stinging reprimand and headed off to the ladies room in search of Anne.

As Beatrice scanned the inside of the terminal, she noticed a light over the Avis booth suddenly illuminate. It had been awkward pushing the wheelchair across the tarmac with one hand cuffed to Kate, so now she reached into her pocket for the key, intending to transfer the cuff from her wrist to the chair. But she couldn't find it. Checking her opposite coat pocket, she still found nothing.

No matter, she thought, *I have a second key in my purse.* However, a quick search with her left hand yielded nothing. At that point, she decided to just deal with the annoyance.

Upon arriving at the Avis counter, Beatrice cleared her throat to get the attention of the agent behind the counter.

"May I help you, ma'am."

"Yes, I'd like to hire a car."

"Do you have a reservation?"

"No, I don't."

"All right, give me a moment. I'm just opening up; I'll be able to tell you what I have available shortly. The young man's fingers danced across the keyboard. "What size vehicle are you looking for?"

"We are four adults."

"Then you'll want a standard size at least."

As the young man scrolled through his inventory, Beatrice lifted her left hand and waved to Evelyn, so she would see where she had gone off to.

"Ma'am, in that size, the only cars I have available are a premium at forty-five pounds a day, or a luxury at forty-nine a day."

"Which is larger?"

"That would be the premium, ma'am."

"I'll take that."

"Do you want insurance?"

"No."

"And how long will you require the car?"

"Two weeks."

"Right. May I see a driver's license and a credit card."

"I prefer to use cash."

"That's fine, but I'll still need to see your license and a credit card."

She realized she had no choice but to comply. "Give me a moment." Turning her back to the attendant, she placed her handbag on Kate's lap and used her left hand to fish out the license and her father's credit card.

Within minutes, the machine printed out the rental agreement. The agent began marking the form with little x's. "I'll need your signature here, and your initials here, here, and . . . here."

Restricted to using just her left hand, Beatrice awkwardly signed her name and initials. Then the attendant compared her signature to the one on the credit card.

"It's my husband's card," she explained. "He's gone on ahead and left me his card to use."

"Very well, but your signature doesn't match the signature on your license."

"My arthritis is really bad today, and I can only use my left hand. Really, that's the best I can do."

The attendant then looked at the picture on the license and saw that it matched her face. "No problem, ma'am. The keys are in the car; space thirty-six. Bring the vehicle back with a full tank of petrol and you'll avoid any additional charges. Oh, and leave the yellow copy of the rental agreement in the glove box."

Beatrice nodded and took the papers, then awkwardly wheeled the chair over to where Evelyn and Anne were sitting. As soon as she reached them, Evelyn stood up. "Let's get something to eat. I'm famished."

"We're not going anywhere, until I find the damn key to these cuffs," Beatrice growled. Again, she checked both pockets in her jacket. "Damn it! I just had it in the plane, I must have dropped it when I was struggling with this one." Beatrice took in a deep breath and let out a long, exasperated sigh.

"Evelyn, be a dear, and run back to the plane. See if I dropped it in the aisle, will you?"

As soon as Evelyn left, Beatrice reached over to her sister and began rubbing Anne's back with her left hand. Her voice was soothing, yet insincere. "Anne, are we feeling better now?"

Anne, didn't respond; she only stared into space. Like so many times in the past, Anne had retreated into her private imaginary world, one where Beatrice wasn't allowed to enter at any cost. It was a fantasy world she had created as a young child, a world where Beatrice couldn't touch her, and certainly couldn't hurt her. It was a place where she was in charge, her safe place, her mental sanctuary.

Fifteen minutes later, Evelyn returned. "Nothing, nada. It wasn't on the plane."

"Did you ask the pilot? Maybe one of them found it."

"Of course, I asked. I'm not *stupid*!"

The exasperation on Beatrice's face was clearly visible. "*Now* what am I going to do?"

"You have a second key. When we're in the restaurant, I'll help you look through your purse."

Upon hearing the word "restaurant," Kate realized how hungry she was, not having eaten since Anne had brought dinner up to the attic. It seemed so long ago. Knowing that she would blow her cover if it appeared the effects of the drug had finally worn off, she reached deep inside herself for inner strength and continued the ruse.

WITH THE EXCEPTION of a few mechanics in coveralls, fresh off the night shift, the restaurant was empty. Evelyn looked around. "Looks like it's cafeteria style, girls."

"Brilliant. And how am I going to carry a tray while pushing the chair with this one attached to my wrist?"

"Anne and I will get you something, Beatrice," Evelyn said. When they reached the table, Beatrice dumped the entire contents of her handbag out on the table. Evelyn began spreading the contents out and soon held something up.

"Is this it?"

"YES! Thank you! I *knew* there was another key in there. Without missing a beat, Beatrice removed the cuff from her wrist, secured it to the wheelchair, and then rubbed her wrist. "Let's get something to eat. I'm buying."

They all walked away, leaving Kate alone at the table, slouched over in the chair, her eyes apparently closed.

Anne debated whether she should get anything for their captive. To avoid incurring any more of Beatrice's wrath, she ended up only putting an extra muffin and two Slim Jims in her pocket, hoping at some point, she might be able to smuggle them to Kate.

Beatrice was the last one to return to the table and sat down. "Eat up, ladies, we need to move on."

At that point, Anne hesitated. "I haven't actually decided if I'm going to continue along with you."

Beatrice looked at her sister and cleared her throat. "Anne, look at me. This isn't only about *you.* We're all in this *together*; we need to *stay* together and see this thing through together, as a *team.* You want to be part of the team, don't you? Remember how everyone always referred to us as the triplets? I hope you aren't going to spoil that for us, Anne. Are you?"

Evelyn reached over and placed her hand on Anne's forearm to try some charm. "Anne, please. Everything will work out, you'll see. There's a reason they called us 'the triplets,' remember? It's the three of us, together again, just like it's always been. Please say that you're with us."

Anne closed her eyes and took a deep breath. Then, very slowly, she nodded.

"Wonderful," Evelyn said, then turned to Beatrice. "How far is it to where we're staying?"

"Does it matter?"

Again, the comment and tone of Beatrice's voice made Evelyn feel totally invalidated. She looked down at her plate. "I was only trying to make conversation."

For the first time, Beatrice realized that, perhaps, she needed to use a softer approach. "We're not staying on Guernsey," she said.

In unison, both Evelyn and Anne looked up and waited for Beatrice to say something more. But she didn't. Finally, Evelyn had the courage to ask: "Then *why* did we fly to Guernsey?"

Ignoring the question, Beatrice said, "We're taking the ferry over to Jersey."

"But why?"

"I've decided to use the house in Guernsey as the drop point. It's remote, and we'll be able to tell if anyone is watching the house."

Evelyn smiled. "So, we're going to play the end card. Good, I'm getting tired of being on the run. How long will we stay in Jersey?"

"That depends on how long it takes for them to make the drop."

"How long did you rent the place for?"

"I rented both houses for two weeks."

Evelyn tilted her head to the side. "You already *have* a place in Jersey?"

"Yes."

"Does it have indoor plumbing?"

Beatrice ignored the question and continued eating. After a pause, Evelyn asked, "If we're in Jersey, how are we going to know if they've dropped off the ransom money?"

"Because, Evelyn, *you* will be going back and forth to check." She held up the Avis car keys. "That's why I rented a car for two weeks."

"So, how do I drive a car back here if we're staying in Jersey?"

"The same way we're going *over* to Jersey, on the ferry."

Not moving a face muscle, Kate smiled to herself. She knew that soon, the number of people watching her every move would become fewer. The fact that Evelyn would be traveling back and forth would only improve her chances of overcoming her captors and escaping. Her biggest challenge now, was staying hydrated and nourished.

"Come on, ladies," Beatrice said. "Let's go drive by the drop location and see what it looks like. Then we'll head over to Jersey."

WHEN THEY REACHED the car, the handcuff attached to the wheelchair was removed, and Kate's hands were once again secured behind her back. Unlike the wheelchair they had stolen from Shannon Airport, there wasn't a tall rod attached to it, it collapsed, and it fit easily into the trunk.

The Guernsey residence was an old farm house. It was located off by itself in the middle of acres upon acres of old pasture land. As they pulled into the driveway, Evelyn rolled down the window and took in a deep breath of air. "Ahh, not a whiff of peat!"

"We're close to the ocean," Beatrice said. "You should be able to smell the salt air from here."

"I can."

The long driveway was covered with crushed clam shells, which the sun had bleached to a bright white. As soon as Beatrice had parked the car, she turned and faced the back seat. "Anne, dear, would you like to come inside, just to see the house?"

"No."

Choosing not to make an issue, Beatrice and Evelyn got out of the car. Anne looked over at Kate, wondering if she was awake and might eat the extra muffin and beef jerky. But Kate still appeared to be out of it.

"Don't you just love the look of the silvery grey weathered shingles?" Evelyn said as soon as she exited the car. "I think it's a perfect cottage."

"Evelyn, we're *renting* it, not *buying* it." Beatrice had never been sentimental about anything. "They said the key was behind an oval plaque under the light fixture by the door."

"Here?" Evelyn pointed to a light on the wall.

"I imagine; lift it up."

"I see it," she said, almost triumphantly.

"Well, *take* it, and open the door."

Inside, the house was clean, albeit sparsely furnished. A large farm kitchen took up most of the first floor, but a sitting room and full bath was just off the kitchen area. Upstairs were three bedrooms and a half bath.

While Evelyn toured the house, Beatrice sat at the kitchen table creating a text message on her phone. When Evelyn returned to the kitchen, Beatrice looked up and saw her walking toward a very ornate wooden chair set against the outer kitchen wall. "Don't sit there."

"Why not?"

"It's bad luck."

"How?"

"That's the witch's chair."

"The *what*?"

"The witch's chair," she repeated. "Back in the day, everyone on this stinking little island believed in witches."

"Surely, you jest."

"No. That's the big thing about this island. The locals once believed the island was home to fairies and that witches gathered here at certain times of the year. Every house had to have a special witch's chair."

"Why?"

"Because if a witch came and knocked on your door looking to rest, and you didn't have a place for them to sit, the witch would cast a spell on your animals and your crops."

"That's *utterly* absurd."

Smiling at the intended pun, Beatrice replied, "Perhaps."

"Beatrice, you don't actually *believe* in that nonsense . . . *do* you?"

"It was just something I read about this island on the Internet, that's all."

"Well, I don't believe any of it." With that, Evelyn sat down in the witch's chair. "It isn't all that comfortable."

"I wouldn't think it would be. I doubt anyone would want a witch to get *too* comfortable," Beatrice said.

Evelyn stood up and stretched, then looked back at the witch's chair. "Ignorant peasants."

"Okay, I've just sent a text off to the bitch's husband."

"What did you text?"

"I texted him that I'll send the address for the drop point shortly. I told him I want the money within the week if he wants to see his little wife alive, again."

"Do you think he'll do it?"

"He will . . . if he wants his wife back."

Evelyn stretched a second time. "I'm getting stiff from all this sitting and now my back hurts from this demon chair."

"All right, we've seen enough here; let's go. Remember to put the key back each time you come here, otherwise, they won't be able to get in to put the money on the kitchen table."

As they returned to the car, Evelyn made a comment. "I like the location; it is remote. I wouldn't even have minded staying here."

Suddenly, Anne spoke up. "*I* can stay here! I won't even mind if I'm alone. I'd *like* to stay here."

"No, Anne. We're all going over to the island of Jersey together."

"Beatrice, I said I would *like* to stay here. I could stay here and wait for the money. I could answer any questions they had."

It was then, Beatrice realized her sister was no longer thinking with a rational mind. "No, Anne. We're all staying together; you'll like this next place, it's much nicer."

"Well, I think *this* is a nice place, and I'd like to stay here and play. I'm going to ask father if I can stay here when we get home."

Beatrice looked at her sister in the rearview mirror. "Anne, none of us are staying here. You'd be all alone and trust me, you wouldn't care for that."

"Yes, I would," Ann said in almost a sing-song, little girl's voice.

"Anne, remember how Father would tell you to put on your big girl pants and play nicely? Don't you want to make Father happy?" She was well-aware of what was happening to her sister. But Anne ignored Beatrice's comment and continued staring at the house.

I wonder how I can return here on my own. Somehow, Anne thought, *I'll find a way,*

Chapter Twenty-Eight

BACK IN LIMERICK, Duffy received a call from an unknown caller. "Hello?"

"Yes, am I speaking with William McDuffie-Ferguson?"

"You are."

"This is Archibald Grey, second administer to the Sergeant of Arms for the House of Lords. I'm returning your call, sir."

"Ah, yes, thanks for returning my call." Duffy said. "We're working on a kidnapping case and I need some information regarding a member of your House of Lords."

"I see; go on."

"Do you have any way of finding out whether the Earl of Surrey is presently attending a wedding on the Channel Islands?"

"Sir, I can assure you with the *utmost* confidence that the Earl of Surrey is *not* attending a wedding on the Channel Islands."

"You are certain of that?"

"Quite so."

"And why is that?"

"The Earl of Surrey has taken up residence in the Royal Burial Ground, sir."

"He's *dead*?"

"Very much so, I'm afraid."

"How long ago?

"It's been at least a fortnight now."

"Interesting."

After a slight pause, the "second administrator" asked, "Will that be all, sir?"

"Yes, thank you." As soon as Duffy hung up, he clicked on his phone's contacts and scrolled down; when he reached a certain listing, he pressed the call button.

"Allied Merchant Services. How may I direct your call?"

"Fraud detection, please."

"Will you hold?"

Duffy never understood why people asked him if he would hold, it was never really a question. He was somewhat surprised when, after only a few seconds, his line was answered.

"Fraud detection, Charles Winston speaking."

"Yes, hello. This is William McDuffie-Ferguson, Royal Canadian Mounted Police. We're speaking on a recorded line; I have a question."

"Go ahead, governor."

"How soon after a person dies is their credit card closed to further transactions?"

"That would depend upon when we are notified, now wouldn't it? Some people continue to use the card, others don't."

"Is that legal?"

"Is what legal?"

"Continuing to use a card after the card holder has died."

"It's not that *unusual*. Often a widow, or widower, will continue to use a card with the deceased spouse's name on it. As long as someone pays the monthly minimum amount due, no one seems to care."

"I see. Well, we're working a kidnapping case. I need to know if there's been any recent activity on a card issued to an 'Aaron Yardley,' Earl of Surrey?"

"What's the card number?"

"I don't have it."

"What brand of card?"

"Not sure, could be a VISA."

"Give me a moment and I'll search the file by last name. You said 'Aaron Yardley,' right?"

"Correct."

Duffy noticed a text had just come in, but ignored it. When the man came back online, he said. "I'm showing two recent charges."

"Can you give me details on those charges?"

"We're not authorized to give that information out over the phone, sir, unless we can verify you are the cardholder. But then, you said you were a copper?"

"Yes, Royal Canadian Mounted Police."

"Where are you?"

"I'm at the Irish Garda station in Limerick, Ireland."

"I'll fax the transactions right over."

"Hold and I'll get the fax number for you."

"I have it on file."

"Good. One last thing. Can you send me a text if there's any further charges made to this card?"

"I'll transfer you to Criminal Support; they handle that

sort of thing. They may want further proof that you are who you say you are."

"Thanks."

"Stay on the line, please."

As Duffy waited on hold, he sent a text to Lou, letting him know he'd be calling shortly. Then Fran-O walked over to him.

"Duffy, here's a fax that just came in for you."

That was fast, Duffy thought.

"Are your lads doing okay?"

"They've closed the gap, Fran-O, but they're still chasing them."

"Remember now, two people can shorten the road. So, be a good lad, and let me know if there's anything more I can do to help."

"I will Fran-O, trust me, I will." Just then, a voice came on the line. "Criminal Support, how may I help you?"

WHEN THE THREE women kidnappers and Kate left the farm house on the isle of Guernsey, they headed toward the island's capital city of Saint Peter Port.

"Evelyn, pay attention to the way we're going; this is how you'll get back to the ferry."

Evelyn rolled her eyes. *I'm not a child, Beatrice.*

Saint Peter Port was not a very large city, but like many old ports, it was picturesque and a popular tourist destination. But the only thing the city offered of interest to Beatrice was the Condor Ferry Service which sailed from Julian's Pier back and forth to the island of Jersey.

"Beatrice, just where is the island of Jersey?"

"It's southeast of here; about fifteen miles off the coast of Normandy."

"It's that close to France, but the British own it?"

"Evelyn, the Channel Islands have belonged to us since the time of William the Conqueror. Why do think we didn't need passports to travel here? You would have known that if you had paid attention during history class."

Evelyn ignored the put down.

NOT LONG AFTER the kidnappers reached the city of Saint Peter Port, Beatrice pulled into a lot marked Ferry Parking. "Wait here, this shouldn't take long."

Entering the terminal, Beatrice saw a line in front of the ticket window. However, things moved along rather quickly and before long she was standing at the front of the line.

"Next."

As soon as she stepped up to the window, the agent asked, "How many tickets?"

"I have a question."

"Yes?"

"Are the tickets to Jersey good for any day or are they only valid for the day issued?"

"If you're bringing a vehicle onboard, the ticket is only good for the day. If you buy it online, you can choose the date. Are you bringing on a vehicle?"

"No."

"Then you're a foot passenger. Foot passenger tickets are good anytime on any trip. You just need to show up."

"Do they come in books?"

"Foot passenger tickets are available in books of ten; you save ten percent."

"Each ticket is for one way travel?"

"Yes, ma'am."

"I'll take two books."

"I'll need to see some identification first."

"Why?"

"Company security."

Realizing she had no choice, Beatrice presented her passport.

After glancing at the document, the agent said, "That'll be five hundred pounds, plus twenty for the crown. Cash or charge?"

Beatrice presented her father's card to the agent. He took the card, never looked at the name on it, ran it, and gave her the slip to sign. Once she signed, he slid the tickets under the glass window.

"Thank you, ma'am."

"I'd like to leave my car in the Condor Ferry lot. Does it cost anything to leave a car there?"

"You can reserve a spot, or you can take your chances that one of the free spots will be available. There's not a lot of tourists this time of year, so you might not have any trouble finding one of the free ones."

"How much is a reserved spot?"

"How long are we talking, ma'am?"

"Two weeks."

"It's a hundred pounds a week, plus seven, ma'am."

"I'll take the reserved parking, too, but I'd like to use pound sterling for that."

"Price is the same."

"That's fine." She placed the correct amount on the counter and the agent slid the parking pass under the glass window.

"Place this on the front dash and you won't be towed."

"How long does it take to reach Jersey?"

"In good weather, the regular ferry usually makes the run in a little over two and a half hours."

"Do you have a schedule?"

Without saying a word, the agent passed a schedule under the glass partition.

"Thank you."

Two and a half hours each way. Ha! Well, Evelyn, it looks like you're going to be spending a little time on the water, she thought.

Before boarding the ferry, Beatrice, finally sent a text to Lou:

Drop point is 34 Tiverton Rd, Guernsey. Leave the money on the kitchen table this week.

Chapter Twenty-Nine

WHEN LOU'S PHONE rang, he recognized Duffy's number. "Whatcha got, Duffy?"

"Lou, Aaron Yardley, the Earl of Surrey, died two weeks ago. I just spoke to somebody in the office of Sergeant of Arms over at the House of Lords."

"So, who's using his card?"

"We suspect it's Beatrice Hastings, she was a Yardley before she married Lord Clark Hastings."

"It didn't take her long to start using daddy's money, did it?"

"Well, technically, it's *her* money now; he only had the two daughters."

"I didn't think British nobles stopped siring kids until they had a male child?"

"I think that's only in the movies. So, how close were you this time?"

"Ten, maybe fifteen minutes, no more than that."

"They're on the island of Guernsey now. Avis just ran a

credit card belonging to Aaron Yardley at the airport." Lou didn't say anything.

"What's your next move?"

"Whaddya think? We're flying to Guernsey," Lou said.

"Right. Stay in touch, and don't forget to save your receipts. This is going to be one helluva expense report I'll be submitting to Fletcher."

"I have them."

"Where's Jake?"

"Right here. Need to speak with him?"

"No, just take care of yourselves."

When Duffy shut down, Lou, turned to the agent who had made the flight arrangements for Beatrice.

"What's the fastest way to get to Guernsey?"

Pointing across the terminal, the old man said. "Do you see the Blue Pelican Air counter over there?"

"Yeah."

"They fly jets."

"Thanks." He looked at Jake. "Let's go . . ."

"Right behind you."

No more than five minutes went by before Lou's phone rang again.

"Lou, Aaron Yardley's card just purchased twenty tickets for a ferry that goes back and forth from Guernsey to the island of Jersey."

"I was just about to call you. I received another ransom note. They've identified the drop point as 34 Tiverton Road, Guernsey. Jake says GPS has it as a private residence. Instructions say we're to leave the money on the kitchen table within the week."

"What's that tell us?"

"The ferry tickets put a wrinkle in it, but my guess is that the island of Jersey may be where their base is, and they'll be using the ferry to check the drop in Guernsey."

"Yeah, that's what I'm thinking, too. What's your next move, Jersey or Guernsey?"

"We're heading to Guernsey."

"Not Jersey?"

"No, we'll stake out the drop site. When someone comes to check it out, we'll follow them back to their lair in Jersey, that's where they'll be holding Kate."

"Be careful."

"Always. See if you can find out where they're staying in Jersey."

"We're already working on that."

WHEN BEATRICE RETURNED to the car, she told Evelyn, "We have reserved parking now; let's park the car and head over to Jersey."

"How far is it to Jersey?"

"In miles, I'm not sure, but it's about a two-and-a half-hour trip on the ferry."

"Beatrice, I'm telling you right now, if you to expect me to be the only one going back and forth, guess again. In case you haven't noticed, there are *three* of us. So, you need to come up with a better plan for sharing the load."

Beatrice was momentarily speechless. In all the years she had known Evelyn, she had never pushed back. Now, she took a long look at her co-conspirator.

"I'm serious, Beatrice."

"All right, Evelyn, we'll do something different." Knowing she couldn't trust Anne, she said, "You and I will swap off on it. Does that make it better?"

"That's better, but it would have been a whole lot simpler if we were just *staying* in Guernsey."

"Staying at the drop point is too risky."

"We could have found another place on the island for us; you've had your nose in your damn laptop often enough."

Beatrice decided to let the snide remark pass. She couldn't afford to alienate Evelyn now that she could no longer trust her sister, Anne.

The ferry trip from Guernsey to Jersey went smoothly, albeit it dragged. When they arrived at the landing, Beatrice was the first to stand up. "Evelyn, I'm leaving you in charge; I'll meet the three of you outside the Avis rental office.

When Beatrice stepped off the ferry she headed over to the ferry ticket window.

"May I help you, ma'am?"

"How much faster is the crossing on the high-speed ferry to Guernsey?"

"It's an hour and a half shorter travel time, ma'am."

"How much more are the high-speed ferry tickets, than the regular ferry tickets?"

"Twelve pounds."

"I have sixteen tickets for the regular ferry. Am I able to upgrade these to the high-speed ferry."

"The agent did a quick calculation, "For an additional one hundred-and ninety-two-pounds, I'll exchange those tickets for the high-speed ferry."

Beatrice reached into her purse, intending to take out her father's credit card. Instead, her hand found the envelope with the cash they had withdrawn from the ATMs in Dublin.

"How much did you say?"

"One hundred and ninety-two pounds, plus eight, the crown takes a share too, you know."

"Here are the sixteen tickets, plus two hundred pounds sterling."

"Give me just a moment and I'll have you on your way."

After upgrading the tickets, Beatrice, walked over to the Avis rental office, and hired yet, another vehicle.

Shortly after they all loaded into the new rental, Kate decided it was time to begin showing subtle signs of recovery. First, she let out a loud sigh. Evelyn turned her head. "Well, look, the bitch is finally coming around."

"Good," Beatrice said, "I'm worn out dealing with her dead weight."

"Yes, she is coming around," Anne said. "We need to feed her and get some liquids into her."

Beatrice looked into the rearview mirror, glad to see the normal Anne was back. "Anne, dear, when we get to where we're going, I'd like taking care of her to be your responsibility. Are you willing to do that?"

"Yes."

"Thank you, Anne."

Evelyn, was going to say something else, but Beatrice motioned with her hand not to say a word.

In the back seat, Kate smiled to herself. Anne was still somewhat of an ally, but just how much she could help was still an open question. Kate suspected Anne was frightened of her sister and would avoid challenging her directly at all costs.

Like many abused siblings, Anne had learned early in life how to shield herself from her narcissistic sister. Whenever Beatrice had tormented her, she mentally retreated into her imaginary world, a world where her sister didn't exist. It had helped her survive over the years.

AFTER LEAVING JERSEY'S capital city, the kidnappers drove along a lengthy causeway without speaking. The vehicle's GPS device finally broke the silence. "In one-half mile, take the next exit; at the roundabout, take the second exit onto Beach Haven West Boulevard."

The house Beatrice had rented in Jersey was on the outskirts of the island's capital city, Saint Helier. Unlike the house on Guernsey, it was a single story building that sat on a small lot by a canal in the middle of a subdivision. Beatrice had requested a week's worth of provisions be delivered to the house.

When they pulled into the driveway, Evelyn said, "Nothing like hiding out in the open for a change."

The house appeared to be more of a summer home than a year-round residence. The owner had made the lot as maintenance free as possible; whatever grass may have originally been on the lot, was now covered over with a thick layer of pea stone stretching all the way back to the massive wooden bulkhead that ran along the canal. Beatrice was surprised she had found it available for the short money she had paid.

"Let's go ladies, everyone out. This is home for a while."

"How long have you rented it?"

"We have it for two weeks. Let's go. Anne, help the bitch out of the car. Evelyn, get the key; it's on a nail, inside the shed." Both women did as they were commanded, yet again.

Chapter Thirty

BLUE PELICAN AIR had both a Gulfstream G150 and two pilots available for an immediate take off. In less than twenty minutes, Jake and Lou were buckled into their seats and gaining altitude at well over two thousand feet a minute. As soon as the sleek, arctic white jet reached forty-one thousand feet, it leveled off and raced across the sky at close to five-hundred miles per hour toward the island of Guernsey.

While approaching the northern coast of Wales, they picked up a slight turbulence which was hardly noticeable inside the opulent cabin. A few minutes later, they crossed into England and the pilot announced they were approaching the English Channel. While it had taken well over an hour and a half for the turboprop the kidnappers had flown to reach Guernsey, the Gulfstream was in radio contact with Guernsey air traffic control thirty minutes after takeoff and beginning to descend.

As they entered the terminal in Guernsey, Jake saw the

drawn, tired look on his cousin's face. Up until this point Jake had been completely focused on the hunt, now a hint of his old humor seemed to return. "Where to, Raven Claw?"

Lou smirked upon hearing his Abenaki name and responded in kind. "First, we need a set of wheels, Spirit Fox."

"But before we do anything, cuz, let's get some breakfast."

Lou looked at his cousin. "An army travels on its stomach, eh?"

"Hey, all they had on the plane were eight small bags of macadamia nuts. I gave you three. That, a meal does not make."

Lou smiled; the two cousins turned toward each other and clasped forearms, acknowledging the bond between them. In that moment, the warrior spirit within each instinctively stirred as if they sensed the quarry they hunted was near, the game was on.

DURING BREAKFAST, LOU sent a text to Duffy inquiring about the ransom money. A text came back: *When do you want to set the trap?*

Lou texted back: *no longer than three days.*

Duffy responded: *A courier will deliver a package in two days.*

Lou responded with a thumbs-up emoji, then looked across the table. Jake had just finished eating.

"Let's go, Spirit Fox, we're burning daylight. We need that set of wheels."

As Lou filled out the rental car agreement, he turned to his cousin, "Jake, pull up your GPS app and punch in 34 Tiverton Road. See what you get."

"Is that where we're headed?"

"That's the drop site. I'd like to check it out first."

"That sounds like something we ought to do."

As Lou stepped away from the Avis desk, Jake asked, "So, what are we driving?"

"A silver Mustang convertible."

"*Whoa*, dude! Are you serious?"

"What'd you want, a black SUV with tinted windows, so we could scream 'police?'"

Jake smirked, "Nah, you da man . . . we're gonna *blend* with those wheels like butter melting on hot toast!"

Lou let out a sigh. "Will you shut *up* . . . it's the only friggin' thing they had."

As soon as they took off, Jake pulled the travel app, WAZE, up on his cell phone. Shortly after punching in the address, an automated voice announced: *"At the round-about, take the first exit. In two tenths of a mile, take the exit onto Oceanview Road."*

"Jake, how many miles?"

"One point nine."

"It has to be near the coast; the island's not very wide at this end."

"The name *Oceanview* kinda gives it away."

Lou glanced at his cousin, but ignored the comment.

The road wasn't much more than a narrow country lane meandering through acres of greenery. On either side of the road, crisscrossing stonewalls divided the land as far as the eye could see.

After traveling about a mile, Jake turned to his cousin. "Some mighty good-looking cattle in these fields, Lou, I could go for a nice, thick, juicy steak tonight, topped with a couple globs of melted blue cheese, with a healthy dollop of Grey Poupon on the side!"

"Those aren't cattle, Jake, they're Guernseys."

"What the hell is a 'Guernsey?'"

"It's a prized milk cow."

"Now that I think of it, they do kinda look like Daisy on the front of the Borden ice cream carton."

Lou simply shook his head. "Jake, her name was 'Elsie,' not Daisy and *she* was a Jersey heifer. We're on the island of Guernsey, these are *Guernseys*."

"Well, aren't you just a glowing encyclopedia of useless bovine information."

"Besides, Daisy was the name of Dagwood's dog, and Donald Duck's girlfriend."

"How do you remember all this shit?"

"We played a lot of trivia over in Afghanistan."

"I guess you did!."

Just then, WAZE announced: *At the next intersection, turn right onto Tiverton Road. Your destination is zero point four miles ahead, on the right.*

When they crested the next hill, they could see a single house standing off from the road, surrounded by fields.

"Place looks kinda lonesome, just sitting there all by itself, eh, Lou?"

"It's farm country, Jake."

"Got a plan, yet?"

"We'll do a drive-by."

"That's one helluva plan ya' got there cuz."

Lou smirked. "Connect the dots. The kidnappers are staying in Jersey. They bought a slew of ferry tickets. Someone will be traveling over periodically to check if the money's been delivered."

"And?"

"And they'll be coming up this road, just like we are. A

car parked off to the side of the road will spook them. So, let's go a little further and find a place where we can ditch this thing."

"What, you don't think this chariot is gonna blend in?"

Lou looked over at his cousin and smiled.

Beyond the driveway leading to the farmhouse, the road curved to the left and went up and over a steep hill. When they reached the opposite side of the hill, Lou pulled over.

"By the looks of these overgrown pastures, it doesn't appear there's been any farming going on here for a while, Lou."

"There's no barn near the house either."

"Might have burned down."

"Set the stop watch on your phone; let's see how long it takes us to hike down to the house."

"What the hell are we doing *that* for?"

"Because I wanna figure out the distance."

"Lou, you wanna know the distance? It's two football fields to the driveway and another in off the road. We have an excellent view of the house from the top of this rise, as well as the road coming in."

"I was just thinking the same thing."

"Yeah, well . . . good. We could build a 'duck blind' off to the left here. That chariot you're driving might not blend in, but *we* sure as hell will. No one will even know we're here."

"I always did like your way of thinking, Jake."

"Have the kidnappers said anything about how they plan to make the exchange?"

"No, that's their blindside. They're only focused on the money."

"Sounds like it might be our ace in the hole, cuz."

"Let's get back in the car," Lou said, ignoring his cousin's comment. As they approached the driveway leading to the house, Lou pulled over to the side of the road. "Let's check out the drop site. Maybe we can learn something."

The driveway to the house proved to be damn close to the length of a football field as Jake had predicted. "Looks like fresh tire marks off to the side of these clam shells, Lou."

"I see that."

"Do you know where the key is?"

"Yeah."

"Any chance of booby traps?"

"Jake, they're not trained insurgents, they're three women on the run, barely staying ahead of us."

"I was just asking for a friend."

After finding the key, they entered the house and did a thorough search. Lou was mainly looking for any additional messages from the kidnappers.

"Seen enough?"

"Yeah, there's nothing here."

Before Lou left, he placed an envelope on the kitchen table. But as soon as they walked outside, Jake said: "Stop."

"What's up?"

"Hold still."

Jake found a long hair on Lou's head and plucked it out.

"Ow! What the hell are you doing?"

"I wanna try something."

With that, Jake ran the strand of Lou's hair across his tongue, reached up and stuck one end of the hair to the door and the other end to the doorframe. "There, now when we come back, we'll be able to tell if anyone's been here."

"Where the hell did you learn *that*?"

"From Sean Connery. He did it in the movie *From Russia with Love.*"

Lou looked as his cousin, shook his head, turned around and walked back to the car. *We're so much alike, yet, we're so totally different,* he thought.

Chapter Thirty-One

WHEN THE KIDNAPPERS arrived at the Jersey house, Beatrice and Evelyn quickly laid claim to their individual bedrooms.

When Anne walked in with Kate, the first thing she did was escort Kate over to a chair, then call out to her sister. "Beatrice, I need the key to these cuffs so I can make her more comfortable."

Beatrice emerged from the master bedroom, which she had claimed, and handed Anne the key. "I want her cuffed to that chair, Anne, and be careful with that key, it's the only one I have now." With that, Evelyn walked out from the bedroom she had claimed. "I really like the mattress in my room; it's comfortable."

Anne called out, "How many bedrooms are there?"

"Three. We each have one."

"Well, there are *four* of us, Beatrice; did it ever occur to you that there are *four* of us?" Anne pointed to Kate. "Do we have to draw straws to see who gets to sleep in the remaining bedroom?"

Beatrice paused just long enough to collect her thoughts. "Anne, dear, she's not one of us, she's not our equal. It doesn't matter to me where she sleeps. She can sleep on the damn couch or standing up, for all I care."

"No, that's not fair! That's not fair at all, and I won't have it! You knew perfectly well there were four of us. You should have *insisted* on four bedrooms."

"Anne, will you relax! She's our *captive!*" Beatrice took a breath and softened her tone. "Anne, honey, she's *not* one of us. We're holding her for ransom, remember?"

Anne locked eyes with her sister. "Beatrice, I'm *warning* you, any more of this cruelty and *father* is going to hear of it."

When Beatrice heard the word "father," she had a momentary flashback. It was the image of their father on the floor gasping for air while her bloody fingers were pressing against his windpipe.

Then as quickly as the image appeared, it disappeared from Beatrice's mind. Their father no longer meant anything to Beatrice; she dismissed the memory without even the slightest semblance of remorse.

But she could see that Anne was no longer rational. She needed to placate her sister. "I'm sorry Anne, this is all my fault. You're right; I messed up. I'll get it fixed." She turned to Evelyn. Tossing her head, she said, "Check the closets. See if there's a rollaway in one of them."

Before long, Evelyn came out of her bedroom pushing a fold-up bed. "Here we go, ladies, one bed already made up."

Beatrice turned to her sister. "There, see? Now everyone has a bed. We'll make a little space out here for her to sleep."

"Thank you," Anne replied, obviously relieved. Beatrice

turned around now and took a deep breath. "Evelyn, I'm starved; pull something together for dinner, will you?" she barked.

ON A DIFFERENT Channel Island, the two cousins were seated in an upscale restaurant where Jake was enjoying a perfectly cooked, medium-rare ribeye with a double portion of blue cheese butter melted on top that ran down onto the platter, forming a pool; a generous dollop of Grey Poupon was on the side.

Lou sat opposite, enjoying his own entrée. "Jake, I doubt they'll be sending someone over every day just to check the drop. But I'll put money down that if I dangle a carrot, they'll take the bait."

"So, you figure no one's coming tomorrow?"

"Exactly."

"Good, then tomorrow we'll build ourselves a duck blind on that hillside."

"Yeah, I like that idea. Once we see someone pull into the driveway, we'll go back to the car and boogie on down closer to the house. That's where we'll wait while they're inside."

"Lou, ya' gotta give this a little more thought . . . otherwise we're gonna stand out like a couple of whores in church!"

Lou was briefly lost in thought before saying, "Point taken."

"So?"

"So, if they come over on the ferry, they'll be going *back* on the ferry, right?"

"Right."

"So, we'll go over to Jersey with them and end this cat and mouse game."

"All right, let's think this through. They most likely will have a car on the other end, and we won't."

"So, we follow them to their car, get the make, model, and license number and *then* we track 'em down."

"You and I can follow a trail, but this is a little different forest from what we're used to. You think that's enough for us to go on."

"Are you serious? Come on, we've tracked down lost hunters and hikers with a lot less to go on our whole lives."

"You're right. Let's just cut to the chase and find where Kate's being held."

"All right, so, we'll follow 'em back over to Jersey."

"That's the plan. No sense in dragging this thing out any more than necessary."

Lou cut into his steak. "I can't believe…that we've…." He forked a large piece into his mouth.

Jake stared at his cousin, waiting for him to finish his thought. When Lou just continued to eat, Jake finally said, "You can't believe what?"

"What?"

"You said, 'You can't believe that we've . . .' and then you stopped."

"Oh, yeah! I guess I was thinking . . . actually, I don't know *what* I was thinking. All I know is I can't believe the two of us . . . "

Jake waited again as Lou cut into another piece of steak. Finally, he said, "That the two of us *what*?"

"That we've been getting jerked around like we have been. I'm worn out."

Jake stared at his cousin, thinking, *I've never seen him like this before; the strain from worrying about Kate, and the lack of sleep is getting to him.*

Jake decided to change the subject. "Lou, what time do you plan on being up and out tomorrow?"

"Early. I don't expect them to travel over tomorrow, but I also don't want them to catch us with our pants down while we're building a damn duck blind, either."

Jokingly, Jake asked, "Do you think we could run electricity over to the blind from the house so we could watch a little television?"

That snapped Lou back to reality as he frowned at his cousin.

Jake reached across the table and grabbed his cousin by the forearm. "Cuz, I'm *kidding*! I'm taking this just as seriously as you are. I'm just trying to help you *relax*."

Lou smiled. "I know, and there's no one other than you I'd want as my wingman on this."

"Ditto"

"Okay, let's finish up. I wanna get back to the hotel and start playing the part of the hound on this."

"Say more?"

"It's time we start rattling their cage with a few text messages of our own for a change."

"I'm okay with that."

Later, when they had returned to the hotel, Lou sent a text to the number that had been texting him:

A good faith envelope was left at the drop today. No more money until we agree on the hostage exchange."

KATE HAD PAID close attention to the landscape as they drove to the house Beatrice had rented in Jersey. She knew she needed to develop another plan of escape while the memories of the landscape were fresh in her mind.

She reflected on what she'd seen: *No sidewalks. So, anyone on foot is going to stand out. That could work against me, or maybe in my favor. I just need to play it right.* Then, as if someone had thrown a switch, Kate's mind went totally blank. Maintaining focus had never been a problem for Kate before, yet over the past few days, she'd noticed it happening.

Kate hadn't had much to eat or drink over the past few days, nor had she been able to get much sleep; she was physically and emotionally drained. Yet, now that her hands were no longer constantly cuffed behind her, she'd be able to catnap now and then. Today, she felt a little stronger. While she was eating the small amount of food she was given that evening, she kept thinking, *I need to pace myself and control the amount of food I take in . . . but, I need to drink more water throughout the day.*

As the evening wore on, Kate began to feel less lethargic although still very much in a weakened state. Her will to survive was strong and she was obviously beginning to adapt. She no longer cared about modesty when she needed to answer nature's call. She no longer cared that her hair was a mess, or that she needed to wash or have a change of clothing. However, the one thing she refused to let go of was her will to live and regain her freedom.

Anne continued to be an ally for Kate, at least from a nutritional standpoint. But beyond caring for her, Anne had little influence on what was going on. Periodically, Beatrice and Evelyn would come over to Kate and verbally harass her, but the abusive hitting that she had suffered earlier in the ordeal had ceased.

That evening, Beatrice noticed that Kate was listening in

as they discussed their plans to return to the drop site on Guernsey. Later, after Beatrice had received a couple of text messages, Beatrice said to Evelyn: "Let's go into my room to talk about this." Kate let out a sigh, wondering, *I must have showed a little too much interest in their earlier conversation, I'll need to be more subtle going forward.*

Although she was unable to make out exactly what was being said in the next room, Kate sensed neither woman seemed especially happy about the text messages. From what she had pieced together earlier, she knew Evelyn would be the first to take the ferry back to Guernsey. Then two days later, Beatrice would make the trip.

So, Anne gets a pass on the back-and-forth trips to Guernsey, she thought. *That works in my favor.*

Later, as Kate lay awake on the rollaway cot, the fingers of her right hand closed around the key she had stolen from Beatrice. *I could free myself now, but what then? I'm too weak to run very far. My chances of escaping are better if I wait until there are only two of them here. They're moving around a lot. I wonder how long we'll be here. I know Lou will come for me. I need to do a better job of leaving signs for him to follow.*

THE NEXT MORNING, Lou and Jake were up early and heading toward the old farm house that would serve as the drop site. Lou parked the car on the far side of the hill overlooking the farm house. In less than an hour the two men had created a structure identical to the duck blinds their Abenaki forefathers had used for generations to hunt waterfowl along the rivers and marshes of New Brunswick. Once they finished the blind, it was virtually invisible to the naked eye by anyone traveling up the road.

"Jake, this is exactly where we needed to be," Lou said, satisfied with their efforts.

"I'll take the compliment, thank you," Jake said, then after a pause, he added, "The only thing we forgot to pack in was a beer cooler and some cushions. I'll remedy that tomorrow." Then he smiled. "Incidentally, Grey Poupon is delicious with pressed duck; did you know that?"

Lou looked at his cousin. "We're not here to hunt ducks."

"Did you know that merely a pinch of Grey Poupon is sufficient to amplify the succulent flavor of the sauce made from the juices pressed from *any* duck."

"No, and frankly, I don't give a shit."

"My pallet seems to be drawn to the wood duck, I think that's the tastiest, but a golden eye is tasty, too, and more common. Mergansers are just too oily for me."

"Will you put a lid on it."

"I was only making a culinary statement."

"Yeah, well, hold that thought for Angelo. I need to give Duffy a call."

"Hmmm, Kemosabe, wise to counsel with Chief before battle."

Although Lou rarely admitted it, from the time they were kids, he'd always enjoyed the comic relief his cousin brought to the table. He just wasn't in the mood for it right now.

After exchanging strategies over the phone with Duffy, Lou, sent a few more text messages to the kidnappers.

OVER ON THE island of Jersey, Beatrice stood up. "Evelyn, join me outside."

"What's up?"

"I just received a couple of text messages."

"Who's texting you?"

"Who do you think? The people with the money."

"And?"

"They've left an envelope on the table, but, they're not going to hand over any money until they see the bitch."

"Well, that puts us in a pretty vulnerable position, doesn't it?"

"Yeah, far too risky."

"So, text back that if they want to see the bitch in person, they need to hand over half the money in advance, as a show of good faith," Evelyn said.

"Then how do we get the other half?"

"Four and a half million pounds is a pretty good haul. We could kill the bitch, or leave her someplace, and take off."

"That's only one and half mill apiece. That's not enough for us to disappear."

"Who said anything about disappearing?"

"Evelyn, think about it, they *know* who we are by now!" Beatrice pointed out.

"No, they don't. We've been using aliases."

"They've seen through that by now. They have our finger prints and they've seen us on security cameras any number of times.

"Well, we're using burner phones."

"And that may be the only piece of cover we have left."

"So, how much money do we *really* need?"

"We could walk away with six million," Beatrice said, "but not with half."

"Then, let's tell them we want six mill up front, or the bitch gets knocked off."

"We can't play that card."

"Why not?"

"We *can't*, that's why."

"It'll show them we mean business."

"No, it won't. Because we'd just end up walking it back."

"Then *you* figure it out."

Ignoring Evelyn's comment, Beatrice began thinking out loud. "Maybe, on the day of the exchange, one of us is somewhere with the bitch while the other one goes over to the drop site and picks up the money."

"Beatrice, that is way too risky; we need to tell them we want the money deposited into a bank account."

"I've been thinking about that. I need do more research on it, though. Let's stick with the drop site for now."

"I've decided to take the early ferry over tomorrow," Evelyn said. "I'll see what they've left on the table and should be back around one."

Beatrice looked at her friend in silence. *Was she paying attention to what I just said, or was I talking to myself?*

MEANWHILE, ON THE island of Guernsey, Lou was on the phone to Duffy. "Duffy, here's the plan: We have an observation point near the drop site where we're able to monitor anyone coming or going."

"Then what?"

"When someone shows up to take the bait that's on the kitchen table, we'll follow them back to the ferry."

"That's it?"

"Hell no!"

"Are you getting on the ferry?"

"Yeah. You said they had foot passenger tickets right?"

"Yeah, that's what they bought."

"Then they must have another car in Jersey to go back and

forth to the ferry. Hopefully something hits one of their credit cards and we'll get a line on the vehicle. Once we know the car, we'll be able to track 'em down."

"Are you taking a vehicle over?"

"Yeah. We'll take the car over and Jake will follow them on foot to their car."

"Sounds logical, then what?"

"It all hinges on getting the car off the ferry quick enough to tail them."

"How realistic is that?"

"We'll see."

"What if you lose them?"

"Then we drive around looking for the car. The island's not that big. We'll know what we're looking for at that point."

"What if it's in a garage?"

"Then we'll do a stake out; they gotta go out for milk and bread at some point. Not a helluva lot different from sitting on a deer stand. We're close, Duffy, I can feel us closing in on them."

"All right, I'm not sure what other options you have without causing them to go on the run again. Is Jake agreeable to this?"

"Yeah. By the way, give me an update on the ransom money."

"We loaded it on a prop plane about an hour ago. The pilot has been instructed to deliver it to you, and only you, at your hotel. You'll need to sign for it."

"Is he a cop?"

"No, but the co-pilot is."

"Do they know what they're carrying?"

"I suspect they have an idea. They're both bonded."

"All right, anything else, Duffy?"

"Only that Fletcher sends his best. He asked me when we were coming back. I told him not until we had Kate."

"Good. I'll keep in touch."

As Duffy placed his cell phone back in the charging dock, he thought, *I sure as hell wouldn't want to be playing the role of the fox with those two hounds on my trail.*

THE FOLLOWING MORNING, Evelyn was out of the house early and standing first in line at the high-speed ferry landing. She waited impatiently for the deckhands to give the signal for cars and foot passengers to begin boarding.

Across the bay, at a different landing, a few cars were already lined up for the less expensive regular ferry. The regular ferry wouldn't even begin taking on vehicles for another forty-five minutes.

AS LOU AND Jake walked across the lobby toward breakfast, Jake asked, "What time does the first ferry get in from Jersey?"

"Seven-forty."

"Then we need to get our asses in gear, it's ten after seven now."

"They won't be on that ferry."

"You know that?"

"Yeah, that's the high-speed ferry."

"And you know they won't be on that?"

"Duffy and I had that conversation. He said that based on the cost that hit the credit card, it was twenty tickets on the regular ferry. The amount wasn't enough to cover any denomination of tickets on the high-speed ferry."

"So, when does the regular ferry arrive?"

"Schedule says the first one comes in at nine-ten. I'll have the kitchen make up a couple of sandwiches for us while we're eating breakfast."

"Make mine a ham and cheese on pumpernickel, and tell them to throw in a few extra packets of Grey Poupon. They probably won't trim the crusts off the bread unless you ask. I'm only guessing they'll have pumpernickel, if they don't, get any whole grain. Pumpernickel's only necessary when it's liverwurst."

Ignoring his cousin, Lou said, "They'll check the drop sometime today; when they do, we'll follow them back to the ferry and home to their lair." After a pause, Lou continued with, "We're gonna find Kate today!"

AS THE HIGH-SPEED ferry approached the dock at Guernsey, Evelyn maneuvered herself around the other passengers so she'd be the first one off. Glancing at her watch she thought, *right on schedule.*

At seven-forty the gang plank came down and Evelyn was hustling toward the reserved parking area.

This is going to be tight, she thought. *I've got roughly fifty minutes to get to the drop, grab whatever is there, and make it back to the landing. I'll need to really fly, otherwise, I'm stuck over here until the one o'clock one.*

Chapter Thirty-Two

THROUGHOUT THE BRITISH Empire, traffic flows on the lefthand side of the road and Guernsey is no exception. The difference from other locales in the empire is that the roads in Guernsey are exceptionally narrow and hilly. As a result, the speed limit posted throughout the island is thirty mph/forty-eight km.

The following morning, Lou was anxious to get moving, and made sure they left the hotel just after eight o'clock. Traffic was light as they traveled over to the drop site. However, when they crested the first of many hills on Oceanview Road, a sedan came barreling over the top of the hill directly at them and in the middle of the road.

Lou reacted instinctively and veered as far left as he could. The other car came within inches of knocking the side view mirror off their car as it raced by.

"*Shit,* that was close!" Jake yelled. "Set your alarm earlier tomorrow, *asshole!*"

"Damn narrow road to be driving like that friggin' idiot!"

Lou said. Within minutes, they had passed by the farmhouse on Tiverton Road, crested the hill just beyond, parked, and settled into the duck blind.

"What time is it, Lou?"

"Twenty before nine."

"So, if they took the first ferry over, they should be here in three quarters of an hour."

"Exactly."

"They'll most likely go right back."

"I would think, there's nothing here for them, but the drop."

"Well, heads up, something just turned onto the road."

"Too early for them, the ferry hasn't even landed yet."

"So, let's just pretend and see who they are."

Both men reached into their backpacks, pulled out binoculars and focused on Tiverton Road.

"I can't make out if it's a car or a truck, yet."

"We'll know as soon as it comes over the next rise."

Once the vehicle crested the hill, Jake said, "Truck . . . think that's them?"

"No, it's too early."

The truck drove past the driveway leading to the house and continued up Tiverton Road without slowing in the least. It passed within twenty feet of their blind.

Thirty minutes later, Jake nudged Lou. "There's a cloud of dust on Oceanview. Something just turned onto Tiverton."

"I see it."

This time it turned out to be the mail truck.

By ten o'clock, when no car had turned into the driveway, Lou said, "They must be taking the one-thirty ferry over."

"Either that, or they're not coming."

Although the duck blind had a roof, it offered only partial

protection from the blazing sun. Around mid-afternoon, Lou stretched his arms out. "We'll need to expand that roof and rub some peppermint on our exposed skin next time; these friggin' green head horseflies are taking chunks of meat out of my hide."

Ignoring his cousin, Jake said, "Do you have the ferry schedule with you?"

"Yeah, you want it?"

"No, just tell me what time the regular ferry arrives from Jersey?"

Lou, looked at the schedule, "Nine-thirty and three-thirty."

"And what time does the ferry go back to Jersey?"

"Ten-thirty and four-thirty."

"So, they've got roughly an hour to get off the ferry, fetch their car, drive over here, check out the drop, drive back, park the car and run like hell to make it back for the ferry . . . that's pushing it."

Lou thought to himself, *Yeah, but it's doable.*

"So, if they don't make it back for the four-thirty, they're stuck here for the night."

"I'd say."

"Well,, if no one shows by four-fifteen, they're not coming today. Would you agree?"

"Most likely."

A few minutes later Jake said. "On second thought, let me take a look at that schedule."

AS THE AFTERNOON went on, two more vehicles turned off Oceanview Road onto Tiverton. Neither vehicle even let up on the gas as they drove past the driveway leading to the farm house.

At four-fifteen, Jake stood up. "Ready?"

"Yup, no use sitting here in the middle of nowhere waiting for something to happen that ain't happening."

When they returned to their car, Lou said, "Let's check the drop site before we leave, just for shits and grins."

When they pulled up to the farm house, Lou put the car in park and left it idling. "I'll be right back; I'm just wanna peek inside." As he walked up to the door, he shielded both sides of his face with his hands and leaned up against the glass.

"DAMN IT!"

Jake was out of the car and standing next to his cousin before Lou could even retrieve the key from behind the welcome plaque. The first thing Jake did was check to see if the hair he had placed on the door was still intact. It wasn't.

"How the *hell* did they get in and snag that envelope without us seeing them?"

"We weren't here, Lou."

"What the hell are you talking about?"

"My guess is that car that almost hit us this morning was them."

"How the hell could that have been them?"

"Maybe they came yesterday and stayed over."

"Bullshit."

"Then they came over on the high-speed ferry."

"No way! Duffy specifically said they bought tickets for the *regular* ferry, not the high-speed."

"Maybe they have an accomplice here on the island."

"Now *that's* a friggin' stretch, even for *you*, Jake. You drive on the way back. I need time to think this through."

When they arrived at their hotel, Jake pulled over to the curb saying, "I'll meet you inside in a few minutes."

"Just leave the car here; nobody's going to touch it."

"There's something I wanna do."

"What?"

"I'm going over to the ferry ticket office."

"What the hell for?"

"I've got a question, that's all. I'll be right back."

KATE WASN'T A LIGHT SLEEPER, but she woke when Evelyn left for the ferry that morning. As she lay on the lumpy roll-away, she thought, *Anne won't interfere when I make my escape, but whoever else is still here certainly will.*

She lifted her head and glanced at the clock above the kitchen window. It was almost quarter past six. Smiling, she thought, *By day's end, I'll know how long I have when one of them travels over to the drop site.*

It wasn't long after Evelyn left when Beatrice walked into the kitchen and fired up her laptop. First on her to-do list was qualifying a few offshore banking opportunities. After surfing the net for a couple of hours, she had seen enough and had already decided against using any bank located in a banana republic, or the Arab world, purely on the basis of her own personal bias.

International banking laws had forced a number of changes. Switzerland was no longer the safe haven it once was. Banks that held the most appeal for her were in the Cayman Islands, and Montenegro. The only wrinkle was both countries required the personal presence of a foreign national to open an account.

In Beatrice's mind, Montenegro had an edge over the Cayman Islands since it steadfastly refused to participate in the automatic exchange of information with other nations. Montenegro also didn't require disclosure of the source of funding for an account.

It was only a few minutes after ten o'clock, when Beatrice heard the unmistakable sound of a car pulling onto the pea stone covered yard. When Evelyn came into the house she was waving an envelope.

"I'm back, and look what I have."

"I didn't expect you back so soon."

"It was crazy! I almost didn't make it back to the landing in time for the eight-thirty return. If I hadn't, I wouldn't have been back until later." She waved the envelope in her hand. "Take a look at what was waiting on the kitchen table."

Beatrice grabbed it from her and opened the envelope. "Two fifty-pound notes. What the hell does this mean?"

"Well, read the message."

Beatrice opened the paper and read it aloud: "No ransom money will be paid until we have an agreement on the hostage exchange."

Evelyn danced across the living area as she made her way over to the kitchen with the car keys. "Our plan is coming together, it's *happening*," she sang out loud.

"Maybe, but we still need to nail down the sticky little details about the hostage exchange, *and* how we get the money."

"Did you find any off shore banks?"

"Yes, but there's a catch."

"What?"

"Foreign nationals need to be present in order to open an account."

"So, let's find one that doesn't."

"It seems to be a rather consistent requirement within the banking industry, deary."

"Oh."

"I believe our best bet is Montenegro."

"Really?"

"The Capital Bank of Montenegro, actually."

"So, what's the plan?"

"I'm going to tell them to hold off on delivering the money. One of us will need to fly over to Montenegro and open the account. Once we have the account, we'll let them know where they can wire the money."

"And?"

"And when the money is deposited, we take off."

Clapping her hands together like a twelve-year-old, Evelyn smiled. "Perfect."

"Not quite; we still need to agree on the hostage exchange."

"Once the money is in our account, we'll just text them and let them know where to find her."

"We'll have to negotiate that."

Kate had listened to everything that was being said. But even more importantly, now she knew where Evelyn hung the car keys, and how long it will take one of her captors to go over to Guernsey and return.

"So, we don't need to go back over to Guernsey again?" Evelyn asked.

"I don't see the need."

"That's too bad; it was fun watching the whales on the way over and back."

Beatrice dismissed Evelyn's comment about the whales as being trivial. "I'll see if I can get a refund for the rest of the tickets; we can use the cash."

Anne had also been listening and finally spoke up. "Don't do that. I'd like to go on a whale watch and see whales."

"Anne, dear, it isn't a whale watch. Evelyn just happened to see them while she was on the ferry."

"I don't care! I'd still like to see the whales."

Ignoring Anne, Evelyn kept talking. "Coming back, we passed the regular ferry chugging along on its first trip over to Guernsey."

"Hold that thought, Evelyn, I need to text them and tell them to hold off on the drop.

WHEN LOU READ the latest text, he made a move like he was going to throw his phone against the wall. "Damn it!"

"What?"

Handing the phone to his cousin, he said, "Take a look!"

Change in plans, do not deliver money to drop. will text bank acct soon.

"Sounds like the drop site is history."

"I'll change that."

"Plan B?"

"You got that right."

Lou punched in Duffy's number. Duffy picked the call up on the first ring.

"Yeah, Lou?"

"The kidnappers just threw us a curve."

"How so?"

"They want us to wire the money to an account."

"What's the name of the bank?"

"They didn't say."

"Do you have a routing number?"

"Not yet."

"Where are they?"

"Jersey, I guess."

"I was expecting to hear from you earlier. Did they come over today?"

"Yeah, but we missed them."

"You missed them? How'd that happen?"

"I'm not sure. Jake figures they came over on the high-speed ferry, not the regular ferry."

"No way. They bought tickets for the regular ferry. Twenty tickets for the high-speed run would have been a couple hundred pounds more. Nothing else has hit their credit cards."

"Jake talked with the ticket agent, they could have upgraded to the high-speed boat using cash. He thinks that's what happened."

Duffy thought about it for a moment. "It's possible, they could have used cash; they hit a few ATMs in Dublin."

"Duffy, we need them to come back over to Guernsey."

"Any ideas?"

"We haven't agreed on the hostage exchange yet, I'm thinking we can leverage that."

"Say more."

"We stonewall on agreeing to any wire transfer until we reach agreement on the hostage release."

"I'm missing something. How's that going to get them back to Guernsey?"

"I'll send a text that the procedure we insist on is outlined in an envelope at the drop site."

"That's pretty weak, but it might work."

"I'm open to suggestions."

"Let's talk about the release first, any thoughts?"

"It'll need to feel safe for them. I haven't worked this out 'eight ways from Sunday' yet, but I have an idea."

"I'm listening."

"I thought we could insist they drop Kate off *outside* police headquarters on the island of Jersey. Once the police confirm that it's Kate, and that she's okay, we'll wire the money."

"Won't work. They're not going to give her up without getting anything."

"Okay, so here's what Jake suggested: We wire a small, good faith deposit in advance saying it's to test that the wire transfer will work. Then, when they send a text with a photo of Kate walking into the police station unassisted, we'll wire more money. Once the police confirm that it's Kate, and she's okay, we'll wire the balance."

"That's too simple, Lou," Duffy said, "I don't think they'll go for it." But after a pause, Duffy corrected himself. "Maybe that *could* work. Text me the phone number they're using. I need to talk with some folks here about the wire transfer."

"So, you're okay if I tell them we'll do a wire transfer?"

"Yeah, let's see if they go for the exchange."

"Their initial demand was nine million pounds. I'll lowball that in the proposal."

"*No*. Don't put the nine million in play, keep it simple."

"Right."

"All right, I gotta go talk to a few people. Let me know if you hear anything else. I'll be working on Plan B."

"I will."

Within minutes, Lou keyed in the text message. As he did so, he said every word out loud. "No wire transfer until we agree on exchange. Proposal will be at drop site tomorrow morning."

"Think they'll buy it, cuz?"

"We'll find out, Jake. They've only got one card to play, and we've only got one card to play.

"How do you want the exchange to go down?"

"Let's think this through . . . maybe we wire a half million pounds into their account, as a show of good faith. When they text us a photo of Kate walking into the Jersey police station, unassisted, we'll release another million. Once the police confirm Kate is alive, we'll wire the balance into their bank."

"They'll push for more on the front end."

"That's when we start negotiating. The more we load on the backend, the greater chance Kate will be unharmed."

"Given that they came over on the high-speed today, they'll most likely do that again. We should drop this off tonight."

"Yeah. Let me hit 'send.' then I'll write out the proposal and stick it in an envelope."

"So, what are we going to do with the nine million in cash you signed for today?"

"Just leave it in our room, it'll be fine."

"Are you *nuts*?"

"No."

"Lou, I think we should take it with us."

"Nah, it'll be fine, just leave it."

"You're *serious*?"

"Yeah."

"Lou, what the hell is the friggin' matter with you? That's a *helluva* lot of money!"

"No, it's not."

"Nine mill, isn't a lot of money to you?"

"It's monopoly money."

"*What*?"

"It's counterfeit."

Jake was silent. "Then . . . then why did you have to sign for it?"

"Duffy didn't want to tip his hand to the delivery boys."

"Okay, so what's the plan?"

"We're gonna drive over to the drop site and I'm gonna leave a copy of the exchange proposal on the table."

"Then, what?"

"Then, we're having dinner."

"And after that?"

"I thought we'd just come back here."

"That's it? That's your *plan*?"

"Well, for tonight, it is."

Jake thought about if for a minute before asking, "Are you carrying?"

"Of course. Kate told me to treat any service issue like an American Express card."

"Now, what the hell does *that* mean?"

"Never leave home without it."

"Gotcha."

Chapter Thirty-Three

T HE INSIDE OF the Jersey isle house was typical of many seasonal seaside cottages. It was furnished with low maintenance, recycled furniture capable of holding up to any and all abuse from the salt air and sun. Every piece of wooden furniture had been painted with either a glossy bright yellow, a honking orange, or a high gloss green best described as a color similar to a praying mantis.

The extent of Kate's ability to move about the house was defined by the length of a single chain joining two handcuffs. During the day, she was cuffed to a chair; at night, she was cuffed to the rollaway cot which was set up next to the chair. Kate would stand up and stretch, but without exercise and proper nutrition, she was becoming noticeably weaker.

Kate sat, ate, and slept in full view of everyone. Beatrice and Evelyn paid little, if any attention to her; it was Anne who was her attentive caregiver.

The second night Kate was at the Jersey house she stayed awake, waiting for everyone else to fall asleep. It was well after midnight when she released herself from the handcuff securing her to the rollaway. Moving silently, she worked her way around the furniture and entered the kitchen area. She knew exactly where the rack was that Evelyn had used earlier to hang the car keys. When she reached the rack her fingers danced from hook to hook, only to find that the rack was empty.

Damn, she thought, *Evelyn must have already taken the keys. Do I dare try to find them in her room? No…I might wake her and she'd sound the alarm. They'll know I have the other key.*

With her hopes of driving off in the middle of night now dashed, she returned to the rollaway. Using the key she'd stolen from Beatrice, Kate painstakingly scratched the words 'Raven Claw' into the arm of the yellow chair. Once she was satisfied she'd left a clue for her husband, she reluctantly clicked the open cuff back around her wrist.

EARLIER THAT VERY evening, on the island of Guernsey, Lou and Jake headed toward the drop site with another envelope. Uncertain as to whether anyone might be inside the farmhouse, Lou doused the headlights and drove the last half mile in the moonlight. When they reached the crest of the last hill before the driveway, he stopped and both men took out their binoculars.

"I'm not seeing any lights, Lou."

"Neither am I, and there's no vehicle in the yard, but just to be sure, we'll leave the car out on the road and walk in."

A short distance from the driveway, Lou pulled over and shut the engine off.

"Don't open the door yet."

Squinting, Jake asked, "You see something?"

"Nah, I just need a second to disconnect the dome light. No sense messing up our night vision when we open these doors." As soon as both men exited the car, they separated and melted into whatever shadows were available from the large Hunter's Moon illuminating the landscape.

As Lou retrieved the key, Jake whispered, "No one's been here since we were here last."

"You know that?"

"Yeah, the strand of hair I put on the door is still there."

Lou ignored his cousin's remark. "Move aside, I need to go in and leave this on the table."

When they exited, Jake pulled out another strand of Lou's hair, ran it across his tongue and placed it on the door frame.

"Jake, do me a favor?"

"What?"

"Use your own hair for that."

ON THE DRIVE BACK, Lou turned into the driveway of the Hogs and Heifers Saloon. The front parking lot was full. "Busy place for a weeknight, eh, Lou?"

"Yeah, looks like we're parking in the overflow lot."

"With all this sitting, the walk will do us good. I've been getting a little antsy knowing I haven't been getting my ten thousand steps in every day, let alone my daily fruits and vegetables."

Lou shook his head and muttered, "How the hell did you and I ever grow up in the same household?"

As soon as they stepped inside the lobby, a very attractive hostess greeted them. "Welcome to Hogs and Heifers, gentlemen! Just the two of you?"

When Jake didn't say anything, Lou said, "Yes, two."

The hostess immediately picked up two menus, smiled and said, "This way, gentlemen." As soon as they were settled, she said, "They're really shorthanded here tonight. May I start you off with something to drink?"

Lou didn't hesitate. "Yeah, I'll have a bone-dry vodka martini, straight up, shaken, with a twist."

She nodded and turned to Jake. "And for you, sir?"

Jake had been mesmerized from the first moment this raven-haired young woman smiled at him in the lobby. Now, realizing that the dulcet tones of her voice were being directed solely at him, he was speechless. His mind was racing as he checked off all the boxes in his head. *She's articulate, poised, definitely pleasing to the eye, educated, obviously works out . . . she is gorgeous.*

When Jake didn't respond to the hostess, Lou glanced across the table. His mouth was open and his eyes seemed to have glazed over. Sensing the awkwardness of the moment, Lou blurted out, "How's the ribeye here?"

"Oh, I'm told it's really good here."

"You're *told*?"

Seeing the quizzical look on Lou's face, the hostess added, "I don't actually work here; I'm just filling in tonight as a favor for a friend."

Turning to Jake, she asked again. "Sir, is there something you'd like from the bar?"

Finally coming out of his trance, Jake nodded as he pointed across the table saying, "Yes, I'll have what he said."

Throughout the evening, whenever the perfectly tanned, shapely hostess entered the dining room, Jake's eyes followed her every move.

There's no way she's unattached, he thought.

When they were just about finished eating, Lou leaned

into the table saying, "Jake, I've had as much as I want, and I need to use the restroom; take care of the bill, and get the receipt. I'll meet you outside."

When their server arrived with the bill, Jake asked, "Can I take care of this in the lobby?"

"Oh, that would be a big help if you would sir, just see the hostess."

When Jake left the table, he knew he had one shot at best to impress her. He took a deep breath when he entered the lobby, and walked directly over to what could be the-girl-of-his-dreams.

"May I help you?"

Her smile sent a thrill through him. "Yes, my . . . my server said I could pay the bill here."

"Oh, yes, you certainly can; it's no problem at all."

As Jake handed the hostess his credit card, then he said, "I'm curious, was your father ever a boxer? Did he fight in the ring?"

Furrowing her brow, she said. "What did you just ask?"

"Was your father ever a prize fighter?"

After running the card, she handed it back to him, along with a slip and a pen, saying, "I'll need your signature on this . . . and no, I don't believe my father ever fought in the ring."

"That's...that's really surprising . . . "

She tilted her head. After a pause she said, "Why do you say that?"

"Because I really think you're a *knockout!*"

She closed her eyes and thought, *I don't believe he just said that.*

Jake countered with a laugh. "I figured I'd give it my best shot."

Laughing the hostess said, "*That* was your best shot?"

"I'm a little out of practice," he smiled. "So, do you come here often?"

The right corner of the hostesses' mouth twitched ever so slightly. After a short pause she said, "No. I'm visiting friends. I have a break between assignments and the Channel Islands was half way . . . that's the only reason I'm here."

"What do you do in *real* life?"

"I'm a marine biologist . . . among other things. You're Canadian, aren't you?"

"Is it that obvious?"

"Totally. I did my junior year at McGill."

"I did my *undergrad* work there."

"Really, well, we have something in common, then."

He liked that. He wanted to have something in common with her, *more* than in-common; he wanted to know everything about her.

"My name's Jake, Jake Gault."

She held out her hand. "Koby, Koby Callahan."

When he touched her hand, he felt an excitement race through him. He wanted to keep touching her, and never let go. "I'm trying to figure out your accent."

"You won't," she said. "My parents sent me to private schools and my teachers came from various places around the globe. I have this totally weird hybrid accent thing going on . . . and, just so you know, my mother wasn't a boxer, *either*."

Jake laughed at that. *Oh, God, she has my sense of humor. I'm in trouble here.*

"Koby, I'm not trying to come on to you . . . well, actually, I am. Look I'm only here for a short time, too. Is there a chance we might get together before we both leave?"

Koby took a long look at the man standing before her. Jake gazed back, wondering what was going through her mind.

The only thing he was sure of was, *this* moment was his *real* shot.

"It *might* be possible," she said, "but I'm taking off tomorrow. We're in Provence for the week. After that, I'm back here before I head out on my next assignment."

"I'm not here for long, either," he said, " . . . but we *could* make it work, if you wanted to."

As she retrieved the credit card slip Jake had signed; there was a slight smile on her lips. He liked the shape of her mouth . . . really liked it.

"You said you were a marine biologist 'among other things,'" he said. "Do you mind me asking what the 'other things are?'"

"I don't mind, but what about you? What do *you* do?"

"I fly planes."

"Big ones?"

"Sometimes, but I really like the little ones."

"Interesting."

"So, how do I get in touch with you?"

Without saying a word, she reached down under the podium, opened her purse and took out a business card. "I'm not a hundred percent sure I should be doing this, but you don't look like a stalker, so here's my card. No promises, Jake-who-likes-to-fly-small-planes, but if you give me a call next week, I might answer."

"I will, Koby who-does-other-things. Thanks."

As Jake walked outside looking for Lou, he glanced at the business card in his hand. It read: *Koby Callahan Ph.D., RN. Oceanographic and Marine Biology Consultant.*

"YOU CERTAINLY TOOK your sweet time getting out here," Lou said. "Let me have one of those fancy cigars of yours."

"Damn! I left them in the car . . . wait here, I'll be right back."

"Nah, I'll go with you. It's a nice night and the walk will help me settle the meal we just had."

The lot closest to the restaurant wasn't anywhere near as crowded as it was when they had arrived, but the overflow lot was still packed. Although the back lot wasn't lit, the bright Hunter's Moon more than compensated for the lack of artificial lighting.

When Jake saw all the empty parking spots, he said, "We could move the car up closer, if you want."

"It's fine where it is."

As they entered the overflow section, Lou noticed movement ahead. "Off to the left," he whispered.

"I saw; looks like two of 'em."

"Think they're carrying?"

"If you mean baseball bats, then . . . yeah, they're carrying."

The two thugs kept bobbing their heads up and down as they moved between cars trying to gauge the distance between themselves and their intended quarry. It hadn't dawned on the thugs that they had lost the element of surprise.

As the two cousins continued walking toward their car, they nonchalantly widened the distance between themselves. Then using a loud voice, Jake said: "Wait a minute, my shoe's untied, I need to fix it." Bending down, he grabbed a handful of dirt and stage-whispered to Lou, "I'll take the one on the right."

When both bat-wielding thugs stepped out from between the line of cars, the one on the right quietly said: "Surprise!"

"Hand over your wallets and nobody gets hurt," the bigger of the two said, "unless you wanna play rough. Your choice."

Lou and Jake stood motionless which the two thugs mistakenly took as a sign of submission.

Standing almost shoulder to shoulder to each other, the two assailants were facing Jake when he tossed the mixture of sand and grit from his hand directly at their eyes. Wasting no time, he delivered a powerful kick into the knee of the one closest to him, shattering the joint with a sickeningly sound. As the man collapsed on the ground, in agony, Jake kicked the bat to the side.

Lou had no difficulty subduing the second man. With lightning speed, he drove the knuckles of his right-hand deep into his opponent's solar plexus. Next he grabbed the wrist of the arm holding the bat with his left and twisted it up and behind his attacker's back, dislocating the shoulder before bringing him to the ground.

With his knee digging into the back of his assailant, Lou called out: "Jake, frisk your guy for iron, then dial 999."

"He's clean, but you mean 911, right?"

"No, it's 999 over here!"

THE GUERNSEY POLICE responded quickly. After taking the two assailants into custody, they obtained statements from both Lou and Jake; the injured men were transported to the island's hospital under guard.

When the last police car exited the parking lot, Jake turned to his cousin. "Let's go have that smoke."

As they sat on an outdoor bench, Lou reminisced. "I don't think I've seen that old dirt-in-the-eye trick since we were kids wrestling over at the village."

"Me, neither."

"Was it White Fox or Long Toe who always did that?"

Jake lightly tapped his cigar. "Long Toe, and he was damn good at it, too. I never could tell when he had something in his hand."

"What made you decide to use it?"

"I saw the baseball bats and I really didn't feel like having 'Louisville Slugger' tattooed on my forehead."

"You could have drawn your Glock," Lou smirked.

"What's the fun in that? Besides, I figured if we let the tiger out, just a little, we'd shed some of the frustration we've been feeling."

Lou drew on his cigar, tilted his head back, and slowly blew a cloud of smoke skyward. "I think you made the right call, cuz."

"Speaking of calls . . . we should let Duffy know about tonight's adventure?"

"Nah, let's just enjoy the smoke; we'll do that in the morning."

AT THAT VERY same moment over on the island of Jersey, Evelyn and Beatrice sat outside on a picnic table under the light from the Hunter's Moon.

"One of us needs to travel to Montenegro."

"Well, it's not going to be me, Beatrice. You need to do some of this running around."

"Shush, keep your voice down."

"Why? There's no one else around; every house is closed up."

"Sound travels over water."

"I don't care, I'm tired of all this; besides, Montenegro is a long trip."

"Okay, Evelyn, I get it. Let's not allow this to come between us. I'll be the one who goes to Montenegro."

"Thank you."

"On one condition."

"What?"

"That you continue to check the drop."

"Fine."

"And you keep an eye on both Anne and the bitch."

"That's more than one condition, Beatrice. You *always* want more."

Beatrice stood up, ignoring her friend. "I need to go figure out my itinerary and book some flights."

KATE HAD BEEN straining to listen in on the conversation going on outside. She was surprised when the screen door opened, and quickly feigned being asleep. Anne had gone to bed earlier and Kate mistakenly expected the other two would remain outside a while longer. Kate had taken the key she had stolen out of her pocket, intending to loosen the cuffs around her wrist a notch or two.

In her haste to feign sleep, Kate inadvertently left her key to the handcuffs she was hiding fully exposed, on the huge arm of the yellow chair.

Through the slits of her eyes, Kate saw Beatrice walking directly toward her.

Chapter Thirty-Four

WHEN BEATRICE SAW how the rollaway bed blocked her path to the kitchen, she turned around and entered the kitchen a different way. As soon as her back was turned, Kate reached out and scooped up the key she'd left on the arm of the chair.

The following morning, Kate was awake early and listening to the conversation between Beatrice and Evelyn.

"Were you able to book a direct flight over to Paris?" Evelyn asked.

"Yes."

"What time do you get into Montenegro?"

Beatrice ignored the question. "I hate that Anne will be left alone today," she said. "I just don't believe we can trust her."

"She won't be alone all that long," Evelyn answered. "If I can return on the one o'clock ferry, I'll be back here by two-thirty."

"Make sure you do that," Beatrice admonished. "After

that fiasco Anne pulled in the attic, I'm just not comfortable leaving her alone with the only bargaining chip we have."

"What time do you think you'll be back?"

Out of the corner of her eye, Beatrice saw Anne helping Kate move from the rollaway cot to the yellow chair. "Hold that thought, I need to get something straight with Anne."

Beatrice walked over to her sister, sat down on the edge of the rollaway and touched her on the arm. "Anne, dear, you're going to be alone for a few hours today. You can go outside and get some fresh air if you'd like, but I don't want you to leave the yard. Do you understand me?"

Anne closed her eyes and slowly nodded her head.

"No, I need to hear you say it, Anne. Do you understand what I'm saying?"

Anne took a <u>moment</u> before nodding her head and responding, "Yes, I'm not to leave the yard."

Kate watched the exchange in horror. *My God, Anne sounds like a schoolgirl who's being reprimanded by the principal. Is she using mental regression as a defense mechanism?*

Having heard what she wanted, Beatrice stood up and walked back over to Evelyn.

"I have to treat her like a child, now, she's totally lost it," Beatrice whispered.

"Yes, I sensed that, too," Evelyn agreed.

"Now, then, what was your question?"

"Oh, I was asking when do you think you'll be back?"

"It'll be sometime tomorrow; I just don't know how late."

"Give me a call when you come in; I'll meet you at the airport."

"No! Absolutely not, I'll take a taxi. I want you here with Anne."

THAT SAME MORNING, Lou's phone rang early; he knew instantly from the unique ring tone that it was Duffy. Sitting on the edge of his bed, he raked his left hand through his hair and across the back of his neck, while reaching for the phone with his right.

"Yeah?" he answered.

"You awake?"

"Getting there, what's up?"

"British Airways ran Earl Yardley's credit card at the Jersey airport."

"When?"

"Not more than ten minutes ago."

"Have you talked with British Air, yet?"

"No, that's my next call. I wanted to give you a heads up first."

"I appreciate that."

"What's your plan for today?"

"I'm waiting for you to tell me where the hell they are on Jersey."

Duffy paused for a moment. "Lou, I've been up most of the night; I'm a little too tired to play games this morning. If I had that knowledge, I'd be sharing it with you right now."

Lou took a deep breath. "Sorry, Duffy. I was out of line . . . I'm just frustrated. This isn't going the way I thought it would."

"We all are. What's your plan for today?"

"We're on stakeout. Hopefully, they'll take the bait we planted last night and then we'll follow whoever shows up back to Jersey."

Duffy was silent.

Lou looked at the screen on his phone to see if the call had dropped. "Duffy? You still there?"

"I'm still here." Duffy paused before continuing. "I got a call from our Sergeant Major during the night."

Lou noticed the change in Duffy's voice. "And?"

"He wanted a briefing on the ruckus you two got into last night."

"How'd he find out about it? I hadn't even told you."

"Exactly, and I'm pissed about that! He got a call from Scotland Yard. They wanted to know what two of his Mounties were doing on the island of Guernsey carrying Glocks."

"He didn't *know* we were here?"

"Oh, he *knew* you were there. I've been keeping him up to speed on your whereabouts. But I got a pretty good ass-chewing for not giving him a heads up about the ruckus you two managed to get yourselves into last night, which, oh, by the way, I didn't even know about until *he* told me. Thanks for making me look bad."

Lou lowered his head, thinking. *Shit, it was pretty stupid of me not to have called Duffy last night. I should have listened to Jake.*

"He made it pretty damn clear he wasn't pleased," Duffy said. "I was told to get my act together, or he's replacing me."

"I'm sorry, Duffy, I didn't mean to blindside you. It won't happen again." After a pause, Lou continued. "Have you made any progress on Plan B?"

"Some. They're still working on it; we'll run a test once we know the bank they're using."

IT WASN'T MUCH later, when Lou and Jake were in position at the duck blind. Lou looked at his watch. "The first high-speed ferry is about to enter Guernsey's harbor."

Neither man said anything, as they sat alone with their thoughts. Lou was stressed out worrying about Kate. Jake looked as though he, too, had something on his mind.

At quarter after eight, Jake stood up and stretched. "Looks like they didn't take the early ferry this time."

"Any number of things could have happened," Lou said. "They might still show; there's time for them to make the one o'clock back over to Jersey."

Around noon, Jake broke into the cooler. "Lou, you want your sandwich?"

"Yeah, let me have mine."

"I thought they were damn skimpy on the Grey Poupon yesterday. I picked up a squeeze bottle, if you want more."

"Yeah, I know…pass me the bottle when you're through."

No sooner had Lou finished the first half of his sandwich when Jake elbowed him. "Something's coming."

"I can see the dust."

Within minutes, a car came roaring over the hill on Tiverton Road, turned on two wheels, and headed up the driveway to the cottage.

"Let's go, Jake. Game time!"

In a heartbeat, both men were moving to their car. Lou had deliberately parked the vehicle just below the ridge, facing back toward the direction they had come. In less than two minutes, they were driving past the driveway and heading toward the ferry landing at Saint Peter Port.

As they passed the driveway Lou said, "Did you get the make and model of the car?"

"No, but it's a tan car, being driven by a maniac; shouldn't be too friggin' difficult to spot when it comes roaring into town."

"Okay, here's the deal: When we get to the landing, I'll

park the car and get tickets. You stand by the entrance to the parking lot, and wait for them."

Jake nodded. "Got it."

"She'll have to really move her ass to make it back in time for the one o'clock ferry."

"I won't board unless I see her board."

"Good. When we do board, let's avoid telegraphing that we're together."

"Right."

Lou ignored the thirty mile an hour speed limit as he raced back to Saint Peter Port. Just as he approach the ferry landing, a parking space opened up directly in front of the ticket office. They both exited and moved into action.

Lou went into the ticket office, and bought both a foot passenger ticket and a vehicle ticket. Jake had taken a position at the entrance to the ferry parking lot. As Lou passed Jake, he rolled down the driver's side window, handed him his ticket and waited to enter the queue for the ferry.

Literally six minutes before the ferry was to leave the harbor for Jersey, a tan KIA came screeching into the reserved ferry parking area. As soon as the driver's door shut, the lone occupant ran toward the gangway waving her arms and yelling: "Wait, wait, don't leave! Please, wait for me!"

When Jake saw the KIA enter the parking lot, he waved to his cousin and was in motion walking toward the ferry. Lou drove his car on board hoping that even though he was the last to board, he might somehow be the first to exit. In the rearview mirror he watched the lone woman running toward the ferry.

No sooner had Evelyn stepped aboard than the horn sounded from the wheelhouse, signaling the ferry's departure. As the huge twin screws started rotating, the vibrations shook the vessel from stem to stern. Ever so slowly, the ferry began to move away from the landing.

Jake quickly positioned himself on the forward top observation deck at the rail, facing the bow. It was sunny, but the breeze off the water had a chill to it. After pulling the hood of his jacket up over his head and donning his sunglasses, Jake's appearance was completely different from the sentinel who had stood next to the parking area. Moments later, Evelyn appeared on the observation deck and leaned against the rail no more than six feet away.

Lou had followed Evelyn up the ladder, and positioned himself a short distance from her on the opposite side from Jake. As the ferry left the harbor, Evelyn rose up and down on her tiptoes, saying to no one in particular, "I do hope we get to see more whales today."

Jake picked up on the queue. "Is there a chance of that happening?"

"Oh, yes,! We saw a mother and her calf on the trip over earlier."

"What species of whale was it?"

"Oh, I don't know; someone said they thought it was a humpback," Evelyn answered.

Jake waited a moment before saying, "Well, perhaps, we'll see some."

"I hope so!"

Without turning to face Evelyn, Jake asked, "Do you take this ferry often?"

"No, this is only my second time. Well actually, it's my second-round trip."

Continuing to look straight ahead, Jake said. "It's my first.

I've never visited the island of Jersey before. Any recommendations for restaurants?"

"No, we're. . .we're in a cottage; we've been eating in."

"I see."

After pausing, Jake asked, "How long are you here for?"

At first it didn't appear Evelyn was going to respond, but then she said, "Just a couple of weeks, then we head out."

"Me, too. I've been on the road way too long. I'm looking forward to putting my head down on my own pillow again."

"Aren't we all!"

Evelyn fingered the envelope in her pocket that she had picked up at the drop. She was anxious to open it and see what the terms were for the hostage exchange, but she was far more excited about the potential of seeing more whales.

Jake had hoped to keep the conversation going, but he wasn't able to come up with any more safe open-ended questions. So, rather than cross an imaginary line, he remained quiet.

After a few minutes, Jake cupped both hands around his eyes. "I think I see a spout ahead on the portside."

Evelyn was immediately up on her tiptoes, leaning forward. "Which side is that?"

"Left."

"Oh, good! I think they like that side. They were on that side earlier when we came over."

Jake rolled his eyes at the idiocy of her comment. Lou had moved slightly closer.

As if on cue, Lou cupped his hands around his eyes, and pretended to look out to sea. "I think I see a spout, too, but it's quite a distance off," he said, holding back a smile.

Then, he decided to give Evelyn a little positive

reinforcement. "For some reason, it seems they *do* appear to favor swimming on the port side."

Chapter Thirty-Five

TWO-HUNDRED AND fifty miles to the east, Beatrice had arrived in Paris, passed through Customs, and was standing ready to board her connecting flight to Podgorica, Montenegro.

Transavia Republic Airlines wasn't her first choice, but given her tight schedule, it was the only option that made sense. Like most low fare carriers, the accommodations were, at best, spartan, and the inflight service was virtually non-existent. As soon as the plane was airborne, Beatrice sat back, closed her eyes, and reminisced about the many pampered flights she had taken to Montenegro with her husband in their private Gulfstream. She hadn't really appreciated how posh those trips were, at the time.

After passing through Montenegro Customs with ease, Beatrice headed directly for the taxi stand. She entered a waiting taxi with a curt, "First Capital Bank of Montenegro." It wasn't in her nature to say "please," and for some reason, she had always looked down upon the people of Montenegro."

The driver acknowledged her with a simple wave of his hand and shifted into first gear. The drive from the airport into the city brought back memories of happier times; nothing seemed to have changed since her last visit. The narrow cobblestone streets were still under repair; colorful, yet faded awnings still jutted out from the shops lining the main street; motor scooters still beeped their horns incessantly as they swerved in and out of the traffic, and the same number of pigeons seemed to roam around the base of the fountain at the central piazza looking for a handout.

Beatrice had made it known to the bank, well in advance, that she was traveling to the capital city of Montenegro specifically to open an account as a foreign nationalist. The populace of Montenegro spoke several Slavic languages, none of which Beatrice spoke or understood. But the representative at the bank had assured her that someone who was fluent in English would be assigned to assist her, and expedite the process.

Upon entering the bank, she boldly approached the first desk she saw and announced, "My name is Beatrice Hastings. I am here to open an account. I was told someone who spoke English would assist me. Is that *you*?"

Before the young lady sitting at the desk could respond, an older man sitting nearby, stood up. "Ah, Madam Hastings, it is a pleasure to meet you. Please, come over here and have a seat. I have everything prepared for you."

After less than ten minutes, Beatrice was informed that every requirement for a foreign nationalist to open an account had been satisfied. Normally, a person would have been pleased that so much red tape had been eliminated beforehand, but Beatrice was livid.

"That's *it*?" Beatrice fumed. "That's all I needed to *do*?"

"Yes, Madam, everything is now in order. Your account is fully functional."

"I was told this would take an hour. Do you take me for a fool?" She scolded. "Do you have any *idea* how much you have inconvenienced me?"

"Madam, please, I am sorry, but I do not understand *why* you are so unhappy."

She had reluctantly passed on an earlier return flight to Paris to allow ample time to satisfy the bank's regulatory requirements. Now, it seemed, taking a later flight had been unnecessary.

THE EARLIER RETURN flight Beatrice could have taken was now fully booked. So, she had an extra hour to kill on top of the three she already expected to have before she could board a flight back to Paris. Exiting the bank with all the venom of a scorpion, she walked directly over to the taxi stand. She cut to the front of the line, ignoring everyone else, and entered the lead cab, shouting "Chateau Bella Luna."

It had been well over a year since Beatrice had last visited the chateau owned by her husband and his two partners in crime. The British courts were still attempting to take control of the estate, however, the government of Montenegro was unwavering in its refusal to cooperate. It seemed that Anne's husband, Solicitor Richard More, had placed the property in a trust which included an unusual paragraph. The trust bequeathed perpetual first rights to the residents of the surrounding villages to work the fields and the harvests. The wording of that peculiar clause effectively *nationalized* the annual harvests which the government of Montenegro was unwilling to relinquish to a foreign country.

When the taxi approached the gated entrance to the estate, a rare smile appeared on Beatrice's face. "Pull close enough to the keypad so I don't have to get out." In a matter of minutes, the two metal gates swung inward with the familiar squeak that Beatrice knew all too well. The sound of the gates conjured up an image in her mind of entering a secret hideaway, a safe house, if you will. For reasons known only to Beatrice, she somehow believed Bella Luna was hidden from the outside world.

"Drive up to the chateau on the hill," she commanded.

When the taxi arrived at the intricate front entrance to the chateau, Beatrice stepped out of the cab. "Wait here," she said.

AT THAT VERY moment, a worker told the estate manager that a taxi had just arrived. The estate manager lived on the grounds of Chateau Bella Luna in a modest, but handsome, stone cottage which was only a short distance from the chateau. This same manager had overseen the annual harvests and cared for the property for the past forty-one years. Like everyone else in the village, he referred to the new owners as "*The Brits.*"

Now, his thoughts raced. *They did not tell me they were coming! I must hurry to gather the staff. We will need time to stock the pantry and ready the rooms. At least Manuel is here. He will help me ready the courtyard. I can always count on him.*

It had been over a year since the owners had been in residence. As the estate manager hurried up the drive, his thoughts drifted back to the night when a helicopter suddenly landed in the courtyard and the owners of Bella Luna had been forcibly taken away at gunpoint.

During the raid that night, the chateau had suffered some physical damage. It had taken several weeks before the necessary repairs to the entryway and the interior rooms had been completed.

As he approached the chateau, his mind sought answers. *Perhaps they have come to watch us harvest the olives, and see how we press the oil.* The estate had always generated a profit from the unique wines and rich olive oil that it produced.

Beatrice had long ago fallen in love with the chateau with its view of the Adriatic, the elegant gardens surrounding the courtyard, and the way she was pampered from the very first moment she set foot on the grounds. Whenever she had traveled to Bella Luna, it had been a joyous, carefree escape. Next to the loss of her husband, losing this retreat had been among her greatest disappointments in life.

Now, upon returning to the chateau, it seemed that nothing had changed. But the main reason she had come was to satisfy her curiosity about her husband's vague references to a stash of gold coins, supposedly stored in a vault beneath the building. It took her a while before she found the hidden door to the secret staircase which lead to the vault. Although she had no idea what the combination was, she was now at least satisfied that the vault existed, and that it seemed to have remained untouched.

By the time she returned to the main floor of the chateau, the estate manager was standing in the foyer. "Ah, Madam Hastings, it *is* you. I am surprised. I was not made aware that you would be coming. But that is no matter, it will only take a few hours to assemble the staff."

"There is no need for that, Alphonse, I am not staying."

The disappointment on Alphonse's face was noticeable. "That is unfortunate, Madam. Soon we will harvest the olives and press the oil. The villagers will come as they have every year. During the day, everyone works, but at night it is like a festival of joy, a carnival. There is happiness everywhere; even the children come."

Beatrice walked over to the window overlooking the pool and the piazza. She allowed her mind to momentarily drift back to happier times spent at Bella Luna. It wasn't until the clock in the foyer chimed that she was brought back to reality. "I need to go, but I will return soon," she said to Alphonse.

When she stepped back into the taxi, she said, "Take me to the airport."

FIFTEEN MILES OFF the coast of France, the ferry from Guernsey sailed into the main harbor on the island of Jersey. Throughout the journey, Jake and Lou had kept a close eye on Evelyn while maintaining their distance from one another. As they approached the landing on the Isle of Jersey, Evelyn was still excited that she had seen a couple of whales on the crossing. As she walked over to the gangway, there was a noticeable bounce in her step. She had absolutely no idea she was being followed by two expert trackers.

As soon as Evelyn disembarked, she went directly to the reserved ferry parking area. Jake followed at a safe distance and stood at the entrance to the parking lot with his head down. To any casual observer, Jake appeared to be completely focused on his smart phone. Lou had tried to convince the ferry boat captain to back into the landing, so he could exit first, that didn't happen. The best he was able to arrange, with the limited amount of cash he had with him, was that the line of vehicles he was in, would unload first.

As Evelyn pulled out of the lot, Jake used his cell phone to take pictures of both the front and back end of her vehicle. It wasn't long after he took the pictures, when Lou pulled up beside him.

"Did you get the make and model of the car?"

"Metallic bronze, four door KIA Cadenza sedan, license DBD3-81-946"

"Which way did she head?"

"Go straight, she's no more than six cars ahead of us."

EARLIER THAT DAY, Kate had been all ears when Evelyn was getting ready to leave. She had walked over to Anne to talk with her. "Anne, I have to go now. I'm going to take the ferry over to the other island. I need to check the drop site, but I'll be back in a couple of hours."

Anne shrugged her shoulders. "We'll be here. Beatrice said I'm not to leave the yard."

As soon as Evelyn walked out the door, Anne went into the bathroom and closed the door. Kate fingered the key in her pocket as she waited to hear the car back out of the yard. When she heard the car leave, she took the key out and undid the cuff holding her wrist and slipped out the back door.

Kate's only plan was to put as much distance as possible between herself and her kidnappers. Once outside, she raced across the rear of the house, down the short driveway, and turned right. Then, she put on a burst of speed and began running up the road as fast as her weakened state allowed.

Kate had always kept herself in excellent physical condition. She had alternated a strenuous exercise routine on even-numbered days with a grueling three-mile run along the forest trails at Havre de Poisson on odd days. But her days of captivity had taken their toll and she was pushing herself to an extreme on pure fear and adrenaline.

Her biggest concern was that Anne might walk to the end of the driveway and see her before she was out of sight.

It wasn't long before Kate was thoroughly winded and at risk of collapsing. She knew that if she remained on the road, she would be exposed. After passing dozens of shuttered homes, she opened a gate and snuck into a storage shed where she could safely rest, regain her breath and her energy.

THE CARS THAT were between Lou and the KIA were strung out, but he was staying as close as possible to the car directly in front of him. Evelyn was six cars in front. The oncoming traffic was heavy, that combined with the narrow road, hadn't given Lou any real opportunity to move forward in the line. It was Jake who first noticed the flashing red lights.

"We're coming to a railroad crossing Lou, and from the looks of the blinking lights, a train's coming."

"When we stop, I'm jumping the line and pulling in right behind her."

As soon as the line of cars in front came to a stop, Lou pulled out and drove to the front of the line.

"Where the hell is she? Where's the friggin KIA?"

Jake shifted in his seat as he tried to get a glimpse between the box cars as they passed by. "Maybe she made it across the tracks before the train came through."

"*No*, they can't be that friggin' lucky!"

Jake opened the passenger side door, saying, "Wait here."

"Where are you going?"

Without saying a word, Jake approached the first car in line and motioned for the driver to roll down his window. After flashing his badge, Jake said, "Were you behind a KIA?"

"I was, but they gunned it, and got across the tracks before the gates came all the way down."

When Jake got back in the car he simply said, "They made it across."

By the time the slow-moving freight had passed, Evelyn and the KIA were nowhere in sight.

As the gates lifted Jake turned to his cousin, "Lou, there's a luncheonette on the other side of the tracks. Let's get something to eat while we figure this out."

The palms of Lou's hands were red from pounding on the steering wheel. He pounded the wheel one more time. "Food! Is that all you ever friggin' think about?"

"Hey we left our half-eaten lunches back at the duck blind. You got a better idea?"

As they entered the luncheonette a burly-looking cook poked his head out from the kitchen. "We're about ready to shut down, boys, so make it snappy."

Lou slumped into his seat. As he raked his hand through his hair and down across the back of this neck, he looked at Jake. "I'm too pissed off to think about food; order for both of us." The emotional drain, the feeling of guilt and continual lack of sleep, were all taking a toll on Lou.

Long after the food was delivered, Lou sat there picking at his meal. "Jake, when you finish, tell this guy you'd like the check. I'll be outside. I need to give Duffy a call; he'll be looking for an update."

"Are you okay? You didn't eat much."

"Yeah, I'm okay; I'm just thinking about Kate."

"An empty sack can't stand up, cuz."

"I know that . . . I'm . . . I'm fine, I'm just tired of all this."

Lou found an isolated bench off to the side where he could have a conversation without being overheard. When Duffy picked up the call, his first words were: "Ah, so you *are* still alive."

"Hey Duffy, the phone rings on both ends, you know that, right? Besides, I'm not sleeping well, and I'm in a rotten mood; so, just know that."

Duffy ignored the pushback. "What do you have to report?"

"We rode over on the high-speed ferry with one of them, and we have a positive ID on the vehicle they're using in Jersey."

"I thought you were going to tail them."

"We were."

"You *were*? What does *that* mean?"

"Jake eyeballed her, but I got hung up getting the car off the damn ferry. We were a few cars back when we got nailed at a friggin' rail road crossing. Talk about a cluster..."

"Who was it that you followed?"

"It was one of them."

"Describe her."

"Average height, average build, talkative, sunglasses, pretty nondescript. Actually, she didn't seem all that bright to me; had a kind of childish obsession about whales. I don't see her as being the planner."

"Did she have large earlobes? Earlobes that seemed to be way out of proportion to the rest of her face?"

"No, not really."

"Then that was Evelyn Maxwell."

"Gimme a break! You can tell who she was from the size of her *earlobes*?"

"Yeah, the Brits tell me it's pretty simple really. For some reason, noticeably large earlobes is a physical trait that seems to consistently appear in the Yardley family tree. Maxwell's not a Yardley, so she'd have what's referred to as non-distinguishable ears.

"Yeah, well, just text me their mug shots and I'll make a positive ID."

"I don't really have mug shots, Lou, but I'll text you what we do have."

"Thanks."

"So, what's the plan now?"

"We're going to drive around Jersey until we find the KIA she was driving. Anything on your end to share?"

"There was a second charge to the credit card, this time in Paris."

"What the hell are they doing in Paris?"

"Seems it's only one of them. Whoever it is, flew to Paris, then took a flight to Montenegro."

"So, they've split up?"

"No, whoever it is booked a round trip."

By this time, Jake had joined Lou and had been listening. "Montenegro's a long way to go for milk and bread Duffy. Whaddya think they're up to?

"We're trying to figure all that out, Jake."

"It has to be connected to the bank account," Lou said.

"That's my guess too; we'll run it down. Montenegro would be an attractive option for them since it's somewhat of a rogue nation, especially when it comes to cooperating with the international community. The only time they seem to share information is when it benefits them."

"All right, you've got the story from this end. I'll let you know when I get another text message."

"Good enough. I've got enough going on over here to keep me busy, but I'm going to call the top cop in Jersey just to let him know you're over there."

"Is that necessary?"

"After what you two pulled in Guernsey, yeah!"

"That was a fluke."

"Oh, one last thing, Fran-O sends his best and told me to wish my lads, 'Godspeed.'"

Jake said, "Tell the old war horse we said, 'Thanks.'" To that, Lou added a few choice adjectives.

"I will, but not in those exact words; I still need to work with him."

As Lou put his phone away, he said, "Let's drive over to the Jersey's Police headquarters and check in."

"Yeah, a little professional courtesy will go a long way."

"I can't friggin believe you said that with a straight face, Jake."

"Hey, somebody's gotta look out for Duffy. We've got him broken in, no sense putting him at risk with 'the powers to be' back home. Hell, if Fletcher pulls him, we could end up with some damn desk jockey that wants to do everything by the book."

WHEN LOU AND Jake walked inside police headquarters, the desk sergeant looked up. "Can I help you?"

"We just got in from Guernsey and we're checking in. Name's Gault, Lou Gault, Royal Canadian Mounted Police."

"Just got word to expect you two. Step over here in front

of the laptop, so I can take your pictures, then you'll be good to go."

After snapping a couple of photos, the sergeant looked up, again. "That's all I needed, fellas. Here's a laptop. Go to our website and you can pull up a street map of the island. There's an option where you can set up a search grid. We'll let you know if anyone spots the KIA."

"Thanks."

"We're here to help. So, call in when you find them, and we'll provide you with all the backup you'd ever want."

As they walked back to their car, Jake said, "That was pretty easy, I didn't expect that."

"Yeah, kinda makes you wonder what Duffy had to give up in trade for that to happen."

"Yeah, he's a keeper."

Chapter Thirty-Six

WHEN ANNE EMERGED from the bathroom, it only took her a moment to realize the yellow chair was empty. Immediately a wave of panic swept over her. Trembling and confused, she ran through the house from room to room, looking under beds, behind doors, behind curtains, and in every closet hoping to find Kate.

Then, as if a switch went off inside her head, she bolted outside and ran around the house, twice. Then, she stopped and began tip-toeing, almost playfully, toward the outdoor storage shed.

When she reached the door of the wooden structure, she grabbed the latch, swung the door open and shouted, *"Aha!"*

There was no response. She knelt down to look underneath the furniture stacked neatly inside, nothing. Next, she stood on her tiptoes thinking Kate may have climbed on top of the furniture, nothing.

Again, like a switch went off in Anne's head, she left the

shed and ran back into the house. Once again, she checked every room, underneath every bed, behind every door, and inside every closet…no Kate.

I can't believe she left the house AND the yard, Anne thought, as she stood at the back door, shaking her head. *She was sitting right next to me when Beatrice told both of us we were not to leave the yard. She's going to be in a lot of trouble when Beatrice gets back.*

Then, for no apparent reason, Anne walked down to the edge of the canal, sat down on the pier and began humming a tune as she rocked back and forth. It was a comforting tune, one her father often whistled.

IT WAS AFTERNOON when Evelyn returned to the house in Jersey. When she entered through the back door and saw the empty yellow chair, her first thought was that Anne had taken their hostage to the toilet.

After hanging the car keys on the rack in the kitchen, she walked across the main part of the house toward her bedroom. It wasn't until she passed the bathroom that she realized no one else was in the house.

"Mother of Jesus! Where the hell *are* they?" Evelyn rushed outside yelling, "Anne, are you out here?"

No reply.

Anticipating the worst scenario, Evelyn walked over to the shed and hesitantly opened the door, expecting to find Anne's body inside. But, aside from furniture, the shed was empty.

Evelyn searched the yard with her eyes. At first she didn't see Anne. It wasn't until a couple of sea gulls attracted her attention that she saw Anne sitting alone down by the canal, next to a stack of grey weathered lobster traps.

Evelyn had a sinking feeling in her stomach as she walked over to Anne, somehow, either willingly, or unwittingly, Anne had set their hostage free. When she reached Anne, she grabbed her ahold of the shoulder.

"Anne, where *is* she?"

Anne mumbled something that Evelyn couldn't quite understand.

"*Anne*, snap out of it! Where *is* she?"

Again, Evelyn couldn't understand Anne's mumbling.

Evelyn decided to squat down so she was eye level with Anne and grabbed her friend by both shoulders. "Anne, *look* at me. Where *is* she?"

Anne turned her head "I don't know. I've looked everywhere. She *knew* we weren't supposed to leave the yard. She heard Beatrice say that."

Evelyn slapped her friend across the face. "Anne! Snap out of it. She didn't just leave the yard; she's *escaped*!"

Anne looked at Evelyn and suddenly scooted further backward from the edge of the canal. "I didn't do it! It's not my fault!"

Without saying another word, Evelyn ran back to the house and grabbed the car keys. As she backed the car out of the driveway, her mind was racing.

The bitch couldn't have gone far on foot. I didn't pass anyone walking when I drove in, so there's only one direction she could have gone.

But no sooner had she backed out of the yard, when she pulled back in, left the car running, and ran over to Anne.

"Give me the key to the handcuffs."

When Anne didn't immediately respond, Evelyn shouted, "I want the bloody *key!*"

Anne took the key out of her pocket while mumbling something about being punished. Evelyn ran back to the house, undid the cuff that was still attached to the yellow chair, put the key in her front pocket and stuffed the handcuffs under her belt. Then she jumped into the car, backed out of the yard and roared up the street.

KATE HID IN the neighbor's shed for few hours. She was paranoid about getting caught again, and exhausted from the burst of energy she had used to escape. It wasn't until she finally decided to move on, and rounded the last curve in the road that she found out Beach Haven West Boulevard ended in a Cul-de-sac. In the distance, beyond the circle a huge stone jetty extended out into the water, defining and protecting the harbor. The boulevard itself ended at the cement barriers placed in a half circle at the end of the road. Off to the right stood a marina; it's parking lot was a little over half full with empty boat trailers attached to the back of pickup trucks. To the left was an impenetrable marsh.

The distance from the house where Kate had been held captive to the end of the street was only three quarters of a mile, however, getting there had exhausted her.

When she saw the sign for the marina, Kate smiled thinking. *They'll have a phone. I'll end this nightmare now.*

To save herself a few steps, she cut across a section of grass that separated the road from the marina's parking lot. The trucks with the larger boat trailers had parked at odd angles, forcing her to weave back and forth as she headed toward the marina office.

Just as she reached the last row of vehicles, a car came screeching into the gravel parking lot, taking the turn on only two wheels. Kate's immediate instinct was to get low.

Evelyn came to a screeching stop in front of the office door. She jumped out, left the car running with the driver's door open, and raced into the office. In what seemed like no time at all, Evelyn was back in her car, had scrubbed out of the parking lot, and had the gas pedal buried as she traveled down Beach Haven West Boulevard.

Knowing that Evelyn was now on the prowl, Kate remained where she was, sitting on a boat trailer between two oversized trucks. Having been tricked by her captors the first time she escaped, she wasn't going to allow that to happen again. She waited in place for a good fifteen minutes, for no other reason than to see if Evelyn might come roaring back.

Without money, identification, or a cell phone, Kate had no plan beyond asking whoever was inside the office to call the police. When she regained her courage, she stood up and walked toward the office door. The first thing she noticed when she stepped onto the small porch, was a faded "Help Wanted" sign that covered close to half of the upper portion of the screen door. The sign had obviously been there for a while.

When she opened the screen door, the rusty hinges announced her presence.

The man sitting behind the old wooden desk glanced up and over a pair of black half rimmed reading glasses that rested on the bridge of his nose.

"What can I do for you ma'am?"

Kate took two steps forward, looked him straight in the eye, and then inexplicitly wavered.

"I need to . . ." She hesitated, baffled why the rest of the words weren't coming out.

She tried to speak a second time, but still couldn't finish her sentence.

The old man cleared his throat and set down the pencil he had in his hand. "I figured you'd show up sooner or later, after that other one came in here asking about you."

Kate's eyes widened and her confusion seemed to clear. "I don't know what you're talking about."

"Oh, I think you *do* know what I'm talking about. That other woman came in here asking about you; she told me to call her, if I saw you."

Kate froze, thinking, *Can I trust this old man to help me, or will he just call Evelyn?*

"Are you the one she's looking for?"

"No. I'm, I'm looking for work . . . that's why I'm here. I need a job."

The old man smiled. "What *kind* a' work are you looking for?"

Kate hesitated, her eyes scanned the man's desk looking for a phone. "I saw the sign out front."

"Any experience working on a *boat*?" His smile showed a perfect set of pearly whites.

Kate still wasn't sure whether she could trust him. "Some . . . I like to fish, and I'm a quick learner."

The old man slanted his head as he looked Kate up and down. Her hair was unkempt, her clothes looked expensive, but they were soiled and rumbled. Her skin was too pale for her to be a homeless person, and she had a look of desperation in her eyes.

"You running from the law?"

"No, sir."

"You running from your *husband*?"

"No, sir."

"Working on a boat ain't easy."

"I'm not afraid of hard work."

"Maybe not, but you're damn sure afraid of that other woman who came in here earlier, aren't you?"

Without hesitating, Kate answered. "Yes, I suppose I am."

"Figured that. So, get yourself in the closet behind me."

"Why?"

"Just do as I say. That other woman is back in the parking lot. Go on now, do as I *say!*"

Kate moved quickly and closed the closet door just as Evelyn came storming back into the office.

"Are you *sure*, you haven't seen the woman I told you about?"

The old man looked up. "*You* again, huh?"

"Have you seen that woman, the one I was talking about?" she demanded. "She *had* to come this way. Did you see her in the parking lot?"

"Missy, I got a number of things I have to do around here, but paying attention to who's coming and going in the parking lot sure as hell ain't one of 'em."

Evelyn walked over to the wooden desk and stared down at him. "Listen, if you see that woman, I want you to *call* me. I'll make it worth your while. Here, here's a fifty-pound note. If you see her, and you *call* me, I'll make that two *hundred* pounds. Do you have my number?"

The old gent looked Evelyn square in the eye. "I've got *your* number."

"Good."

The old man waited until he saw Evelyn pull out of the

parking lot before calling out. "You can come out now, missy; that other one's gone."

Kate stepped out of the closet and walked over to the window overlooking the parking lot.

"I said she was gone."

Kate let out a sigh. "Can I use your phone?"

"Ain't got one."

"You don't have a *phone*?"

"Nope, used to have one, right over there on the wall in the corner. You can see the outline where it was. Folks used to wait in line to use it. Some of 'em fed coins into that thing like it was a damn slot machine. Hell, there was a time, I thought about getting a second phone, but then everybody switched to carrying cell phones."

Kate looked behind her and saw the outline on the wall where the pay phone had once been.

"One day, I heard that phone ringing. It'd never done that before. It was some young fella from the phone company calling to tell me he was going to start charging me a *convenience* fee, that's what he called it, for the privilege of having his phone on my wall."

Kate tried, again. "Can I use your cell phone? It's a local call."

"Ain't got one."

The old gent began to chuckle. "I told that young fella he could come over at *his* convenience and take that damn thing out before *I* started charging *him* a convenience fee! Took 'em a while, but they got around to it; fella that took it out said that's all he'd been doing . . . taking out pay phones."

Kate stared at the old man in disbelief before saying, "You don't have a cell phone either?"

"I don't."

"So, if you don't have a phone, how do people charter boats?"

"They call the skippers. Every damn one of 'em has a cell phone! They all work for themselves; hell, all I do is rent 'em dock space, sell 'em gas, and charge 'em for the fresh water and electricity they use."

"But when she asked you to call her, you just said you would."

"I did not."

"You *did*, I heard you."

"No. What she *asked* me was if I had her number."

Kate noticed a slight twinkle in the old gent's blue eyes. "What I said to her was that *I had her number*, and I do! Missy, I've run across a few of her kind along the way."

Kate smiled. "May I *please* use your cell phone?"

"I already told you, I ain't got one."

"You really don't have a cell phone?"

"Don't need one."

The old gent's simple approach to life reminded Kate of Lou.

"You still interested in that job?"

Now knowing that every boat captain carried a cell phone, she answered, "Yes, I am."

The old man smiled. "Well, go down and see the skipper of the *Knot on Call*."

"Where is he?

"Boats are feminine ma'am. *She's* tied up down on pier four, third boat in; you can't miss her, it's the worst looking of the lot down there."

"Are any other boats looking for help?"

"*The Dirty Oar* was short a deck hand this morning 'fore they shoved off."

"Are they coming back soon?"

"Not likely. They caught the early tide and went out with the rest of 'em this morning. There's a big fishing tournament off the coast of Scotland. They'll be up there chasing salmon around the lochs for a while. I don't expect them back for four, maybe five days, now. Go on down to the *Knot on Call*."

Kate walked over to the desk, leaned over, and gave the old gent a kiss on the forehead.

"What was that for?"

"For hiding me."

As she turned to walk toward the back door, the old gent yelled out. "Hold it right there!"

Kate wasn't sure what was about to happen. As she turned around, the old man tossed her a sweatshirt.

"It gets chilly out there. You can turn it inside out if you don't like the advertising on it."

Kate held the garment out at arm's length, on the back, stenciled in large letters, were the words, "Bud's Marina."

"Are you Bud?"

"I am."

"Thanks, Bud. I love it."

Chapter Thirty-Seven

A S SOON AS Kate pulled the sweatshirt over her head and walked out the back door, the sights, sounds, and smells of the harbor welcomed her into an entirely different world. Off to the left, the sky was filled with approaching storm clouds. The sea beyond the break wall was a blanket of whitecaps. The waves crashing against the seaward side of the jetty were sending sprays of white foam up into the air. Yet, for the moment, inside the harbor was entirely calm.

As she walked along the path toward the dock, she sensed the colder weather and felt bits of rain in the wind. Directly across from the marina was the upscale Flying Bridge Restaurant. Most days, at this hour there wouldn't have been an empty table on the deck; but today, the umbrellas were tied down and seat cushions taken in. Other than the sound of small boats coming in and the ever-present gulls squawking among themselves in the wind, the harbor was quiet.

Only three boats were tied up at Bud's Marina, and they were all in slips at the far end of pier four. Even from a distance, she could tell they each had seen better days. The first in line was a large center console named *Reel Fisherman*. Next, was a blue water yacht named *Atsa My Boat*. A small Italian flag fluttered from the stern. Last in the row, sat the *Knot on Call*.

Bud wasn't kidding when he said it was the worst looking of the lot, she thought.

The boat stood tall in the water. In its heyday, it would have been considered the flag ship in many harbors. Although she looked seaworthy, whoever owned her now had fallen behind with the routine maintenance every boat required. The hull needed to be scraped and painted. There was a thick growth of algae visible at the waterline which swayed back and forth as the waves lapped up against the hull. What originally would have been bright work, had been painted over; the sun and constant exposure to the salt air had clouded the plexiglass windows to the point they were opaque. The cleats on the gunwales had oxidized, and the lettering on the stern was beginning to peel at the edges.

On the positive side, the bilge was running and pushing out a steady stream of water. A sign nailed to the piling next to the boat read: *Knot on Call*, Captain Sam T. Barber, Full day or Half. A phone number was listed.

Well, at least he has a cell phone, she thought as she walked down to midship, stopping where a ladder hung over the gunwale.

"Ahoy, *Knot on Call*!"

There was no acknowledgement.

"Hello! Captain of the *Knot on Call*."

The wind was stronger out on the dock, so Kate cupped her hands around her mouth and yelled: "Hello in the boat!"

Still no answer.

She looked around; the only sound was the whistling of the wind, the lapping of water against the hull, the gulls, and a bell from a buoy anchored at the entrance to the harbor. Suddenly, she felt very alone as a shiver ran through her.

Then she noticed what seemed to be a light on inside the boat's salon. She decided to board the vessel, expecting that any moment someone would appear. As she stepped onto the main deck, a piece of paper taped to the cabin door caught her attention.

The cryptic handwritten note merely said: *Back on Friday - Sam.*

She stared at the note wondering what day of the week it was. Just then, the wind picked up and large droplets of rain began to splatter the deck. Kate pressed herself underneath the narrow overhang attempting to stay dry. But when the full fury of the storm hit, she tried the handle and the hatchway opened.

"Hello?" she called inside. "Anyone here?"

Silence.

Nobody's home, she thought, *well, at least I'll be dry and I have a place to ride out the storm,.*

The salon was rather spacious; the seat cushions were somewhat worn and bleached from the sun; other than that, it was clean and devoid of clutter. She turned and noticed the galley, just below on the port side.

Kate hadn't eaten anything since dinner the night before and her stomach had been growling for a while. When she entered the galley, she thought, *well it certainly looks well used, but at least it's clean.*

When she opened the small refrigerator, the only thing she saw was a carton of eggs, half a loaf of bread, and a jar of something. Rummaging through a few cabinets, she found a tea kettle and a frying pan. Once she got the hang of the marine faucet, she filled the tea kettle, lit a burner, and began looking for a toaster. While she was waiting for the water to boil, she reached into the refrigerator and took out the jar. To her surprise it was a jar of lemon curd, one of the few things she truly missed since she had left Ireland.

Her thoughts roamed to the fishing lodge where Chef Angelo would occasionally include an ample number of lemons in his weekly replenishment order, and create a batch of the rich curd exclusively for her. The delicacy was a breakfast staple she had grown up enjoying every morning, spread over warm, freshly baked scones.

Outside, the storm was picking up. The boat actually began to rock and more than once, Kate felt the need to grab hold of the counter. The sensation caused her to feel a flutter in her stomach and she began to feel queasy. When she heard the rain pelting against the deck, she instinctively looked at a porthole. *It's coming down heavy now*, she thought. Then, as if to validate her, there was a flash of lightning, followed by a rolling clap of thunder.

As the dark clouds moved in, the defused lighting which had been coming in through the opaque portholes abruptly went out, as if someone had turned off a lamp. Being unfamiliar with the ship, it took time before Kate found the interior light switches. Once she had sufficient light again, she explored the forward sleeping quarters.

There were three staterooms on board, one on either side and another in the bow. The stateroom on the port side was the largest; it was obvious someone was living there. The one on the starboard side was filled with boxes. The forward stateroom wasn't quite as large as the others, but it was empty, and after testing the mattress, she found it far more comfortable than the rollaway she'd been sleeping on. When Kate, heard the tea pot whistling, she returned to the galley.

Outside, the lines securing the boat to the dock weren't as tight as they should have been, given the weather conditions. As Kate sat at the table eating, she was jolted several times as heavy winds slammed the hull up against the dock on the starboard side. Off and on, she could hear a faint crackling noise which sounded like static from a radio.

After finishing her simple meal, she decided to brave the elements and climbed the ladder leading to the bridge. As soon as her head cleared the deck, she smiled. Mounted to the dash among a number of other instruments, just to the side of the ship's wheel, was a maritime weather radio. She reach over and turned the volume up just in time to catch the tail end of a broadcast.

"…especially in the Channel Islands and the coastal regions of west Normandy."

Familiar enough with weather radios, Kate knew that warnings were continuously broadcast and updated on the hour. She sat back in the captain's chair waiting for the report to cycle back.

"This is a message from the Channel Maritime Alert System for Thursday, October 25th. A severe storm warning has been issued for the north coastal regions of Brittany, The Channel Islands, Normandy, and surrounding coastal areas. A small craft advisory is in effect. Gale force wind conditions are expected for the next five to seven hours. Winds in excess of eighty kilometers, gusting to over one hundred. Seas six to eight feet above normal with potential storm surges at high tide. Possible flooding in low lying areas,

especially in the Channel Islands and the coastal areas of west Normandy."

Kate pursed her lips. She had learned two important things: a major storm was approaching, and today was Thursday, October 25th.

While she waited for the storm report to repeat again, she scanned the bridge looking for an electronic device with a microphone. Then she saw the empty docking station mounted to the roof truss directly over the ship's wheel. *Hmmm, the owner must have taken the ship-to-shore radio with him.*

Disappointed, Kate returned below deck and prepared herself for the long night that lay ahead. She had some knowledge of small boats and knew the bilge pump worked off either a battery or electricity. She wasn't sure if the boat was connected to an electrical line, or if the pump was working off the battery. In any event, before she settled in for the night, she made sure everything but the bilge pump was off.

During the night, the howling winds woke her twice; each time, she made the sign of the cross, as thoughts of the banshee crossed her mind.

Chapter Thirty-Eight

BEATRICE LEFT CHATEAU Bella Luna early enough to avoid late afternoon traffic that often clogged the streets of Montenegro, and arrived at the airport with ample time to board her flight to Paris.

There, she was detained in Customs only a short time before pre-boarding her flight to the isle of Jersey. When the flight attendant advised passengers that there would be a thirty-minute weather delay before take-off from Paris, Beatrice plugged her cell phone into the receptacle under her seat and drafted a text message to Lou containing the account details she had established with the bank in Montenegro.

After double-checking the numbers of her new account, she keyed in Lou Gault's phone number, pressed the send key, and turned off her cell phone. Once she adjusted her seat belt, she put on her sleep mask and settled back, hoping to enjoy a little uninterrupted shuteye.

BEATRICE WOKE WITH a start when she sensed the plane was rapidly losing altitude. Moments later, she heard the pilot announce: "Flight crew, please prepare for landing."

Once the plane was on the ground, the flight attendant picked up the intercom and announced: "Welcome to *Saint Malo*, France. Local time is two-fifteen a.m. Thank you for flying British Airways. We look forward to serving you on your next trip."

Beatrice immediately reached up and slammed her fist into the call button above her seat. The attendant made eye contact with Beatrice and motioned that she'd be there shortly.

Before the attendant could turn off the call button above her head, Beatrice snarled, "Saint Malo! Why we are still in *France*?"

Slightly taken aback by Beatrice's abruptness, the attendant put on her best smile and politely responded, "We were diverted to Saint Malo."

"Well, I'd like to know *why*." Beatrice said with pursed lips, obviously annoyed.

"It's weather-related, madam. Jersey closed its airport after we were in flight. The captain made an announcement, but you must have been asleep. If you have any checked luggage, it will be at carousel three." With that, the attendant turned her back to Beatrice and walked back down the aisle.

Furious with the unexpected delay, Beatrice whipped out her phone; her fingers raced violently across the small key pad as she crafted a text: *Evelyn, my return delayed due 2 weather*. As soon as the symbol indicating the message was being sent displayed at the bottom of the message, she exited the phone app.

What she didn't see was the second message: *Undeliverable . . . please check the number and try again.*

For the next few hours, Beatrice was on her cell phone hellbent on finding alternate transportation to Jersey.

BACK ON THE ISLAND of Jersey, Evelyn repeatedly drove up and down Beach Haven West Boulevard looking for Kate.

The bitch is hiding in someone's yard. She's waiting for nightfall, Evelyn thought. *Ha, you think you're clever, but you're not clever enough. I'll find you, bitch!* She didn't really notice the dark clouds overhead.

When the full force of the storm hit, Evelyn made two final runs up and down the street before finally packing it in.

In the short time it took Evelyn to run from the car to the house, she was drenched. Once inside, she walked directly into the bathroom, grabbed a towel, and began drying her hair. When she came out, she noticed Anne sitting in the yellow chair, "Anne, did you make anything for us to eat?"

There was no reply. However, at the sound of her voice, Anne got up and began setting up the rollaway bed.

"Anne, what in heaven's name, are you doing?"

"I'm getting the bed ready."

"For *who?*"

"For her."

"Anne, she's not here. She's gone."

"No, she's not . . .she's here; she's in the bathroom, I just saw her go in."

That was the point at which Evelyn finally understood something deep inside Anne had snapped. Dreading the inevitable confrontation that she knew would occur as soon as Beatrice returned, Evelyn went into her bedroom, sat down on the bed, opened the envelope she had retrieved from the drop site and read the contents to herself.

On the day the hostage is to be released, one half million pounds will be wired into your account as a show of good faith. When we receive a text with a photo of the hostage standing on the steps of the police station in Jersey, unassisted, we will release an additional one and a half million. Once the police confirm the hostage's identity, the balance of your demands will be wired.

Evelyn folded the letter up and put it back inside the envelope. *All we've been through, and now we'll end up walking away with nothing. I can't even go back to the miserable life we've been living.*

The thought of how Beatrice would receive this news was unsettling.

Well, Beatrice, when you get back here, you'll find out soon enough that we have nothing to trade.

Evelyn's thoughts were interrupted when she heard what sounded like a child's voice coming from the living area. She walked over to her bedroom doorway and looked out. Anne was rocking back and forth in the yellow chair, singing something that sounded like gibberish..

NOT LONG AFTER the storm hit, the desk sergeant at police headquarters reached out to Lou and Jake, directing them to shelter at the island's main fire station until the storm passed.

The morning after, Lou was up early. He waited until just after five a.m. before calling Duffy.

"Morning, Lou."

"They sent me a text with the bank information. I'll forward it."

"Any word on the hostage exchange message you left for them?"

"Not yet, but that may be weather-related. One helluva storm went barreling through here last night."

"I heard. There's actually a question whether the one who traveled over to Montenegro made it back to Jersey."

"Jake heard both Jersey and Guernsey closed their airports."

"Yeah, we're checking on whether the flight from Paris even got off the ground. So, what's your next step?"

"We're just gonna continue patrolling the streets; that KIA is here somewhere. Everything else is on hold until I hear back on the money exchange."

"Expect a text saying they want more upfront money."

"Is there any way you can trace their GPS from a text?"

"I asked Fran-O about that. He said he'd have one of his lads check into that. Meanwhile, what kind of back up do you have?"

"We don't."

"Lou, they've given us the slip too many times; you need backup."

"Duffy, I'm sure the cops here are nice guys, but they're not trained in hostage rescue situations."

"Well, for that matter, neither are you."

Lou paused to let that sink in. "Yeah, but we're trackers."

"I hope so."

"So, what's the deal with the wire transfer?"

"We've got the plan all worked out. We've tested it locally and it's set to go."

"Are we gonna test it with the kidnappers' account?"

"Wouldn't hurt."

"When I hear back from them, I'll let them know we're

going to test the wire transfer, just to make sure it works. How much do you wanna play around with?"

"It's a test, doesn't friggin matter, go with a nominal amount."

"Got it."

MEANWHILE, AT THE far end of the island, Kate was awake. She sat on the edge of the bunk in the forward birth, both hands gripping the rail that kept the mattress in place, her head was bent over and her legs were dangling over the side.

Between the wind howling and the constant jolts every time the boat slammed up against the dock, she hadn't slept well; now she was groggy. To truly understand if the grogginess was sleep related or lingering effects from the drug Beatrice had forced upon her, would have required lab tests.

She shook her head, trying to clear the cobwebs and regain her focus. When she finally got up, she headed straight toward the galley. The first thing she heard was the bilge pump. She let out a sigh of relief, realizing the boat still had power.

After pumping fresh water into the tea kettle and turning on a burner, Kate, sat down at the table. When she went to pull a napkin out of its holder, she noticed a colorful brochure. She picked it up thinking she'd learn a little about the *Knot on Call.*

Instead of being about the *Knot on Call,* the brochure was a promotional piece for a two-day jazz festival held in Saint Malo's *Parc de Bel Air.* Inside the brochure was a list of featured musicians and the dates they would be performing.

Someone had circled seven performances. Three of them were on day one; four were on day two of the event, which was a Thursday.

Hmmm, Kate thought, *the note on the door said whoever this Sam is, he'd be back on Friday . . . today.*

As soon as Kate finished fixing her tea, she decided to go topside to get a look at whatever damage the storm may have caused. The boat itself looked none the worst, but the harbor was filled with shredded seaweed and other floating debris. Across the harbor, the restaurant was missing a few shingles, but other than a bright red dingy aimlessly adrift in the harbor, everything else seemed to have made it through the storm.

The conundrum Kate now faced was whether to remain aboard the *Knot on Call,* or strike out and try to find someone with a phone to finally call the police. The only concern she had about leaving the safety of the boat was the fear of falling into the hands of her kidnappers once again.

SAM T. BARBER, skipper of the *Knot on Call,* considered himself to be a jazz aficionado. At least three times a year, he traveled to festivals on the mainland and had amassed an extensive collection of jazz recordings, which he constantly listened to on the sophisticated speaker system he had onboard his boat.

Sam hadn't always been a jazz fan, he'd grown up loving heavy metal. It wasn't until he was diagnosed with chronic back pain, totally brought on by stress, that his physician encouraged him to listen to jazz as a way to unwind. In short order, smooth jazz proved to be the cure-all he needed to truly relax, once that happened, he was hooked for life.

On this particular morning, Sam was sitting in the Saint Malo ferry station, coffee in hand, reading the newspaper, waiting to board the ferry back to Jersey. For the past two days, he had left the world behind and mellowed out, listening to some of Europe's finest jazz musicians.

Being semi-retired, Sam didn't feel any urgency to return to the isle of Jersey. Like his competitors, his charter boat business pretty much ended when the tourists went home. Yet, he was a creature of habit and had awakened early, intent on making the first crossing.

It came as no surprise to Sam that there was only one other soul waiting for the ferry when he arrived at the terminal. The early crossing was predominantly used by commercial traffic. On the other hand, the late afternoon ferry was just the opposite. It was always jammed with foot passengers and personal vehicles returning to Jersey after having spent the day visiting the monastery known as *Mont Saint-Michel*.

When he left Jersey for the music concert, Sam had purchased a round trip ticket. Upon entering the terminal, he went directly over to the waiting area and sat down on one of the uncomfortable wooden benches.

Shortly after Sam arrived, a mother with two young children entered the terminal, purchased tickets, and also sat down.

At precisely ten minutes before the ferry was set sail, a man dressed in a light grey uniform with burgundy piping and a colorful shoulder patch, exited the door adjacent to the ticket window. He walked directly over to the gate, and changed the signage over the door to read: *Embarquement Immediat.* Then, he announced in an authoritative voice: *"Jersey traversier."*

By the time Sam folded his newspaper and stood up, the mother and her two children were already moving toward the gate. As he walked past the lone woman who had arrived at the terminal before him, it appeared she was asleep.

Sam stopped, and cleared his throat. "Excuse please, are you traveling to Jersey?"

The woman sat up a little straighter and opened her eyes.

When she didn't respond, he repeated himself, "Are you traveling to Jersey?"

After a pause, the woman replied, "Yes. . . I am."

"Then you'd best come along; we're boarding now."

With that, Sam walked toward the gate and Beatrice Yardley Hastings stood up, grabbed her carry-on luggage, and sluggishly followed behind him.

Chapter Thirty-Nine

T HE PASSENGER LOUNGE onboard the ferry was everything one would expect it to be on a no-frills commuter carrier. There were rows of blue plastic contoured seats bolted to the deck, theatre style. Next to the windows on either side were booths. The concession stand consisted of several vending machines, none of which looked like they had been cleaned in years.

Sam took a booth on the port side, mainly so he could spread his newspaper out. The mother and her children chose seats near the hatchway leading out to the observation deck. The lone woman selected a booth on the starboard side and from her posture, obviously intended to sleep.

The two children who boarded with their mother were typical kids. They amused themselves by constantly going in and out of the hatchway to the open deck, chasing each other around the rows of chairs, and otherwise just being kids.

About half way through the ninety-minute crossing, Sam finished reading his paper, got up, tossed his paper in the trash receptacle, and stepped out onto the observation deck. He was surprised to see the lone woman who had been in the terminal standing against the rail.

Sam stopped about six feet from her, rested his forearms on the rail and took in the seascape before him. The blue-green water was calm in the aftermath of the storm. Without turning to the woman on his right he said: "Beautiful day for a cruise, wouldn't you say?"

The woman paused and looked at him. "I thought I saw a spout a moment ago."

"You very well may have; most of them are migrating to warmer waters this time of year, but there's still a few out there."

"Oh, look! There's another spout!" She sounded excited.

"That's a Fin Whale. They're commonly mistaken for Humpbacks."

"How can you tell?"

"By the shape of the spout."

The woman looked at Sam for a moment. "Really?"

"Absolutely. Every species of whale has a different size blow hole, and that's what defines the shape of the spout."

The woman didn't respond.

After a pause Sam continued, "Fin whales are pretty social; if there's one out there, there could be as many as a half dozen more."

"Why, there's another."

"You'll only see two types of whales in these waters now, the Fin and the Sperm."

"Sperm is such a vile name for a whale."

"They're named after the waxy substance in their heads; it's called 'spermaceti.' Back in the day, it was used in lamps, and as a lubricant. They even made candles out of it."

Beatrice turned slightly toward her fellow passenger. "You seem to know a lot about fish."

"Well, a whale is *not* a fish. But I run a sport fishing boat out of Jersey."

Beatrice snorted before saying, "Really? You own a boat and you're taking a ferry?"

"I needed to have a little fun."

"I don't find this ferry the least bit fun."

Sam ignored the caustic remark. "I wasn't referring to the ferry; this is my time of year to have fun."

After a lengthy pause, Beatrice said, "I thought fishing was supposed to be fun."

"It is, but I charter out my boat, and the season's over now."

After another pause, Beatrice continued. "Is your boat very large?"

"It's a sixty-five-foot sport fisherman."

"Is that large enough to cross the English Channel?"

Surprised that the woman suddenly seemed interested in having a conversation, Sam answered. "It most certainly is. I've made that trip more than a few times. She rides high in the water, so it's an easy crossing, as long as you stay in the shipping lanes."

"Interesting,"

With that Beatrice stepped away from the rail. "I'm going in; it's far too windy out here for me."

BACK ON THE ISLAND OF JERSEY, Kate spent most of the morning sitting in the galley, drinking tea, reading the ship's log, killing time, waiting for this fellow 'Sam' to return.

She had a headache and her stomach felt queasy after

eating a minimal breakfast. When she tired of sitting in the galley, she climbed up the ladder to the bridge, if for no other reason than for a change of scenery. The opaqueness of the windows below had diffused the light to such an extent that it wasn't until she went topside that she realized how bright it was outside. The sudden light seemed to intensify her headache and she instinctively reached for a pair of sunglasses hanging directly above the wheel on the bridge.

As soon as she put the polarizing lenses on, she saw a couple of people fishing along the jetty. Then it clicked. *Those fishermen are bound to have cell phones.* The Jetty looked to be only about a half mile from the boat and the shoreline looked like she could walk along the water's edge without being seen from the road.

Without hesitating, Kate backed down the ladder, grabbed the sweatshirt Bud had given her and donned one of the baseball hats hanging next to the hatchway.

FOUR MILES SOUTHEAST of where Kate was making her way along the shoreline, the ferry from Saint Malo was pulling into the landing on Jersey. Foot passengers were allowed to disembark as soon as the gangway was lowered, and today was no exception.

Beatrice had attempted to reach Evelyn several times while in Saint Malo, but to no avail. She knew there wouldn't be any cell service once she was out to sea, and had been resigned to wait and call Evelyn once she had returned to the island. But now, even though she was ashore and standing at the taxi stand on the isle of Jersey, she still was unable to get through to Evelyn.

Sam had left his jeep at the parking lot earlier. When he

saw his fellow passenger standing at the taxi stand, he pulled over. "If you get in. I'll give you a lift."

"No, thank you."

"You'll wait here all day for a taxi."

Beatrice let out a sigh before reluctantly, getting into Sam's vehicle.

"Where to?"

"I'm staying on Beach Haven West Boulevard."

"Ha, that's the street *I'm* on. What's your name?"

After a brief hesitation, she responded, "Beatrice. And you are. . . ?"

"Sam. Sam T. Barber."

"I had the impression you might have lived on a boat."

"That I do. I have a slip at the marina at the far end of the boulevard."

"You're a Yank, aren't you?"

"Did my accent give me away?"

"Yes. Why are you here on Jersey?"

"I came here for the water."

Beatrice paused before saying, "There's nothing special about the water here."

Sam smiled. She had played right into his hand, and responded: "I guess, I was misinformed." The classic movie Casablanca, was one of Sam's favorites and he loved setting up the conversation so he could use one of Bogart's famous lines. Beatrice didn't connect the dots, and continued looking straight ahead.

The island was small and it wasn't long before Sam turned onto Beach Haven West Boulevard.

"What number?"

"I don't recall; it's a yellow house, single story. The whole yard is covered with stone."

"Ah, I know the one; it's just a little further on."

As they continued down the street, Beatrice turned to Sam. "I'd love to see your boat."

"Well, then we'll swing down there before I drop you off."

As Sam passed the house Beatrice had rented, he pointed to it. "Is that the place you're at?"

"Yes."

"Thought so. The marina's just up the road."

WHEN KATE REACHED the base of the jetty, she was surprised at how massive it actually was. From a distance, the rocks hadn't looked so large, but up close, they were humongous blocks of granite. Kate decided the easier route to the top from the shoreline was to scale the grass embankment.

It did prove to be the easier path, but along the way, Kate slipped a few times on the wet grass and ended up with serious green stains on both knees.

Once on top, Kate boldly walked up to the first fisherman on the jetty. "Sir, do you have a cell phone?"

"It's back in the truck."

"Is it far? Could you get it? I need to make a call."

The man looked at her. "Not now, honey, the fish are coming in."

"Seriously?"

When the man didn't respond, Kate walked about twenty yards down the jetty to the only other fisherman on the jetty. "Sir, do you have a cell phone with you?"

"I do."

"Can I borrow it? I need to make one quick local call."

"I wish you could."

Kate didn't quite understand what the man was saying, so she rephrased her question. "May I *please* use your phone to make a call?"

"It's not working; the cell towers are all down, the storm knocked 'em out."

Kate closed her eyes and took a deep breath. "Any idea when they'll be up?"

"Nope, no way of telling. The crews have to come over from England."

"Can you drive me to the police station?"

"Not now, girl, the fish are running."

"Please? I need your help."

In between reeling in his line and making another cast, the fisherman glanced at the disheveled grass-stained woman standing next to him. "Hey, go bother somebody else, will ya."

"Please, I really need your help."

The man stepped away from Kate saying, "Go away, I came here to fish."

When Kate heard that response, her shoulders slumped and a wave of frustration flowed over her. Whatever hopes she had of being rescued were dashed. As she retraced her steps along the jetty, she looked over at Beach Haven West Boulevard.

I wonder if any of the houses along the canal might have landlines, she thought. Yet, the more she pondered it, the more she realized that whatever phone service the seasonal houses would have was probably suspended.

When she stepped off the jetty, she followed the path to the parking area and leaned against the railings that defined the lot. Kate was more than a little surprise at how often not getting caught, versus being rescued was foremost among her thoughts.

I have two options, she thought. *I can wait here and hope I can catch a ride with one of these fishermen, or I can take charge and go over to the marina and see if Bud has a car.*

When it didn't appear that either of the fishermen were about to call it a day, Kate stood up and headed toward the marina. It was a short walk across the overgrown field separating the jetty from the marina's parking lot.

At the exact moment Kate was about to step up onto the wooden landing and enter the marina's office, a jeep came careening into the parking lot and pulled up to the front door. Time seemed to stand still as Kate watched a man exit the jeep and speak to someone in the passenger's seat.

"Come on, we'll go in through the office," she heard him say. "My boat's tied up on the other side."

With that, Beatrice Hastings stepped out of the passenger side of the jeep and locked eyes with Kate O'Grady.

Chapter Forty

KATE STOOD FROZEN in place. She couldn't believe her eyes. What were the odds that her second chance at freedom would end exactly the way her first escape had?

Beatrice was less than ten feet away from Kate when she stepped out of the jeep and looked directly at her; yet, arrogance prevented Beatrice from recognizing the person standing before her. She saw what she wanted to see, a homeless person looking for a handout and thought, *even Jersey has to deal with these wretched beggars.*

The baseball cap, sweatshirt, sunglasses, and Beatrice's own self-centeredness combined with a personal distain for the less fortunate, prevented her from seeing the reality of who was standing before her.

On the other hand, Sam gave Kate a closer look as he walked around the front of his jeep. It struck him that the hat and the sunglasses were quite similar to ones that he owned.

If Beatrice had a longer look at Kate, things may have

turned out differently. But when Sam opened the door to the marina, his body completely blocked Kate from Beatrice's view.

"After you, ma'am. We'll go straight through and exit out the back." With that, Beatrice stepped across the threshold, oblivious to the fact that she had been within arm's reach of her escaped hostage.

Once Beatrice entered the building, Kate backed away from the doorway and looked for a place to hide. The parking lot was empty. The only possibility she saw was the dumpster next to the building.

Inside, the old gent sitting at the desk looked up as Sam and Beatrice entered the building. "How was the festival Sam?"

"Fine, Bud, we'll talk later,"

When Sam reached the rear door he opened it, saying, "Here we go, ma'am, step right out. My boat's the last one down there on pier four."

Upon seeing the *Knot on Call*, Beatrice raised her eyebrows. "Is it seaworthy?"

"She may need a little TLC on the outside, but she'll get you across the channel."

"What would you charge?"

"This time of year? I'd do a channel trip for three thousand pounds."

"Do you take credit cards?"

"I do."

Nodding her head, Beatrice replied, "I'll think about it. How much notice do you require?"

"If I'm not committed, I can be ready to set sail in as little as two hours."

"Do you have a business card?"

Sam opened his wallet and pulled out a card.

"Thank you. I've seen all I needed to see. Now, if you'll be so kind, you can drive me back to where I'm staying?"

"Let's go."

As Sam walked past Bud, he winked. "Be right back."

WHEN KATE HAD come face to face with Beatrice so unexpectedly, it had rattled her to such an extent that she inexplicably lost her ability to process what was happening. Now that Beatrice was inside the building, Kate hunkered down, hidden behind the dumpster.

Kate had no idea who the man with Beatrice was, her first thought was that Beatrice had hired a private investigator to find her. Now, she closed her eyes and her thoughts raced in several directions as she pressed up against the back side of the metal garbage bin. But only one of her thoughts was encouraging. *I know Lou will come for me,* she thought. *But he won't find me unless I leave him clues.*

When Kate heard the screen door open and close a second time, her body stiffened and she pressed herself against the back side of the dumpster even harder.

One side-effect of the drug Beatrice had forced upon Kate was temporary paranoia. Oddly enough, pharmaceutical trials had shown it to only show up once the drug was no longer being administered.

They weren't in the office very long, she thought, *but long enough to up the ante with Bud. That has to be why they came here.* She closed her eyes. *This marina is no longer safe for me.*

Even after hearing the jeep leave the parking lot, Kate continued to remain hidden, pressing herself against the dumpster. Not even five minutes later, she heard the sound of a vehicle entering the parking lot and come to a stop near the door. Once she heard the office door open and close again, she edged around the corner of the dumpster to see if it was the kidnapper's car. It wasn't, it was the same jeep Beatrice had been in.

When ten minutes passed, and no one came out of the office, her instincts told her it was time to put some distance between herself and the marina.

She glanced at the *Knot on Call* one last time, dismissed it, and moved toward the jetty.

BOTH THE ISLE of Jersey and the Isle of Guernsey had taken a direct hit from the storm. However, because the towers on Guernsey had recently been replaced with a design specifically engineered to withstand gale force winds, the island never lost cell phone service.

When Lou's phone rang, he knew who was calling by the ring tone.

"Hello, Duffy."

Without fanfare, Duffy said, "They're using the Capital Bank in Montenegro."

"Well, that explains the trip to Montenegro."

"Security cameras at the British Air counter in Paris confirmed Beatrice Hastings was the traveler."

"So, Hastings was traveling and Evelyn Maxwell was with us. That left only one person guarding Kate."

"Yeah, Anne Moore, twin sister of Hastings. She's been maintaining a low profile so far. She may be just playing the role of jailer."

"Twins, huh? Funny, looking at the pictures you sent over, I'd never have known that."

"They're fraternal, not identical. Have you heard anything back on the exchange?"

"No, and that's a concern."

"The cell towers on Jersey are all down; that's the reason."

"How long before they're up?"

"Not sure. We're pressuring Vodaphone to get on it."

"Let's hope. What else?"

"We believe Hastings may still be enroute. The flight she took out of Paris was diverted to Saint Malo. Also, from everything we've been able to piece together, it appears she may be the ring leader."

"Where the *hell* is 'Saint Malo?'"

"It's south of you, on the coast of France. Jersey hasn't reopened their airport yet, but the ferries are running again."

"You think she may be on a ferry?"

"We don't know that. She could be waiting for Jersey to reopen their airport. We've notified the French authorities."

"What's the hold up with the airport?"

"The control tower is out. It'll take a while before they reopen.

"Duffy, this is Jake."

"Yeah, Jake?"

"Any progress figuring out where they're staying in Jersey?"

"We literally just got a search warrant for the rental agency they went through. When we weren't able to reach anyone at the agency by phone, a car was sent over. The business is being run out of a private residence. From the looks of things, the owners must have taken off, but a car is on the way over there now, with a search warrant."

WHEN BEATRICE ENTERED the house she had rented on Beach Haven West Boulevard, she saw Anne, not Kate, sitting in the yellow chair.

"Evelyn! What's going on?"

Evelyn emerged from her bedroom looking like she'd been through the mill. "The bitch is gone. She wasn't here when I returned from the ferry."

"And you didn't go *after* her?"

"Don't start on me. Of course, I did! I'm not a complete *idiot*. I drove up and down this stupid street for *hours* trying to find her, even during the storm. I went out again this morning looking for her. I have *no idea* where she went! For all I know, she wandered into the marsh area across the street and drowned."

Beatrice looked at her sister, Anne, then turned back to Evelyn. "Didn't *she* tell you how it happened?"

"No, she's been like this ever since I came back. She keeps mumbling that it wasn't her fault . . . and something about 'not leaving the yard.'"

Beatrice walked over to her sister and knelt down. "Anne, dear, I need to know what happened. Tell me what happened, Anne."

Anne mumbled something which Beatrice wasn't able to understand.

"Anne, how did she escape? You're not in any trouble Anne, nothing's going to happen to you. Just tell me how she escaped."

Anne started rocking back and forth. "You said not to leave the yard, and I didn't."

"Evelyn, where are the cuffs?"

"They're in the car; I had them with me in case I found the bitch."

Beatrice got up off her knees. "Anne's delusional, she's having another one of her episodes."

"Her *what*?"

"It always happens when she's stressed."

"I never knew that."

"Remember how I would tell you she was visiting our cousins in Scotland."

"Yes."

"Well, she never went to Scotland."

"Where was she?"

"Father shipped her off to a treatment center."

"For what?"

"She's psychotic, just like my mother; she can't handle stress."

"I never knew that about Anne."

"Of course not, we kept it hidden. It was our little secret." Changing the subject she asked, "Was there anything at the drop?"

"It's on the table. They've proposed conditions for the exchange."

"I texted them the bank information. Let's see what they want."

"It doesn't matter, we're screwed. Without the bitch, we don't have anything to trade!"

After Beatrice read the proposed conditions for the exchange, she sat back in her chair. "This is just a wrinkle."

"A wrinkle? You call this a wrinkle? This not a *wrinkle*!"

"I need to think about it."

"Yeah, well you go ahead and think about it."

With that, Evelyn stood up and stared out the kitchen window. "We've come all this way, *all this way*, and for what? For *what*, Beatrice? We've gone through all of this for *nothing*! Now we can't even go back to the miserable lives we had!"

Beatrice continued to stare at the message, totally ignoring Evelyn and her rant. "There is a way," she finally said.

"Sure, all we need to do is find the bitch."

"No, there's another way, but we'll need more money up front."

"So, what's the way?"

"We'll use Anne."

"Yeah, like that'll work."

Beatrice turned and stared at her sister rocking back and forth in the yellow chair, mumbling to herself.

"Anne is nothing more than a liability now. They want a picture of the bitch going into the police station. Fine. We'll give them one of *Anne*, going in."

"Be serious, Anne doesn't look anything like her."

"Not true, the two of them have similar body types, who's going to know it's not the bitch if she has her back to me when I take the picture?"

"Her hair is the wrong color."

"Evelyn, we can fix that."

"You're bloody well serious, aren't you?"

Beatrice thought for a moment. "It's the only way. Otherwise, you're right, we walk away with nothing."

"Once she goes into the police station, they'll know."

"By then the money will be in our account; like I said, we just need more money upfront."

"There is no way we can drop Anne off at the police station, and get off this island."

"Yes, there is."

"How?"

"We're taking a boat."

"Oh, yeah, like they won't be watching the ferries."

"I didn't say ferry."

"Oh, great, now we're going to steal a boat? Yeah, sure, like nobody will notice *that*?"

"We're not going to *steal* a boat. I met someone who *has* a boat."

"So?"

"So, let's think about this exchange. You're right, once Anne goes into the police station, that's the end of any more money being wired. That's why we have to front load the deal."

"They said they're willing to wire a half million as 'good faith.'"

"That's not enough. We'll counter with *four* million in good faith, and *five* mill when they get the text photo of her standing on the steps at the police station."

"Think they'll buy it?"

"No, but they'll come back with something better than what they're offering right now."

"Won't the police be waiting outside for us, you know, when we're supposed to be taking the picture of Anne on the steps?"

"I would hope so."

"That doesn't worry you?"

"No, because we're taking the picture *earlier*. Let's go get some hair coloring."

RETURNING TO THE marina, Sam entered just as Bud looked up from his desk."Where'd you get the *gigolo* shoes?"

Sam, looked down at his feet. "What, you don't like my

velvet slippers? I bought them in Provence three years ago at the jazz festival."

"They make the outfit."

Sam flipped his brother the bird. "Here, shake hands with the French," he said.

"You missed the fun last night."

"I heard; any damage?"

"Restaurant across the way lost a few shingles, that's about it."

"And the cell towers went out."

"Well, that's always a given."

"Yeah."

"Someone came by looking for work."

Sam ignored Bud's comment. "You got much petrol left?"

"I thought you were done for the year."

"I may have a charter."

"There should be enough."

"Good, that'll save me from going all the way over to East Harbor."

"You didn't hear me before, I said someone came by looking for work yesterday."

"I heard you."

"I sent them down to that sorry excuse you have for a boat."

"I left a sign saying I'd be back today."

"I think she may have spent the night there."

"It was a 'she?'"

"Yeah."

Sam tilted his head to the side as he remembered seeing the woman wearing a hat and sunglasses earlier . . . and made a mental note to check if his hat and sunglasses were still aboard the boat.

Chapter Forty-One

WHEN KATE WAS nearly halfway across the field between the marina and the jetty, she looked up and saw the two vehicles which had been in the jetty parking lot leaving. When she reached the lot, a lone angler was resting against the guard rail.

"Sir, do you have a cell phone on you?"

"Towers are out, ma'am."

"Are you waiting for a ride? I could use a lift," she said.

"I'm just waiting for the tide to go out a little further so I can walk across the mud flats to my house."

"Why did everybody just leave?"

"Slack tide. Fishing's no good during a slack tide. But they'll be back here when the tide comes in again."

"How long before that happens?"

"Twelve hours. But folks will be pulling in here long before that; ya' know, to claim their spot and get set up."

Totally disheartened by the news, Kate gave a wave of thanks and walked over to the guard rail where she leaned her butt against the hard metal and rested her chin on her chest, completely disheartened. *What now?* she wondered.

The only thing she felt was frustration and exhaustion.

I can't go back to the boat again . . . I need to find someplace else to shelter for the night.

She remained in the area around the jetty until it was dark enough to feel safe enough to move about. The field separating the jetty from the marina though overgrown, still did not offer much concealment. Twice, she dropped to her knees to avoid being caught in the headlights when a car came to the end of the boulevard and turned around.

Finally, when she reached the end of the field, she slid into the drainage ditch that ran alongside the road on the opposite side from the houses and the marina. At a distance, in Kate's mind, any one of the houses were likely candidates to shelter in, but the closer she came to them, the less sure she was of that. After lying low and studying the houses, she decided on the fourth cottage from the marina.

As dusk turned to twilight, Kate crossed the street with the stealth of a ninja, walked around to the rear of the house, broke a pane of glass, and let herself in.

Once she was inside, it was obvious the house had been closed up for the season. Still, she picked up the receiver on the wall phone just to be certain it was disconnected. There was no dial tone. Next to the phone was a thermostat. The temperature was set at fifty-five. Kate cranked the thermostat up to seventy-two degrees.

The refrigerator had been cleaned out, but not the pantry. The owners had left a package of granola bars, two cans of tuna fish, an unopened box of crackers, a few tea bags, and a six-pack of bottled water. There was a tea kettle sitting on the stove. Kate removed the lid, walked over to the sink to fill it, only to find that the water had been turned off. Smiling, she walked back into the pantry and poured two bottles of spring water into the kettle. Unfortunately, the stove was gas, and it, too, had been turned off.

FURTHER DOWN THE street, Evelyn was finishing up blow drying Anne's now chestnut brown hair.

While Evelyn was in the bathroom with Anne, Beatrice worked up a few numbers. Now that Anne would be the sacrificial lamb, the ransom only needed to be split two ways.

When she had returned from her journey, Beatrice had shared with Evelyn the fact that she had visited Bella Luna and the secret vault in the cellar seemed to be intact. Now, smiling to herself, Beatrice thought, *With the cache of gold at Bella Luna, we only need enough money to get there.*

"Evelyn, when you're finished with her hair, put Anne in the yellow chair and come into the kitchen."

As Evelyn entered the room, Beatrice brightened. "We don't need more than *two* million to disappear; then we'll find our way to Bella Luna. Actually, we could do it with only a million pounds."

"Won't they come after us there? That's where they nabbed our husbands."

"Evelyn, our husbands were big time operators, we're small fry. They're not going to come after us."

"What if the bitch never shows up, and the charge goes from kidnapping to murder?"

"They'll have Anne. She'll take the fall for us. Relax, everything's going in our favor; besides, it would cost them too much to extradite us. And once we're in Montenegro, we'll apply for citizenship, which will make it even more difficult to be extradited."

"Two million is a far cry from *nine* million," Evelyn complained.

"We don't *need* nine million. There are millions at the chateau. We just need enough money to stay under the radar until we can get there."

Just then, Beatrice's cell phone beeped.

"The phones must be up. Let's text our demands for the exchange."

"All right, but I think we should go for more than two million up front."

Beatrice ignored her friend and typed in a text message:

Tomorrow @ noon, wire 2 mill in good faith upfront . . . once we have proof of deposit, we'll text a picture of hostage on the steps of the police station . . .once proof of a 7 mill deposit is verified, we'll release hostage.

When Beatrice was satisfied with the text, she hit 'send.'

A FEW MILES AWAY, Lou's cell phone chirped. He picked up his phone and read the text, then smiled. "Jake, take a look at this."

"I'm surprised they didn't ask for more up front, Lou. Interesting that they went for the photo op on the steps of the police station."

"Yeah, I'm curious about that, too. They want the exchange tomorrow. I better pull over and forward their text to Duffy."

As Lou forwarded the text, Jake said, "So, they somehow think they can let Kate out of the car, have her cooperate in a photo shoot on the steps of the police headquarters, and then she's gonna walk *back* to their car?"

"They have to have a different plan in mind."

"Yeah, they must. They're just not showing their hand. Maybe they're dumping Kate somewhere after they get the initial payment."

"That doesn't give them a lot of up-front money once they split it three ways."

"Maybe they're planning on taking the picture beforehand."

"Maybe. But if Kate gets anywhere *near* a police station, with her training, she'll bolt."

"You don't think she's gonna have an escort?"

"Not sure, but knowing Kate, if she senses even the slightest chance of freedom, she'll go for it. Especially if there are cops around, she'll be yelling to attract attention."

"Unless she's drugged, or they have someone close by."

"One person guarding her, no handcuffs? Kate could take 'em out."

"Not if she knows there's a rifle that'll put a bullet in her back."

"Good point." Both men looked at each other, thinking about that possibility.

"Lou, I think she'd know if there was a shooter aiming a rifle at her." Lou's phone rang before he could respond; it was Duffy.

"I got your text."

"And?"

"What do you make of it, Lou?"

"I think the ransom just went from nine down to two, Duffy."

"I think you're right, but we're playing with monopoly money, anyway."

"What aren't they sharing?"

"That's what we've just been kicking around over here. They must figure Kate's gonna bolt if she gets near a police station; and once she's inside, it's over."

Duffy chose not to add the possibility that Kate might not be in very good shape.

"They want the exchange tomorrow. I'm going to text back that we agree to the date, time, and money."

"We're ready."

"Right. I'll be in touch."

As soon as Lou hung up with Duffy, he sent a text: *accept your terms.*

WHEN BEATRICE'S CELL phone chirped, she opened the text and read it. "They took the bait."

"What did they say?"

"Just that they accepted our terms."

"How much do you think we're leaving on the table?"

"It doesn't matter."

Beatrice picked up her phone and quickly sent a reply. *Fine.*

LOU AND JAKE had been using a grid pattern to canvass the island. As far as brands go, KIAs proved to be a pretty popular vehicle on the island. Yesterday, they had stopped a number of times checking out KIAs and had just about finished with the island's southeastern quadrant. Early this morning, they were starting on a new section.

"Lou, we've passed quite a few houses with garages."

"Yeah, but keep in mind they're using a rental. What are the chances of a rental being garaged?"

"If Duffy has a copy of their rental listing, he might be able to tell us if there's a garage."

"Worth a call."

It was close to 6:30am when Lou pulled up Duffy's number and pressed call.

Duffy picked up on the first ring. "I was just getting ready to call you. We just got the address from the search warrant of the realty office…we know where they're holding up."

"Wait a sec, I'm putting you on speaker . . . okay, go ahead."

"They're at 1187 Beach Haven West Boulevard. It's a single-story ranch."

"Does the place come with a garage?"

Duffy paused for a moment. "Lou, why does that matter?"

"It doesn't now, but does it?"

"I don't know; I'm checking the listing. All it says is there's off street parking."

As soon as Jake heard the address he entered it into his GPS app. "Lou, we're on the wrong end of the island, ya gotta bang a U-ey."

Lou immediately pulled over and began making a three-point turn.

"Okay Duffy, we're on our way."

"All right, listen up, when you get there, you are to call for backup before you go in. Ya got that?"

"We will."

"I'm dead serious Lou, no heroics."

"Understood."

As the call ended, Jake looked at his cousin, "This is it, Lou."

"Let's hope so."

It wasn't long before they reached the address and Jake yelled, "Lou, pull over!"

"You see something?"

"Yeah, there's the KIA."

After parking down the street, they doubled back and stayed low, going through several backyards. By the time they reached the house, again, the KIA was gone.

Chapter Forty-Two

EVERY MORNING, beginning around 6:30 a.m., the parking lot behind the Jersey police station began to fill up as officers arrived for the first shift. Like clockwork, at exactly seven, every officer was assembled for roll call in the station's briefing room.

At exactly 7:05 a.m. Beatrice pulled the KIA up in front of the Jersey police station and parked on the deserted street. The city of Saint Helier had a reputation for being a bustling resort town during the summer tourist season, but off-season, it was just another sleepy little seaside town.

Beatrice turned to Evelyn. "Walk with Anne. Once you're on the steps, make sure she has her back to me before you move away; then, I'll take the photo."

"Got it,"

Beatrice stepped out of the car and walked around to the rear door.

"Anne, dear, I need you to get out of the car and take a little walk with Evelyn."

"No, I'm not going."

"Anne, *please*, just do this one tiny thing and I won't bother you again for the rest of the day, I *promise*."

Anne folded her arms defiantly over her chest. "No."

"Anne, it will please *father*, if you do this." After a slight pause, Beatrice continued. "Wouldn't you *like* to please father, Anne? You *know* how much father *adores* you."

At the mention of her father, Anne looked at her sister.

"Anne, come on, we *need* to do this. . . to please father."

Without saying a word, Anne stepped out from the car and walked across the street with Evelyn. Then, when prompted, she stood by the entrance with her back to the camera just long enough for Beatrice to capture the photo she needed.

ON THAT SAME morning, as sun leaked around the window shades in the house where Kate had taken refuge and slept, she now stirred. Her body still needed sleep, but she was more determined than ever to find a way to end this ordeal. Her only problem was that she just couldn't seem to wrap her head around a plan of action.

The side effects associated with the drug Beatrice had used on Kate were still impacting her ability to think clearly. The drug itself was promising and was potentially a low-cost anesthetic for patients undergoing a lengthy surgical procedure, however, it was still in clinical trials. The governing bodies that had regulatory oversight for the pharmaceutical industry had requested additional testing due to the many side effects that had surfaced. The most notable one being short-term paranoia and abnormal behavioral swings which ran the gamut from high anxiety to complacency. Normal protocols were in place and distribution of the drug was only authorized for test purposes.

That said, a small quantity of the drug had somehow disappeared from the controlled testing environment, and became available on the black market, which is how Beatrice had found it.

The drug's side effects were beginning to take their toll on Kate; paranoia had definitely set in.

NOT LONG AFTER the sun came up, Bud left the one-bedroom apartment he used on the second floor of the marina and walked over to the *Knot on Call*. As he entered the salon, he called out to Sam, "Ya' got breakfast going, yet?"

"Coffee's ready, got hash fries going, and the bacon is cooked. How do you want your eggs this morning?"

"Looking up at me. Did you have the police radio on this morning?"

"Nah, I've been listening to the sweet sounds of Dizzy Gillespie's trumpet."

"Cops are looking for some kidnappers. Sounds like they've been on the run for a while."

"Pour yourself a coffee. . . cream is in the ice box."

Bud shook his head. "Sam, you don't have an 'ice box,' it's a mini fridge."

"Dad always called it the ice box; what's the problem?"

Bud just shook his head. It wasn't long after they had finished breakfast when Sam's phone rang.

Who the hell is calling me this early? he thought. When he hesitated taking the call, Bud said, "Answer it, will ya'? It could be Angela."

"Who the hell is *Angela*?"

"She's the one selling extended warranties for cars."

Ignoring his brother, Sam picked up the phone.

"This is Sam."

"Yes, Mr. Barber, this is Beatrice Hastings. We met on the ferry yesterday."

"Oh, yes . . .yes, good morning. What can I do for you?"

"I'd like to engage your services."

"All right. . . when and where would you like to go?"

"I'd like to travel to Saint Malo, France; can you be ready to depart at one o'clock today?"

Sam looked at his watch; it was approaching 7:30, he had plenty of time to fuel up. "Certainly. Meet me in the marina office at a quarter of one."

"That will be fine. Do you require a credit card now?"

"No, we'll run your card at the office."

"Fine."

When he hung up Bud asked, "Was that the woman you said wanted to go across the channel?"

"Ya, only now she's going to Saint Malo."

"Easier trip for you."

"As long as they pay, I don't really give a damn."

"Bring your boat around to the pump after you clean up here and we'll top her off. What time do you figure on getting back?"

"I'm not sure. It'll be late though."

"Then you're on your own for dinner, little brother."

"WHERE'D THE KIA GO?" Lou asked.

Jake shrugged his shoulders. "They must have just left as we were parking."

The warrior spirit deep within Lou released a menacing growl. "There's still a chance some of them are inside, with Kate."

When Jake took out his cell phone, Lou whispered, "Put it away."

"No backup?"

"Listen to how quiet it is. The slightest noise will spook 'em. We can't risk a firefight if Kate's inside."

Jake whispered, "Duffy won't be happy."

Ignoring his cousin's warning, Lou whispered, "The only entrance seemed to be in the rear."

"I saw that."

"Alright, let's deploy."

It was early morning, the position of the sun cast a shadow behind them as they slowly made their way along the side of the building. When they reached the back edge of the building Jake signaled that he'd open the door and Lou would enter first.

Glocks in hand, they 'duck-walked' across the back of the building. When Jake opened the door Lou dove into the porch area, rolled to the side and jumped up into a Chapman stance. Jake followed suit and they soon realized the house was empty.

Lou holstered his pistol saying, "Are they psychic? How the hell do we keep missing them?"

"Come here, look at this."

"What?"

"The yellow chair."

Lou smiled as he ran his hand across the words his wife had etched into the arm of the yellow chair.

"Well, they *were* here, Lou. We're only minutes behind them now."

"Yeah, but the question is, where the hell did they go?"

"Wanna stake this place out?"

Lou thought about Jake's question. "No, I think they're on the move again."

"Then let's go see where this street goes."

When they reached the end of Beach Haven West Boulevard Lou turned around in the circle and faced the marina.

"You see a KIA?"

"All I'm seeing are pickups and empty boat trailers, Lou."

"Me, too. Let's go and keep our eyes out for this KIA."

"We need to close the loop with Duffy."

"Give him a call, tell him the place was deserted."

TWENTY MINUTES LATER, the KIA returned to Beach Haven West Boulevard, and pulled into the driveway at number 1187.

Chapter Forty-Three

WHEN ELEVEN-FIFTY A.M. arrived, Duffy's system sent both a text message and an email to Beatrice's cell phone, confirming that that two million pounds had just been deposited into her account at the Capital Bank in Montenegro.

When Beatrice's phone beeped, she smiled, "It's working Evelyn, the money is flowing in."

"Good, then we're out of here!"

Beatrice immediately sent the photo of Anne, masquerading as Kate, standing at the steps of the Jersey police station, in a text message to Lou.

"All right Evelyn, let's go."

"I thought you said, one o'clock?"

"So, we're early, do you really give a shit at this point?"

"What about Anne?"

"Just leave her in the chair; they'll take care of her," Beatrice said, "Come on, we need to go. I don't feel safe staying here any longer."

INSTINCTIVELY, LOU KNEW it wasn't Duffy when his phone chirped. He handed his phone to Jake. "See who this is."

"It's a text message. It's a picture of a woman standing on some stairs. I can't tell if it's Kate, she's got her back to the camera."

Lou pulled over to the side of the road saying, "Let me see." It took less than a second before Lou said, "That's not Kate!"

Lou's left hand swept through his hair and across the back of his neck. After taking a deep breath, he pulled up Duffy's number and pressed "call."

Duffy answered saying, "We just wired the two million. Have you heard anything?"

"Yeah, they just sent a photo of a woman with her back to the camera standing on the front steps of the Jersey Police Station."

"Is it Kate?"

"No. It was a set up."

"You're sure of that?"

"Kate's thighs are different. Besides this picture was taken earlier."

"How do you know that?"

"I'll forward it. The woman in the picture is casting a shadow. If they'd taken the picture shortly before noon, the sun would have been directly overhead. There wouldn't have been a long shadow."

"Hold on, let me see what this text says that I just got." Duffy came back on the line saying, "Beatrice Hastings just used her credit card."

"Where?"

"Hold on and I'll pull up the coordinates . . . Bud's

Marina, 3807 Beach Haven West Boulevard."

"Crap, we were just there. They're trying to get off the island on a boat. Do you think Kate's with them?"

"Lou, my guess is no. They think they have two million in the bank, Kate's just baggage at this point. Let's talk through what the plan is." Duffy suddenly sensed that the line had dropped. "Hello? Lou . . . Lou, are you still on the line?"

Duffy tried to reach Lou several times, only to bounce directly to voicemail.

AFTER SAM HAD taken on sufficient fuel to make the run, and tied up at the pier, he walked over to the office expecting to spend a little more time with Bud.

When Beatrice, walked in at twelve-fifteen, he looked up saying, "Mrs. Hastings, you're early."

"Better early than late."

Bud, immediately recognized the second woman, but said nothing.

Sam smiled, saying, "Well, we've got a good tide, so, we should make Saint-Malo in good time."

Beatrice smiled. "Fine," she said.

"Well, let's run your card, and we'll shove off."

Beatrice took out her father's credit card and Sam ran it through a device he had on his smart phone. The system prompted him for additional information. "What's the zip code for this card?"

"The what?"

"The postal code, I need to enter the postal code."

Beatrice panicked. "I . . . I don't remember. It's so long ago that we took this card out and we've moved a few times. Can't we skip that?"

"Afraid not, the card won't process without it."

Beatrice reached into her purse and took out her own credit card. "Here, use this one."

Sam exchanged cards with her and asked again: "Postal code?"

"GU18"

He punched the code in and the system took it.

Beatrice held out her hand waiting for her credit card back. As Sam placed it in the palm of her hand, he looked around. "Where's your luggage?"

"Oh, we travel light . . . that's the beauty of credit cards, don't you agree?"

Sam just smiled. "Then we're good to go, ladies; follow me."

Once they left the marina office, Bud stood at the back window and watched them walk single file down the path running along the water's edge and over to the pier were the *Knot on Call* was tied.

Sam led his passengers into the salon, made sure they were comfortable, blew the bilge, hit the button to start the powerful inboard engine, then went topside to release the lines.

AS SOON AS the marina's parking lot came into view Jake said, "There's the KIA."

"I see it. We're going in with Glocks drawn."

"Give me a chance to get around back."

The car no sooner came to a stop, when both men were out and moving into position. Lou waited for Jake to circle around before he entered.

"Police! Put your hands up!"

The old man, sitting behind a desk, wasted no time putting his hands up in the air.

"Jake, search the room."

"No need to, there's no one else here Lou."

Motioning with his pistol, Lou said, "Stand up. What's your name?"

Not seeing any real option other than to comply, the old man stood up. "Name's Bud. This is my marina."

"Where's the woman who just ran a credit card here?"

"She's on the *Knot on Call*."

"On the what?"

"That's the name of the charter boat she just went out on."

As both men holstered their weapons, Lou asked, "How many people are on that boat?

"Three."

Lou spread pictures of Beatrice, Evelyn, Anne, and Kate across the man's desk. "Which of these people got on that boat?"

Bud looked at the photos before pointing. "These two just left on the *Knot on Call*."

"You said three people got that boat."

"Third one's the skipper."

Pressing, Lou asked, "What about these other two?"

Kate no longer looked even close to the picture Lou had of her after all she had been through. Anne had never been to the marina. "Nope, don't recognize either one of them," Bud said, shaking his head.

"So, it's just these two who boarded the ship?

"It's a 'boat,' but yes."

"No one else?"

"Just the skipper."

"Can you reach the skipper?"

"I can, by radio."

"Good, then tell him to return to port."

Bud walked over to his ship-to-shore radio, pressed the button on the handheld mic and said: "Base to *Knot on Call,* come in *Knot on Call.*"

In between a little static, they heard a voice came over the radio, "This is the *Knot on Call;* Go ahead base."

"Buoy one niner is out; repeat, buoy one niner is out . . . proceed with caution."

Sam immediately knew that was Bud's distress call; something was wrong. He backed off on both screws and threw one into neutral.

In a heartbeat, Beatrice appeared at the base of the ladder leading up to the bridge. "What just happened?"

"One of our propeller shafts kicked a prop. We'll need to go back and get that fixed. It won't take long; we'll be back out in twenty minutes. I have a spare at the marina."

Beatrice could feel the boat turning around. She had overheard the radio call from Bud on the auxiliary speaker located in the galley and suspected that it was a signal of some sort as they were already in deep water, well beyond the last buoy.

Raising her pistol, she fired a shot. The bullet struck the ship-to-shore radio then ricocheted upward ripping a hole in the canvas canopy directly over Sam's head. "Get back on course, and stay on course for Saint Malo."

Sam could tell from her stance that she knew how to fire a weapon; he complied.

Once Beatrice was satisfied that Sam had returned to his original course, she demanded, "Now, unplug that radio.

Sam pulled the radio just far enough out of the docking

station so it disengaged. Whether it was still operable after being grazed by the bullet, was another story.

"Now, unplug the microphone from the radio and toss it overboard."

Again, Sam complied. "You can put the pistol away, we're headed to Saint Malo."

WHEN THE *KNOT ON CALL* failed to acknowledge the message and return to the harbor, Lou punched in Duffy's cell number.

"Duffy, two of the kidnappers are on a small craft that just left Jersey. Is Kate at police headquarters?"

"There's been no message from Jersey headquarters yet, Lou. What's the name of the boat?"

Lou turned to Bud, "What's the name of that boat again?"

"The *Knot on Call*, out of Jersey."

"Did you hear that?"

"Yeah, where are they headed?"

Lou looked at Bud who called out, "They're headed to Saint Malo, France."

"Got it," Duffy said. "We'll alert the proper authorities and have our people standing by."

"Good," Lou said. "Now we have to find Kate. She can't be far away."

"Lou make sure someone is stationed at the marina, just in case they do come back."

While Jake waited for Lou to call for backup he walked over to Bud. "Bud are you sure you've never seen either of these other two women?"

Bud took a careful look at both photos before he pointed at the one of Kate. "There's something about this one's eyes that reminds me of a gal who came in here just before the storm. She was definitely afraid of one of them other two… but I can't be sure if it was her."

"Which one was she afraid of?"

Just as Bud pointed to a photo, Lou ended his call.

"Jake, we gotta go."

As Lou and Jake walked out of the marina Lou pointed to the jetty. "Let's see if we can find out anything from those fishermen."

"Okay, but given that the third kidnapper and Kate are still out there, let's check out the house they were using on the way over, just for kicks."

"Good call."

Chapter Forty-Four

T HE TWO COUSINS APPROACHED the house at 1187 Beach Haven West Boulevard with every bit of caution they had used earlier in the day. When they reached the back edge of the building they again "duck-walked" across the rear of the building to stay below the window ledges. As soon as they entered the screen porch they heard a voice coming from inside. Lou pointed with his pistol, signaling which way he'd go.

The sound seemed to be coming from a bedroom. When they reached the hallway both men pressed up against the wall. Jake held out his hand and on the count of three stepped into the doorway.

Sitting in the middle of the bed, rocking back and forth, babbling incoherently was Anne More.

Jake quickly searched the rest of the house, the shed, and the dock area, hoping he wouldn't find a body. When Jake returned to the house, Lou was on the phone talking to the

Jersey police. This time the call was to take a suspect into custody.

BY THE TIME Lou and Jake reached the jetty it was slack tide, there wasn't a fishermen in sight.

As Lou pulled the keys out of the ignition he looked at his cousin. "Jake, let's split up and take a look around, maybe the ground will tell us something."

It wasn't difficult for either of these skilled woodsmen to recognize fresh tracks that wove in and around the mix of assorted wild grasses, milkweed, stands of thistles and scrub bushes. The footprints all appeared to be made by the same person, but they seemed to either go toward the marina or come from the marina.

Finally, Lou picked up a single set of tracks that took a different trajectory. Once the tracks left the parking area, they swerved away from the marina and headed toward the far side of the field. Lou cupped his hands and made the sound of the whip-poor-will. Before long Jake was standing beside him.

"Whatcha find, cuz?"

"Looks like the same tracks as the others, but they don't head to the marina."

"Lead the way."

The tracks continued in a straight line diagonally across the field to the far side, then down into the gully that ran along the length of Beach Haven West Boulevard. A large marshy area bordered this side of the street, and the ground was fairly wet. The further they traveled, the more signs they began to see.

"Whoever we're following is struggling with the terrain."

"Yeah, I've seen their hand prints a couple of times."

Neither man flinched when they turned a bend in the trail and four pintail ducks, that had been resting among the tall reeds, took flight.

"Lou, if you're traveling parallel to the road, why would you walk down here and not on the road?"

"I'm either hunting the marsh, or I don't want to be seen."

"I think we can rule out hunting."

When Lou didn't respond, Jake said, "I showed that marina fella the photo of Evelyn Maxwell. He said she was one who came into the marina a couple of times looking for someone."

"What's that tell ya?"

"That the person we're tracking doesn't want to be seen."

"That's what I'm thinking, too."

The footprints were small enough to belong to a woman, but neither man was ready to ask the other if they thought they were tracking Kate.

Not long after the tracks passed beyond the marina, Lou held up his hand. "Whoever we're following, stopped and waited here."

Jake knelt down to get a closer look. "Maybe last night. Whaddya make of it?"

Lou knelt down beside his cousin, "Let's think; for some reason they laid down on a slope. It's gotta tell us something we don't know."

Jake laid down next to where the grass was matted down on the slope. "Well, depending on how tall the person is, they woulda had a pretty good view of anything going on over at the marina, without being seen."

"Maybe so, but I don't think that's it, Jake. If it was about the marina, they would have stopped directly across from it. There's something else going on we're not getting."

"All right, so, where do the tracks go from here?"

Lou stood up and walked a little further down the gully. "They don't."

"Then they either crossed the road here, or decided to *use* the road, because they sure in hell didn't backtrack."

"Whichever it was, it looks like the decision was deliberate. I don't see any sign of a struggle."

"Those toe prints are pretty deep."

"Yeah, but if there had been a struggle we'd see a second set of tracks. And the ground would have been really disturbed. My guess is that whoever it was, they were just pushing themselves up to get a better look at something."

Jake looked up toward the road. "I'm gonna go across the street, just to look around.

"I'll see if they continued down the road."

LOU WALKED A considerable distance, scanning the pavement and the edge of the road for signs of anyone having traveled recently in that direction.

Jake walked directly across the street and scoured the soft shoulder looking for signs. As he skirted a puddle, something caused him to glance across to the far side; and there it was, a single footprint.

When Jake made the sound of the whip-poor-will, Lou doubled back.

"I think I found were the chicken crossed the road, cuz."

Lou nodded. "Let's go."

Like many of the homes on the street, the yards had been

covered with pea stone, but this one had a wooden walkway that led around to the rear.

Circling the house, they saw a broken pane of glass in the rear door which immediately put them on high alert.

Lou peered through the upper panel of the window. "It's pretty dark in there, Jake. It'll take a while for our eyes to adjust."

"Understood."

"We don't know who broke in, or if they're still inside. Let's go in with Glocks ready."

"Okay. But we need to give our eyes a chance to adjust. As soon as we enter, make yourself as small as possible."

"Right."

Lou reached through the broken pane, opened the door and both men slipped into the cottage, melding into the darkness.

Crouched motionless, with his eyes closed, next to the wall, Lou listened for even the slightest sound. After thirty seconds, his eyes had dilated sufficiently that he was comfortable enough to move forward. Passing through the kitchen, Lou paused under an archway leading into what he guessed was the living room.

Without warning, a figure lunged at him from a corner of the room. He managed to see the glint of a butcher knife as the smaller figure came at him. Blocking the downward strike, he grabbed the assailant around the waist and felt a familiar figure under his touch.

"KATE!" he yelled. "It's ME!"

The sound of her husband's voice snapped Kate out of her panic. Still not sure, she froze in mid-motion.

"Lou?"

He lowered his weapon, "Kate! It's me, honey!"

Hearing her husband's voice, a second time, she dropped the knife and collapsed into his arms.

Lou held her tightly as their emotions took over and tears of relief streamed down their cheeks. Lou could feel Kate's body shaking as everything she'd bottled up throughout the ordeal began to flow out.

JAKE TEXTED THE Jersey police and requested an ambulance, then he positioned himself outside to flag down the first responders. Within minutes, emergency vehicles stationed at the very beginning of Beach Haven West Boulevard were in motion. It was only after paramedics entered the dwelling that Lou released his wife from his arms.

"Kate, we need to get you to a hospital."

With tears in her eyes, she trembled. "Don't leave me, Lou."

"Not a chance, babe, I'm going *with* you every step of the way."

As the EMT's strapped Kate onto a gurney, Lou turned to Jake. "Jake, this is *far* from over. I want the *bastards* who did this."

"Me, too! I'll stay on it."

At that moment Lou's phone rang. It was Duffy. Before Duffy could say anything, Lou blurted out, "We have her!"

"Is she okay?"

"I don't know. She looks pretty rough; she's been through a lot. The EMT's are here now. We're transporting her to the hospital."

"Where are you?"

"We're down near the end of Beach Haven West Boulevard, close to Bud's Marina."

"We've alerted the French Government. They're standing by, ready to pick up the kidnappers as soon as they step foot on Saint Malo."

Out of the corner of his eye, Lou saw the first responders begin to lift Kate into the back of the ambulance. "Duffy, I gotta go."

"Right, we'll talk later."

THE HIGH-SPEED ferry usually made the run from Jersey to Saint Malo in two hours. This day, Sam, never let up on the throttle and the *Knot on Call* approached Saint Malo's harbor in just over ninety minutes.

When land came into view, Beatrice appeared at the foot of the ladder leading up to the bridge. "What port is that directly ahead?"

"That's Saint Malo, France."

"Then turn left, we're going to *Mont Saint Michel*."

Sam knew that when he failed to return to port, Bud would have alerted the French authorities, and they'd be waiting for them at Saint Malo. Keeping his eyes on the channel, he said, "I thought you wanted to go to Saint Malo."

"Just do as I say."

From topside, Sam glanced down at his passenger and saw the twisted face of someone who was willing to kill. The pistol she still held was now pointing right at him. Without a word, he swung the boat to port and headed toward Mont Saint Michel, France.

He had no doubt she would try to put a bullet in him at some point. But he wasn't about to let that happen, especially since the largest jazz festival of the season was in another month and he had platinum level patron tickets.

Having sailed into the harbor of Mont Saint Michel a number of times, Sam was familiar with its tides, especially the tricky mud flats lining the narrow channel. Now Sam figured, if he played his cards right, he could avoid getting shot and maybe even save the *Knot on Call*.

The water surrounding Mont Saint Michel was basically a shallow tidal harbor, but navigable at low tide as long as one stayed within the channel markers.

When the *Knot on Call* reached the fifth buoy marker going in, Sam saw the markings on the buoy, it was low tide. In one swift movement, Sam turned the rudder full starboard, cut the powerful engine, and dove off the bridge into the water.

In less than twenty seconds, the *Knot on Call* had beached itself and sat precariously balanced on top of the mud.

Sam swam for all he was worth back to the number five buoy, knowing it would give him some degree of cover if the one with the pistol got trigger happy.

In seconds, Beatrice and her companion appeared on deck.

"Beatrice, what happened?"

"Our brave little captain scuttled the ship, deary, that's all."

"What'll we do?"

After letting out a sigh of disgust, Beatrice nonchalantly said, "We flag down one of these passing boats." With that, Beatrice stepped up onto the narrow transom, steadied herself by holding on to the flimsy elevated stern light and began waving with her free arm.

It wasn't long before she attracted the attention of several boats. "See how easy this is? It's actually working out to our advantage, we'll be coming ashore on a boat they won't be looking for. Look, see, two boats are coming to rescue us already."

"Where?"

"Right there."

When Evelyn moved closer to Beatrice to get a better look, her added weight altered the boat's center of gravity and the hull rolled a little further to starboard. When that happened, Beatrice lost her balance and unceremoniously fell from her perch, landing face down in the mud.

Thrashing about trying to right herself, Beatrice soon realized her flailing was only drawing her deeper into the odiferous muck.

"Help me, you fool! Can't you see I need your help? Evelyn, give me your hand!"

Evelyn leaned over the rail as far as she could, extending her arm. "I can't reach you. Oh, my God, this muck smells even worse than that wretched peat does. Hold on, I'll get you something to grab on to."

When Evelyn went into the salon, the boat that was nearest to them veered aside allowing the vessel behind it to come forward. With that, a voice came over a loudspeaker: *"Rester immobile! Rester immobile!"*

When Beatrice saw the reflection of the flashing blue lights bouncing off the wet hull beside her, she gave way to her *flight instinct* and began to "crab-crawl" away from the beached boat.

Noticing the name on the stern was written in English, the metallic sounding voice switched to English: "Remain where you are! Police! Repeat, remain where you are!"

Beatrice continued to ignore the command and tried

scampering further away from the boat. Ironically, the only thing she was able to accomplish was to imprison herself even deeper into the stink and muck of the slimy tidal flats.

OUT IN THE CHANNEL, Sam managed to lift himself up onto the buoy in time to watch the harbor patrol secure a line around Beatrice's mud-caked body and literally drag her kicking and screaming off the tidal flat with an electric winch.

Eventually, Sam was picked up by a passing boat. The first thing he did when he arrived on shore, was to walk over to the harbor police station. He was ready to testify.

Chapter Forty-Five

AS SOON AS THEY arrived at the hospital, Kate was wheeled into the emergency room. The staff immediately began examining her and ordering a series of routine tests. It was obvious she was dehydrated and within minutes, after taking her vitals, a saline solution was infusing into her arm.

Other than chaffing from the handcuffs, and a few bumps and bruises, she had physically come through the ordeal remarkably well. The true story would remain unknown until the test results were back.

As the day went on, the lingering effects from the drug forced upon her began to subside. The question now was whether she could put the ordeal behind her mentally.

While the hospital staff continued to go about the usual poking and prodding, Lou sent text messages off to Alessandra and Kate's cousin, Claire, letting them know she had been rescued and was undergoing evaluation in a hospital on the Channel Islands.

It took close to three hours before the results from every test the doctor on duty ordered were back. Shortly thereafter, Kate was wheeled out of the ER and into a private room.

Lou stood at the doorway of Kate's room, quietly staring at his wife, wondering how much moxie and what kind of mojo she must have inside her to have endured such an ordeal. During their ride in the ambulance, she shared how she'd tried keeping her wits about her, and had escaped *twice* from her kidnappers.

Kate was sitting up in bed, but her eyes were closed. She was still hooked up to a few monitors and the side rails on the bed were up. Earlier the aides had helped her shower and wash her hair; she looked tired, but she was a far cry from the disheveled, desperate woman he had found hours earlier. The only thing Lou saw was the beautiful woman he loved.

As he leaned again the doorframe, Lou also began to feel the stress and worry beginning to leave his body. When an aide brought in a tray of hospital food, Kate opened her eyes.

"Kate, if you don't mind, the next time you decide to fly over to Ireland, I think I'll just tag along," Lou said.

She looked up and smiled. "The next time I fly *any*where, you can damn well *bet* you're tagging along."

"You'll get no argument from me on that, sweetheart."

As he leaned over to kiss her, he heard someone clear their throat. Turning, he saw a tall, distinguished man in a white lab coat standing in the doorway holding an iPad.

"Lou, this is Doctor Odgren; he's been examining me," Kate said, introducing them. "Doctor, this is my husband, Lou."

After shaking hands, Lou asked, "How's she doing, Doc?"

"She's still dehydrated, so we'll continue getting more fluids into her and some nutrition into her stomach. Her vitals are good, but we're going to run a few more test and keep an eye on her for a few days.

"She's been though a lot," Lou agreed. "I'm all for taking our time."

"From everything we can see at this point, aside from a few bumps and bruises, both she and the babies appear to be doing fine."

The room went silent. . .as time stood still.

Lou looked at Kate while Kate looked at Doctor Odgren. "Would you say that last part again?"

"I said 'you and both babies appear to be doing fine.' Of course, we'll need to continue monitoring things. We did an ultrasound when we determined you were pregnant and everything appears to be normal. I would suggest you see a prenatal care specialist when you return home though. You're just past the middle of your first trimester."

The doctor saw the blank look on their faces.

"Oh, you didn't know?"

Kate shook her head. "No!"

"Well, then, let me be the first to say: Congratulations."

Lou leaned down and kissed his wife. "Looks like your cousin's negligée hasn't lost its touch."

Kate started to laugh.

"What's so funny?"

"My cousin, Claire, she said she wanted to borrow it back."

"So?"

"She already has enough kids to field two soccer teams."

ONCE JAKE WAS assured that Beatrice Hastings and Evelyn Maxwell had been taken into custody by the French government, and that Kate was in good hands, he bid Lou adieu, and flew back to the island of Guernsey.

When Jake walked into the lobby of the hotel where he had previously stayed in Guernsey, Percival Bodine, the manager who had checked him in earlier, looked up.

"Ah, Mr. Gault, you are back. Will you be staying with us again?"

"That's what I'm here for."

"Let me see what I have available. Is it just yourself?"

"For the time being."

"And how long will we have the pleasure of your company?"

"That I don't know."

"I see." After scrolling through his computer Bodine looked up, "Sir, one of our bungalows is available, I can put you there at the same rate. Will that be suitable?"

"That'll be just fine."

"Good, this way you can avoid going through the lobby during your stay." With that, Bodine motioned for a bell hop. "Take Mr. Gault's luggage, he's in number seven."

Jake reached across the desk saying, "Thanks Percival"

"It's a pleasure to have you back."

AS SOON AS JAKE and the young bell hop left the lobby, Jake said, "Son, I can carry my own bag. Here's a tip for your willingness to help, just point me in the right direction."

"Hey, thanks Mister. Number seven is the last one on the left. Just follow this path."

Once Jake set his luggage down on the bed, he took the business card from Koby Callahan out of his wallet and punched her number into his phone.

"Hello?" she answered after a few rings.

"Hi, is this Koby?

"It is. Who's this?"

"Jake Gault. We met last week at the Hogs and Heifers. I'm the guy who flies small planes, and went to McGill University, remember?"

She hesitated, then laughed. "Yes, I do remember, actually." The sound of her voice sent a thrill through him.

"Well, my business is wrapped up and I was hoping you and I might get together."

"It's possible," she said. "What did you have in mind?"

"I thought maybe we'd start with dinner and conversation. Would that work?"

"It could. When were you thinking of doing that?"

"Tonight, actually, I could pick you up in an hour. Would that work?"

A huge red flag went up for Koby. *This guy's coming on way too fast, I need to think about this,* she immediately thought.

When she didn't respond right away, Jake counted with, "Or we could get together *tomorrow,* maybe for lunch."

"Okay, lunch tomorrow," she said. "I can make *that* work. Do you like Greek food?"

"Who doesn't?" Jake lied.

"Great, then let's do Opa's on Seaside Avenue . . . say 11:30? That's early enough for us to beat the lunch crowd. I'll meet you there."

Jake hid his disappointment in the delay, saying, "Works for me. I'll see you then."

THE FOLLOWING DAY, lunch was enjoyable for both of them and it led to dinner that evening. Dinner that evening led to lunch and dinner the next day. The conversation at the table never seemed to lag, nor did either of them feel it was forced.

It wasn't long before they each realized they had begun subtly mirroring the other's body language and sharing personal stories which they rarely talked about with others.

For the remainder of the week, Jake and Koby were pretty much inseparable. They spent their days lounging on the beach together or cycling, in the evenings; they enjoyed each other's company over dinner and a bottle of wine.

At one point Koby sensed the chemistry between them was so strong, she literally flashed back to a conversation she'd had with her mother, years earlier: "Koby, the best people show up unexpectedly," her mother had said..

Toward the end of the week, Jake decided he'd take a risk. He reached across the lunch table, took hold of Koby's hands and looked her straight in the eyes. "I'd like to ask you something."

Koby had no idea where this was going, but she was curious enough that she said, "Go ahead and ask, but don't be surprised if the answer is 'no.'"

"I'd like to invite you to my cousin's wedding?"

"When?"

"Right now."

"Wait, you're cousin's getting married right *now*?"

"No, no, I mean I'm asking you, *right now*."

Tilting her head slightly, a smile appeared on her face. "Oh, well then, when is it?"

"It's this Saturday . . . in Ireland."

Koby mulled the date over in her mind.

Jake stared at the woman who sat across from him, waiting for a response. The longer he waited the more he realized how beautiful she was, not only physically, but on the inside as well. The beauty he saw in her wasn't anything as temporary as her looks; it made him want her even more.

"I'm committed to being in Nantucket on Saturday," she said, "but I can push my arrival date out a little."

"Then it's a 'yes?'"

"Yes, it's a 'yes,' Jake-who-flies-small-planes. But the following day I'm off to Nantucket."

Without skipping a beat, Jake said, "Now, *that's* really a coincidence."

"What is?"

"That you're flying to Nantucket."

"Why?"

"Because *I'm* going there, too…right after the wedding."

"Seriously?"

"Yes,"

"I didn't know you were planning to go to Nantucket."

"I am now."

Epilogue

K ATE O'GRADY-GAULT spent two additional days in the hospital under the watchful eyes of Dr. Richard Odgren before she was given a clean bill of health and discharged.

The drug that Beatrice had used on Kate proved to be an anesthetic. She took comfort to learn that research had shown if anesthetic medications, generally used for surgery, were administered early in the first trimester of a pregnancy that it only presented a minor risk to a fetus.

Lou and Kate left the Channel Isle of Jersey and flew to Dublin on a Blue Pelican Air charter. They met with the priest and entertained numerous members of her family in the days before they exchanged their wedding vows in Abbeyfeale, in the presence of no less than two hundred and thirty-eight members of Kate's extended Irish family. After the ceremony, the celebration at The Tankard Inn was one that will be remembered for years to come.

Before leaving Ireland, Kate met with an OB/GYN

specialist and was given a thumbs up. They spent the next week relaxing on the shores of Lake Como in northern Italy. Following that, they took their time traveling down Italy's west coast, spending a few days on the Isle of Capri before heading up the Adriatic side of 'the boot.' When they reached Venice, they boarded the Orient Express and took the train to Paris. After exploring 'The City of Light' and surrounding French countryside, they returned to Abbeyfeale a few days before heading home to Havre de Poisson.

LOU GAULT'S status with the Canadian Mounties reverted back to 'inactive auxiliary' status while he was touring Europe. Upon his return to Havre de Poisson, he was pleased to find that every end of season project he had initially launched, had been successfully completed.

BEATRICE HASTING was arrested by the French authorities when she was taken off the Harbor Patrol boat in Mont Saint Michel.

She was extradited to Ireland where she has been charged with two counts of kidnapping, two counts of murder, two counts of assault and battery, two counts of grand larceny (theft of a motor vehicle), and conspiracy to commit wire fraud. Her British passport was revoked and she has been charged with kidnapping by the United Kingdom and 'piracy on the high seas.

Additionally, the French government has charged her with attempted murder, piracy on the high seas, and one count of reckless endangerment with a firearm.

Currently, Beatrice Hastings is confined in *Fleury-Mérogis* a maximum-security prison south of Paris. Both the Canadian and the Irish governments are in negotiations with France to extradite her. In all likelihood, Beatrice Hastings will spend the remainder of her life in prison. Which country will have the honor of hosting her will be determined by the courts.

EVELYN MAXWELL was also detained by the French authorities in Mont Saint Michel after being taken ashore by a Harbor Patrol boat when she was unable to produce proper identification.

Subsequently, she was extradited to Ireland where her British passport was revoked, and she was charged with the identical crimes levied against Beatrice Hastings.

Currently, she is behind bars awaiting trial in the Irish penal system. She has been labeled a flight risk and is being held without bail. A crown-appointed barrister has been assigned to represent her.

The Canadian government has also charged Maxwell with the abduction of an officer of the law and kidnapping. Evelyn Maxwell, like her husband, will undoubtedly spend the remainder of her natural life in prison.

ANNE MORE was picked inside the rental house where Beatrice and Evelyn had abandoned her. Following a thorough psychiatric evaluation, was found to be incompetent to stand trial.

Anne's world had finally closed in on her and she was no longer able to function independently.

She has been admitted to Broadmoor Hospital, a high-security psychiatric hospital in Crowthorne, Berkshire,

England. Undoubtedly, Anne will spend the remainder of her natural life in England, most likely completely unaware of the events which lead to her being placed in custody.

JAKE GAULT returned to the Isle of Guernsey once the kidnappers had been apprehended. When he flew to Ireland to witness his cousin renew his vows, the young marine biologist who captured his attention at the Hogs and Heifer's restaurant, accompanied him.

Once Jake returned to New Brunswick, he resumed flying the mail plane. His classification with the Royal Canadian Mounties has been changed to 'inactive axillary' status.

On weekends, he now regularly flies to the island of Nantucket, off the coast of Massachusetts.

KOBY CALLAHAN, the young marine biologist who captured Jake's attention on the Isle of Guernsey is currently leading an international research team, commissioned by the North Atlantic Institute of Marine Sciences.

WILLIAM MCDUFFY-FERGUSON (a.k.a Duffy) was promoted to the rank of sergeant, for the third time upon his return to Canada. He now serves on the newly created Canadian International Abductee Advisory board.

SERGEANT MAJOR FLETCHER MARTIN, was presented with a budget-breaking expense report. To cover the costs submitted by Duffy, Sergeant Martin had no choice but to defer replacing eighty-seven patrol vehicles by a full year.

SERGEANT FRANCIS O'CONNOR, (a.k.a. Fran-O), has since announced his intent to step away from the Irish *Garda*. Plans are currently underway to honor him with a retirement party. The celebration will certainly be attended by all the lads who have served under his command, over the past 50 years. As usual, he has tasked his lads with pulling the event together.

CHEF ANGELO successfully managed the renovation and expansion projects of the kitchen at Havre de Poisson. He oversaw all the modifications to the dock and the replacement of mattresses to Lou's specifications. It is assumed that next year's clients will rest better at night.

ALESSANDRA, wife of Chef Angelo, is currently enrolled in an online class leading to certification as a midwife. Currently, she is anxiously awaiting the arrival of the twins.

SAM T. BARBER was released on his own recognizance by the Mont Saint-Michel harbor police. The *Knot on Call* was pulled off the mud flats during the next high tide and towed to a boat yard. The grounding on the mud flats did little more than clean the hull of the *Knot on Call*. After replacing the zinc plates, Sam sailed his boat back to the island of Jersey and mothballed it for the remainder of the season.

BUD, owner of Bud's Marina, finally decided embrace technology and now has a cell phone.

DOCTOR RICHARD ODGREN, the physician who attended to Kate while she was on the island of Jersey turned out also to be a pianist of note. Unbeknownst to Sam T. Barber, at the upcoming jazz festival, he would listen to an artist known within the world of jazz as Dick Odgren.

Please Give a Review

If you have liked this book, please take a moment and give a review on Amazon.com.

Here's a Sneak Peak into Book Four of the Lou Gault Chronicles, entitled, *Sabotage*, when revenge goes out of control.

When revenge goes out of control
SABOTAGE
A Lou Gault Thriller
Dave McKeon

Sabotage - Chapter 1

The only audible sound inside the parking garage came from the soles of Dominic Martino's fashionable Italian leather shoes hitting the concrete floor. As the echoes bounced off the inside walls of the cavernous cement building, his assassin waited in the shadows.

Martino was a gifted prosecutor, as well as a creature of habit. The killer had studied him for weeks and knew his routines. He also knew Martino would be the last to leave his office, and oblivious to his surroundings as he walked toward the parking garage.

As Martino approached his vehicle in the area reserved for the district attorney and staff, his mind was elsewhere . . . as usual.

Earlier in the month, a jury had handed him a hard-won victory. He smirked, thinking to himself, *why was I even concerned this one could end in a hung jury? I had a solid case . . . the jury listened . . . and justice prevailed. As it should.*

Days earlier, the assassin had scoped out the garage. Choosing a location where he would take someone's life was never a random act. It was always a deliberate one which gave him the advantage over his prey. The element of surprise also seemed to sexually arouse him as he lay in wait for the kill.

The assassin's given name was Vincenzo, but after years of working the waterfront, his forearms had become grossly distorted. His massive forearms resembled those of the cartoon character Popeye the Sailorman. Those who worked beside him on the docks referred to him as "Popeye." Only a few select people knew of his avocation as an assassin-for-hire . . . and of his allegiance to Santino Varni.

Now, as Martino approached a large puddle of oily water directly between him and his Mercedes Benz, he sighed. Clearly frustrated, he circumvented the water to avoid damaging the expensive soft leather shoes he wore. As he brushed up against a support stanchion, he thought it was a spider's web that touched his face, until he felt a sudden tightening around his neck.

Within seconds, his briefcase fell to the floor and both hands instinctively reached for his throat. At the 10-second mark, his head began jerking wildly from side to side. He was desperately seeking to locate and confront his attacker. But Popeye's massive forearms had already become an extension of the garrot, and Dominic Martino was being manipulated as if he was a papier-mâché marionette, on a string.

Within 20 seconds, Martino was gasping for air. His fingers were frantically digging into the sides of his own throat in a futile attempt to release himself from the constraint that was cutting off his airway.

After 30 seconds, his eyes were bulging. His mouth was open now, and his tongue was grotesquely extended.

At the 60-second mark, his brain was being denied lifegiving oxygen; he could feel the strength draining from his extremities.

After 90 seconds had passed, his lungs felt like they were on fire. He tried to scream . . . but the only noise he made, was in his head.

At the 120-second mark, the intensity of his struggle began to fade. Deprived of oxygen, his body was shutting down.

After another 60 seconds had passed, Dominic Martino lost consciousness, and lay slouched against the chest of his killer.

The assassin looked at the Rolex stretched across his massive wrist. The elapsed time was reaching four minutes, the average length of time for someone to die once their airway was blocked. Yet, Popeye strained to maintain the tension on the garrote for a full six minutes, after which the chance of survival was nil. His victim would have succumbed to both an air choke and a blood choke. The blood choke was more critical. Once the carotid arteries were unable to supply the brain with oxygen rich blood for a sustained period of six minutes, clinical death would occur.

In one smooth motion, the assassin released the garrote and slipped his arm underneath his victim's left armpit. Then, he grabbed the right armpit for leverage and dragged the lifeless body of Dominic Martino into the darkness as if he were a rag doll. With his right hand, he slid open the panel door of an unmarked van. He had covered the cargo area with sheets of plastic. Then, in one swift motion, Dominic

Martino's body was unceremoniously dumped inside the van.

But just before closing the door, Popeye noticed the exquisite pair of Italian leather shoes on Martino's feet.

Stepping out of his own shoe, he tried on one of Martino's. The hand-made loafer fit Popeye's foot like a slipper. As he kicked off his other shoe, he removed Martino's second shoe and whispered, *"Grazie."*

As he closed the door, he blew a kiss at the body sprawled in the back of the van. Whether the shoes would remain a *trophy* . . . or a curse . . . only time would tell.

Sabotage - Chapter 2

JUST UNDER FIVE HUNDRED miles to the northeast of Boston, most of the men who had come to the fishing resort known as *Harve de Poisson* had been on the water for well over an hour. The sportsmen who had made the journey this far into the Canadian wilderness were true outdoors men. They willingly accepted the morning chill and the heavy dew, clinging to the open boats, in exchange for the chance to haul in a trophy fish. It mattered not that the stars were still visible when they left the dock. These men came to fish and early morning was prime time to hook into a monster that might rise from the depths to feed.

The mist coming off the surface of the lake in the morning this late in the season, was a sure sign that the temperature of the air was dropping faster than the warmer lake water. But summer wasn't ready to give way to autumn, not just yet anyway. The forest's canopy was still green, and the wavering sound of loons, calling to their mates, still announced the coming of every new day.

Once the last boat had left the dock, Lou Gault, proprietor of the resort, closed the door to the bait house and headed back along the path toward his cottage.

Ten years had now passed since Gault fought in the Afghan wars. Shortly after he returned to New Brunswick, he had inherited the resort from his paternal grandfather, Grey Elk, along with forty-five square miles surrounding the deep glacial lake. The land that was passed along to him was all that remained of the ancestral lands once belonging to an eastern band of Abenaki since the beginning of time. Gault led a peaceful life now, far from the carnage of war. Yet, the warrior spirit that defined him in battle still remained within him.

AS LOU OPENED the screen door to the porch that spanned the front of his cottage, he turned and looked across the lake; his eyes searching the horizon for anything that might be a threat to the environment, for anything that seemed out of place or different.

Over the years, Harve de Poisson's reputation had spread across Canada and well south into the States. To the truly avid fisherman, the allure of landing a trophy fish *never* went away. To the serious hunter, the *potential* of bringing down a record-sized buck worthy of being listed in *Boone and Crockett* was like "the call of the wild."

The number of record-breaking trophies that had come from Harve de Poisson was a record unto itself. That achievement, combined with the pristine environment, the first-class accommodations, and the exquisite menus served by Chef Angelo, it was no wonder so many sportsmen irreverently referred to it as, "Mecca."

Although the very essence of Harve de Poisson, itself,

hadn't changed over the years, life at the resort certainly had. The year-round residents now numbered nine, three of whom were under the age of five. The number of cottages available to guests and the size of the dining lodge had doubled. Cellular and internet service had become a reliable amenity, and every year by early April, there was a waiting list.

SHORTLY AFTER LOU entered the porch, Kate, his wife of seven years, called out from the kitchen.

"Lou, are the boats all out?"

A slight smile appeared on Lou's face as he savored the sound of his wife's Irish brogue. "Yeah, everyone seemed pretty eager to get an early start this morning, Kate."

Moving to the doorway leading into the cottage, she asked, "Do you have anything special going on this morning?"

"Not really. Well, there's a couple of things I need to do. Luigi Secondo is flying up."

"And what time is that?"

"Around ten. Why?"

"I'd like to get my run in. Could you watch the kids for me?"

"Yeah, sure. Are you just doing three miles?"

Without saying another word, Kate stepped out onto the porch, and up on her tiptoes, planted a passionate kiss on her husband's lips. When she finally broke away from him, Lou placed his hands on her shoulders. "Kate, I can't believe how much it turns me on just to be your man."

"Well, hold on to that thought, because that's all we have time for until tonight. As soon as I'm back and showered, I'm on the phone for the rest of the day pulling next year's budget together for the Major Crime Unit."

"Are the twins up, yet?"

"Up, fed, dressed, and watching 'Odd Squad' on PBS." With that, Kate was out the door.

As Lou watched the love of his life jog down the path, he thought: *Just about as fine a figure as any woman could have, beautiful on the inside, smart as a whip, a wonderful mother, and still as friggin' sexy as ever.*

KATE HAD BEEN somewhat of a *city mouse* most of her life, but she had adapted quickly to life in the Canadian wilderness. She enjoyed the serenity of the forest and used the solitude it provided during her frequent runs to clear her thoughts and prepare for whatever was ahead.

When Kate returned from her run and began to stretch out, she said, "Lou, how many times has Luigi Secondo come up here this year?"

"Ha…I've no idea. Luigi comes and goes as he pleases." After a pause, he said, "Maybe every third week he's up for a few days."

"That man must have more money than he knows what to do with!"

"I don't know about that."

"Well, for the last three years he's taken a cottage for the entire season, and he's hardly ever here. Now, *that's* a waste. He's always alone. Never once has he ever come up with anyone. If ever there was a man chasing the will-o'-the-wisp, he's the one."

"Maybe so, but it's his life."

"Does he ever put a line in and fish?"

"Once in a while. I think he comes up here mainly to get away. He and Angelo are a twosome."

"Well, of course they are! Luigi brings Angelo all kinds of

delicacies from Italy. The man needs to find a good wife, settle down, and be happy."

Lou smiled. *Kate, a man can be single and still be happy,* he thought.

"Lou, what is it that Luigi does?" Kate asked, using a more serious tone.

"I haven't a clue."

"In all the years he's been coming up here, you've never talked about that?"

"Nope."

"I find that hard to believe."

"Well, believe it. I don't talk about that topic with other fellas who come up here. Hell, they're trying to get away from the world they live in."

"You're always chatting with this one and that one; what in the world *do* you talk about?"

Lou shrugged his shoulders "Well, we talk about fishing, we talk about hunting…tackle…bait…the lake…the weather…the guides…Chef Angelo…ya know, guy stuff."

"And you're not the least bit inquisitive about what Luigi Secondo *does* for a living?"

"I am not."

"Well, this Irish colleen you married would certainly like to know."

Lou looked at his wife and smiled. *No kidding,* he thought, *that's why the Mounties recruited you to head up New Brunswick's Major Crime Unit.*

Eight years earlier, INTERPOL had loaned a young Lieutenant Kathryn O'Grady to Canada, helping the Mounties bring down an international smuggling ring that was operating in the Bay of Fundy. Her investigative skills proved to be so effective that the Mounties ended up making her an offer she couldn't refuse. Shortly thereafter, she transferred from Ireland's Directorate of Military Intelligence, to the Royal Canadian Mounted Police.

"Well, it may not matter to *you* what he does, but I'll put money down that Angelo knows."

"Kate, don't go sticking your nose where it doesn't belong," Lou said.

With that, there was knock on the door. It wouldn't be long before Lou Gault realized his resolve to live a simple, peaceful life was about to be tested…once again.

Praise for the Lou Gault Thriller Series *Five Star Reviews from Amazon Customers*

- "Almost impossible to put down." *- Jack J.*
- "Intriguing read drew me in." *– Ron N.*
- "Fast reading intriguing crime story with well-developed believable characters and excellent descriptive scenes." *– Ben H.*
- "Riveting international thriller"*– Patricia M.*
- "Readable and action packed"*– Bill G.*
- "Exciting and action packed"*– Andrea N.*
- "Lou Gault is the man." *- Customer*
- "Very engaging, good read." *– Kathleen Z.*
- "You are the New Clive Cussler. Can't wait for the next one." *– Ed P.*
- "An exciting and intriguing read." *– Rev. Mark N.*
- "Lots of intriguing themes woven together to make a very good read." *– Bay B.*

Books by Dave McKeon

Relentless Pursuit

War Chief

Howl of the Banshee

Future Books

Sabotage

The Red Road

RELENTLESS PURSUIT

When the Canadian Mounties join forces with MI6 and INTERPOL seeking to uncover a ring of international smugglers, Lou Gault, a war-weary ex-commando, must decide whether he is willing, once again, to put his life on the line.

But when a team of Mounties goes off the grid and operates from a remote sportsmen's lodge deep in the wilds of New Brunswick, it becomes a deadly game of cat and mouse with only one outcome . . . Winner takes all.

The intrigue of international smuggling

RELENTLESS PURSUIT

An AMAZON BESTSELLING ACTION THRILLER

A Lou Gault Thriller

Dave McKeon

AMAZON #1 BESTSELLING AUTHOR

WAR CHIEF

When two game wardens are killed and scores of deer found slaughtered with only their antlers taken, the action ramps up in this crime thriller. When a developer threatens the ancestral lands belonging to the Abenaki native people, the warrior spirit within Lou Gault awakens.

Crooked politicians, outcasts of society, conniving developers, and rogue pharmaceutical interests all challenge the sovereignty of the Abenaki lands. When the tribal elders remain silent, Lou Gault can no longer remain quiet. WAR CHIEF is the tale of a crusader driven to save his people at the risk of losing what he loves most. The underlying question becomes: Has the clock run out?

WAR CHIEF

A Lou Gault Thriller

Dave McKeon

AMAZON #1 BESTSELLING AUTHOR

Acknowledgments

A special thank you to my early readers: Barbara Cheney, Barry Covin, Carl Johnson and, Tom Mullin. Your continued willingness to carve out time to review my early drafts and offer your unabashed critiques truly opens my eyes to what I am unable to see.

Again, a shout out to Paula Howard, my editor and publisher, for the tireless effort she puts into bringing my stories to the public. Thank you Paula, you are a joy to partner with.

Lastly, a tip of the hat to Bob Hurley, the talented graphic artist who designs my covers.

About the Author

Dave McKeon is an award-winning author of short stories and creator of the Amazon best-selling Mystery, Action, Adventure series, *The Lou Gault Thrillers*.

His stories reflect a diverse background of life experiences and an unquenchable love affair with the outdoors.

A native New Englander, he has hunted, fished, hiked, camped, skied, and traveled in the eastern United States and throughout New Brunswick and Quebec, his entire life.

A Vietnam-era veteran, Dave has formerly held both a Top-Secret Clearance and the Department of Energy's "Q" Clearance. His stores are influenced by his experiences working with the NSA, the EPA ,and the Department of the Navy.

To Learn more about Dave McKeon
Visit www.avillagewriter.com

www.ingramcontent.com/pod-product-compliance
Lightning Source LLC
Chambersburg PA
CBHW062109290726
48975CB00001B/167